Maggie Ford was born in the East End of London but at the age of six she moved to Essex, where she has lived ever since. After the death of her first husband, when she was only twenty-six, she went to work as a legal secretary until she remarried in 1968. She has a son and two daughters, all married; her second husband died in 1984.

She has been writing short stories since the early 1970s.

A Soldier's
Girl

Maggie FORD

EBURY
PRESS

3 5 7 9 10 8 6 4 2

Ebury Press, an imprint of Ebury Publishing
20 Vauxhall Bridge Road,
London SW1V 2SA

Penguin
Random House
UK

Ebury Press is part of the Penguin Random House group of companies whose
addresses can be found at global.penguinrandomhouse.com

First published in 2001 as *Brenda's Place* by Judy Piatkus (Publishers) Ltd
This edition published in 2016 by Ebury Press

www.eburypublishing.co.uk

A CIP catalogue record for this book is available from the British Library

ISBN 9780091956295

Typeset in India by Thomson Digital Pvt Ltd, Noida, Delhi

Printed and bound in Great Britain by Clays Ltd, St Ives PLC

Penguin Random House is committed to a sustainable future for our business,
our readers and our planet. This book is made from Forest Stewardship
Council® certified paper.

For my children, Janet, John and Clare

Chapter One

Balanced on a wooden chair brought up from the kitchen for better stability, Brenda Wilson stared down at the hem of the long white dress she had on.

'It's not right, Mum. It's dipping all to one side.'

Her mother did not look up from inserting pins around the fine hem ready for handstitching. 'Well, if yer keep leaning over like that, then it will, won't it? Stand up straight.'

Obediently Brenda lifted her head, pulled back her shoulders and stretched her slender waist, returning to her true height of five foot four inches. Even so, looking at herself in the long mirror of the wardrobe, she saw not the light brown hair that hung in loose waves about her shoulders, nor the oval face with its blue eyes, but the still-offending hemline.

'It's still dipping,' she accused.

Her mother looked up at her briefly, then sat back on her heels to survey her work. 'Where?'

'On the left.'

'It's because yer still looking down. It's the way yer standing. Yer'll 'ave ter stand up straight in church next week.'

'I am up straight.'

'You ain't. Yer all one-sided, Bren. Yer keep going all saggy. Pull yer left shoulder up a bit.' Brenda obliged.

'That's better. See, it's level now.'

Brenda frowned. 'Stand like this in church and people will think I'm deformed.'

'Course they won't. And stop frowning. Yer supposed to be 'appy on yer special day.'

'I will be,' retorted Brenda. 'On my day. But not with one shoulder stuck higher than the other.'

'Not if yer walk properly.'

Before her daughter could make any further protests, the door of the poky little bedroom she shared with her sister, Vera, burst open, admitting the girl, two years younger than she and very like her in looks except that at this moment her lips were a tight line of pique.

'Bren! Take a look at this blinking 'eaddress.'

She'd been downstairs trying the thing on over and over again, all the time moaning and exclaiming. They could hear the infuriated squeaks through the thin walls of the house in a series of high-pitched oh's and ow's. Mum had grinned several times at the sounds but had said nothing, knowing how tense her older daughter was three days before her wedding.

From her elevated position on the chair, Brenda glared down at the intruder. She had her own problems with this blessed hemline Mum kept insisting was all right. The bridal gown, in a sleek white satin, had been bought cheap in Roman Road market two Saturdays ago. Mum

2

had altered it to fit, and now it looked a picture but for the blessed dip to the left side of the hem.

'What's wrong with the headdress?' she demanded and saw Vera's pretty little nose wrinkle in disgust.

'I hate it, that's what's wrong. It looks daft, pink flowers, I look like a bloomin' village maiden. And pink don't go with me fair hair at all.'

'You said you was happy with pink when we was in the shop. I did say blue, but you wouldn't listen.' They'd gone there again last Saturday to get her veil and tiara of wax orange blossom as well as the bridesmaids' dresses and headdresses, circlets of artificial pink flowers. Posies to match would be coming on the morning of the wedding. 'We can't start changing it all now. It's too late.'

'It looked all right in the shop,' Vera complained. 'Under their electric light it looked lovely. But in daylight it looks awful, me with me fair hair. All right for you – all in yer white, yer bouquet all cream carnations an' lilies an' fern. But me . . .' Running out of steam, she broke off and yanked the headdress from her head, probably for the sixth time, to glare down at it.

Had Vera's hair been a touch darker, as Brenda's was, there'd have been no cause for complaint, but she seemed to have forgotten it was she who had gone overboard for the pretty shade, gazing in rapture at the other bridesmaid, their cousin Sheila, on whom pink looked quite stunning against all that dark brown hair. Seeing herself in Sheila she had forgotten how much lighter her own hair was.

Trust Vera to be awkward. She had been so adamant in the shop that this was what she'd wanted. And to come over all prima donna at the eleventh hour, or almost,

3

was exasperating. If they'd been well off, it might have been possible to go back and get something else. But they weren't well off, none of them, and she and Harry were getting married on a shoestring as most everyone did in Bow or anywhere else in the East End of London. All right, Deacons in Roman Road was no Harrods, but he stocked stuff just as nice as any posh shop, and certainly far cheaper. But even he wouldn't go changing purchases after they'd been bought and paid for. At shops like that you paid up and took pot luck which was why Mum had had to alter it slightly, taking it in at the waist and lifting it at the shoulders, just as she'd had to take in both bridesmaids' dresses at the waist.

Brenda's solution to her sister's dilemma was brief and impatient. 'You could dye yer hair a bit darker.'

'What?' the reply was flung back at her. 'I don't want to go darker.'

'It's just for the day. You can use the stuff what washes out.'

Brenda worked at Alfio's, an Italian hairstylist's in Bishopsgate. She had been there six years, since she was fifteen. Before that, leaving school at not quite fourteen, she had worked in a cake factory, which she had hated. Her life, she had felt, was worth more than sitting at a bench slopping cream on the lower half of an endlessly moving belt of Victoria sandwiches or packing almond slices into boxes. Her fingers were dexterous, her mind lively; her leanings inclined towards the creative. She'd ambitiously and innocently enquired after any possible vacancies for a starter at Alfio's, which she had been passing at the time, to be told in very good English with only the slightest Italian accent that he was taking on no

4

one. However, seeing potential in her presentable appearance and eager expression, he had said he'd be willing to train her.

His next words, 'For which I will require a fee for two years of training,' had swept excitement right out of her system.

Hiding shock and disappointment she had asked how much this fee would be and if she would get paid. He had beamed at her naivety (she was to find out that he was a man who beamed at everything even as he scolded and upbraided and criticised) and said blithely that she didn't get paid, and at her bleak expression added that the London Academy of Hairdressing charged three times as much as he. At his fee, she'd blanched, seeing all her hopes disappear – she with no money, no savings, a fourteen-year-old with no job. By then her wish to be a hairstylist had so overwhelmed her that she had hurried home on the bus and run through the streets to speak to her parents, to beg them help her, so sure that they would.

Her dad's first words had been, ''Ow can we pay that kind of money?' Her world collapsed around her and she hadn't been able to eat for a week. Her parents became thoughtful, then troubled. She caught them talking together in low whispers. Then her dad had said, 'We might just be able ter manage it, but if yer don't work 'ard an' make a fist of it, then yer out! Don't let us down, Bren. We ain't rollin' in dough, yer know.'

His only stipulation had been that he pay her tuition fee on a monthly basis rather than as the one whole down payment Mr Alfio Fichera had demanded. To this day, Brenda never could fathom out why the man accepted the terms, but he did.

Those two years had nearly crippled her parents, skimping and scraping for her, and she spent the time alternately overwhelmed by gratitude, consumed by guilt, knowing what they had sacrificed for her, and fighting the jealousy it provoked, especially from Vera who, if denied some small thing, would hold Brenda up as an example of favouritism.

Once her two years were up, she'd stayed on at Alfio's as a qualified hairstylist and his chief assistant. She could have gone up West and got a position with a high-class salon but she always felt she owed Mr Fichera a debt of gratitude for his generosity in taking her on as he had in the way Dad had stipulated. When she had told him that she was getting married and would obviously be leaving, he had said sadly, 'What a fool. What a waste. A single woman could have her own salon in time – become so very successful. But there . . . If ever you need any advice, any time, come to me.'

He was right, it could be looked on as a waste. Between Mr Fichera and Dad she reckoned she'd become as good as any top-class hairstylist. With her tutor, she had Dad to thank. How he ever managed to keep her those two years she would never know.

Like most people round here, they were far from well off. Her father was employed by a small firm making record and photograph albums; his money wasn't so bad, though with two girls and two boys to feed, rent to pay, clothing and all the other bits and pieces that ate into a wage, they still lived somewhat close to the bone. A week in Margate in August on three days' paid holiday money, with Bank Holiday Monday as an extra paid day, took a year to save up for. They would stay at a boarding house, and Mum would buy the food for the landlady to cook for their breakfast and evening meal. If it rained, that was too bad. You made the best of it; guests were allowed back only for a meal and for bedtime. But Dad had always made sure they had that holiday. During the worst of the Depression, he had been luckier than some. With millions out of work his boss had kept him, painting the factory when no work came in.

Even so, there had been times when Mum and Dad had feared they might have to find somewhere to live with a lower rent. Brenda remembered praying until she cried that they wouldn't have to. She'd had all her friends here, and her school. The thought of changing schools, being among strangers, had been too awful to contemplate.

It hadn't come about, but she'd been dragged out of school at thirteen and a half to work in the cake factory so that her small wages could help to boost the family income. She was never allowed to forget how lucky she had been to secure a job when so many were on the dole.

That was in the past now. In 1937, things were at last looking up. Even so, getting married on the low wages Harry earned as packer in a warehouse was still proving tough. But she was proud of him. He'd managed to pay the holding fee on a flat above a shop in Bow Road. It wasn't much – living room, kitchen, bedroom, boxroom, access by an external wrought-iron staircase, a backyard toilet to be shared by them and the shop's proprietor. But she'd have her own home, hers and Harry's, their own little love nest.

Just under a week and she'd walk down the aisle of St Mary's on Dad's arm, all solemn, to stand beside

Harry. She'd return on Harry's arm, all smiles. The congregation, his family one side, hers the other, and friends, would be congratulating them both, following them out for photographs, and she would no longer be Brenda Wilson but Mrs Harry Hutton.

She recalled the first time of seeing him. She and a group of girls had been outside a chip shop exchanging banter with a group of boys. Then he'd asked if she'd like to go to the pictures. Taken by his handsome looks, she'd said yes, something about him making her hope it wouldn't be just a fling. It hadn't been. After three dates with him, a feeling began to stir that got her mulling over a new name for herself, Brenda Hutton, hearing in her head the nice ring of it. She'd even written it down on bits of paper, screwing them up afterwards and throwing them away in case, discovered, she'd be laughed at. The mention of his name would bring twinges of excitement in much the same way as she had once shivered to the names of Tyrone Power and Clark Gable.

And now, come Saturday, she would be Brenda Hutton forever, his ring on her finger, one thought only in her head, that they leave as soon as possible for their own little home and make love to each other as man and wife, in fact to make love to each other for the first time ever.

Underneath that chirpy exterior he had displayed on their first meeting, Harry had proved to be a shy person. For all his hearty attitude with his mates, in with the best of them for ogling the girls, once on his own with her he'd been uncertain of himself. So much so that though she'd felt sympathy for him, it had added to his charm rather than lessening it. But once he had regained his self-confidence, he proved himself to be as strong-minded as any man, and she loved him for it, knowing he'd make her happy. Every girl needed an assertive man for a husband.

There was, however, one fly in the ointment of all this contentment – leaving her job. After Thursday, having Friday off to prepare for the wedding, she wouldn't be going back. It was perhaps her only regret.

'It's a respectable job,' she'd pleaded with Harry. 'Not like working in a factory.' But he'd been adamant.

'I'm not 'aving me wife going ter work. We ain't that 'ard up and if I can't provide I'd rather not be wedded. I ain't 'aving people pointing a finger at me saying yer got ter work ter 'elp keep us. No, Bren, once yer married ter me, your place is 'ere, in the 'ome. That's as it should be.'

She was proud of him for saying that, not expecting her to keep him while he loafed as some men did. And she looked forward to playing housewife, meeting other housewives. This was the dream of nearly all single working girls, to get married and never have to go out to work again. They would look enviously at their married counterparts and long for the day when they too could get their man's breakfast, see him off to work before settling down in their kitchen with a nice quiet cup of tea and a leisurely cigarette. Then they would flick a duster around their new wedding presents and wash up their gleaming new crockery and saucepans, also wedding presents. No more taking orders from a boss. No more rushing off to catch the workman's bus. No more clock-watching apart from timing the evening meal. Utter bliss. Every girl's dream. Yet Brenda couldn't help viewing the loss of her job with a small pang of regret. She loved hairdressing but she was giving it all up. In an odd way she felt obsolete, left behind, as if the world were going on without her and someone else would take her place.

Of course the friends she'd made there would come to her wedding if they could. Mr Fichera would definitely be there. One or two of the girls might visit her new home, which she would parade proudly before them. But eventually they would stop coming, get on with their own lives, befriend the new person who would take over from her. In time even her name would be forgotten as if she had never been. It was inevitable.

Oddly disconsolate, she turned her head away from Vera and Mum and glanced out of the window. From here she could see almost the whole way along Trellis Street. Not that there was much of it to see. A dozen or so houses stood on each side ending at the archway over which the Great Eastern ran, deafening the ears with rattling trains that boomed over the empty space below and filled the street with stinking smoke. Houses were terraced, with tiny front gardens that grew little and that blackened by soot from the trains. Each front door was set into a dark brick porch; beside it protruded a single, slightly bayed downstairs window, its stone mullions also blackened by soot; two upper windows were also stone-framed, unpretty, without character, each exactly like its neighbour, front and back, as with every other street in this district. Maybe it was better than Shoreditch or Whitechapel or Stepney or many other East End areas, but it still looked dull and dingy.

At the moment the street was full of kids. August meant they were on holiday and all seemed to be here in this one street. Brenda took a deep breath and did her best to brighten up and endure her mother's attentions to the hem.

Trellis Street had seen three major events this year. In May there had been the street party for the coronation of King George and Queen Elizabeth with the women bringing a little something to help fill the trestle tables they'd set up, with nearly fifty kids sitting down to sandwiches, cakes and jelly. The men had brought the beer for later, dragging a piano out from one of the houses for a sing-song and a booze-up.

Earlier this year, in January, had been the funeral of Tim Goodings with whom she had gone out for a while when she'd been eighteen. He had died from pneumonia; that and TB ran rife among people with little money. His funeral had been done by the Co-op, a single hearse and one following car, all his family could afford from years of putting into the Co-op funeral divi.

After the coronation do had come the still-talked-about fight between Mrs Cummings and Mrs McNab, one a fierce Cockney and one an equally fierce Irish woman, each yelling the other down, each as fast-talking as the other. It had ended with the two women rolling in the gutter, tearing out each other's hair. The police had had to be called. Rumours had gone around but no one ever knew the rights of the argument. Something to do with kids – it usually was – ending up with both insulting the other's husband. Arguments did go on, but never normally to the point of rolling in gutters and letting blood, no matter how little.

Now there was to be a fourth event. Her wedding. On Saturday, the eleventh of September, she would emerge from her home, arrayed in shimmering white satin and step into the waiting car paid for by her father. All the neighbours would stand at their doors watching her go. They'd grin and wave and call good luck to her. And she would shine.

Happy again, she craned her neck to see further down the street.

'Hold still!' came the command. 'Stop wrigglin' or I'll end up gettin' one of these bloomin' pins in yer skin. Then yer'll yelp. And stand up, will yer?'

Brenda brought herself back to attention. Vera was still standing in the doorway, carping, glaring at her headdress. Brenda just hoped she'd cheer up on the big day.

'Right!' Her mother's conclusive tone brought her sharply back to the fact that she was still balancing on the kitchen chair in the bedroom. 'Does that suit your ladyship?'

But Mum's voice was kindly and Brenda dutifully looked down. Yes, that looked better. Much better.

'Mum, you're a marvel. You really are,' she exclaimed and from the corner of her eye saw Vera's nettled figure disappear abruptly from the doorway, the door closing with a sharp click behind her.

Vera would be all right on the day, would smile with the others and cause no trouble to mar her sister's wedding. And pink suited her fine. She would give that hair just the tiniest of tints to make it work.

Chapter Two

She lay in their new bed in their new flat, trying her best to come to terms with this new experience. And by his very lack of movement as he lay beside her, she knew Harry was doing the selfsame thing.

It had been a lovely day, a perfect day, which had gone without a hitch. Although the church was crowded with family and neighbours and friends, more people than she had expected, only her and Harry's immediate families – about all his parents' house could hold – had been invited back for the wedding breakfast and party afterwards.

The sun had shone without a break, the day had been just warm enough to be comfortable, almost balmy one could say. Everything had sparkled. The bridesmaids had been gorgeous. Vera had submitted to having her hair tinted a couple of shades darker than its natural blonde; she had said she liked it and was thinking of keeping it that way, though Brenda knew she wouldn't – too much trouble and expensive as well for a girl earning only twenty-one bob a week as a shop assistant. But she and

Sheila had looked truly lovely in that pink she had moaned about so much, both girls like two peas in a pod with such a strong family resemblance and their identical height.

And Vera had smiled all through the ceremony, through the wedding breakfast too, finding herself attracting the attention of a friend of Harry's brother and best man. Vera could be stunning when she smiled. Pity she didn't do it more often, then maybe she'd keep a boyfriend. Boys went for her, invited her out, but after a while they'd drop her and find someone else. Brenda knew why – if she'd only stop carping about everything – but you could hardly tell her and upset her. Maybe one day she'd learn. But at least she had taken that one's eye. They had been together the whole evening.

'Did you see the way yer brother's friend was looking at Vera?' she whispered to the motionless figure beside her.

His voice came low, muffled by the sheet pulled up around his chin despite the warm night. 'I think 'is mate is sweet on 'er. Told me 'e was finking of asking 'er out.'

'That's nice,' Brenda said softly and lapsed into silence again, her eyes wandering about the room which was faintly lit by street lamps, closed curtains stirring in the night breeze that came through the half-open sash window.

There were sounds too, making the room seem even more still: some way off a dog barking; faint passing footsteps from the pavement below, someone on their way home at this late hour; now and again a passing car, all public transport having long since stopped. She wished Harry would move or at least put his arm round her. He lay like a log. But she did understand. And they'd not long got into bed. It needed time.

14

It had been traumatic to say the least, this business of actually going to bed. One could almost have described it as a shock to the system – it had been to hers. She still wasn't sure what she for her part was supposed to do, having no example to go by. Mum had never told her the facts of life. 'Just do what comes natural,' she'd said sharply on being asked and had turned away, her narrow cheeks reddening – and she was now sure that Harry too hadn't much of an inkling. She could be relieved that he hadn't, proof that he'd had no experience with girls before her.

Both she and Harry were innocents. Though it didn't help now. If only someone, Mum for instance, had enlightened her just a tiny bit on what was expected of newlyweds. Maybe it was awkward for a mother to explain such things to her daughter. How would she explain when her own grew up and got married? It was a delicate subject, not easy to broach. Staring up at the faintly lit ceiling, Brenda silently forgave her mum.

She remembered the girls at the factory where she had started work, at nearly fourteen. An uncouth lot, some of them. On one occasion someone had related *having it off* with a bloke and how she had handled the biggest dick you ever saw, her audience of five girls screaming with laughter and making comments of their own. Innocently she'd asked what was a dick and had been told to take a peek at a horse when it sees a mare.

She had gone looking at all the horses she could find, those that pulled the coal carts and milk floats, but there was nothing to tell her what she should be looking for. Intrigued, she'd asked Mum and had seen that thin face go bright crimson. The next minute her mother's hand had struck out and connected with her cheek in a sharp stinging smack. She was told to keep a ladylike tongue in her mouth and to shut her ears to the things filthy people said. It was years later, to her extreme mortification, that she finally discovered what it meant.

The girls she had worked with at Alfio's had been too nice to talk about anything crude or relate what they got up to with boys outside work – if they got up to anything at all. She had got married today knowing nothing and that too in its own way now seemed somehow mortifying.

Did he feel the same? Was that why he lay so still and quiet beside her? Neither of them had looked at each other as they crept into bed; she felt very conscious of being in her new nightdress, of him being in his pyjamas. She had undressed in the living room, he in the kitchen. From there he had called softly, 'Ready, Bren?' and suddenly all pent up and shy, she'd replied that she was. He had already clicked off the bedroom light switch by the time she came in. They'd clambered into bed in the dark.

So far, with the covers pulled up to their chins, he had kissed her, briefly, leaning over her, and had then fallen back into the position he still retained beside her.

'Orright, Bren?' he'd asked and she'd nodded vigorously so that he'd be aware of it if he couldn't see her in the dark. Now they lay side by side, aware of each other's closeness – or she was of his – neither of them with anything to say, and with each passing moment embarrassment grew, since neither of them felt ready to make the first move. Of course, it should be him to make it, not her. She lay wondering what was going to happen, and how, this consummation of marriage that the vicar had spoken of.

It was ridiculous after all those evenings they'd said their goodnights to each other while they were courting, when he would cup her breasts in kissing her and she would love it, not drawing away, feeling the wonderful sensation that passed over her, even though a blouse or dress lay between his hand and her flesh. There'd been hardly ever more than that; she, determined to save herself for her marriage, had felt gratified that he hadn't made too intense an advance. But they'd always been at ease with each other. Until tonight.

From the start of their relationship she had been surprised by the diffident way he behaved. From his apparently knowledgeable attitude when she had first seen him with his mates, she'd taken him to be a bit of a woman-chaser and had hoped he'd behave himself on that first date. He had. He hadn't even kissed her. Encouraged, she'd let him take her out the following Saturday to the pictures, at La Boheme, the big imposing cinema on the corner of Burdett Road. He'd seen her home to the top of her turning, and had actually *asked* if she'd mind him giving her a goodnight kiss. It had been that gentle and tentative kiss of his that had sent little needles of joy pinging through her, invoking the love she still felt for him.

Harry hardly dared to breathe. His mind was in a whirl, indecisive, and he felt sick. Hell sometimes being a bloke. All right for a woman, all she had to do was wait her cue and follow his unspoken instructions. It was him

17

what had to make the first move, and it was like jumping off a bloody precipice. Worse: with that all you had to do was jump, your lights going out as soon as you hit the ground. With this, you knew you'd be spending the rest of your blinking life forever being reminded of the bleeding blunder you made of it all.

He'd never been a one for girls, not until Brenda. For all his displays of bravado, of discussing girls with his mates, they made him uneasy. They were wily and clever, got there before you and shied away making you feel a bloody fool. If they didn't, they were all over you, scaring the life out of you.

He had turned twenty-two before he found any real self-confidence to take on a girl seriously. The girl had been Brenda and after a couple of dates he'd seen no reason to change her. He was comfortable with her, and he was a man who preferred things easy. She was the sort a bloke could let do the thinking. He was proud of her too. She had everything: brains, looks, poise, bags of charm, and a sort of calmness about her. She was not your soppy sort who squealed and frisked about, showing a bloke up everywhere they went. Yet she could be the life and soul of a party. Everyone liked her. And now he was married to her. Now he must show how strong and virile he was, that he was boss . . . Well, not exactly boss, he didn't think she'd stomach that, but worthy of his role as husband.

He drew in a deep fortifying breath and felt her body grow taut. The nerve that breath was supposed to fortify collapsed instantly. What should he do now? If he put his arm under her head? That meant lifting it, making a big thing of it. Perhaps if he leaned over and kissed her again? He should never have lain back after kissing her that first time. Bugger it!

To think of all the times he'd fumbled her breasts as they stood locked in each other's arms inside her parents' dark porch, hardly even daring to whisper in case her dad came to the door and hurriedly yanked her indoors, being protective of his daughter's honour. As if they could do much inside a poky little porch! Or her mum would invite them in for a cup of cocoa before he went home. A real passion-killer, cocoa, as was her mum, nattering on, seeing him to the door when it was time to leave, saying to Brenda, 'Now don't stay out here too long, luv, yer dad an' me want ter go ter bed.'

What chance did a bloke have after that?

Not that he'd ever have touched Brenda against her wishes. Naturally a girl wanted to be intact on her wedding day. It wouldn't have bothered him if she wasn't, so long as it wasn't by some other bloke. But the truth of it was, he'd never had the courage, and God knows he had his needs all right, that tightening and swelling down there every time they said goodnight making him feel he might go potty if he wasn't relieved. He'd go home feeling downright frustrated like he'd been dropped into a bucket of cold water. But he'd never given way to it. Imagine losing Brenda – and she'd certainly have given him his marching orders – it would have been the end of the world. Yet now, when it was all right to go all the way, he couldn't even begin. Not so much as a stir down below.

Nerves. If he made a hash of it, how would she react? He dreaded even thinking of it. The mere thought of her contempt, of maybe hearing her giggle, was a threat to his tackle. Soft as a bloody overripe grape. Something had to be done. He reached a hand across his body and felt his fingers touch the smooth, slippery satin of the nightdress just above her breasts. They felt so firm under his fingers. A split second later he heard, 'Oh . . . Harry . . .'

It took no more than that. She was in his arms and he at last felt in total command. This their first night as man and wife was grand, perfect. Apart from the business of hurriedly pulling on protection – she'd warned earlier that she didn't want any babies too soon, not until they'd saved a bit – yes, it was great. How could he have been so blooming stupid as to even think it wouldn't be?

Brenda awoke with a tingle of excitement, but not because of their love-making last night. That hadn't quite been what she had imagined, although she had not really known what it was she had expected.

Lovely, of course, being explored all over, experiencing the thrill she had always felt whenever Harry held her close, his hand wandering as he kissed her, but surely there had to be something far more when a man and woman really became one, as it were?

The sensation of him slipping himself inside her had for a moment been a bit alarming. In fact, she had found herself praying it wouldn't do her an injury, which was silly because this had gone on ever since man walked the earth, and women had never come to any harm by it, had they? After the first thrill of his hands touching her there, it had sort of gone off, so she lay there while he did what he needed to do. Much more enjoyable had been the long and ardent kiss he had given her when he'd climbed back into bed after disposing of that thing he'd worn to stop babies happening. After that they had fallen asleep.

No, this excitement stemmed from the anticipation of going off on the honeymoon this morning. The suitcase was already packed. And now would come the rush to catch the train to Eastbourne where they were spending a week before coming home next Saturday.

Bringing herself fully awake, she gazed down at Harry, who was just beginning to stir. Her husband. It did seem funny, as if they had magically come by this state. He looked so handsome lying there. Pity to disturb him. In fact she could easily have sat here watching him forever.

She dropped a kiss on his firm, narrow cheek. 'Time to get up,' she whispered, and saw him stretch, screwing up his face.

'Ahh . . .' He yawned mightily, then opening his eyes, he turned and smiled at her. 'You orright, old gel?'

She gave him a push. 'Old gel? And us just married. Give us at least a chance to get old!'

She leapt out of bed before he could catch her, even though it would have been nice to be caught and make love all over again. There wasn't time. On the narrow mantelshelf over the tiny oval-topped firegrate, their new alarm clock, a wedding present from one of his aunts and uncles, showed eight fifteen. Its tinkling had woken her up but for some reason it hadn't been that loud and had ceased of its own accord. Well, cheap and cheerful, Harry would have to tinker with it later to make sure it behaved itself properly when he had to get up and go to work. But not until they returned from their honeymoon.

'Come on, love,' she scolded. 'We've got ter be out in half an hour or so. Mustn't miss our train.'

She heard him singing in their bedroom as he dressed while she made the breakfast – her first-ever breakfast for them – a bit of bacon, egg, and fried bread. Mum had got in a few provisions on Friday before the wedding.

Harry had got under her feet, washing and shaving in the sink behind her as she busied herself around the gas stove; he had said sorry several times. But it was lovely to know that this was how married life would be from now on, getting in each other's way, saying sorry to each other.

Breakfast was a rush, and the washing-up got done hurriedly. She put everything away tidily, and made a last-minute visit to the loo in the yard to empty out so as not to be caught out before getting on the train; her heart pounded from all the preparations to be off.

Soon, once they had their going-away togs on, Harry carefully locked the door of the flat as if it was the most precious thing he would ever do, putting the key carefully into his pocket before picking up the suitcase.

'You got our door key safe now?' she asked.

He grinned at her, which showed him to be very pleased with himself. 'Yer saw me do it?'

She grinned too, happy that he was happy. 'Yes, but I just wanted to make sure you'd remember where you put it.'

He took her arm with his free hand. 'You leave it all ter me. Come on, let's be orf.'

He helped her down the iron staircase to the side gate that took them out on to Bow Road, very quiet at this time of a Sunday morning; in a way she was sad at leaving their home so soon for a whole week, but their honeymoon beckoned, and they needed to hurry. There weren't that many tube trains running on a Sunday, though the excursion train to Eastbourne would be crowded on such a sunny morning. People would be taking maybe a last trip to the south coast before September with its uncertain weather put an end to any more days out.

Harry, a little ahead of her, looked anxious to get going. She hurried along watching his long gangling form leaning away from the heavy suitcase as it bumped against his leg, his other arm held away from his body to counter-balance the weight. She carried the two smaller bags, one with various bits and bobs that hadn't fitted too well in the case: another hat, her envelope handbag, a spare cardigan in case the sea air was chilly when they stepped out of the train at Eastbourne. The other bag held sandwiches, a bit of their wedding cake and a flask of tea to tide them over on the train journey.

They were catching the ten twenty from Victoria. She hoped they'd have enough time to buy the tickets without too much of a rush, perhaps even get a cup of tea in the station buffet. That remained to be seen. Getting there was the most important thing. Once on the train they could relax. She only hoped they wouldn't look too much like newlyweds and have to endure the covert smirks that would embarrass her and spoil her journey. Well, she'd look the smirkers straight in the eye until, embarrassed themselves, they'd have to turn away. She would put her arm through Harry's, cuddle up to him and show them all that she was proud to be his wife.

They were going to have a lovely honeymoon.

Chapter Three

In the kitchen Mum was buttering the slices Brenda had so far cut from a large crusty bloomer.

'I must say, Bren, yer look as if yer've settled down nice enough.'

Brenda chuckled as she sawed at the loaf. She'd bought the week's provisions yesterday, an hour or two after she and Harry had arrived home from Eastbourne. Tired from the journey, she'd still had to go out shopping, cutting her first teeth as a new housewife. It was as yet a labour of love, as was this Sunday tea to which they had invited both their parents with one or two relatives popping round later to celebrate their homecoming.

Harry and both their fathers were at the moment in the front room, the two older men lounging in the nice if second-hand armchairs while Harry sat on the small sofa that didn't match. Soon she would buy some strong fabric to cover all three pieces and make them match. The men, taking full benefit of the September evening sunshine slanting through the window, were talking and smoking as they waited for tea to be laid.

'We've hardly 'ad a chance yet,' Brenda answered her mother. 'Say that again after we've had tea. I'm still new to all this.'

'You 'ad enough practice at 'ome.'

'Not all on me own, Mum,' Brenda laughed. It was nice having her parents to this, her first effort at entertaining. 'All I ever did them days was ter help you.'

Harry's mum popped her head round the door. 'Anythink I can do?'

Wedged between a wall and the little wooden baize-covered kitchen table, Brenda glanced around the pocket handkerchief of a kitchen. 'Well, not really, Mum.' She had to get used to calling her Mum, though with her own mother there it made her feel awkward doing so. 'There ain't hardly any room for two of us out here.'

She saw Harry's mother's expression change and hastily rectified her mistake. The woman mustn't feel shut out.

'But if yer could lay the table, the tablecloth's on one of the chairs in the front room still wrapped up in fancy paper. And if yer can take in that nice cutlery and the tea set you and Harry's dad bought us. Thanks ever so much for them. They really were a lovely wedding present and we just can't wait to give them an airing. You'll be the first of our visitors to use them, you and my mum and dad.'

The woman's face brightened as she went to the little leather box whose open lid displayed the gleaming cutlery. 'I'll come back for the other things.'

It was her own mother's turn to look a bit down as the other woman departed bearing the box of cutlery. 'I 'ope yer liked our present, Bren.'

Brenda beamed at her. Mum and Dad had bought them a radio set. 'It's the best present anyone could wish for, honest. We can occupy all our evenings listening in, being as we won't be able to afford to go many places.'

She saw her mother's face relax, but it grew thoughtful too, a slow, deep indrawn breath accompanying it. 'So, Bren, how'd it all go?'

Brenda returned to cutting bread. 'How did what go?'

'You know. Yer 'oneymoon. Did yer . . .? Well, you know.'

'Oh, we had a lovely time. The weather was smashing for September, and we had really comfortable digs. We could see the sea from the landing.'

'Yes, but everythink else – was everythink orright?'

'Of course.' She was falling in to what Mum was alluding to, and not too happy about it. 'Why?'

'Just wondered.' Mum was buttering furiously. 'Yer know, first time fer yer both – that sort of thing.'

A small twinge of irritation made itself felt. *That sort of thing* was her own business, hers and Harry's. She wasn't prepared to share even with her own mother the ins and outs of the cat's arse so to speak, in spite of Mum imagining she had every right to know. But she blinked away her annoyance. Probably all mothers were like this. Concerned for their daughters.

'We had a lovely time, Mum. And me and him – we're fine.'

Either content or realising she oughtn't to pry, her mother went back to buttering bread, now with less agitation, and changed the subject.

''Ope yer don't mind yer Aunt Grace and Uncle Herbert poppin' over after tea. It's natural, them wanting ter black their noses – your new place and everythink. Herbert said 'e'd bring a bottle of whisky. And I've got that sherry in me bag what was left over from the weddin'.'

'Harry's Aunt Ada and Uncle Reg will be here too after tea,' Brenda said, growing increasingly crestfallen at the prospect of all these people in one room hardly large enough for two. They really had no business inviting themselves like that. How was she going to fit them all in?

She had started off inviting both parents to tea, that was all. But when Harry's mum had asked if her elderly dependent mother, who lived with them, could come, how could she say no? It made seven people sitting down to tea. True, the bulky Victorian table that had been his grandmother's now graced her own flat. This gracious wedding gift had been the old lady's treasured possession and had stood unused in two parts against the wall of his parents' bedroom behind a curtain. Accepting it with good grace, Brenda suspected they'd been glad to see the back of it. It was almost too big for here, but she had fitted it in somehow.

'It's only nat'ral,' Mum was saying, 'they'd want ter see yer now yer 'ome safe from 'oneymoon.'

She had no option. 'It's going ter be a crush in this small place.'

'Oh, we'll manage,' countered her mother without hesitation.

Brenda sighed. She'd hoped for an early night. Harry had to be back at work tomorrow morning and would get up at six thirty to be there by half seven.

They'd had an early night last night after all that travelling. Even so, he had proved himself well up to standard in the lovemaking department. She had no doubt by the way he kept looking at her that once they had got rid of their guests he'd show himself equally enthusiastic as he'd been last night. Pity about all this having to take precautions though – go on like this, it would end up costing him a mint on them things he got from the barber's shop. She'd offered to cut his hair for him and save money, but only barbers could provide what he went in there for. At that rate, she found herself smiling, he would soon have the best-cut hair in the neighbourhood.

Her first effort at entertaining was turning out a great success even with seven people crammed round the table in the tight space between the rest of the furniture.

Conversation flowed easily, apart from an enquiry from Mum about what Eastbourne's scenery was like, which brought a wink from Harry's father.

'If I know 'im, he wouldn't of given 'er much time ter look at scenery!'

Brenda felt herself blush and saw Harry's face redden. His mother threw a sharp look at her husband.

'That's enough, Sid! Round a tea table an' all and in company. Leave the youngsters alone.' She turned towards Brenda's mother. 'He can be so blessed coarse when 'e likes. Don't stop ter think. I'm sorry.'

Mum, having hurriedly bent her head to the unnecessary task of cutting her ham sandwich into quarters, lifted her face to smile acceptance of the apology while Dad cleared his throat, and gave the two young people an embarrassed glance.

'Let's just say,' Harry's mother added hastily, 'they 'ad a lovely time.' This only succeeded in turning it into an innuendo, albeit innocent, and she in her turn went pink.

'Eastbourne was lovely,' Brenda volunteered, trying to avert her eyes from Harry. 'We went up on the cliffs quite a few times. They're ever so high and I felt scared. I couldn't go anywhere near the edge, but Harry did. He didn't see any danger. I was so frightened for 'im. It's miles down. The lighthouse looked just like a little toy all that way below. But Eastbourne's ever so clean and tidy. And the sea air smelled so nice and fresh. We was so sad to come away.'

Having finally sidestepped the ticklish subject, she was glad as the conversation settled down with no more personal references. But she knew that when the others arrived after tea, they would all be agog if only showing this in their meaningful if kindly glances. It was understandable, of course. After all, she was the first of the youngsters in the family to get married.

At one time it had been assumed that her brother Davy, oldest out of them all, twenty-four going on twenty-five, would have been first. But he was more happy with his mates, going to pubs and dance halls or cycling in the usual huge group of blokes out into the country of a weekend, with not a steady girl in sight.

At the other end of the scale, Brian, her younger brother who in her estimation was not half as good-looking as Davy, at nearly seventeen was always out with some girl or other to the consternation of Mum in case he ended up getting one of them into trouble. Mum was well aware what he was like, and even Brenda despite her own innocence knew there were girls of that sort about. In fact, Brian's behaviour was the cause of more rows in Mum and Dad's house than anything else. Not even Vera's petulant attitude provoked as many arguments.

It was an unbelievable squash, as she knew it would be. By seven thirty the room was stuffy with heat coming off so many bodies. All she could think of was thank goodness the whole two families hadn't decided to *pop in.* Look how full of relatives the church had been on her wedding day. All that lot and they'd have been lined up the outside stairs like some queue at the pictures. Just as well her brothers and her sister hadn't come, especially Vera, moaning her head off. But they wouldn't have. Too full of their own pursuits, they were: Brian out with a girl, Davy with his mates, Vera with hers.

'If any more,' she whispered to Harry as she watched everyone trying to find space to sit, 'we'd have had to sit on each other's laps.'

He grinned at her as he filled his pint glass from one of the half-dozen bottles of brown ale his uncle had brought along while her guests finally got themselves sorted out, and muttered out of the corner of his mouth, 'I tell yer one fing, Bren, we ain't gonna do this very often.'

From the look on his face she knew he harboured the same thought as her – to get rid of everyone as soon as decently possible so they could both go to bed. They'd been fools to entertain after having been married for only a week. With them just back from their honeymoon, only

30

the inconsiderate would have accepted any invitation this soon, and this was just a third of the family. No doubt in time the rest would trot along. It could go on for weeks, and they would have to put up with it, she supposed. It was inevitable, with no one keen to be left out of viewing the newlyweds' new home. But tonight it was most important, even urgent, to get their guests out as early as possible.

She and Harry needed to be alone tonight and not so late that they'd be too worn out entertaining to do anything. Tomorrow or the next day her periods would start and for the best part of a week they'd be barred the joy of each other. Being made love to in the comfort of their bed was still so novel that she contemplated the coming love-starved week with real feelings of bitterness against this most natural cycle in a young woman's life.

'I'd of thought you'd of found somethink of a bit more roomy than this place,' her Aunt Grace, Mum's sister, was saying. 'Not quite so poky.'

Wedged on the two-seater settee between her barrel-chested husband Herbert and Harry's ample Aunt Ada, Grace, thin like Mum, looked decidedly uncomfortable.

Harry's dad had given up his fireside chair to Harry's grandmother, her own dad vacating the other to Harry's mum. Both men now stood on the iron landing to the stairs enjoying a smoke and a drink in the evening air after the stuffy room. The hard chairs were left for Harry's Uncle Reg who suffered from chronic bronchitis and needed to stay indoors, his wife Ada, Harry's widowed Aunt Carrie who could hardly have been left out as she lived with his mum too, Brenda's Uncle Norman who'd fallen into deep conversation with Reg, her Aunt Kath who preferred to sit higher, Mum and herself. And Aunt Grace had given up the struggle for the constricted if softer sofa seat and moved to the dining chair which Norman had finally felt compelled to give up to her. Brenda watched him wander off to join the other men on the landing.

Under very obvious duress Grace was perched stiff-backed on the hard chair, tight-lipped and sulky and looking so much like her niece Vera when things didn't quite go her way that Brenda had to suppress a grin.

Bringing her chair close to Harry who had perched himself with his glass of beer on one of the sofa arms, she grew aware of its creaking and complaining at his misuse.

'I 'ope that arm's safe,' she said and saw him grin down at her.

'I ain't puttin' all me weight on it.'

That he hadn't gone out with the men but had chosen to stay here with her made her feel protected and she felt his free hand come across her shoulder, a move which caught the notice of nearly everyone, who gave approving smiles. Colouring up, she again prayed they wouldn't make it too late in departing.

Aunt Grace was still going on about the smallness of the flat. 'You should of 'ad a better look round. It don't do to rush into things too quick.'

'We couldn't find anything bigger for the rent we could afford,' she countered, seeing Harry's dad come back inside for a top-up from one of the bottles of beer on the table. 'It's big enough for us.'

'But what about when babies . . .'

'Not big enough fer us lot,' Harry's dad put in with a wink and a big grin as he filled his pint glass. 'Never mind, Bren luv, we won't be leavin' it too late ter be on our way. Leave you two love birds ter yerselves, eh? Bound ter wanna make best use of yer little love nest, still only a week married.'

'Sid!' his wife shot at him, but his grin remained big.

'Anyone want a cup of tea?' Brenda the hostess asked quickly.

They might take it as a bit of a hint to begin preparing for home. Few ever stayed on after evening tea came round, a signal for a social gathering to come to a close. The other two men followed Harry's father in, saying it was getting dark and a bit chilly out there; the general response to Brenda's suggestion was that tea would be nice.

Making the most of it, she added, 'I'll make sandwiches.' That was the deciding factor.

'Then we'll 'ave to go,' Aunt Grace said, not all that happy to sit for much longer on a hard chair. Once the men had drunk up their beer, and the womenfolk had put aside their empty sherry glasses – a wedding present from her Aunt Edie and Uncle Phil who'd had sense enough not to come this evening – Brenda hurried out to the kitchen to make cups of tea and ham sandwiches with pickled onions and gherkins to pick at.

'I'll help yer, dear,' Harry's mother offered, lifting a hand at Brenda's mother as she too rose. 'You stay there, luv. You did it all at teatime. My turn now. We'll be orright, won't we, Brenda?'

Brenda saw her mother's lips tighten but smiled placatingly at her as she submitted herself to her mother-in-law's offer. The woman, in her element, took charge.

'You put the kettle on, luv. I'll cut the bread, and you can butter it. Then I'll finish doing the sandwiches while you make the tea.'

Brenda, though she complied, made a small vow to keep Mrs Hutton senior at arm's length if she possibly could. Keep Mum away too.

Like a clairvoyant, tiny signs of the future eased themselves into her head: visions of mother and mother-in-law, of herself and mother-in-law, of herself and Mum – if she wasn't careful she'd end up piggy-in-the-middle, her married life marred scarcely before it had started. Tomorrow, she thought as she handed round sandwiches, she would start girding her loins against all outside interference. This was her place. Hers and Harry's. Their lives. No one had any right to come barging in but on her, the home-maker's say-so.

Snuggled down in bed, she whispered shyly in Harry's ear that he only had a day or two left before her periods began again and the shop closed down.

'Never mind,' he whispered back after thinking about it for a moment. 'Yer'll still be 'ere beside me, an' we can still kiss and cuddle, can't we?'

It was nice to hear, though not doing anything would probably drive them both mad. Pushing it out of her mind, she turned her thoughts to this evening and the squash there had been in their tiny flat.

'What if our whole families had turned up? We wouldn't of been able to move at all.'

She giggled suddenly, her mind picturing an influx of people shuffling in a line slowly round and round the front room. 'Bad enough those what were here. Any more and it would of been standing room only, all the way up the stairs outside, everyone taking turns coming in and going out.'

She heard him chuckle as her words resurrected his own thoughts on the day, but in a while, because he felt pleasantly tired after having made love to her, she heard his breathing regulate, slow, each breath caught on a gentle snore that had become so comforting to her ears – a reassurance of his constant protection. After that she heard no more until the jangling of the alarm clock brought her awake to a wet Monday morning and the knowledge that she must get up and get Harry off to work. At last she was a real wife. And it felt good as, with him shaving at the kitchen sink, she made his breakfast.

Chapter Four

'No sign of any family then?'

Brenda forced a nonchalant smile as she sat in her front room with her Aunt Grace, the woman having decided to pay her a visit this Thursday afternoon. She had simply come up the staircase, knocked on the kitchen door and announced, 'Just thought I'd pop round, see how you are.'

Too many relatives just *popped round,* even after eight months since her wedding. It was about time they got tired of it, although it did help while away the time between Harry leaving for work in the morning and coming home in the evening.

As the first flush of being married and looking after a new home wore off she'd started to miss Alfio's. In her head she heard them chatting among themselves, chatting to their clients. She would recall that lingering, slightly stale fragrance on entering the shop first thing in the morning and the stale tang from the hairdryers switched off from the day before. There was always the lovely sweet scent of soap and perfumed hair lotions and the peculiar taint that came from the process of permanent waving – a mixture of heated hair, the perming solution itself and something electric emanating from the wires suspended from plugs above the customer's head. The memories seized her at the oddest times with a sort of a pounce, and she would sigh and look around her quiet flat and hurriedly go and make herself yet another cup of tea and have a puff on a cigarette.

Knitting helped. Keeping the fingers busy, and the mind. She had knitted Harry no end of Fair Isle jumpers these last eight months, the more intricate the pattern the better to keep her from too much thinking. With no babies in the offing as yet, she could have at least gone part-time at Alfio's. But Harry wouldn't hear of it when she mentioned the possibility. 'I ain't 'avin' no wife of mine workin' and that's that.'

'I take it you two 'ave been *tryin'* fer a family,' her aunt was saying.

Brenda shrugged, sipping at her tea. 'We're not in any hurry. We just want a little bit more savings to give our kid a good start. There's time.'

'Not as much as you think, love. A family ain't a family without little 'uns about.'

Brenda retained her smile. 'Give us a chance, Aunt. We ain't even been married a year yet.'

'Only four months off it.' Her aunt surveyed her with a look of censure. 'I'd of thought yer'd of gone some way towards it, at least clicked by now. Oughter be thinking about it, yer know.'

'We are thinking about it,' Brenda countered and took an abrupt sip of her tea, in her agitation spilling a few drops down the bodice of her blue crêpe dress. 'Oh,

BUM!' Alone, she'd have said something far stronger but Aunt Grace wasn't one for swearing. She liked to put on airs.

Leaping up she hurried into the kitchen for a flannel, and returned with the front of her dress darkly damp but no harm done. The incident however did put a stop on her aunt's interest in babies for the moment.

But it wasn't so much the spilled tea that had annoyed her as those small stabs of disappointment each time her periods showed up. She and Harry had begun trying around Christmas but so far nothing had happened.

Even as the family gathered for Christmas Day at her mother's, Boxing Day at his, and again on New Year's Eve with his people, she had noticed eyes straying to her middle in hopes of seeing a tell-tale bulge there.

Harry had noticed too. 'S'pose it is time we thought of a family,' he'd said a day or two after the New Year. 'S'pose we've waited long enough and I can't see us saving any more than we 'ave. Uvver people manage on less'n what I earn. I s'pose we can.'

With a small surge of excitement, she'd agreed, although a little irked that others were virtually pushing them into making a decision when it should have been solely their own. But, oh, the joy of dispensing with those ugly, cumbersome rubber sheaths which she'd always hated, to make love with such a feeling of freedom, her tender parts no longer rasped by unforgiving rubber that had to be lubricated first to make entry easy; their amour no longer interrupted when he had to turn his back to her to fiddle about fitting it on.

Once she'd offered to help him, thinking it might in some strange way rouse them further, but his face had flushed deep red in the shaft of moonlight pouring through the curtains she'd forgotten to draw fully together and he'd snapped at her saying it wasn't her place to do things like that and to stop being rude.

Their ardour had seeped out of them both and he'd thrown the thing back in its box and lain back staring at the ceiling. She had tried to coax him but it had been no good. She too had got angry and, with tears running from the corner of her eyes, had turned over away from him.

Next morning they'd both been silent and sulky – that was until he was almost halfway down the staircase and she remembered how Mum had always told her never to let the sun set on an argument nor let someone leave the house without making up first.

'You never know,' she'd always impressed on her, 'if they might 'ave an accident and you never see them again. You'd never forgive yerself.'

What if he'd had an accident that day? She had called him back and hugged him goodbye, sending him off with a smile on both their faces.

Of course Aunt Grace was right, a child made a marriage, and there should by now have been some sign of pregnancy. She would be the first to admit disappointment that nothing had so far happened. And another thing, carrying would put an end to those horrible squares of towels a woman had to wear nearly a week out of every month – towelling that had to be soaked in a bucket of salt water, rinsed and boiled, which after only an hour or so of being worn would chafe and often cut the tender inside of the leg as the blood dried along the edge of the folds almost to razor-blade sharpness. The hours of work to get them clean always left behind yellowish stains for all the scrubbing and boiling and bleaching. She had lost count of the times she'd gone out to buy another half-dozen from the haberdashery, all soft and fluffy, but after a few month's wear, harsh and abrasive. Done with too would be that dull pain she got at the start of every period, and sometimes sharp intermittent stabs too. To think, freedom from that for the next nine months. Why did women have to go through it? It wasn't really fair. Men never had to.

Nine month's freedom from all that in itself made pregnancy attractive. Brenda sighed and poured her aunt another tea, the amber liquid all fresh and clear in her still practically new white china cups with their tiny raised rosebuds around the rims. 'I hope it happens soon, too,' she said.

'It ain't turning out ter be the sort of world ter bring kids into lately,' her mother observed when Brenda told her what her sister Grace had been asking. 'The way things is all going ter pot these days – fightin' 'ere, an' fightin' there. Makes yer wonder, don't it? But yer Aunt Grace 'as got too much lip, pokin' 'er nose in where it ain't wanted. I dare say yer'll 'ave yer kids when nature thinks fit and not before.'

She was right about the world going to pot, though it had been doing it for four years or more – Japan and China, Germany flexing its muscles as it marched into the Rhineland, Italy invading Abyssinia, Spain locked in a civil war. Even here, Mosley's blackshirt fascists were parading around East London as if they wanted to own it, trying to raise Cain, skirmishes breaking out between them and Communist supporters, the police having to break them up. Humans were so stupid; they couldn't be peaceful for one minute.

Last year there'd been a headlong rush of idealistic young men off to Spain seeking adventure in supporting either one side or the other. Caught up in the excitement, her own brother Davy had talked of going off to fight Franco's fascists. He had no Communist leanings, and said that the Spanish government forces were only being financed by them but that anything was better than fascism, and hadn't that business of Hitler ordering the bombing of those ordinary people of Guernica during April last year proved it?

It had taken all Mum and Dad's efforts to argue him out of it. In the end it was only hearing the British government was threatening to put in jail any of its countrymen volunteering to fight in Spain that had made him think again. Bravado was one thing. Being jailed by your own government was another. Mum and Dad had breathed a sigh of relief while Brian had scoffed about soppy idealists and how finding himself a girl would soon cure all that. Brian's every solution was a girl.

Had Davy gone, he might have got himself killed in some foreign war that was none of his business. It would have been awful. But now the smell of war had begun to hang over them all. Last month Hitler had annexed Austria, and even though the newsreels showed the people welcoming him with cheering and the Nazi salute, it had an ominous ring to it and everyone was on edge. When the government decreed that English children were to be issued with gas masks, an alarming reminder of the poison gas that had been used in the Great War, the announcement had Brenda's blood running cold. She had heard tales when she was young of her grandfather's experiences in France. He was gassed and several years later died from its effects. Gran, left a widow, had never remarried.

'But we still 'ave kids, don't we?' Mum was going on. 'Mind, I ain't saying you oughtn't start a family. Things 'ave ter go on and it'd be nice ter be a grand-muvver. But let nature take its course and it'll 'appen, Bren – when it's ready. An' don't take too much notice of yer Aunt Grace. Yer know what she's like. Yer sister Vera's just the same.'

But Aunt Grace had left a longing in her that was hard to ignore.

Whitsun Bank Holiday Monday, Hampstead Heath: 'Appy 'Ampstead as the Cockney called the place, the Mecca of the East End Londoner if he wasn't off on a pleasure steamer to Margate or a train to Southend.

For ages Brenda had planned for Harry's twenty-third birthday, falling on Saturday, to be celebrated here on the Bank Holiday Monday with a picnic, their two families present, the sun shining hot and brilliant. She'd been so certain that a wet and miserable April must give way to a decent May. It hadn't. Wet all the previous week, it was still showery, but in sheer desperation she had stuck it out with her arrangements, gratified that the others were as optimistic about it brightening up, even though they were down on the number she'd hoped for. It seemed other people had the same idea as they arrived surprised to find it almost as busy as on any fine bank holiday except for macs and brollies in abundance.

Dodging the showers, the traditional Bank Holiday fair doing its best to accommodate all those with the intention to stay a bit drier under the awnings of sideshows, stalls and fairground amusements, she and Harry, plus his and her mum and dad, several aunts, uncles and cousins, one of his sisters, and even Vera with some boy called Oliver, braved the brisk south-east breeze as they devoured sandwiches, cake, pop and flasks of tea.

Brenda, sitting on his mac close to Harry and pouring tea for them both, couldn't help a smirk at Vera and her Oliver hurrying off hand in hand towards the fairground. How long would she keep this bloke? Until their first tiff no doubt. Brian and Davy weren't here of course. Davy had gone off somewhere else with his mates, Brian somewhere else with a girl.

But it was lovely sharing a day with her family about her, even if it was threatening to rain again. The last time had been at Easter. It had rained all that holiday too. Then there had been a tussle as to which family to spend Easter Sunday with and which to go to on Easter Monday. In a way it felt like a repeat of Christmas, spending Christmas Day with one, Boxing Day with the other, but who took priority, his or hers? She could see how it was always going to be – dispute and decision with one or the other's nose being put out of joint.

'We'll alternate each year,' she'd said judiciously at Christmas. But then had come the priorities. Their first Christmas as newlyweds had upset Harry's people, who were not pleased at being chosen for second place, as they saw Boxing Day. It had almost come to a nasty dispute between her and Harry, and although she had got her way, Boxing Day had been one of tension.

'Nice of yer to come,' his mother had said as though she would have rather stretched the cold welcome to include '*or bother to come at all*'.

Easter had been a complete reversal. Striving to be fair, Brenda had let Harry's family have first pickings, going to them on Easter Sunday while reserving Bank Holiday Monday for hers. Then it had been her own mum who had behaved a bit off. 'I didn't fink yer'd be bovvering, Bren,' she'd said by way of welcome.

'We did come to you for Christmas Day, Mum,' Brenda had returned as huffily, the hello kiss they'd given each other cold, a mere stiff peck. 'We want ter be fair.'

Her reply had been a small sniff from Mum. The matter was dropped as Dad, his stiff moustache pricking her cheek, gave her a resounding smack of a kiss on the cheek as if she'd not been seen for months instead of the odd days she came calling as well as the occasional Sunday dinner with them, but she had felt the tension in Mum as clearly as she had felt it on the Boxing Day in Harry's mum.

'Next year,' she said when they'd got home, 'we'll 'ave Easter on our own and go somewhere nice. A boat trip ter Margate an' blow the lot of 'em.'

'If we've got the money,' Harry had said darkly. 'Might 'ave a kid by then.'

'Then we'll take it with us, won't we?' she'd snapped, suddenly tetchy, and they'd fallen into sullen silence but for terse exchanges when the need arose, till they had gone to bed still not speaking. If this was how married life was, she had brooded, her back to him, there wasn't a great deal to recommend it. And to think how starry-eyed she'd been on her wedding day.

But today everything was different. Her and Harry's families sat all together as chummy as they had been on her wedding day, sharing each other's picnic, chatting together on damp grass, on macs and waterproofs, the afternoon air as full of their camaraderie as it was heavy with the smell of fish and chips, soused herrings and shellfish, ice cream and candyfloss and engine oil from the fairground.

This was the first time of meeting up since the wedding and it did Brenda's heart good to see them as she sat beside Harry on the raincoat he had spread on top of a waterproof sheet over the well-trodden wet grass.

The clouds parted and for a moment sunshine flooded the slopes of fields and wooded areas. Amazing, what a bit of sunshine could do. Brenda felt her spirits lift immediately even though this golden light wouldn't last long. Already clouds were threatening to blot out the sun again and over to the south-east where the wind was coming from looked distinctly black, promising a real downpour before long.

But while the sunshine lasted it invigorated the whole populace. At other times virtually deserted, Hampstead Heath as on any Bank Holiday seethed with enjoyment and despite this year's poor showing in the weather department, the air vibrated to the clatter of fairground rides, a cacophony of tinny music, shouts and shrieks of those enjoying being scared out of their wits and the babble of voices split by occasional laughter.

Then the sun went in. A chill wind came up and suddenly all noise of pleasures seemed to become muffled. Brenda's spirits faded a little, but only a little. Wait till she gave Harry his other present.

Such a pity his birthday weekend had turned out to be a damp squib. He didn't look happy being dragged out in this weather. He looked cold. She was cold too.

She shivered and huddled close to him, sipping her tea from the flask's Bakelite screw-topped cup.

'P'raps after this, we'll make for 'ome. I think I've had enough.'

'Me too,' he said, gazing balefully at the fair sitting on its churned-up area of mud that had once been green grass. Its painted stalls and swings, merry-go-rounds and coloured electric lights tried bravely to glow through the now dull light. He glanced at the clouds. 'It's gonna pelt in a minute.'

Indeed, one or two fat drops of rain had begun to plop down on the heads of the merrymakers. People were beginning to stand up, put on their mackintoshes and capes, to open up umbrellas, gather up their belongings, some to run, most of them leaving behind a litter of wrapping paper, empty cans, bottles, orange peel and banana skins to mark where they'd been.

Harry opened their own brolly up while Brenda quickly put the top on the flask and shaking out the dregs of tea from the cup twisted it back on, shoving the flask in the carrying bag with all the sandwich wrappers. She'd get rid of them once back home, tidily. Why add to all the rubbish left to blow about Hampstead Heath until the garbage men came to collect it up? It made a sordid mess of London's only bit of countryside.

She pulled a face as the rain began to come down in earnest, the rest of their family hastily gathering up what was left of their hopeful picnic.

'It was a silly idea of mine,' she said, but his arm stole round her.

'No it weren't. It was a nice idea if the bloody weather 'adn't buggered it all up fer us. An' I'm really grateful,

Bren, honest. And thanks again fer me present. It certainly is different ter the others.'

Brenda laughed. 'So it should, me being yer wife.'

His parents had bought him a cardigan which he was wearing today for its warmth under his suit jacket. His brother Bob had given him a box of six handkerchiefs, as had one of his two married sisters.

'Yer can't have too many nose wipes,' he had remarked bravely as Brenda's mum and dad presented him with yet another small box of them so that he seemed to be laden down with hankies. Thank heavens his other sister had got him a tie, grey and blue striped.

Brenda, having eked out her housekeeping money for months and with a little from her fast-disappearing post office savings, had used the two pounds on a silver signet ring for him, engraved with his initials. It did her heart good to see how his face had lit up when he'd opened it on Saturday.

But she had another present for him, one she'd kept back especially for today and which she had hoped to present him in glorious sunshine. Well, never mind. She could hardly wait to see his face light up even more.

'Where's Clifford?' The first large drops of rain were moderating to a fine onslaught and Harry's sister Iris was gazing towards the fairground. And there he was, her two children's father, head bent, legging it back with one child in each hand, both protesting at being stopped from enjoying their candyfloss. He arrived out of breath from his run.

'It was bloody sunshinin' when we went there,' he hailed as he came up to the little group.

'We're goin' 'ome,' his wife said at him. 'Get them kids' macs on.' She turned to her mother as Clifford complied. 'Bloody fiasco, this. Who's idea was it anyway?'

Brenda turned quickly away, busying herself with her shopping bag. She felt Harry's arm tighten round her.

'I've enjoyed it anyway, Bren. You 'ave good ideas. Always do.'

Looking across to the rest, she saw Mum smile at her, reassuring her of her own support. Her dad, Harry's father and her uncle were all three standing around while Mum, her aunt, her mother-in-law and Harry's sister busied themselves gathering up their stuff, umbrellas wavering, even though the rain had abated for a moment or two. She turned to Harry who was looking watchfully up at the sky and whispered in his ear the other part of her birthday present to him.

'Harry, I've something to tell you. I was waiting till after yer birthday ter tell you. Sort of delayed birthday present I suppose. An' I wanted ter be sure. I'm six weeks overdue. I'm going to have a baby.'

Being as regular as clockwork with her periods, there could be no doubt about it.

He had been quiet earlier on after she had declined his offer to take her on one of the rides. She felt he'd been sulking a little, at a loss to know why she should refuse. Now he'd realise why. It took a moment or two for the penny to drop as he turned his head to stare at her. Then he was gazing into her face, his eyes truly lighting up. 'Bren . . . You mean . . .?'

She nodded eagerly. The next thing she was in his arms; he let go of the umbrella and gave out a whoop to cause those about them to stop what they were doing and whirl round to stare at them as he planted a great big kiss on her lips. When they broke apart he became aware of their bewildered looks and he held her away from him as though displaying her to them.

'Bren's 'avin' a baby! I'm gonna be a dad!' he shouted, throwing his arms wide like someone coming to the end of a song then catching hold of her did a jig with her while the others crowded around to bestow their congratulations, the rain which had restarted being ignored.

Brenda accepted it all with a heart that beat with sheer joy and pride and a deal of relief. No longer would she have to offer excuses for not being pregnant. Suddenly she was important, the first in her family to make Mum and Dad grandparents, and it felt wonderful.

Chapter Five

It felt so lovely being treated with respect, people enquiring after her, Harry telling her not to lift this, not to do too much of that, worrying about her doing any heavy house-work. It didn't occur to him that she did it anyway when he was at work. How otherwise did his shirts get cleaned, the linen get mangled, the shopping carted home, the bed pulled out from the wall for her to make?

In fact he'd attempted to make the bed for her before going off to work just in case she strained herself. Make it indeed! Once was enough – he tucked in so much sheet at the bottom there wasn't any left at the top to turn it down. As for the blankets, God alone knows what he'd done with them, but they were slipping off all night. Not wanting to hurt his feelings, she let him continue then stripped the whole thing when he was at work and remade it. But few things last forever. Within a week he'd tired of being helpful and she wasn't sorry. All that unmaking and remaking. So much easier doing it the once.

For her in these early days of pregnancy, this summer of 1938 was proving a happy time despite the clouds hanging over the nation. To bring a baby into a world overshadowed by threat of war wasn't something she'd have preferred but babies got born no matter what and she'd protect her own, with all her might. But it was scary and she couldn't help being worried. Who wouldn't be? Why did people have to destroy others' peace of mind with their selfish need for power? Why couldn't Hitler be content to rule as dictator of his own country Germany without annexing other countries?

'Because 'e's like all bloody dictators,' Harry said. 'Never satisfied.'

What with Austria, then Czechoslovakia, they'd come so close to war with Germany. But that was all past thanks to Chamberlain's negotiations with Hitler and Mussolini that Hitler be satisfied with what he now had.

'Czechoslovakia ain't that pleased,' Harry observed darkly. 'A bloody great chunk of their country sawn off it. All Chamberlain's done is sell them Czechs down the river.'

'So long as it stops us going to war,' Brenda told him and relaxed along with the rest of the nation to continue life as before, except that the papers told of the government stepping up its defences, and parks still having trenches dug in them, and gas masks still being issued to school children.

'I 'spect it's just a precaution,' Harry said as he too settled back utterly confident of his little island home remaining safe from Europe's problems.

With the threat of war diminished, his mind was mulling over a way of bringing in a bit more money. And God knows they'd need it with a baby on the way. He hadn't told Brenda about it yet and he wondered constantly how she'd take it when he did. But it was a good idea now that it was certain there would be no war. Even more so the way she was going on about this place. Better not to speak too soon though. Let it bide awhile.

Holding tightly to the railing, the iron cold to her touch, Brenda negotiated the slightly icy stairs with a cautiousness that bordered on trepidation. She was seven months now, carrying all in front and, so she felt, becoming top-heavy. The baby lay on her bladder, necessitating frequent visits to the toilet in the yard. It meant getting down these blessed stairs at least a dozen times a day. What if one day she slipped? The baby could be damaged. There was the rest of November, all December and part of January still to go; all the time she would be getting heavier and more cumbersome. What of these perishing steps when the January snows came? Bad enough in these early November frosts and morning fog, when the bottom of the stairs often became invisible.

She could have used the po up in her flat. Maybe she would have to as a final resort when her time came even nearer. But it meant the thing had to be emptied, carried down to the lavatory in full view of the other flats over the shops. Nor would she have two hands free as she did now. Even easier then to slip on ice or snow and in her condition lose her footing.

'Leave it ter me ter empty,' had been Harry's solution when she'd mentioned it. 'I'll do it for yer when I get 'ome from work. I ain't finicky, yer know.'

'I know, love,' she'd said kindly. 'But I can still manage.'

'Don't want yer slipping down them steps in your state.'

But there was no way she could bring herself to leave it full for him to empty when he came home from work. It wasn't nice, all dark orange and smelly after a day sitting there. Even she couldn't have stood it. And she wouldn't have wished that on Harry. Besides, it was embarrassing.

Mrs Copeland, a woman in her fifties who lived above Patterson's the sweet shop next door and in whom she confided a lot, said to empty the po down the sink, but that was out of the question. She did have standards. As a hairdresser she had become conditioned to absolute cleanliness and, like her own family, she had never been uncouth.

Mrs Copeland was a nice woman, if a little gross. She and her husband lived on their own now their four children were married. She was almost like a mother to Brenda when her own mum wasn't around. 'If yer in need of anyfink, you call over ter me. Just holler across the balcony. Me ole man, Les, can't 'ear yer – goin' a bit deaf – but there ain't nuffink wrong wiv my 'earing. S'don't ferget, anyfink yer want, luv, I'll be over like a shot.'

At least she had one good neighbour. Those on the other side above the chemist's shop, she didn't even know their names, only that they were husband and wife. They kept themselves to themselves. For all that, she had many times been aware of their kitchen curtain twitching, when they nosed at her making her way to the lavatory, the sly, sneaky pair.

'Are you all right, Mrs Hutton?'

The voice to one side just below her, with her halfway down, startled her. Her hand gripping even tighter on the rail, she looked down to see Mr Stebbings, the proprietor of the second-hand bookshop over which she lived, gazing up at her. Immediately she was conscious of the fact that he might have been able to see up her dress through the iron latticework of the open stairs. But his eyes were trained solely on her face.

'You be careful of these steps, Mrs Hutton. They're a bit slippy this morning. It's been a cold night.' His remark was light but earnest as she nodded her appreciation of his concern.

John Stebbings was a widower, who said his wife had died four years before – what of, Brenda didn't know, but she knew they had no children. In fact he didn't seem to have any relatives. She estimated him to be around thirty-six but he appeared to be a rather lonely man, a bookish man, quite learned she imagined. She wondered he'd not remarried, for though thin he was quite good-looking enough to have found himself someone after three years. Maybe he just preferred his own company and his books. That sort rarely made good husbands and who round here would be the sort he'd fancy?

He had put down the empty cardboard box he'd been holding and came to the foot of the stairs. He now held out a hand for her to take as she felt for firm ground, the final step to the cracked and uneven concrete being steeper than the rest, a trap for an unwary foot or a moment's lost concentration.

'Thank you,' she mumbled as she gained her footing.

He smiled and let go her hand. He had a nice smile. 'You shouldn't be going up and down these in your condition, if you don't mind my saying. I can see it being even worse once winter arrives.'

He was well spoken, so had most likely been born and bred in some other part of the country. She always found herself compelled to put on a better accent when she did speak to him, even though as a hairdresser she had taught herself to watch her diction. Customers liked you better that way. So many times then she had wished herself better brought up, not that she'd have wanted to change Mum and Dad for the world. But lately she'd let her speech slip a little, and mostly spoke as Harry spoke. It didn't matter so much these days. Who did she have to impress?

Better enunciation returned quite naturally as she answered him, wanting him only to go away. She didn't relish him seeing her going into the ramshackle wooden toilet even though he must know what her errand was.

'I expect I shall manage. We do, somehow. I'm OK now, thanks.'

Her words were meant as a signal for him to leave her; he understood and, with a departing smile, went back to the box he'd put down under the stairs in order to help her and busied himself stacking it on a pile of others.

Brenda hurried on across to the horrible little lavatory whose wooden door never properly closed but, warped with the years, gaped halfway up. She hated having to use it, was sure the secretive couple in the flat next door could see in by straining their necks. The place was a haven for dark cobwebs and was fearfully cold in winter. It never smelled nasty though. Mr Stebbings, a fastidious man, made sure of it always being clean. But how nice to have had the privacy of a toilet in her own home, she thought, lowering herself on to the wooden seat, uncomfortably aware that he used it too.

She'd been on to Harry time and time again about moving. Unfairly, she rather blamed him deep down in her heart. When he found this place he should have given thought to the inevitability of having children. But then so should she have. But she'd been so overwhelmed, so excited and overjoyed at this home of their own, their first home, she too hadn't thought of the inconvenience she now suffered. She shouldn't blame him.

Even so, Harry was being a real stick-in-the-mud. While she dreamed of a nice little house in a nice little neighbourhood, a few trees in the street and a little back garden full of flowers, he seemed quite content to stay where he was.

As the seat warmed to her flesh, for she was taking ages to pass water with the baby sitting on all her tubes, Brenda mused upon that little house of her dreams. Two bedrooms, maybe three, a nice front room, a dining room and a nice-sized kitchen, and of course an indoor toilet, maybe even a bathroom. No flat-dwellers above shops to see her progress back and forth to one like this.

Only yesterday she'd raised the subject again. 'God knows how I'm going to manage here when the baby's born, love. Bad enough now. If only we could find somewhere else to live. Somewhere really suitable – a little rented home. Couldn't we put our names down on a waiting list for one of them council estates like Dagenham?'

He had frowned. ''Ow can I afford that kind of rent, on my wages?'

He was right of course. A warehouse packer's pay wasn't exactly a bank manager's salary. She'd known that when they'd married. This was all they had been able to afford. It was no better now. And with a baby on the way, there would be an extra mouth to feed. No question now of her begging to go back to work to bring in extra cash. That old argument had gone out of the window the moment she'd fallen pregnant. It seemed they were stuck here.

'In anuvver couple of months, Bren,' he pointed out, 'yer'll be thin as a rake, back ter where yer was, an' running up and down them stairs again like nobody's business.'

Again he was right. Really the baby wouldn't be a problem, except of course when she had to take it shopping with her. That too had been solved with Mr Stebbings offering to let her keep the pram in his unused but dry shed under the outside staircase. And the flat's tiny boxroom would do for the child, probably for years, even if they had another baby. She knew too that finding another place to live such as she'd have liked could land them in all sorts of debt. But it didn't take away her dream of a proper home.

Getting up awkwardly from the toilet, Brenda hoisted her knickers, tugged the hem of her dress straight and pulling the chain noisily enough to tell the whole neighbourhood, made her way back upstairs.

The warehouse was huge, dwarfing those who worked there. It was noisy. In summer air flowed through its loading bays to everyone's vast relief. In winter it was like the Arctic. In the packing bays men shivered despite working like demons folding the flat cardboard to make boxes, filling them with the precise number of required items, not one more, not one less, working against the clock on piecework, impatient vans waiting to take them away. They remained on their feet from eight in the morning to six at night – longer if needed so as to earn overtime, with ten minutes' break in the morning, ten in the afternoon, and a half-hour for lunch. The klaxon blared to stop and start them, like bleeding automatons, so by the end of the day each man felt the weight of his labour.

A scarf round his neck, Harry worked like mad along with the rest, counting the minutes to the sound of the klaxon.

'I wouldn't trust that bleeder no more'n I could throw 'im,' resumed Peter Goodings from an earlier conversation touching on Czechoslovakia, broken off on starting work. World affairs constituted Pete's pet subject. 'I know it's all gorn quiet out there, but you mark my words, that bugger Adolf 'Itler ain't gonna let it rest. He ain't gonna rest till them Nazis is in power over the 'ole of Europe. There's 'im massing 'is troops while we in this country sod abart puttin' up a few anti-aircraft balloons an' diggin' 'oles in parks.'

'There ain't gonna be no war,' Harry told him as they stood side by side in the men's toilets during their ten-minute break. He turned to Fred Banes next to him. 'What d'you fink?'

The man shrugged and stepping back from the yellow-stained urinal gutter, buttoned up the fly of his worn trousers. 'Still looks grim ter me.'

'Yer fink so?'

'Wha' else?'

'Well, 'Itler ain't done nothink else since Chamberlain's chat wiv 'im,' Harry said as they moved away from the urinals.

Pete turned on him. 'What yer mean, he ain't done nuffink else? He'd bloody nigh walked all over Czechoslovakia. Has 'e stopped at Sudetenland what understandably 'ad nearly all Germans livin' in it, like 'e promised that bloody soppy Chamberlain? No. He's gorn straight on, takin' in all the non-German parts too. That's 'ow much 'e can be trusted. Bloody daft, we are.'

'Germany and France 'ave signed a pact on the inviolability of their present frontiers,' Harry pointed out, quoting yesterday's *News Chronicle,* his favourite paper, almost word for word.

Peter chortled as the klaxon to resume work sounded. 'More bits of paper. Meanin'less. You mark my words, we're headed fer war, and we ain't even ready. Bloody stupid country. Bloody stupid government. Next year this bloody country'll be at war, you mark my words.'

Harry remained unconvinced. Things had settled down despite Pete's gloomy predictions. Czechoslovakia and its troubles were far, far away in Central Europe, nothing to do with Britain apart from puny sabre-rattling. When the threat of war had first loomed, he'd hastily shelved what he'd seen as his brilliant idea to bring in some extra money so that eventually Brenda might get her little house. But since 'Peace In Our Time' had been seen to be working, he could see no reason why he shouldn't go ahead with his idea – in fact he had begun to feel very excited about it.

The only problem was Brenda, six weeks off having her baby. How would she feel about his plan? But if it brought in money towards the house she dreamed of, surely she'd not turn her nose up at him being away for the odd weekend here and there? He'd already tested one of his mates about it.

''Ow's it work?' he'd asked. 'What do I do ter get in it?' Bob Bennett had grinned knowledgeably, already in it. 'Nuffink to it. Just sign up an' yer do abart thirty-five drills a year. Yer does 'em in yer local hall an' yer get paid attendance. Yer goes on a few weekend exercises. Yer goes away fer a couple of weeks trainin', somewhere on the Yorkshire Moors or Dartmoor or the New Forest. Means bein' away from 'ome, but it's like 'avin' a blinkin' paid 'oliday really, a bit of adventure thrown in, away from the wife. *And* yer employer's bound *by law* ter pay yer fer the time orf.'

It sounded almost too good to be true, getting paid to attend, getting allowance money, enjoying a bit of adventure at the same time: a two-week holiday once a year, paid for. He'd never been paid for holidays in his life apart from Bank Holidays. Some jobs paid their workers three days' holiday, but his wasn't that kind of job. Here a holiday was recognised, but you took it at your own expense. Joining the Territorial Army, his employers had to honour his wages even though he wouldn't be there working. It sounded like paradise. But first he must speak to Brenda, see what she thought about it. She couldn't help but agree. After all, it was as safe as houses now the fear of war had receded, and to think of that extra dosh coming in. How could she not agree?

Dinnertime at the Wilson household was always a big thing. Dad, Vera, Brian and Davy all worked close by, and all came in for their midday dinner around one o'clock.

Today Brenda had joined them but planned to stay on after they'd gone back to work for the afternoon. If she got back home on the bus around four thirty she'd be in time to cook Harry's evening meal. Allowed only half an hour at midday, he took sandwiches and she would have a lovely big steaming hot meal waiting for him in the evening, come rain or shine. He worked so hard, he deserved really good food.

Today she needed to talk to Mum on her own, with no interference from the rest of the family. Mum would advise her properly. Meantime she let herself join in the light-hearted conversation around the kitchen table.

But Vera, who had come in well after the others and who chattered on after they'd left, seemed in no hurry to get back to work. She too had taken up hairdressing, though not at Alfio's but a so-called beauty parlour where she was learning mostly to do nails. She took staggered dinnertimes and the place where she worked was very near so she saw no reason to rush away until the last minute.

'Bet you'll be glad when the baby's born, Bren.' She eyed her sister's bulging middle, Brenda had only five more weeks to go. 'I'm really looking forward to being an auntie.'

Brenda smiled indulgently. 'How's Oliver?'

'Oliver?' Vera looked puzzled for a second. 'Oh, *him*!' Emphasis was laid on the 'him' in somewhat refined disdain. Vera had started speaking a lot better since starting at a beauty parlour. 'I'm not going out with *him* any more. I gave 'im up at the beginning of autumn.' She still slipped now and again. 'Well, we just parted company really. I'm going with Alfie Woodman. Me and his sister is friends at work and we went dancing together.

That's how I met him. He's a lot diff'rent from Oliver, lots more lively.'

'You like him then?' What she really wanted to say was, 'I suppose he'll last about as long as Oliver did.'

Obviously Vera's natural bent for fault-finding would have driven him away. But a glow had begun to touch her sister's cheeks. Vera was in love. Perhaps for the first time. Brenda hoped so. She was dying to see her settle down. Or even Davy. It was a bit exacting being the only married one in the family. She wanted company so that she could discuss husbands, children.

'Mum said I can bring him here after Christmas dinner,' Vera was gabbling on. 'You coming to us for Christmas Day, Bren? Yer'll meet 'im.'

Brenda parried the question. 'Aren't you going ter be late back to work, Vera?'

It would be Christmas Day with Harry's people this year. She wasn't looking forward to it. She now wished she had spent it with Harry's people last time, then she would have been coming here this year. It would be awful not sitting down to Christmas dinner with them, them carrying on without her.

Vera had glanced up at the clock on the mantelshelf over the kitchen fireplace. It was only a fireplace these days; the old gleaming blackleaded range the girls had known as children had gone and an efficient modern gas stove now replaced it.

'Gawd! Look at the time! Mum, you should of said. I'm gonna have ter run all the way.' She was up from the table, grabbing her coat, hat and handbag off the empty clothes horse where she'd drape them when it was not in use for airing at the start of the week. 'I'll see yer soon, Bren. See yer ternight, Mum.' She was off, the front door making the whole house shiver as it slammed after her.

In the peace that descended with her exit, Mum got up and poured them another cup of tea. 'How's Harry, then?'

It was significant that she made no reference to Christmas Day. Brenda's reply was automatic. 'He's all right – same as always.'

Dispelling what had become air one could have cut with a knife, now was the time to embark on the subject she'd been waiting to confide to her mother. 'It's Harry I need ter talk to you about.'

She squared her chair to face her. 'Mum, Harry's gone and done something I'm not sure which way to take . . .'

'He ain't playin' abart!'

'No-o-o.' Despite herself Brenda had to smile at the question shot at her. 'No, Mum, he's gone and joined the Territorials.'

'The what?'

'The Territorial Army, the TA. About two weeks ago he asked me what I thought about him doing it. He explained about him having ter spend some weekends away from me and p'raps two whole weeks away training.'

Her mother put down the teapot and sat down, drawing her cup towards her, her eyes never leaving her daughter. 'But 'e knows yer goin' ter have the baby in a few weeks. 'ow can 'e go orf and play soldiers at a time like that? What did you say?'

'What you've just said. I told him to at least wait till I had the baby. An' I said too that it remained ter be seen if he should do it even then. I might be needing 'is help once it's born. Trouble is, 'ow can I not let 'im? It's the only way he's ever going ter bring in any extra money. He ain't skilled enough to go finding any other better-paid job, and it do look like we could be stuck in that flat of ours forever. This way he can save a bit towards a better 'ome fer us all. That's what I want, Mum, somewhere better to live. I'm beginning to hate it there. But him taking me by surprise I went off the deep end at him. We had a row. The next day he just went and signed on.'

'You was still at loggerheads next morning?' Her mother scrutinised her, aghast. 'I've always said never leave the 'ouse or go ter bed wivvout makin' up.'

Brenda fell silent. Trust her to worry over something unimportant when something far more crucial was at stake. Yet what was she consulting Mum for? Harry had already signed on. Whatever she or Mum thought, it was too late. He couldn't unsign himself. She just wanted Mum to agree that it had been the wrong thing to do without getting her proper agreement first.

Her mother reached for her hand across the table. 'Don't blame 'im, luv. He thought 'e was doin' 'is best. Ain't as if 'e's goin' orf ter war, now, is it? An' it might do yer both good, 'im doin' somethink. Sometimes I fink you two are thrown too close ter one anuvver in that poky little flat of yours. Do yer both good to be apart every now an' again. Absence makes the 'eart grow fonder, yer know. An' you'd get a bit of time to yerself too. Maybe see a few friends. You ain't 'ad enough friends since yer married. Look up some of 'em yer worked wiv. Or join a muvvers' club. There are some around, talking abart their kids. Yer might find yerself an 'obby. Yer could even take in a couple of people wot wants their 'air cut an' styled a bit cheaper, an' make a bit of money on the side.'

'Harry don't want me to do that,' Brenda said quickly. When he had put up barriers on her suggestion of returning to hairdressing, before she'd had the baby, she had suggested perhaps doing a bit at home to help their income. He had put his foot down to that as well, morose and tetchy, his manly pride dented with her implication that he was unable to keep them.

'I ain't havin' my place turned into an 'airdresser's, me stuck in the kitchen while you muck about wiv someone's 'air in 'ere. Every Tom, Dick and 'Arry traipsin' through, bits of 'air and wet towels everywhere.'

Yesterday she'd raised the question again. 'I just want to help us get a proper house some day. On one of them council house estates.'

He'd shook his head as if she was touched. 'All that way out, yer'd be moaning abart bein' on yer own all day while I'm in London at work. Yer've read in the papers abart them suburban 'ousewives getting depressions what they're calling the suburban blues, no one ter talk to except listen ter the bloody wireless all day.'

'Oh, trust the papers ter make a big thing,' she'd broken in angrily. 'There must be thousands really 'appy on council estates, all that country around 'em, but the papers find the odd neurotic sort. And you believe 'em!'

He had remained stubborn. 'All our family's 'ere. Before long yer'd be cryin' ter come back ter London sayin' yer never see no one. And me wasted me money. That's if I 'ad money ter spend on an 'ouse in the first place.'

'I don't see no one now,' she'd argued. 'All *I've* got is the wireless for company when it comes down to it, till you get home at night.'

'Yer can still see yer family a couple of times a week. Me mum visits yer. We see them at weekends, or your people. Stuck out at Dagenham yer won't see a bloody soul. No one's gonna afford ter go all that way. Yer'll be isolated. An' anuvver fing. It ain't just the rent, it's the fares fer me ter get back and forwards ter work. I'd 'ave ter buy a bike and cycle twenty bloody miles fer the perishin' job I'm in. It ain't worth it.'

'You could get a job locally,' she'd pleaded. 'They put up industry to go with housing estates so men won't have ter travel to London.' But he'd had enough of arguing.

'There ain't no way I'm gonna risk it, Bren. Not wiv a baby comin'. An' I'm not 'avin' you goin' back ter work, even in this flat – me a laughin' stock. I won't 'ave it. And that's it!'

She had flared up. 'Right! We'll stay 'ere! We'll bring up a kid in this cramped little hole and never let it enjoy any fresh air or anythink. Is that all I matter to you – me and the baby? So long as you get your way.'

'Yer do matter ter me,' he'd yelled back. 'You and the baby!'

'Then do somethink ter make me believe it!'

'I will,' he'd bawled at her and had flung himself out of the house, going off to work.

All day she had pined and fretted at what she'd said to him, letting him go off without them making it up. That evening he'd come back with his shoulders hunched. He'd said sorry about the argument. She'd apologised too, had kissed him tenderly, but it had still rankled. She knew he would never let her go ahead with her scheme to make a bit of money, and she did not care to raise it again in case it provoked another row. It was then that he had told her what he'd done.

'Did it in a fit of temper, I s'pose,' he had said by way of excuse as she stared at him, too flabbergasted to take it in properly.

'I know I'm not good enough for yer,' he'd said, his face glum as she continued to stare. 'It's the only way I could see of makin' some extra. The only way I can see of yer getting yer 'ouse some day. I'll put every penny of the allowance and stuff away and p'raps by next year or so we can move.'

'Oh, Harry . . .'

Everything else had been forgotten. What he said had struck at her heart. Even the shock of being told what he had done had been erased as she hurried to cuddle him, crying out, 'Oh, love you *are* good enough for me. I love you. I'd never of married you if I 'adn't thought yer good enough.'

Only when they'd gone to bed had it all sunk in, but she had had no wish to raise it then, with him snoring gently beside her.

Now talking to Mum it came back to her, as it did then, and maybe unfairly, that he might have done it solely to stop her thinking about doing a bit of hair-dressing, even at home, and crushing his self-esteem. Yet she couldn't blame him. He needed to have his pride, like any man. And the very second the notion of him being selfish came back to her, she wanted to hit herself for thinking such unfair thoughts of him. It was as Mum said, he was trying to do his best.

Chapter Six

Brenda's grin was one of affectionate mockery as she eyed her younger brother's sullen face. 'What's the matter, Brian? Girlfriend let you down?'

It was Boxing Day. Mum had got over the pique she felt about Brenda coming here today instead of yesterday, but fair's fair, Brenda debated. Now, with dinner over, washing-up done, and all her immediate family congregated round the cheery front-room fire, Mum was content and glad to have her here.

Brian grimaced at his sister, his face like a kite.

'I got toofache,' he said glumly and now the slight swelling on one side of his face became apparent to all, though it had been apparent to his mother since the day before yesterday.

'Yer should get that seen,' she advised as she cut slices from the Christmas cake already begun yesterday. 'I told yer, 'ave it seen to before Christmas or yer'll suffer all over the 'oliday. No one's goin' ter look at yer at Christmas. Yer'll 'ave ter 'ave an hour orf work termorrer and 'ave it done.'

Brian's grimace became even more pronounced, but his mother was handing her eldest daughter a piece of the cake, having already dismissed his problem.

'Yer'll take a bit of this 'ome with yer, Bren, or I'll 'ave it 'anging about fer ages. Davy don't eat it. Nor do Vera – watching 'er figure.' She looked across at her other daughter who was roasting chestnuts by the fire, then glanced again at Brian. 'And 'e won't eat any wiv a tooth like that. It weren't the same not 'aving you round 'ere yesterday, Bren.'

Brenda looked up sharply from the cake she was nibbling, Christmas cake as only her mother could make it, heavy and moist with fruit and spices, bitterish-sweet and so laced with brandy that its fumes gushed up the nose well before being tasted. 'I told you, Mum, it's only fair ter—'

'Of course it's only fair, luv, but it don't make it feel no better. I was just saying, that's all.' Her voice low, she looked across at Harry chatting in front of the fire with his father-in-law. 'Next year yer'll be wiv us.'

'Of course,' Brenda agreed readily. She too wanted that.

'An' we'll 'ave the baby too. Ter fink it'll be nearly a year old by then. Funny 'ow time goes. Me an' yer dad grandparents. Makes me feel quite old.' Mum came to sit down beside her. 'What d'yer 'ope for, luv? A girl or a boy?'

Brenda smiled dreamily, conflict over Christmas left behind. 'I don't mind really, s'long as it's all in one piece. A boy I s'pose, fer Harry. He'd like a boy. But it don't really matter, do it, s'long as it's all there and 'ealthy.'

'Ow-w-w . . .' Brian's moan took her mind off their conversation. His father glanced sorrowfully towards him while Vera went on blithely picking hot chestnuts off the little fireplace shovel she was using as a griddle, and Davy looked up from the crossword he was doing in last Friday's newspaper to grin unsympathetically.

'He'd rather put up with bags of agony than go orf ter the dentist. Yer a right little coward, Bri, ain't yer?'

Brian glared at him, fingering the swollen cheek. 'All right fer you. You ain't got ter go an' sit in that dentist's chair.' But Davy gave a mocking guffaw.

'I'd be there like a shot. What's the point sufferin' when yer can do somefink ter stop it? Yer got ter look it straight in the eye, Bri, yer coward. That's what you got ter do.'

Davy, always covertly proud of his willingness to look everything straight in the eye, still glowed from his earlier intention to go and fight in Spain against the fascists. But that was over. General Franco held sway. There was Hitler now to contend with, although Britain was sitting back in the glow of Peace In Our Time. But if the call to arms did come he'd be first in line to join up. He didn't see much point in joining the TA as Harry had done. Harry had only done it to get a bit of extra money for his family. As he had only himself to keep, with a decent-paid job what did he want going off to play soldiers? He preferred the real thing.

Brian took his hand from his cheek to round on Davy. 'Well, it ain't you's got toofache, is it?' And immediately returned to nursing the cheek.

Brenda looked at him in sympathy. She knew, they all knew, what a raging toothache was like – the unending hours of grinding agony, which even so were easier to endure than the visit to the dentist, where the evil, suffocating almond smell of raw rubber from the mask would ever be associated with that whirling sensation in the brain as the gas entered the body, all provoking a momentary sense of panic before oblivion took over. She could understand how Brian preferred to suffer a little longer until pain finally drove him there. And to have it over Christmas as well, with the house full of family members all being jolly – it had been quite a gathering at Mum's this year and Brenda ached at having missed out.

But all very well for Davy. If he had to go to have a tooth out, would he be so brave?

She told him so and had him grin at her. 'Well, don't you think it's daft, putting up with three days of that just to avoid a minute's discomfort?'

'A minute's discomfort?' Brian blazed, sufficiently angered to take his hand away from his cheek once more. 'This is a bloody back toof! Comin' through already rotten.'

Brenda raised her eyebrows towards her other brother. 'Then you're right, Davy. He should have it seen to. It could be an abscess.'

'Could be a wisdom tooth,' said Davy before his brother could reply.

'It's a bit early for 'im ter get wisdom teeth.'

'Some do come through early.'

'Why don't you two shut up!' Brian burst in. 'Talkin' over me 'ead as if I was a bit soft in it. I got a toofache – I ain't dim. Talking about me own teef over me own 'ead.'

Brenda couldn't help laughing. Poor Brian. His cohort of girlfriends should see him now, all pale and wan and suffering. No wonder he was stuck at home, not daring to let any one of them to see him like this. But maybe pale and wan and suffering was what drew some girls to a man, wanting to mother and comfort. Right up Brian's street, that.

She sobered with him glaring at her, but she couldn't help feeling so comfortably happy here with all her family. She had not been allowed to do a thing to help Mum; a pouting Vera had been asked to help instead, and she felt like an eastern potentate sitting here in the comfortable chair with her feet on a stool, her stomach stuck out in front of her under the flowered blue smock she wore, and Harry glancing over at her every now and again, he proud as a peacock.

What a contrast it made with yesterday. There was always an awkward feeling to Harry's parents' place. His dad was cheery enough, and there had been a lot of his aunts and uncles and cousins there to temper the atmosphere, but she always had the sensation that his mother was forever summing her up even as she chatted sociably to her: did she treat her son as he ought to be treated – the breadwinner and master of his own home; was she trying to establish her own will over his; would she be a proper mother to his child? It would leave her tense, and afterwards snappy towards Harry into whose ear she could not help suspecting his mother had dropped a casual word while they'd been there.

Not so here. Harry and her father got on ever so well together and Mum was usually all over him like the sun shone out of his backside at times. Sitting here, she felt she could view the future with much more confidence, and Harry joining the TA in November hadn't been as bad as she'd thought, especially after Mum had encouraged her with advice on what she could do during the times he *was* away.

It was true, since he had begun leaving her with one evening a week to herself she'd even started to look forward to it. Once a week he'd come home from work, eat his evening meal then go off to the local drill hall for lectures and things. He'd come back full of it, what he had been doing, the mates he was getting to know. Last week he'd come home clutching one and sixpence for having introduced a workmate who'd signed a paper. Harry had taken her to the pictures on it, in the ninepenny's, to see Gary Cooper in *The Plainsman*.

For the time being, Harry had been given a set of overalls to do his training in, free of charge, and a forage cap. After being in it for six weeks he'd get a proper uniform. 'They don't measure yer,' he'd chortled. 'They just look at yer and give yer the nearest size from the store. I'm gonna look a right prat in it, I bet.' Still, seeing him all dressed up going off to his drill hall equipped with the silver-topped swagger stick she wrongly imagined they'd give him as well – not real silver, but it would look good – she'd be so proud of him.

She *was* proud of him. He was doing something towards getting that little home she hoped for one day, giving her his attendance money which she put religiously away in the post office. There was not much in it yet, but it would accrue. He got paid too for weekends away and for that fortnight at summer camp and his boss would have to pay him as well – yes, their savings would soon mount up.

*

The doctor had given her a rough idea of when the baby could be expected.

'Sometime around the second week of January,' she told her mum and Harry's. 'Or it could be a bit later, it being me first, so he said.'

Harry's mother had cuddled her and said she would be fine. She already had grandchildren from Harry's two sisters, and it came to Brenda that she derived satisfaction now from the fact that this baby would be by her son. Her own mother cuddled her and said she couldn't wait to be a grandmother for the first time ever.

'I'm so proud of yer, luv. I'll be there ter 'elp yer, luv, when it's time.'

'I'm having it in hospital, Mum.' She'd been booked into the London Hospital for months. 'I'll be in good 'ands.'

'Yes, well, of course yer will. But I won't be far orf.'

The kiss Brenda gave her mother was warm and affectionate. If she had been having it at home, Mum would have been right there by her side, helping the midwife. Mum and Dad were paying for some of her stay, bless them, since her own meagre weekly contributions to Hospital Savings benefit could hardly cover it all. She wished she had gone in for the larger amount, but on Harry's pay that had been impossible, what with insurance and other bills going out every week.

Harry looked worried when she told him the possible dates. 'It's all right,' she assured him. 'I'm going ter be fine. Yer mother said.'

She couldn't help adding that last remark a little caustically, if with a laugh. But he still looked concerned.

'It ain't that, Bren. I know yer gonna be fine. It's just that around that time I'll be away on a weekend trainin' course. I might not be 'ere.'

She could feel the shock register on her face. And with it anger that he could be so unhelpful. 'You can't be away, Harry!'

He looked crestfallen. 'I don't want ter be. But I'm a soldier, luv. I 'ave ter do what I'm told.'

'You don't!' she blazed at him. 'You're a part-time soldier, that's all, and we ain't at war. Yer going to have to tell them the situation and ask for compassionate leave, or whatever they call it. You're a volunteer. They can't make yer go away at the very time yer wife's 'aving her first baby.'

They were compassionate. With no problem he was told that should his wife begin labour the weekend he was to go on the training course, he'd be excused. He relaxed. So did Brenda, even though, try as she might, there remained a tiny seed of resentment deep inside that never quite seemed to disappear as January arrived. 'You'd better be here,' a voice inside her kept telling him as he went blithely off to work and on a Friday to his drill hall. Somehow the joy of seeing him in his uniform had now paled.

Brenda lifted her head as a dull ache presented itself around the lower part of her back. She'd had backache before, but this was different.

She'd asked Mum what to expect when the baby started but all Mum had said was, 'You'll know,' a perplexed expression on her face as she tried to recall how she had felt at the outset of her four babies, mixing it up with the sharp agony of the one that had been a miscarriage.

'It's a sort of dull achy sort of feeling from what I remember.'

All she could remember was the vicious contractions of her muscles, producing such pains that she had just screamed her lungs out with it until the birth allowed its blessed relief. How could she tell her daughter what that had been like? What? And frighten the poor little cow out of her wits? She'd find out in time, poor little bitch! What women had to go through. If men had to go through it . . . At those times she had wished with all her heart that they did. Or that they could be there beside the poor sufferer to really see what she was going through. 'Once the baby's 'ere, yer forget all about it immediately,' she said encouragingly, hoping that would suffice.

Brenda waited. It was just before mid-morning. Slowly the pain went and she had no more trouble after that. Maybe it had been just one of those things. She did not tell Harry, there was no point, and had a good night's sleep. Next day the ache returned, at first a mere trace of itself, sometimes almost non-existent. Now it was late afternoon and the ache became suddenly more pronounced, a sort of throb, raising a definite question mark in her head. Yet all she could think was, damn, she was in the middle of doing ironing. A disembodied twinge of annoyance swept through her; it would be inconvenient at this moment to be carted off to hospital. Harry's dinner was cooking. Stew. In the oven a rice pudding simmered, its surface just beginning to brown. With an inborn sense of urgency she unplugged the iron, turned the gas off under the stew on the hob and switched off the oven. She was about to take the rice pudding out when a great stabbing pain caught her in her middle.

'Ooh!' Breath hissed through her teeth. From out of nowhere panic tore through her. Harry! How was she going to get hold of Harry? An hour would go by until he came home. And her mum. How was she going to get hold of Mum? Mr Stebbings downstairs – he had a telephone. 'Use it whenever you have to,' he had reassured her. Well this was an emergency.

Holding her stomach although the pain seemed to have diminished a bit, she opened the kitchen door to the iron staircase. A bitter January wind laced with flecks of snow hit her full in the face, whipping the shining pageboy hairstyle she'd achieved after washing it yesterday into a ragged mass of light brown strands. Wrapping her apron tight about her, realising that she should have gone back to get her coat, she began her descent.

The steps were still ice-covered from this morning and it was taking her ages, with her huge bulk. She descended one step at a time, hands almost sticking to the iron rail as she gripped it with both hands for support so as not to slip. She was sure the skin of her palms might come off on the frozen iron. Twenty steps down, it felt more like two hundred, the ground never seeming to get any nearer. Ten steps and the pain caught her again, this time quite viciously, making her stop and cry out.

Standing there halfway up in the air, in her flimsy slippers, the wind dragging at her hair, her loose apron, her extra-large skirt, her bare legs, tearing her breath away, all she could do was call out a faint and ineffectual, 'Help! Someone 'elp me!'

She hadn't bargained for this, it had not entered her mind. She had pictured perhaps waking up one morning, reaching over to the sleeping Harry and saying with a dart of joy, 'Darling, it's started.' He would go for an ambulance, then pick up her small, already-packed suitcase and help her gently down to the street with the expert assistance of an ambulance driver and nurse.

This reality frightened her. What if she had the baby on these frozen steps? What if it died of cold?

'Oh, God! Help!' The wind carried her voice away. Apart from that, the world lay empty and silent, at least close to, for she could hear the main road traffic building up with people beginning to leave work for home.

There came another alarm with the thought of people leaving work. It was Thursday, and Mr Stebbings' shop was closed for the half-day. She was alone here. All alone.

'Coo-eee . . . Brenda, wotyer doin'?' The call was like a wonderful full orchestra playing the most beautiful music. Joan Copeland was leaning over her landing. Brenda looked up and almost lost her footing in her relief.

'Oh . . . Joan . . . I've started. I've got such pains an' I'm all on me own.'

'I'll come down.' In seconds, despite her fifty-odd years, the woman was down her own stairs through the dividing gate in the fence, the gate never locked, and up Brenda's, and with a lot of huffing and puffing and 'careful-now-dear-take-it-slow,' leading her back into the warmth and safety of her kitchen.

Getting her to a chair, she shut the kitchen door with a bang, leaving the blustery, snow-spattered wind outside.

'Now, you just take it easy, luv. I'm puttin' the kettle on – make yer a warm cup o' tea.'

'There ain't time . . .'

'There's plenty of time. It's yer first. It ain't goin' ter come inter the world not at least till termorrer. We'll wait till yer 'usband gets home. I'll stay wiv yer. What time's 'e 'ome? Then 'e can go fer the doctor what can ring the 'orspital and send an amberlance. Now, you orright, luv? I'll get that kettle on. I bet yer dyin' fer a cuppa.'

She was terribly thirsty, she hadn't realised. Seconds later she was twisting to fresh pain. Mrs Copeland looked startled.

'That's quick. Should of bin 'alf an hour before yer got anuvver one. 'Ow long was yer out on them stairs?'

'I don't know,' Brenda sobbed. 'Ten minutes? It felt longer.'

Mrs Copeland nodded, relieved. 'It could of bin longer then. But yer could of caught yer death of cold standin' out there. Right, we'll get yer that cuppa and warm yer up.' She took a long sniff of the aroma of stew. 'Just done is it? Well, we'll get some of that down yer. It'll 'elp give yer strength fer yer ordeal ter come. You'll need it, luv.'

Not at all encouraged regarding this ordeal, Brenda meekly allowed herself to be given a cup of tea, and ate some of the stew which she had to admit tasted delicious to her, together with a couple of thick slices of buttered bread. 'That'll 'elp too. Blessed 'ard work 'avin' babies.'

She had one pain during that time which convinced her she must have been out on those stairs longer than she'd thought after all. She had stopped shivering by the time Harry came home. Opening the back door he let in a blast, closing it hastily and saying with easy good nature, 'Bloody weather – glad ter be 'ome,' followed by an equally easy, 'Watcher, ole gel!'

Looking up, he frowned to see her sitting white-faced on a chair with Mrs Copeland there in attendance. 'What's the matter, Bren?' he burst out. 'You orright?'

'The baby's coming,' she began, but Joan Copeland intervened.

'What I want you ter do, Mr 'Utton, is go fer the doctor and get 'im ter ring fer an ambulance. This weather, best get 'er inter 'orspital soon as possible. Yer never know, it could worsen and she'd be stuck 'ere.'

Harry's face had gone white. He tore open the door, clattering down the icy stairs with no care that he could slip. Joan turned to her charge, her florid face lit by a big motherly grin. 'Yer orright now. I'll stay till 'e gets back.' And never had Brenda been so glad of a friend as she was at this moment.

Chapter Seven

Harry's face held an expression of proud achievement as if he himself had given birth to the baby.

'They say yer can't call yerself a man till yer've 'ad a daughter,' he announced after he'd kissed her and then, very cautiously, the crumpled little cheek almost smothered by the shawl. He seemed to have forgotten that all along he had referred to the unborn child as *him*.

Propped up with pillows, sitting up as best she could, sore from the stitches, Brenda held her tiny darling to her. 'Where'd yer hear that?'

He was looking at the baby. 'Don't know. 'Eard it somewhere. I feel more like a man than I've ever felt. Sort of protective I s'pose. Responsible.'

He lifted his eyes to his wife. 'And what abart you, Bren? You feelin' orright? The 'ospital said you'd bin fine an' it all went well.'

She nodded. His total confidence in the hospital's assurance meant he had no conception how she felt, how she had been, what she had gone through. It felt as though the baby had been trying to take her insides with it in getting into the world. She was now left aching, and occasionally winced at a small blunt stab. She'd expected to be completely free of all pain, just as she had been the moment the baby popped into the world, and had gone into a panic at this first stab, thinking something awful had gone wrong.

'It's tor be expected, m' daarlin',' soothed the nurse with the Irish accent who had been with her through much of the labour. 'Ah, it'll go in a little whoile an' yor'll be as roight as rain.'

It was as Mum had said, she had forgotten the pain, now a dim memory only, but she could not forget the fear that had gone with it. Fear of the unknown, of being left alone, of feeling certain the gas and air she was being given was doing nothing to alleviate the agony, of being told to bear down, to push when she had no strength left except to give way and cry out, wasting her breath, as they told her. It had taken sixteen hours. And to think she'd had that idiotic illusion of giving birth on those ice-covered stairs at home. Then one last push and out it had popped like a little wet rabbit. The pain had subsided like magic, leaving only these odd twinges which she now knew would soon fade away. With Harry here beside her she felt only joy at what she'd achieved, but the memory of that fear would never leave her.

'It was yor first,' said the Irish nurse when she'd mentioned it. 'Most new mothers don't knor what tor do. Yor'll be orlroight with orl the orthers.'

All the others! She wasn't sure if there would be any others. For the present this was quite enough.

'What'll we call her?' she asked Harry before the rest of her visitors descended on her two at a time to see the little one.

All the fathers were at bedsides the length of the long ward speaking in hushed, whispering voices. In a while it would erupt with relatives and the place become filled with their gabble. Later they would depart, and the nurses would resume their work, quick, efficient and quiet.

She had seen it all as she waited for her pains to restart. All during that quiet night and next day she had waited, embarrassed that it must have been a false alarm. But they'd examined her and said she should stay.

Imagining what lay in store for her, she had sat with empty arms watching the others with their babies until by now she knew the procedure, feeling she'd been in here months instead of only a day, in this other world far removed from all that felt normal – the everyday world had ceased to exist. She'd listened to the faint rumble of distant traffic, but it seemed to have no connection with anything here, like stars seem to have no connection with the earth.

Out there was chaos. In here calm reigned, and an efficiency that was daunting, with everything running on oiled wheels. She couldn't remember in what order but it seemed every hour of the day something was happening. After visitors, babies would be removed to the nursery, then food came round filling the ward with its warm, overboiled smell. When that got cleared away bedspreads were straightened, pills administered to those who needed them, stitches which most women seemed to have swabbed or taken out, basins brought round, mothers asked to express into them any milk surplus to their baby's needs. This took place in order to nourish those whose mothers could not produce enough in spite of being shown, often sternly, how to suckle. Breasts were felt and examined for inflammation or infection. A dozen and one other things needed seeing to. The only respite from it came during the time of enforced rest, with the ward curtains closed and the nurses out of sight. Their voices could be heard murmuring in conversation from the office, and distantly, the fractious crying from the direction of the nursery which caused the mothers to lie worrying and not resting at all, tense and waiting only for their babies to be brought back for their feed. After that they would be put into cribs beside the mother.

Few doctors were seen but at some time during the day crumpled sheets would be restraightened and the ward tidied in a surge of energy ready for the matron's inspection. It had occurred as Brenda had waited for her labour pains to start again, though yesterday morning she had been too busy in the labour ward to care if the matron had done her rounds or not.

In preparation for the woman's appearance, mothers were ordered to 'sit up straight' as if they were staff instead of patients and despite the fierce prickle of catgut-sharp stitches sticking out from the most tender parts. Bed linen stretched like a board across the abdomen revealed not a crease, not a pillow looked out of place, not one item of a patient's belongings was in sight. It was like being in the army, as if the rest of the world pulsed to a different beat, or there *was* no world outside. A sigh of relief issued forth as the dignitary departed after having asked a brief question or so of a few of the mothers, giving each a nod and a distant smile before moving on to the next quarry.

She had bestowed her smile on Brenda. 'Still waiting, I see,' she had remarked and inclining her head graciously, had moved on, leaving Brenda feeling almost guilty that she hadn't produced one twinge of pain to order.

'I've been 'ere two days waiting for mine,' said a woman in a hospital gown who had wandered up the ward towards her, her abdomen so swollen that Brenda wondered if she might not be having twins. 'It feels like two weeks in this place. I don't half miss me own home.'

'I miss mine too,' Brenda said to the girl, whose name was Mavis. Mavis had nodded bleakly, arms folded over her bulging stomach.

She knew how Mavis felt. As they fell into conversation about babies and labour and how they would cope with them when they did get home, Brenda thought of her flat, no longer three poky rooms to her mind, but a haven of peace, seclusion, comfort. There was no comfort here whatsoever – just white efficiency.

'I've got to put up with this for a fortnight,' she moaned to Harry. But he was thinking deeply.

'We've thought up so many names, Bren, I just can't fink of a single one now.'

Yes, names. She brought her thoughts back to the question. 'D'you remember we once said Gerald if it was a boy and I said Adele if it was a girl?' She'd read the name in a book and had liked it. 'Let's call 'er Adele.'

He looked astonished. 'But that was just one you thought up when we was 'avin a bit of fun. She ought ter be named after someone in the family. P'raps after me mum, or yours. They'd sort of expect it.'

Brenda felt a ripple of annoyance run through her. 'Why should they expect it? She's ours, not theirs. I don't want to call her after anyone. And it'd end up upsetting one or the other.'

'She could 'ave both names, after each of 'em.'

'And one get upset because she'd got the other one's as a first name? Anyway, they've both got old-fashioned names. I want her to 'ave a modern name so's she'll feel comfortable with it all her life.'

'Then give 'er your name,' he said mildly, his easy going nature ready on this special occasion to fall in with her wishes. 'It's a nice one.'

It was a wonderful compliment, proving how much he thought of her to have said that, though it had probably been said in all innocence, but she shook her head.

'I'd like to call her Adele. It's different. Harry – she'll love the name. Adele Hutton. Adele Eleanor Hutton. How about that?'

For a moment Harry looked at her, sure she'd lost her senses, but her eyes were all shiny with fervour and she was gazing up at him so happy and so trusting. He couldn't upset her in her present condition. His determination to honour his mother with his daughter's name wilted. But his dilemma only grew.

Mum had been hinting about it for months. 'Let's 'ope it's a girl, eh? And she could even 'ave my name.'

Names! His child, the first girl in the family, should be named after her. His oldest sister had two boys, one named after Harry's father, Sidney, the other after his own dad, Charlie. His other sister had given her boy Dad's other name, Robert. His brother Bob had no children as yet; they had lost their first two months before it was due, a girl as it had turned out – a sad, sad business which Mum had never really got over.

She'd told Harry a long time ago how she had been praying his first child would be a girl. Now he'd made her happy, and now he must go and tell her about Brenda's choice. Bloody stupid name, Adele. Eleanor was even worse. Yet how could he face a great big argument with Brenda at this moment? She would get upset and argue. Better to disappoint Mum than have Brenda upset, so soon after having the baby and him getting all het up as well.

He'd be better biding his time. After all, they weren't going to christen the baby in the next couple of seconds. It could be delayed for weeks. He might get Brenda round to his way of thinking eventually. Meantime he would say nothing to Mum about the name.

It was good to have her home again. Sick of hospital and saying she was feeling absolutely fine, she had signed herself off against all warning that the hospital would take no blame if she had to be brought back. But Brenda was blooming. And so was the baby. The matter of the name had so far been neatly sidestepped even though she was speaking of her as our little Adele.

'Yer might of changed yer mind time we get ter the christenin',' he'd pointed out tentatively, but didn't pursue it after a look from her. He had held his tongue a while longer, just glad to have her back home.

Apart from having a baby waking up in the middle of the night which wasn't half as bad as they had both imagined – Adele seemed a contented baby if ever there was one – he was only too relieved to get back to normal domestic life. Much of those ten days without Brenda he had spent at his mum and dad's. Mum had been getting all his meals, and he hardly needed to go home but for a change of underwear, since she did his washing too. Mum had been so good, so self-sacrificing, and in answer to her questions as to what name they had thought of, her tone full of expectancy, he hadn't found it in his heart to hurt her. He'd hedged and said it was a bit too early to decide.

'You must've both 'ad time by now,' she'd come back at him, once more putting him at a disadvantage.

Everyone around him putting him at a disadvantage. Everyone on his back. All because of a bloody name! He was too easy, that was the matter, at least with women. At work, with his mates in the pub, and especially at the drill hall, in uniform now even if it was still ill-fitting, he was his own man, holding his own views. It was great being a soldier: Brenda worried for his safety, missed him when he left her alone, now even more so with a baby. She wasn't angry – the thought of a few extra quid made the difference, because she still clung to that home of her dreams, and of course one day he, the provider, would get it for her. And having the baby had put those ideas of her doing that hairdressing lark to help bring in an extra few bob and making him feel not worth his salt, all in the past. Life was bliss, with him master of his own house.

There had only been one row – well, hardly a row – even though she had rounded on him like he'd committed a crime.

She'd hardly set foot in the house, holding their new baby. He had been carrying her suitcase and helping her up the stairs. In the front room she'd tenderly laid the baby down in the crib he'd bought, had gazed around then returned to the kitchen, surprised to see everything so tidy. He hadn't needed to tidy. He hadn't been there for it to need doing. But dust lying thick and undisturbed was proof enough that he hadn't been there. So was the oven. As she bent to open it, there, in the centre, sat an enamel pie dish full of very dead rice pudding with fluffy green and black mould covering its entire surface.

'What's this?' She had withdrawn it and had held it under his nose like the prime exhibit in a criminal court.

'Harry! Didn't you notice it there? What've yer been eating these ten days? Surely you must of seen it in there.'

'I ain't bin 'ere,' he mumbled abjectly, inwardly seething. After everything he was trying to do for her, for her to do her nut over a bit of bloody rice pudding left in an oven!

'Look at it!' She had grabbed a knife from the kitchen drawer and with it was frantically digging the solid mass from its dish into the sink.

She was livid and it was so stupid. It was only a rice pudding. What was there to get upset about over one perishing rice pudding? There were more serious things happening in the world. But he didn't say so. It would only have made things worse.

'Where've you been then, if you ain't been here?' she'd shouted at him.

'Me mum's mostly,' he'd mumbled.

She'd gone silent and so he had enlarged on the explanation. 'She offered to get me dinners for me, save me doin' it.'

'And where did yer sleep?'

'Mostly there.'

'And I suppose she did yer washin' too.'

He nodded glumly. But she'd calmed down, leaving the offending rice pudding in the sink and going back to her baby. Having gone through all that giving birth it was natural she'd be a bit on edge. It probably wouldn't be her only outburst, but on the whole life seemed set to run smooth as silk.

'How'm I going ter manage, you being away?' she was bleating at him.

These last few weeks she'd become unexpectedly tearful. It wasn't like Brenda. Not from the very first time of meeting her had she ever resorted to tears at the slightest provocation. But now . . .

'It's only a weekend, Brenda. I don't *want* ter go. I just *have* ter.'

In actual fact he couldn't wait. To be under canvas, a real soldier for once with all the mates he'd made at the drill hall. It was an adventure, roughing it, manoeuvres, all that mock fighting, swinging like Tarzan from ropes over ponds, climbing over ten-foot-high wood frames and pounding along pathways, rifle in hand. Wonderful!

'I'll be back by Sunday night. Have ter be in work on Monday,' he encouraged her with a big display of making an effort to be cheery for her sake and grinning at himself for the cunning liar he was.

'I know.' She wasn't really crying, just bleating a bit. 'I'm just being stupid. It's being left here on me own ter cope with the baby.'

'Yer get on orright copin' with it,' he told her. 'An' I can't just say to 'em, me wife can't 'andle our kid on 'er own, so can I be excused, now can I? I'm in the Terries. I'm a soldier.'

Army regulars referred to them as part-time soldiers but he must nevertheless comply with TA regulations. 'In any case they let me off the previous training course on compassionate grounds when yer 'ad the baby, so I do 'ave ter go, luv. Couldn't yer spend the weekend at yer mum's?'

Brenda nodded and looked up from breastfeeding little Adele. She had got her way with the name, and the christening would take place in two weeks' time. But it had had its repercussions. His parents had come to see the baby twice in four weeks, and when they'd gone round there, though his dad was hearty enough, his mother had remained distant and frigid, not once referring to her hopes to have had her own name included in those bestowed on the little girl. That in itself showed how hurt she had been. But wasn't he hurt too, her behaving like that?

No matter how Mum felt about it, this *was* his baby and her first granddaughter. She could have been a bit more generous. So he'd come to agree with Brenda, and looking at his daughter's round, blue eyes, the alert way they followed his moving finger, and that funny little quirky smile which Brenda said was wind, to have named her Irene wouldn't have fitted her at all. She was an Adele if there ever was one. Mum would come round in time.

'I suppose I could spend Saturday with me mum,' Brenda replied to his suggestion.

He felt heartened. 'Yer should stay the night, Bren. Yer can't come back 'ome in the dark with a baby. If yer stay there, I can bring yer back on Sunday night.'

'An' where do I sleep? There's no room there, and all the baby's stuff is 'ere. On second thoughts, Harry, I'll be all right.' She had brightened considerably. 'I've got ter get used ter being on me own,' she added with such a change of mood that Harry was quite startled, if relieved.

A thought had come into Brenda's mind. She'd have all Friday night and all Saturday to herself, even Sunday up until eight o'clock. What if she invited Mrs Copeland to come over and have her hair cut and set? She wouldn't charge her. It would be a way of saying thanks for her friendship and her help when the baby had begun to come. Not only that, it would be practice, getting her hand in again. And when any time Harry was away for weekends, or even off on Friday nights for two hours at his drill hall, she could start taking in the odd person who wanted their hair done for half the price the hairdressers asked. Her only outlay would be a decent pair of scissors, and some setting lotion. She already had her own hair tongs, which could be heated over the gas ring of the stove. Hair could be washed in the sink, and the customers gone well before Harry came home. If he noticed wet towels hanging about, she could say she'd had her usual Friday night bath in front of the fire. He need never know and she would have some money to put away in her post office savings for the day they could rent their nice new house. The prospect filled her with eagerness and she found herself hardly able to wait for him to go off on his weekend.

Practice on Joan Copeland's harsh grey hair went marvellously, as well as providing a sociable Saturday afternoon after morning shopping. Joan promised to send a friend round on Sunday morning to be styled, this one of course for a two-shilling fee. After all, Joan's hairdo was done out of friendship, but she wasn't prepared to become a charity organisation. The two bob in her savings – ten of them to a quid – would soon mount up. Trouble was it could never be a regular thing, with Harry only away on the odd weekend. But she could give a regular Friday-night service, and an expert trim at one and six wasn't to be sneezed at.

'It looks really nice,' said Joan, admiring the results of the trim and a touch with the tongs in the little mirror on the kitchen wall. 'Yer've done it really nice. Better'n any proper hairdresser.'

Brenda didn't argue that she had been a proper hairdresser, just not allowed to carry on her trade now she was married with a baby. Joan's fifty-year-old head of iron-grey hair had taken some skill to make look bright and fluffy, and it was good to have it appreciated.

'Makes me look ten years younger,' she said. 'I'll tell me friend. She was goin' ter book an 'airdo at the 'airdresser's during the week. But she'll be round 'ere like a shot when she sees it ternight. 'er and 'er 'usband is coming to us ternight. We play whist, yer know, on a Sat'day night, the four of us. Wouldn't miss it. One Sat'day at 'er place and one Sat'day at mine. I'll tell 'er. She'll be 'ere. What time?'

'Say eleven?'

'Luv'ly!'

So Brenda sat down to her midday break, on this occasion keeping the main Sunday dinner aside until

Harry came home. Now she was two shillings better off and already dreaming of that little house in a year or two. Of course, he wouldn't be angry when finally she produced her nest egg for him to put towards the rent until he found a decent local job in whatever council estate they'd decide upon. Meantime this would be her secret and no harm done.

Chapter Eight

Harry was worried. The words 'peace in our time' seemed no longer to be holding much weight with Germany launching her first aircraft carrier and reported to be planning to double her U-boat fleet. In response, the British Navy was said to be undergoing a huge reorganisation to boost its fire power.

Everywhere you looked preparations were being made, especially them lorries delivering air-raid shelters. His mum's road had been told they would get theirs delivered around the end of February which was next week. Anderson shelters, they were called.

'Dunno 'ow they're goin' ter fit in these bloody tiny patches of back gardens,' his dad said. 'No room ter swing a bleedin' cat let alone one of them things.' His sorrow was that his precious flower border would have to go, at the moment bare but for the first green peeping from daffodil bulbs that must have been in ten years or more. Even so Mum had expressed her relief that they'd have something to shelter in if bombs did fall.

'Which they won't,' she'd added. ''Cos we ain't goin' ter 'ave no war. Chamberlain will stop it, like last year. I believe in 'im one 'undred per cent.'

A lot of people did. Harry hadn't their faith. And Mum was looking forward to delivery of her Anderson like it was a bloody birthday present.

It was said families earning less than two hundred and fifty pounds a year, roughly four pounds seven and six a week, got one free, which meant everyone around here. For many it would have been nice to see three quid a week, let alone eighty-seven and six.

People with no garden could get Morrison shelters for indoors, which might mean one for him and Brenda. They were a sort of steel table-like structure to crawl under in an air raid. Though the table his nan had given them for a wedding present was sturdy enough. Other than that brick communal shelters were being built. It all sounded so ominous, yet people continued to go about their business as if there was no thought of war whatsoever.

What worried him was him being in the Territorial Army. At night he lay awake stewing over how Brenda and the baby would get on if he was called up, and he would be. Well-trained and ready, they'd be the first to be inducted into the regulars. He'd been a sodding fool to sign up, but how could he admit that and not lose pride? Instead he vented his fear in rages against the nation in general.

'Don't understand this bloody country!' he burst out, crumpling his evening paper down on his lap. 'It says 'ere, Germany's launched a thirty-five thousand ton battleship called the *Bismarck*. If that ain't planning fer war, I don't know what is. The countries what they've already walked into are bloody landlocked, so why double a U-boat fleet and launch a sodding great battleship if they don't intend war at sea and us a sea-going nation? It all points ter one fing. An' there's us, our heads in the sand, muckin' abart wiv a British Industries Fair and some bloody washtub what does its own washin', as if *that's* a bit of news we're goin' ter be interested in!'

Brenda went on placing his dinner on the table before feeding the baby. She too was scared. She too visualised Harry being swept up in the first consignment of men. It could be the trenches in France all over again, with men used as no more than cannon fodder, being shot to bits or dying of gas poisoning.

She shivered, thoughts flying to the poison gas, her eyes turning to little Adele in her crib beginning to get restive for her evening feed.

'They've give us all gas masks and they're putting up them barrage balloons,' Brenda murmured. Wasn't that proof that a war wouldn't be just in France but that they were expecting civilians to be slaughtered too? There had been raids on London during the last war, and ordinary people had got killed. Since then planes had become much more efficient and high-powered. They could spray the population with gas as well as drop bombs. The gas masks being distributed said as much.

Again she shivered. The thought of getting down those stairs, carrying little Addie, hurrying through the streets to the nearest shelter while bombs fell all around, spreading death and destruction, didn't bear thinking about, and again she felt bitterness rise against the place they lived in – not only inconvenient but now full of danger. But like many people, while frightened and concerned about war, there remained a little voice inside her head that said it wouldn't happen, it was just that precautions had to be taken, just in case, and that Chamberlain could be relied upon to avoid it this time as he had last year. She said so and saw Harry's wan smile which didn't help.

It seemed his belief in approaching war was being proved right as the country's confidence in salvation, often with a tinge of desperation, began to wither. On the fifteenth of March newspaper headlines and the news on the wireless blared of Hitler having entered Prague against all declaration that he had no more territorial interest in Europe.

With no Germans residing there as his excuse to enter Prague, there could be no more doubts: the shadow of war hung over everyone as by the end of March those pale eyes trained themselves on the Polish border. Britain and France had no option now but to pledge to defend that country against any attack.

'Oh, Harry,' Brenda moaned, as they listened to the news, 'What are we going to do?' But Harry had no answer for her.

Mrs Hutton watched the departure of her son and his little family, Brenda pushing the pram, while he kept one hand lightly touching the handle as though he was helping push. How he could still be so considerate after the way she'd bullied him into doing what he'd done, Irene Hutton couldn't believe as she noted the fond gesture. Acknowledging their final wave when they got to the end of the road, she came in and closed the door, going into the living room where Sidney sat with her other son and his wife who had also spent Sunday afternoon here.

Having no family yet, Bob and Daphne had no need to go home so early to put a baby to bed. Irene sniffed back the pang of sadness at the loss of the miscarried baby girl. Almost a year ago and it still upset her.

Daphne leapt up as she came back into the room. 'I'll help you clear the tea things.' She was a good girl, always eager to help. Not like Harry's wife who hadn't even offered, merely sat cuddling the baby as if it were her only calling in life. She bet it was Harry who washed up their dirty plates while she mewed over the child.

Waving her helper back, she sat on the settee next to Bob and took a glance around her front room, warmed by a bright fire and the results of her skills in re-covering the ancient three-piece suite, together with cushions and embroidered headrests. On a similarly re-covered high-seated fireside chair in one corner out of any draughts sat her mother, cushions propped all around her.

'I ain't rushing about clearing away the very second the others 'ave gone,' she announced to all, apart from her mother who had fallen asleep. 'But I'm worried about Harry. He should never of joined them Territorials.'

Sid took his pipe from his mouth. 'It's up to 'im. He wanted ter do it.'

'And I know why.' Her tone took on an edge. 'It's 'er I blame, naggin' 'im into it with 'er wanting ter get a posh 'ouse out in one of them council estates. Taking 'im right away from 'is family.'

'And 'ers.'

Irene gave him a withering look which silenced him and he went back to comfortably puffing his pipe and gazing into the fire while she carried on as though he had never interrupted.

'Too many 'igh an' mighty ideas, that one. Nice cosy little place she's got, all on Harry's efforts, not 'ers, and still she ain't satisfied.'

'They've got a baby now,' put in Bob, keeping his eyes averted from his wife who looked at him with sharp appeal. 'Not much room for a baby.'

'They've got that boxroom.'

'That's all it is, Mum.' He shifted uncomfortably, feeling Daphne's eyes on him bidding him to drop the subject of babies. 'Six by five, innit?'

'It's big enough fer a cot.'

'And when it grows? A girl 'as ter 'ave a chest of drawers and a mirror and a wardrobe. There's no room there.'

'Then'll be the time ter find somethink bigger. But now? With a war coming on?'

'There ain't going to be a war, Mum,' Daphne put in hurriedly. A war would take Bob from her, and she with no children.

Before the fire, Sid's chest rumbled with phlegm. Hawking it up he spat neatly into the fire. Irene drew in a disgusted breath as the thick liquid sizzled briefly and disappeared amid the hot coals.

He worked in a wood yard and sawmill just by the Thames. Breathing in sawdust all day, he was bound to be troubled by phlegm, but there was no need to spit it into the fire in company, especially in Daphne's company. Her parents were quite comfortable, had a nice house in Hackney which put Irene's to shame. She bridled at having them come here and seeing what she had. Even with

Daphne she would polish and dust and examine for any little thing out of place if she and Bob were due to visit.

Daphne kept her own little rented flat off Roman Road as bright as a new pin. Fastidious, she was, you could eat off her floor. And now, Sid spitting into the fire, right in front of the girl.

'Fer God's sake, Sid, not in company!' she couldn't help bursting out, shamed. But he wasn't listening.

'I 'ate ter say it, Daph, love.' Daphne loathed the shortening of her name but he still did it. 'I don't fink we'll get away wiv it this time, not like last year. This time poor old Chamberlain ain't got no legs ter stand on. As far as I can see, 'e should never of 'ad that meetin' with Adolf 'Itler. We'd of stopped that bugger in 'is tracks if we'd declared war on 'im then.'

'Don't talk rubbish!' Irene eyed her daughter-in-law's paling face. The girl was insipid enough as it was, with such delicate skin and fair hair and light blue eyes – as if she had no blood in her whatsoever. But she had such a lovely disposition it was no wonder Bob had fallen for her. Next to her he was vibrant, dark-haired, dark-eyed, strong in body, tanned even in winter from an outdoor job as a roofer. Next to him she was a tender white lily. 'And don't swear, Sid!'

'Anyway,' she went on. 'I wasn't talking about war. I was talking about Harry's wife. She drove 'im to joining them Terries so's they could get a bit more money towards that 'ouse she keeps dreaming of. She should be contented with what she's got. I suppose she won't be satisfied until she's got it, even though he'll be one of the first ter be called up now. I suppose she'll be sorry then and blame it all on him.'

'That's unfair, Mum,' Bob burst in. 'If it do 'appen, then we'll all be dragged into it sooner or later . . .'

He stopped as Daphne let out a little cry, but his mother was already on her feet. 'I'd better get clearing these tea things. Get the place shipshape again. Come on, Daphne dear, let's get it done, shall we?'

Brenda, pushing Addie in her pram to her mother's this Saturday afternoon while Harry went off watching Spurs, his team, playing at home, also thought of war.

April had come; buds on soot-laden bushes in the patches of front gardens had begun to give them a cleaner look with the promise of spring. Pity there wasn't the promise of a happier one. When Harry had read that the Territorial Army was being doubled, its total strength to reach a total of three hundred and forty thousand, he had burst out, 'What the bloody 'ell 'ave I got meself into?' She, full of guilt feelings, had tried to make light of it, trying not to recall her dad's seldom spoken-of recollection of the trenches in France in the last lot.

She knew how Harry must be feeling. Her own blood felt like water in her veins even as she strove to make him feel less despondent. He was trying to be brave about it. He would be brave. But bravery wouldn't save him if he got himself in the path of a bullet, would it? She shuddered and hurried on.

The streets were noisy with kids. She couldn't imagine these streets quiet, as they would be if government plans to evacuate them from the cities took place if hostilities began. Two and a half million children was the number spoken of, a sure sign that London and other cities expected to be bombed out of hand, just like Guernica in Spain had been bombed, innocent civilians slaughtered. It was enough to make the blood run cold.

So much was happening all at once. Decisions to conscript all men of twenty years old, a compulsory national register of youths under twenty-one who'd be given six months' training for transfer into the Territorial Army. If Harry hadn't joined he might have escaped all that, being a married man. Now he was trapped. And it was all her fault.

Her arrival at Mum's found her father digging a three-foot deep hole, six foot six by four foot six, in the back garden with the help of Mr Johnston, their next-door neighbour. Strewn all over what was left of the patch of lawn lay huge heavy sheets of galvanised corrugated iron, the curved end of each side section making them look like beasts that had just died. End sections were propped upright against the rickety dividing garden fence, and on the narrow age-broken concrete path lay a bag of heavy nuts and bolts to fit the whole overlapping assembly together as the sections were dropped into the finished hole.

Mr Johnston already had his in; Dad no doubt had helped him, and now he was returning the favour. One third of his shelter sunk into the ground, bolted together but with no covering of earth yet. It looked like a great wallowing elephant, and as unsightly a bit of construction as anyone ever saw.

She stood at the back door watching them for a moment. All along the row of back gardens that had each been a square of neatly mown lawn with a couple of lovingly tended flower beds, neighbour was helping neighbour to destroy their treasured work for the sake of protection should bombs ever rain down from the skies.

Vain hope, Brenda thought as she stood there. A garden hardly thirty foot in depth put the structure not twenty foot from the house given that it needed to be a couple of foot clear of the back fence. What good was that if a home got a direct hit? Again she felt her blood turn to water.

Having deposited the pram, which Mum and Dad had bought out of their Co-op divi when Addie was born, in the porch, she'd gone through to the back and now stood letting in the chilly April air until Mum said to shut it as it was causing a draught enough to make the smoke from the back room fireplace puff out into the room. 'And I've only just put me duster round in there, luv.'

'Do you think there'll be a war?' Brenda asked Mum, who brought in a tray of tea and biscuits. Little Addie lay on cushions on the floor at Brenda's feet.

Her mother shivered visibly. 'This blessed fire ain't sendin' out any 'eat terday,' she apologised, glaring at it as though it should wilt before her look or blaze up in an effort to please. 'We ain't 'alf gettin' some rotten coal these days. I 'spect they're saving the best stuff.'

She broke off, not saying what for. War was on everyone's mind now.

'Do yer think there'll be a war?' Brenda persisted.

Mum shook her head, sighing. 'I don't know, luv. Don't know what ter make of it all. There's Davy sayin' he can 'ardly wait ter register, though thank Gawd he ain't rushin' orf like he wanted to durin' that Spanish lark. Silly little bugger. Well, I suppose he's a bit older now. An' there's Brian, all upset because he'll be too

104

young ter register. Mind, he's got girls on 'is mind more'n he's got war. Just wants ter make an impression on 'em, wants ter be in uniform and show orf to 'em.'

'I can't help thinking about my Harry,' Brenda said, gazing down at Addie with her little arms going and her china-blue eyes darting everywhere. She was twelve weeks old now and so pretty. To think, if war did break out, she might not see her dad for years, might not even know him when she did.

'I feel terrible,' she said, 'letting 'im go into the Terries just to help us towards gettin' another place.'

'You didn't *let* 'im, luv,' her mother corrected her. 'It was 'im told you he'd gorn and done it. It was 'is choice.'

'But it was me drove 'im to it.'

A key sounded in the front door and Vera came in. She was looking very put out as she dragged off her winter coat and smart little hat to drop them and her handbag carelessly on to a chair.

'Not there, miss!' stormed her mother. 'Take 'em up to yer bedroom.'

Vera ignored her, her pretty mouth working angrily. 'I'm sick of men! Ronnie told me he went and registered, even before it becomes compulsory. Did it this morning. If that's all he thinks of me I might as well tell 'im to take a runnin' jump!'

Ron Parrish was her latest. To Brenda's knowledge they'd been going out with each other for nearly three months, which made him almost a steady bloke. Perhaps he too had got fed up with Vera's ways. But this time, rather than smirking, she was a little sorry. About time some bloke saw something in Vera other than her aptitude for finding the negative side of everything.

105

'He probably feels he ought ter show willing,' she offered. 'He ain't actually going in yet. And if he does, I expect he'll write to yer.'

'Oh, he's promised to.' Vera had brightened. 'He says he'll write to me every day when he does go. If there's a war.'

'There you are then.'

'Now go an' put yer clothes upstairs,' urged their mother, going to call their dad and Mr Johnston in for a cup of tea. They had become somewhat hot despite the chill wind, their faces streaked with soil from wiping them with muddy hands. The earth three feet down was decidedly wet.

'If we ain't careful,' David Wilson growled, 'that Anderson's gonna be sitting in water. I ain't diggin' any deeper, that's fer sure. The bloody thing can take its chances.'

Mr Johnston, nearly six foot, built like a bus, his wide leather belt hardly enough to go round his middle, grinned in agreement.

'That's what I said, Dave, didn't I? When we got mine in. It's a bloody waste a'time anyway. This lot's gonna all blow over and the bleedin' fing'll be sittin' there in me backyard, a bleedin' eyesore, an' all me daff bulbs gorn fer a burton, and me chrysanth roots all bleedin' dried out fer want a' plantin' and no bloody good. Me whole garden spoiled, fanks ter 'Err 'Itler.' Mr Johnston's garden, tiny though it was, had been his pride and joy, a riot of colour in summer, neatly dug and manured in winter, his minuscule garden shed holding all his immaculately maintained tools.

He sat his bulk down on one of the kitchen chairs and with mighty slurps gulped the throat-searing tea Brenda's mother had poured as if it were cold water.

Within minutes he was up on his feet again, smacking his lips and announcing, 'That was taken an' wanted, Mrs W. And ta, very much. Come on, Dave, let's get the rest of that bugger in 'fore me old lady gets me tea on the table, or she'll 'ave me guts fer garters!'

Soon Brian and Davy were coming in, ready for their tea. Harry would not be home from football until six, giving Brenda plenty of time to walk the few streets home with the pram while twilight remained. Harry worried about her being out after dark.

Meantime it was good having a bite to eat here, though not too much because she'd be getting her own Saturday tea when Harry came in. All too seldom could she enjoy sitting down with them all, hearing Davy and Brian arguing light-heartedly, seeing Dad heartily getting on with his food while Mum hovered before sitting down to her own. She even relished putting up with Vera.

'Serious, then, you and Ron Parrish?' she asked Vera as she leaned over Addie's pram, which she'd drawn up close to the table. They were eating in the back room for once and it made Brenda feel very special. Normally Saturday tea was eaten in the kitchen, with no one really sitting down for long; Vera and the two boys were usually eager to be out again for Saturday night's enjoyment.

She laid a smear of margarine from her little finger on the baby's lips, taking pleasure from the attention her child got as the lips smacked at the new taste, the china-blue eyes wide with what could only be seen as wonder.

'Don't want ter get 'er too used to our food yet, Brenda,' said Mum, though she too enjoyed the lovely spectacle. 'Spoil her meal, it will.'

'It's only a smear, Mum.'

'Still feedin' 'er OK? Plenty of milk?'

'Plenty,' Brenda told her proudly, but desisted from smearing any more marge on the little rosebud lips. Her mother watched the child adoringly before she turned her eyes to her daughter. They glowed with pride.

'She's a picture, luv. Yer've done well.'

Brenda prinked inwardly and bit into her jam sandwich, all she would take from Mum without spoiling her own tea when she got home.

'What d'yer mean, Ron and me serious?' queried Vera suspiciously. Her eyes on Brian, who was wont to torment her, she addressed Brenda in a low voice.

'I mean is he the one?'

Vera coloured slightly and, suspicion fading, relented. 'I 'ope so,' she murmured.

Brenda hoped so too. It would be nice to see Vera settling down with a steady boy, and from what she'd heard of Ron Parrish, he was an easy-going sort who'd probably put up with her tantrums and carping enough for them to make a go of it.

It was a good couple of hours she spent there. Brian talked about where he was going this evening, to a dance apparently; Davy was going to the pictures with half a dozen other lads, Vera seeing her Ron. Mum and Dad would settle back in their armchairs by the fire once their children had gone out, keeping each other company, comfortably.

Brenda said her goodbyes long before the boys departed. Vera was already up in her bedroom, the one she and Brenda had once shared, getting herself ready for Ron when he called.

Brenda wouldn't be seeing her family next weekend. She could have, as Harry was going away again for weekend training, but she intended to style a couple of heads on Saturday afternoon, and another on Sunday morning.

Of course she'd get dark looks from her in-laws when she and Harry went there the following Sunday. His mother would wonder aloud why she couldn't have spared an hour or two for them on Saturday afternoon. But she'd face that when it came, smile sweetly and make some excuse.

They, like Harry, had no idea what she was up to, and the less they knew of it, the better. She didn't want any arguments with Harry. Not until she had enough in her savings to proudly put in front of him when the time came, and so dismiss all his objections. While he was away playing soldiers, even though he was bringing in a little bit of money, this was her flat, her place, and when he wasn't here she would do what she wanted in it.

Chapter Nine

Harry was worried out of his life. He was no hero, he knew that. He had been transferred into the *proper* army a couple of months back to be bellowed at by Sergeant Dodds, known with deep disaffection as Ole Doddy. Shaking in his boots he plunged the bayonet deep into the dangling straw sack seeing it as the enemy and believing it too with the protracted scream he was ordered to let out while hurtling full tilt at the thing. On manoeuvres, dodging real live bullets and real live grenades near enough to put the fear of God up him while real live shells burst in front of him and his mates in their headlong and erratic rush, designed to scare the shit out of him, he knew he was not a brave man. If this was as near to real live war as the authorities could make it, God help him when it did finally become real.

''Undred bleedin' times worse!' bellowed Sergeant Dodds in the ears of those returning exhausted, tottering and white-faced beneath the streaky camouflage of dirt.

August and the news was not good. Here in Aldershot he listened to men discussing excitedly how they were going to show them bloody Nazis a thing or two, and felt for those like himself who wished they'd never signed on at all.

How often she regretted what she had done. In moaning so much about her precious dream house she had pushed Harry to join the Territorials in the first place. But for that he'd be safe here at home. They trusted that if war came he as a married man with a kiddie would escape, at least for a while, being called up. It had been said earlier in the year that only *unmarried* men had been ordered to register. If war broke out maybe it wouldn't last long enough for Harry to get conscripted.

Every time Brenda thought of it, she mentally wrung her hands and hoped against hope that it would all blow over like last time and he would come back, maybe even be discharged from the forces. Meantime she fretted, angry that she now had all the time in the world to carry on her little hairdressing business. She no longer had any heart for it, pining for Harry, reproaching herself that it was all her fault that he wasn't here any more.

Perhaps writing and telling him she was doing hairdressing again might alleviate some of that remorse, like confession was supposed to do. Maybe he would understand the justification for it now that she was allowed only a soldier's wife's allowance, which gave her hardly enough to live on. He wouldn't quibble, surely.

'I wouldn't do that,' Joan Copeland advised her when she mentioned it to her over a cup of tea together. 'Wiv 'im away, that's all he needs, ter be told his wife's bin doin' somefink be'ind his back.'

'You make it sound like I was being unfaithful,' protested Brenda. 'As if I was going out with someone else.'

'It'd sound like the same fing to 'im,' Joan said. 'He didn't want yer ter work, an' you 'ave, be'ind his back. Ain't that a bit like bein' unfaithful?'

'It ain't the same at all,' she murmured. 'Every woman what's got a man in the forces will 'ave to get work to make ends meet. They don't give yer much to live on. You 'ave to. He knows that.'

But she didn't write and tell him. And as August progressed she went back to doing hair with a slightly easier heart that she hadn't.

It would have been with an even easier one if the news wasn't so ominous. Polish troops, it said, were rushing to their border as Hitler now began demanding Danzig and the Polish Corridor dividing Germany from East Prussia, and demanding an end to the British and French pact with Poland. If that wasn't a prelude to war, then what was? It seemed it could no longer be averted and Brenda, like everyone else, held her breath.

Five days later while Addie slept sublimely in her cot, the Copelands having popped over to support her following the announcement that the Prime Minister would speak of his failure to win peace, she and they sat in her flat tense and disturbed on the edge of their seats in front of her oval-topped, Bakelite wireless to learn that Hitler had cocked a snook at Britain's threats, had invaded Poland and bombed Warsaw, and thus they heard the tired voice of Chamberlain issue through the speaker informing them that, *as a consequence, this country is now at war with Germany. We are ready.*

'Oh, Joan . . .' Brenda's sigh was a low, drawn-out wail, her gaze flying to her small daughter, just eight months old and utterly defenceless.

Joan leaned forward as the voice died away, touched her hand, then with Brenda and Mr Copeland, stood up as the National Anthem boomed bravely into the room, its initial defiant roll of drums causing little Addie to start in her sleep and whimper briefly and fall quiet as all three looked at each other in silence, none knowing what to say. The silence seemed to go on forever, then abruptly cease with all the effectiveness of a thunderclap.

Brenda's next utterance of, 'Oh Joan!' was an exclamation of even deeper fear as a thin wailing came to their ears followed by a nearer wail and a still nearer one as if it were stalking. This was the first time either of them had heard it but they recognised it immediately for what it was, just as wild prey instinctively know the meaning of a snapping twig. The women stiffened, the man swore. Breasts rising and falling in near panic they gazed towards the window and the man let out yet another epithet.

'Bleedin' air raid!'

Adrenaline rose in them as if for flight, but where?

'Under here!' yelled Brenda, and grabbing a half-wakened and now crying Addie, scrambled with her under the big Victorian table that had stood the test of fifty years' continuous use, the sturdy top and the heavy, bulbous legs offering an immovable shelter.

Below in the street, people could be heard shouting, running, no doubt for the nearest communal shelter. Then all faded away to silence.

Under the table the three crouched, Addie making sure this room would not be anything like silent for the next twenty minutes, as Brenda did what she could to quieten her.

Distantly came another wail, this time one even note. The all clear! Creeping reassuringly nearer. Those under the table let out a great sigh of relief and crawled out. The street outside came alive; they heard voices talking animatedly, calling out, even laughing as Britain continued about its business.

'Thank Gawd we're all in one piece,' breathed Joan. She turned to Brenda. 'Look, we'd best be getting back 'ome.' She didn't add that they'd feel safer there, their own walls about them. She gazed at Brenda with something like appeal in her washed-out grey eyes as if for forgiveness that she was deserting her. 'Yer do understand?'

Brenda nodded reassuringly. 'Of course I do. I've got things ter do anyway.'

'Yer sure yer don't mind?' Again Brenda nodded. 'Yer'll be orright?'

'I've got to get something to eat, and feed Adele.'

Joan's gaze dropped to the baby Brenda was still holding. 'She's a little dear. She took it all well, didn't she? Well, I suppose being only a baby she'd know no diff'rent. Yer sure now?'

'Yes, I'm sure. Go on. And thanks ter yer both for coming in ter be with me.'

After dinner she had a lady coming whom Joan herself had put on to her, to have her hair trimmed. It would mean another few pence to add to her coffers. That was if the lady came now that war had been declared. But little could stop most women from wanting to look their best.

Brenda smiled, and with the others gone, got herself something to eat and gave Addie her bottle. Her own milk was fast drying up. After that she would lay down an old sheet to catch the trimmed hair, bring in a chair from the kitchen and set out the comb and scissors from her hair-dressing days. The scissors were sharpened by the old knife grinder who came round once a week.

It was mediocre work. How she longed for the days when she would give someone a lovely permanent wave, see the results all silky and bouncy. But she had no equipment for perming and no room for it, and no hair-dryer. No room existed for that either, even if she could have afforded it. Maybe one day she would. All she could do was wash, dry with towels, trim, style and curl, using tongs laid to heat up across the gas ring.

The results were always appreciated and it was cheaper than a proper hairdresser's. And sometimes a client would leave a little tip. It all helped, though in her heart she yearned to be able to do so much more. But even if she did have room, Harry would see it and not be too happy, feeling that his self-esteem was being undermined.

Brenda sighed and went out to the kitchen to wash up her dinner things and make everything nice and tidy ready to wash her first customer's hair over the sink. Thank God she had an Ascot for hot water and the little metal hairspray she had found it necessary to spend a little of her hard-earned profits on. Swiftly she fished in the cupboard under the sink and brought out the spray to fit on to the Ascot's nozzle.

Ethel Briggs would be here shortly. She was a young girl from across Bow Road who worked all week and went out all day Saturday. She came twice a week, Sunday afternoon ready for Monday, and on a Thursday evening ready for Friday and Saturday. She always requested the same style, her long blonde hair swept up from her small oval face, the curls pinned on top of her head. She brought her own hairpins though Brenda nearly always had to add a few from her small stock, for which she charged a little extra. No point giving them away – she'd had to buy them in the first place and it didn't take long that way to eat into the savings.

Ethel Briggs said she modelled in a big store in the West End which was why she was hardly ever home. She never said which West End store, but she wore lots of vivid make-up, and Brenda, looking out of her flat window, often saw her getting out of a taxi quite late at night. She was beautiful. Oddly, Brenda had never seen her leave for work in the mornings, or had always managed to miss her.

After Ethel Briggs she would have Mrs Bickham, who came regularly every Sunday afternoon, rain or shine. Hers was a simple wash and trim, her iron-grey hair stiff and harsh, but Brenda suspected she came here mostly for the company. Mrs Bickham was a naturally chatty old soul and it seemed a terrible shame when such people lived alone. Poor old thing had lost her husband years ago in an accident where he'd worked in the docks. Fell into a ship's hold, she said. She'd had one child who'd died young, and few of her family came to see her. Sundays could be long for those on their own and she really used these appointments as an excuse to fill an hour of the day. She always left a little tip. 'Fer the pleasure of yer comp'ny,' she'd say.

It made Brenda think of Harry; she too was alone these days. But she had Adele and she had her hair-dressing, and she still had Harry even though he was away and could only come home when allowed. She thanked God for all three as she pushed the end of the hairspray tube on to the nozzle of the Ascot.

It was a mad rush to get everything put away out of sight. By the time Harry walked in the door and she flew into his arms full of joy at seeing him home on his weekend leave at the end of September, no one would ever have suspected what she had been doing in his absence.

Getting his letter last weekend she had hurriedly cancelled all three regular appointments for this weekend, steeling herself against her disappointed customers' looks of pique and hoping they'd continue patronising her. After all, she cost a third of what they'd have to pay in a shop. She also prayed no one who might have been recommended to her and didn't know what was going on this weekend would come tapping on her door on the off-chance of having their hair seen to. It did happen from time to time, thus her reputation was spreading.

She'd dusted and swept, searched every nook and cranny for tell-tale traces of hair snippings, had rear-ranged chairs, and, thinking of the tidy sum she'd accrued in her post office savings, hugged Harry in his rough-textured khaki uniform to her.

It was worth losing money to have him home, to cook for him and see him eat with relish what she had cooked, to have him look at little Adele and remark how she'd changed and grown in the weeks he'd been away.

He'd changed too. She could hardly take her eyes off him, he looked so well and fit. He'd filled out in a muscular way that made her shiver with delight, hardly able to wait for the time when they clambered into bed, together again.

'Missed me?' he whispered as he got in beside her. The house lay quiet. Adele slept. She was very good at night, there'd be no interruptions.

She felt solid muscle beneath the pyjamas. 'What d'you think?' she breathed, aware of the mounting excitement inside her.

'I don't know,' he teased.

His voice had become lower, fuller, exciting her even more as she responded to his banter, teasing back, 'Well I ain't missed yer, so there!' Then, because that sounded so awful, she pressed herself against him, wrapping her arms about him, adding hurriedly, 'Yer don't know just how much I've missed yer. I don't know how I got through these last couple of months.' And she meant every word of it.

'Well I'm 'ere now,' he murmured, his voice growing hoarse, and with bodies entwined time became lost in a tide of pleasure, relief, and finally, deep and utter contentment as they relaxed, the long absence forgotten.

'We thought we'd pop in ter see yer, son. Didn't fink yer'd 'ave much time ter come round ter see us on twenty-four hour furlough.'

'They call it leave these days, Sid, not furlough.'

Harry opened the door to his parents' knock, they came in talking as if picking up exactly where they'd left off when Harry had gone into the forces. No how are you, son? No welcome home, love. No glad to see you.

'Brenda told me you was coming home this weekend when I came round on Wednesday.'

Mrs Hutton always dropped in to see her for a couple of hours on a Wednesday afternoon. Brenda made sure to

118

keep that afternoon free of hairdressing appointments, since her mother-in-law still had no idea what she was doing. Had she known, she would have written to Harry about it, and Brenda guessed the way she'd have put it too: '*Did you know your Brenda is . . . hasn't she told you?*' etc., making it sound as though she'd caught her doing something underhanded. Brenda was sure she would receive no praise for her efforts to help swell the kitty. Perhaps she was being a little unkind, but she'd come to know Mrs Hutton by now, and was aware of her conviction that her daughter-in-law did nothing but harass her precious son.

'I'm not being rotten, Mum,' she confided in her own mother. 'I 'ave tried to be nice. I must be turning into a right resentful whatsit, but she acts as if I'm always hounding him to get me own way. I ain't. I just want us to 'ave something better than we've got. What's so wrong about that? I feel she's always judging me – the way I bring up Addie, that I come to see you more than I see her, for wanting a bit more out of life, all sorts of things.'

At least Mum was on her side. 'Don't tell 'er too much – that's my advice,' she cautioned.

But Brenda needed an ally, needed to explain how she truly felt. 'I know I'm being selfish and I know she thinks I'm carping on about wanting my house so much. And I know there's a war on and many of us'll never get what we want. I know I should be thinking, "Let's just get through this bloody war, that's all", but when it is over, I want to 'ave saved enough, or helped Harry save enough, for us to get that nice house. After all, even if this war is over by Christmas, I think we both will 'ave deserved something better. That ain't a crime, Mum, is it, ter think like that?'

119

She had been gratified by her mother shaking her head in agreement. 'Well, ter see his mum, yer'd think it was,' she'd added.

So in came Harry's mum and dad, interrupting Harry's precious few hours with her, spoiling their last Sunday afternoon alone together for God knows how many months to come. They sat at her table drinking her tea, his mother holding Addie on her lap and demanding Harry's entire attention.

His dad wasn't so bad. After a while he fell into conversation with her, leaving his wife to commandeer her son.

'Makin' ends meet?' he asked, lighting a hand-rolled cigarette while Brenda took one from the packet Harry offered. She nodded to her father-in-law's enquiry.

'Sort of.' She wasn't going to tell him of her little sideline. In fact that didn't help her make any ends meet, being put away for something far more important. They would assume immediately that she was rolling in it if they knew; at least Harry's mother would, she was sure.

Without moving her body, Mrs Hutton turned her head to glance at her. 'Hope little Adele ain't goin' short.'

'No, Mum, she ain't.' It was hard to disguise the edginess in her voice. 'Do she look as if she is?'

'They should give army wives a bit more,' his dad said. 'After all it's our boys fightin' fer their country . . .'

'No one's done any fighting yet,' Brenda put in hurriedly, controlling a shiver at the thought of Harry being sent off to fight.

'We 'ad that air raid the day war was declared,' Mrs Hutton reminded her.

'That was a false alarm,' Brenda said. 'Turned out ter be an ordinary plane crossing the Channel which no one identified.'

'Even so,' Mrs Hutton went on, 'they must be expecting somethink, what with all them children evacuated out of London and all the big cities. Enid and Iris's boys 'ave gone. Didn't even know where they was going, and my 'eart bled for them two girls ter see the look on their faces when they came 'ome after seein' 'em off. You're lucky, Brenda, your little Adele ain't old enough ter be ripped from yer like my Iris and Enid's was. They weren't told where they'd ended up until two days later. *Two days later!* On some farm it was, near some village called Blighstone in Huntingdonshire. They're not sure if they like it there or not, but they're already 'omesick, poor little devils, torn from their 'omes ter live with strangers. An' now, everywhere yer go the streets feel all dead without the kids. Sort of eerie. It must mean they expect us ter all be bombed in the very near future. And you're saying there's not been any fighting yet.'

'Well, so far it seems a bit of a farce,' Brenda protested. 'They'll be sending the kids back 'ome again before long. I don't think Hitler's got the stomach ter take us on properly, not this time, or he'd of 'ad a go already. In fact some people are calling it the Phoney War.'

'Let's 'ope it stays that way,' Harry's dad remarked with a significant ring to his tone before taking a long, slow, meaningful drag of his cigarette, so thinly rolled that its tip hardly glowed, while a now-thoughtful family took in his words.

Chapter Ten

Wartime made a strange Christmas. But for Brenda it made a lovely one, if freezing cold, with Harry home on seven days leave and already in civvies.

'Can't wait ter git out of these bloody army togs!' he grunted, perched on the edge of the bed to drag his legs out of his harsh khaki trousers. 'Wot a bloody relief!'

Brenda stood watching on this Christmas Eve, remembering how he'd held little Addie to him seconds after clumping up the iron stairs, bursting into the kitchen to dump his kitbag so as to enfold her in his arms.

'Bloody 'ell!' he'd exploded as she presented him with Addie. 'She ain't 'alf bloody grown!'

'Well, she's nearly a year old,' Brenda had laughed.

'But it makes yer fink just 'ow long yer've bin away. I ain't seen none of 'er growin' up, 'cos of this bleedin' war. S'pose I've been lucky not to've been sent orf ter France wiv the Expeditionary Force or I wouldn't of got 'ome fer Christmas.'

After the so-called Phoney War much had happened in quick succession since October. Tons of merchant shipping being sunk daily by U-boats had caused the government to announce that butter and bacon had to be rationed in mid December, which at last made it feel like a war was on. Then war had really been brought home to everyone with the devastating sinking of the *Royal Oak* in its home base with the loss of eight hundred men. Not long after had come a general call-up of all single men over twenty.

Davy had been called up and, away from his old mates, had realised there *were* girls in the world and that, according to his letters, his uniform was attracting them like flies.

There was the blackout, of course, and the business of having to stick strips of gummed brown paper across all windows to safeguard against flying glass if there were air raids. So far, however, it looked as though more people were being injured by the blackout itself, not seeing icy patches on pavements or walking into things or being knocked down by vehicles with their lights covered and nothing to show up a pedestrian. Silly things were being done: white paint added to mud-guards and, according to some newspapers, in the country black cows having white stripes painted on them. People too put little strips of white paper on their sleeves so as to be seen by vehicles.

Abroad, the RAF, dropping leaflets on Germany urging the people to surrender, was at least bombing the German fleet at the same time. And a few days ago came heartening news that the battleship plaguing merchant shipping in the South Atlantic, the *Admiral Graf Spee,* pride of the German fleet, had been scuttled after British warships had trapped her in the mouth of the River Plate.

Thankfully there had been no ground fighting so far in France. But the one thing that mattered to Brenda was that Harry was still in England, still safe, and today here over the Christmas holidays.

She looked at him slipping into his civilian trousers and standing up to fasten them about his waist. They were slightly loose, but he had grown leaner rather than thinner, his physique brimming with full health, his muscles forming ripples beneath his skin as he reached for his clean white shirt which she had washed and ironed in readiness for his homecoming. They were going to have a glorious seven days together.

'I tell you what,' he said as he slipped a pullover over his shirt. The weather had turned freezing cold and the flat only had the one fire in the parlour. 'When we've spent Christmas at your parents and mine, we'll pop off up the West End an' see a show. We'll get your mum or mine ter give eye ter Adele. 'Ow about that?'

The theatres that had closed at the declaration of war had all opened again. Piccadilly and its surrounding areas might be blacked out, but inside each theatre the management had more than made up for it with brilliant lighting. Brenda's heart leapt at the suggestion and she clasped Harry to her.

'What would yer like ter see?' he asked. 'We'll 'ave ter line up though and take a chance. I can only afford ter go up in the gods.'

'I'd really love ter see that musical, *Me and My Girl*. I could do with a bit of cheering up. If we can get in.'

'We'll get in,' he said in a sure tone. 'I'll put me uniform on. It might 'elp the commissionaire to give it anuvver thought if he starts ter put 'is arm down as we get ter the 'ead of the queue – he might lift it ter let us two in if he sees me in khaki.'

He chuckled and draped an arm about her and she felt with pleasure the smoothness of his civvie clothes, the strength of that arm, and smelled the fresh scent of shaving soap on his cheek.

This year Christmas Day was being spent with her family, it being their turn and Brenda keeping to her rigid stipulation of alternating her festive-season visits.

Harry's mother wasn't too pleased. 'I thought being as Harry was 'ome, you'd of stretched a point this year.' But Brenda was sticking to her guns, offend or please. Harry, it seemed, was content the way things stood. He would get his share of petting from his mum the next day.

Davy was also home on leave, proudly displaying the corporal's stripes on his sleeve. 'I'm really enjoying it, Mum,' he said, despite the accepted notion that no one enjoyed being in the forces. But then he was athletic, an enthusiastic and, so it was turning out, natural leader of men, having honed his leadership skills in the group of friends he'd gone around with since school days. But now, of course, he'd found girls at last and stripes had proved an added attraction for them.

Mum was pleased and concerned all at the same time, ever protective of her sons. 'I 'ope you ain't getting in wiv the wrong sort, Davy.'

To which he smiled covertly, knowing what she was getting at, and said to Brenda, 'Yer'd think I was fifteen instead of twenty-five wouldn't yer?'

'Enjoying yourself then?' Brenda countered meaningfully and he nodded as he swigged from a pint glass of beer.

'I'm watching it. She thinks 'cos I never bothered wiv girls, I don't know what I'm about, but I know what ter pick and choose from, and I ain't ready ter go down with a dose of clap. Now where's our mum's mince pies?'

They were all here this Christmas, almost as if they were making the most of it while they could. Mum had excelled herself with her festive fare – sugar promised to be put on rations three days after Christmas, so she'd gone to town with her Christmas cake, pudding, mince pies and sherry trifle, and damn the expense. If rationing became really tight, she'd be saving money on food anyway for a long time to come. It now looked as though the war was going to be a long drawn out affair after all and things would get even tighter according to the government.

Mum's table groaned under its weight of delicious goodies. It practically sagged with the numbers sitting around it for Christmas dinner, all the aunts and uncles, nieces and nephews not in the forces as yet. In the evening the Johnstons from next door came in with their own family; the two houses were thrown open so that the drink was stored in one house along with the leftover food for the evening. The dancing and general merrymaking took place in the other, as both houses were accessible by way of the gate that had been made in the dividing wood-stake fencing years ago. That's how neighbours were around here, Brenda thought as she and Harry went next door, he for a beer, she for a gin and orange.

Adele had been put to bed among all the visitors' coats, along with the other tots in the family, all curled higgledy-piggledy, a heap of tired-out little forms, while the older children in the other bedroom slyly consumed the dregs of beer glasses and half-empty beer bottles which they'd pooled. The parents knew, but turned a blind eye. They'd learn! Tomorrow with heavy heads, they'd learn. But come next year, they would probably be at it again, the little sods! The parents smiled and got on with their own jollifications.

Boxing Day with Harry's people was equally jolly, but for Brenda, though she laughed and chatted with everyone, not quite the same as at Mum's. She wondered if Harry felt the same way about her family. He was bound to and she couldn't blame him, because she couldn't blame herself.

As with Brenda's people, little Adele was made much of by her grandparents, being unique on both sides, with one family the first grandchild, with the other the first granddaughter.

Brenda could see Harry's sisters' noses put out of joint, since their boys were virtually taking a back seat in favour of a sweet little baby girl. Rather than embarrassment, Brenda knew a certain tinge of triumph but did her best to hide it. She never saw them much, but she had nothing against them.

Both had brought their sons back home. The evacuation at least with them had not lasted long. A wailing letter from her boy had sent Enid hot-foot to Huntingdonshire to drag him away from the couple who'd looked after him. They were left in tears, having become attached to him and feeling they had failed in their efforts to do their duty.

Seeing her sister's boy home, Iris had made her own tracks to the farm where her sons were, only to find them contentedly stuffing themselves on home-made pork pies around a blazing farm kitchen fire and talking about how they had enjoyed themselves in the straw barn during the autumn, throwing straw at each other, and how they helped feed the pigs and chickens. They were even happy to rise at dawn having gone early to bed in the winter evenings.

They had been enthusiastically talking about Christmas with all the fare a well-kept farm could provide when their parents appeared at the door. Iris had been in tears. An argument had ensued between her and the wife of the farmer – so the story went – with Iris indignantly accusing the woman of setting young children to work contrary to the law and demanding of her boys that they pack their belongings and come home with her.

Brenda had stemmed a chuckle as the story was relayed to her and managed to keep a straight face. She could just see Iris laying down the law, very much like her mother.

Her brother-in-law Bob was altogether different, rather like his father, and chatting with him and his wife Daphne, she spent a more pleasant time than she'd expected, feeling more at ease than usual in the Hutton family, as she did with Harry's grandmother who lived with his parents.

It was a houseful on this Boxing Day and two days later with his mum willingly taking charge of Addie it was good to be on their own up in the crowded gods of a packed theatre, enjoying the music and dancing and joining in with the words of 'The Lambeth Walk'.

They spent New Year's Eve alone, happy to be so though Harry was due back off leave the following morning.

'I'll see you soon,' he said as he left, kissing her and the baby. It was a formal farewell. They'd said their goodbyes the evening before as the clock struck midnight, making love as if they might never see each other again.

Harry's return to his unit left Brenda unsettled and listless. It was going to take a while to get back into her stride and she had to push herself to do so. If she wanted to keep her little business, as she liked to call it, going she would have to take herself in hand and get on with the job. What upset her more was that apart from Joan Copeland she had no one to tell.

It came out while sitting round the Sunday dinner table at Mum's, with Dad, Vera and Brian there. She spent a lot of time at Mum's, trudging through the streets with frozen slush getting into her shoes and sending brown splashes up Addie's pram.

'It's a wonder yer find enough ter do in that little flat of yours, up there all by yerself, except fer little Addie,' Mum remarked after Vera had asked if she ever went out with friends and she had answered very seldom, her only friend being Mrs Copeland.

'That old thing?' Vera had scoffed, immediately putting Brenda's back up.

She ceased eating abruptly. 'I'm not like you. I can't go gaddin' about – I'm a married woman with a baby. I've got responsibilities. I can't just pop out for a bit of enjoyment just when I feel like it.'

'Don't this Mrs Copeland offer to 'ave Addie for yer so's you can?'

'She does lots for me.' Brenda returned to eating. 'I couldn't ask her.'

'What about Harry's mum? Don't she ever give eye to 'er?'

Brenda stopped eating again. 'What, and 'ave her asking me where I'm going and what for and making me feel as if I'm 'aving a swell time while her poor son's away? No thank you!'

Vera grinned. 'So yer 'appy ter let yerself become a recluse? It's no good pining after Harry, Bren. Yer've got ter 'ave a bit of life or you'll go daft. Making a martyr of yerself, that's your trouble. It ain't being disloyal wantin' ter go out and enjoy yerself sometimes. Ain't as if yer was goin' ter make an 'abit of it. Ain't as if you're goin' ter mess about with someone else or something like that. Yer've got ter go out an' meet people or yer'll go crackers.'

It was then Mum asked her question after saying she'd always have Addie. Hot under the collar from Vera's observations, she blurted out that she was all right and that she saw plenty of people when she did their hair.

It was Mum's turn to stop eating. 'Do their 'air? Yer mean yer doing 'airdressing again? Yer didn't say. What d'yer do with little Addie while yer out? I told yer I'd always look after 'er.'

Now she had to admit it. 'I'm doing it at 'ome, privately. Harry don't know. He didn't want me ter start working. Said he can provide well enough fer us all.'

'We know 'e didn't.' Her pale eyes took on a sly gleam that suggested collusion. 'But 'e ain't there now ter say, is 'e?'

Brenda smiled too. 'No, he ain't.'

'And what he don't know won't hurt him, will it?'

Vera gave out with, 'Ooh,' but Brenda was quickly on to it all.

'I don't mind you knowing, Mum, but Harry's mum don't know. And I'm not going to tell her if I can help it. She'll only start going on about me not telling Harry and how underhanded that is, and hinting I might not be looking after Addie as I should. As if she imagined me making pots of money to spend on meself. What I do make, and it ain't that much, I'm saving. Every penny. Every last ha'penny is going into me post office savings fer when Harry comes home and we can find ourselves a proper house to live.'

Mum went back to her meal. 'I think that's really commendable, luv, and I can see 'ow yer feel about yer muvver-in-law. But I wish yer'd of told me sooner. I wouldn't of disapproved.'

'I know you wouldn't,' Brenda said, cutting into her baked potatoes with nervous energy.

'Yer should go out more,' Mum was saying. 'Yer don't want ter be stuck up in that flat working yer bottom off all the time. Everyone needs a bit of a break. If yer want ter go out any time, don't ferget, I'm always 'ere ter look after Addie for yer. I'm surprised you ain't asked me before.'

'There's really no one to go out with, Mum.'

'Yer can always come out with me,' Vera offered.

'Or me, even,' added Brian.

It was wonderful. All these offers. She felt so cared for here in the bosom of her family, the house redolent with the aroma of Sunday roast, all warm and comforting, this year's fierce winter weather left outside.

'You've got yer boyfriend,' she said to Vera who was now going steady with Ron Parrish. He was just twenty-two, she had celebrated her twenty-first birthday last October, so they were of an age and, it seemed, well away. But at her words she saw Vera's face change. There was a chance that their relationship might end, this time through no fault of Vera's. Her Ron had received his call-up papers, as from last month all nineteen to twenty-seven-year-olds were being summoned. Any mention to Vera of her having a boyfriend would provoke her displeasure. The war was beginning to hit all of them.

Brenda turned quickly to her brother, chiding him affably. 'And you got all them girls yer go out with – I've no intention of playing gooseberry, I can tell yer.' She saw him look just a fraction relieved at her refusal of his offer.

'Not fer much longer,' he stated brightly. 'At least not round 'ere.'

Brian too, nineteen last October, came into the age group liable for call-up. In his case he couldn't wait to go; it made him feel a man at last. Only Mum and Dad would feel it, Davy already having volunteered.

'Whyn't yer join that young wives' club,' her father muttered suddenly into his dinner plate. 'The one what's formed itself in that little tinpot hall in Malmesbury Road? I 'ear a lot of them's got 'usbands in the forces. Yer might find someone ter go out wiv occasionally. Yer never know.'

'I might do that,' Brenda said.

She felt relieved, despite hearing the hollow note in her father's voice as he changed the subject back to her. Her secret was out in the open at last and she felt much better. It had been on the tip of her tongue to tell them on Addie's birthday last month, but Harry's parents had been there and she had found no way to mention it without his mother overhearing. Ears like a bat, that woman had.

Adele's had been a nice little first birthday party, held in the flat with only the grandparents on both sides there. She'd done a nice tea with a little cake she had made herself. Sugar and butter had gone on ration by then – four ounces of butter and twelve ounces of sugar per week per person wasn't much to allow for the luxury of a birthday cake, but she had managed. Everyone had said how good it was. But the whole thing was marred by Harry's absence. His daughter's first birthday party and he hadn't been there.

It was hard to be jolly, but she'd made the best of it. Adele in her second-hand high chair looked a bit bewildered as everyone tried to get her to blow out the single pink candle. Finally they blew it out for her. But she enjoyed her bit of cake, her face and dress got smothered in it. Brenda had saved Harry a slice, stored in greaseproof paper and then an empty Oxo tin with an airtight lid. When he did come home on leave she would present it to him. The gesture alone helped make him seem that much nearer.

'But God knows *when* he'll be 'ome again,' she remarked to Joan Copeland later.

So much was going on to lower people's spirits. Everything seemed to have come upon them all of a sudden – German troops gaining ground on a hundred-and-twenty-mile front north of Paris, the liner the *Union Castle* sunk by a mine with a hundred and fifty-two passengers dead, the weather enough to depress anyone with snow drifts, high winds, freezing temperatures and coal in short supply. Even the Thames was frozen over for the first time in over fifty years; and at the end of January the worst storm of the century swept the country while everyone huddled indoors feeling everything was against them.

Spring brought a bag of mixed feelings – irritation, encouragement, and for Brenda at least, brief elation. People felt irritation at meat going on ration, but encouragement in May with Churchill taking over as Prime Minister from a worn out and dispirited Chamberlain, warning that he had nothing to offer people but blood, toil, tears and sweat, at the same time declaring his determination to achieve ultimate victory.

'We're all right be'ind 'im,' her father said, his voice ringing with that pride the whole nation had begun to feel. 'We'll show them bleedin' Nazis!'

As for Brenda her elation had come after a letter from Harry saying he was returning home on leave. But it was short-lived as, hugging him in an ecstasy of welcome, she saw the extra-large kitbag and the weighty pack he'd dropped on the kitchen floor to embrace and kiss her.

She broke away. 'Why've yer brought *everything* 'ome?' But she knew even before his face clouded over.

'Somefink I got ter tell yer, Bren,' he began.

She didn't let him finish, her cry sounding to her like it belonged to someone else. 'They're sending you abroad? This is embarkation leave.'

She saw him nod.

'Where?' cried the voice again. Her mind seemed to visualise an infinity of dread, horror, grief, bereavement. She fought to control it. She saw his wan smile.

134

'Can't tell yer, me love. Not allowed. "Careless talk costs lives!"' he quoted from the posters that had gone up all over the country. 'None of us know, and they won't say.'

France! her mind shrieked. Or Belgium. The newspapers that had been full of Hitler invading Denmark and Norway now blazed a new name for English ears – Blitzkrieg – and told of Belgium and Holland invaded, of Belgian and Dutch troops being pushed back and back, of an unstoppable advance of the German war machine.

'I'll be orright,' Harry said to her fear. 'Yer know me, I know 'ow ter look after number one. Let's make the best of the time we've got tergevver.'

But it wasn't a happy leave. Mostly they brooded silently when not trying to cheer each other up. They went to her parents and attempted to be lighthearted. They went to his, and Brenda had to watch his mother fawning over him, monopolising him, her eyes watery and sad. 'I see little enough of him as it is. I won't see nothink of 'im when he goes away. I'm just 'aving ter make the most of 'im while I can. What if anythink happens to yer? If only you 'adn't joined that blessed Territorial Army, yer'd be like yer brother now. Yer wouldn't of got called up, you with a wife and baby. An' all because yer wanted somethink yer couldn't 'ave. That's what comes of yer both being too ambitious, Harry love. I don't know what I'd do if I lost you.'

'Ain't gonna lose me,' he said. But it was sickening to watch, even more having to listen to those thinly veiled insinuations that it was she who had driven him into the Territorials. How anyone could even think to display that sort of mawkish emotion when what he needed was for

135

them all to be staunch so that he could hold firm? Even so it was a job to hold herself back from tears as she saw him off when the time came for him to say goodbye. He wouldn't let her go to the station with him.

'It'll knock yer fer six,' he said. 'All them couples and families sayin' goodbye to each other. All them tears. All them dads cuddling their kids. No, I'd sooner say goodbye in the privacy of me own 'ome. I'll write ter yer as soon as I know where I am. And don't worry, nuffink's gonna 'appen ter me.'

That last kiss, that, 'Now you look after yerself, now,' had torn the heart out of her, making it feel as if he was taking it away with him. She was sure he felt the same about his own heart. 'I'll be back before yer know it, yer'll see.'

Watching him clump down the iron stairs in his heavy boots, she noticed his greatcoat and his kitbag and pack impeding his progress. His forage cap looked too jaunty as he turned at the bottom to wave a final goodbye.

Holding back tears, Brenda returned the wave and then he vanished from her sight through the yard gate leaving her to scurry back to the front window to catch a last glimpse of him from there. A few seconds before melting into the hordes of early-morning workers making their way towards Mile End Station, she saw him wave up at her.

Pushing up the sash window, Brenda leaned far out in an attempt to keep him in sight a little longer but all she saw was a hand shoot up from the moving body of people. She knew it was his. Then that too disappeared. And he was gone.

Chapter Eleven

There was no way to combat this anguish still tearing at her a whole week after Harry went back. Not a word so far and nowhere to get in touch, yet she must force herself to get on with her life as if everything was normal.

'I've got to, for Addie's sake, for Harry's sake,' she told her mother. 'But I'm going to pieces here all on me own.'

The reply she got was, 'And 'ow would he feel,'im sent Gawd knows where, if he knew yer was allowing yerself ter go ter pieces?'

'He won't know if I don't tell him.'

'Yer written to 'im? Yer know where he is?'

'How can I if I ain't got an address ter write to yet?'

Just as well he didn't know, but it didn't make her feel any less as if she was letting him down. 'Do we all feel like this?' she asked.

There was only one answer, go and find out. Taking her dad's earlier advice she went along on Thursday afternoon to the young wives' club. At least it might take her mind off herself.

Walking in through the unpainted door of the ramshackle little hall with Addie in her pram, she found the place not overfull but a-buzz nevertheless with lively chatter, the tinkle of spoons against teacups, while one or two tots hung around their mothers' feet or stared out from their prams. It was obvious that not all these women had men in the forces.

Someone came up to her, asked her name, bent and tickled Addie under her chin and, beckoning over a young woman, announced, 'This is Doris Osborne. She's new too – came first time last week. I'll leave you two to get acquainted with each other, all right?'

It felt strange getting to know someone from scratch and Brenda realised what a recluse she had become, stuck in her flat. She blamed it for lack of company apart from Joan Copeland, and sometimes Mr Stebbings who she might bump into from seeing her parents or Harry's, or on going shopping. She did see the two or three people who came to have their hair done on the cheap, but that wasn't the same. The last proper friends she'd had dated back to before she'd been married, girls from schools and then girls from work, but they'd all drifted off. It was nice to sit with Doris over a cup of tea chatting about husbands and family during the rest of the afternoon.

Doris, a thin waif of a girl with extremely blonde hair, definitely not a bottle blonde with such a pale skin, said her husband, John, was in the Air Force stationed somewhere in North Essex. Dutifully she withheld the name – careless talk, as the posters pointed out. Brenda wasn't that much interested anyway. But it was nice to find others all of the same ilk, alone, depressed, anxious,

138

sometimes full of fear for those they loved and could not be with, but most managing to hide it under a cloak of bright and friendly chatter.

The shabby little hall reflected their efforts. A trestle table covered by a white cloth had home-made cakes to buy and large enamel pots of tea. A smaller table held a doll to be raffled, someone having made all the clothes for it. The proceeds would go towards forces' comfort. A group of women sat in a little circle in one corner busily knitting khaki wool into what appeared to be scarves, gloves and balaclavas, in a sort of help-our-boys-out-there pool.

Apart from that little else seemed to go on except for standing around chattering. Even so, she came away promising to see Doris next Thursday, more heartened and determined to shoulder her lot and get on with things for Harry's sake.

His letter, arriving a week later and which she grabbed from the postman as if the man might take it away again if she didn't, said he was OK, was just somewhere in Belgium. The envelope with the words ON ACTIVE SERVICE on it was marked with a large censored stamp, so he couldn't say where. He hoped she was all OK too and had she tried to write?

She read it with a touch of anger. How could she with no address to send it to? Now of course she would, care of the unit scribbled on top. But anger turned quickly to fear. Was he in the thick of fighting? After saying he was fine, he'd mentioned he was looking after himself. What did that mean? All she could do was cling to hope for his safety, as armour against the anxiety his letter had provoked. News was all of Dutch and Belgian armies being pushed back, of German troops reaching the Somme, of the Belgian army beginning to fall apart before a terrific enemy onslaught.

She told Doris of her fear and anxiety for Harry. Doris nodded, adopted sympathetic expressions and said he would be all right, and that she must keep cheerful. But Doris's husband was cosily stationed at an air base not too far away, still coming home quite regularly. She wasn't going through what Brenda was going through, and her sympathy and encouragement were a bit hollow and gave little comfort.

Only half listening to the light but monotonic voice of the news announcer over the wireless, Brenda went on doing the middle-aged woman's hair. It was someone who had heard about how little she charged and was taking full advantage of it.

Brenda supposed she should be happy to get clients, but she wasn't very happy about this one. The tongs were raising a stink of grease. The woman had had a perm two weeks ago and fearing to lose the tight lines of waves she'd been so pleased with, hadn't washed it since.

'No, luv, I don't want ter touch it yet,' she said as Brenda suggested it be washed first. 'It'll last fer anuvver couple of weeks, then it can be done. I will come back ter you fer that.'

'You'll have to pay again just to have it washed,' Brenda warned but the woman grinned, revealing two missing front teeth.

'That's orright, luv. I'd of saved up a couple more bob by then. Yus, call it false economy if yer like, but it's the only way us sort can manage one week to anuvver.'

She'd laid out enough on the perm, she told Brenda quite openly, and could only afford to have it livened up by a touch or two of the tongs – which she couldn't do herself.

'Me arms is a bit stiff, luv. Yer know, at my age, a bit of arthritis an' all that. Just can't get me arms up far enough. Better 'aving someone else do it while I got a bit ter spare in me purse, though me ole man don't know or I bet 'e'd dock me 'ousekeepin'. He finks it comes by magic, this hairdo. Now I've 'ad it done, he don't fink it'll ever come out. Best keep 'im ignorant.'

And of course she cost far less than a salon. 'Just abart afforded it, I did. But now it's bin permed I don't want ter lose it too quick. Me ole man likes it. An' yer 'as ter keep yer ole man 'appy, don'tcher? I'll bring me own shampoo when I come next time, luv. Best not ter take chances wiv a perm wot corst me the earf. Took a lot of savin' up for this.'

Deftly, Brenda wielded the tongs, longing to have the job over and done with as the woman chatted on.

'First one I've ever 'ad, yer know. 'Ated it. Scared the wits outta me, all them iron fings stuck on me 'ead, me strung up ter that machine fing. Never again. Only 'ad it done fer me daughter's sake. She keepin' on at me. But me old man can go fer a funny run once it goes straight again. Never no more, I say. It was fer me daughter's weddin', yer know. She got married to a sailor. Gorn away now, 'e 'as. On 'is ship. Ain't heard from 'im since, she ain't, poor luv. But she will, soon. I just 'ope he keeps safe – fer 'er sake.'

141

Brenda's mind turned instantly to Harry. She hadn't heard from him either since that last letter, and that had really been hardly more than a note.

Trying not to breathe in too much, she manfully applied the tongs. It was then she became aware of what the newscaster was saying. Something about British forces being cut off with their backs to the sea as German troops took Boulogne.

Brenda felt her heart become like a piece of concrete inside her ribcage and it was all she could do to hold herself together as Mrs Stokes, her client, made a face in the little oval hand mirror propped up on the kitchen table for her to see in.

'Our poor boys, eh? Sons an' 'usbands out there. It's a shame.'

Brenda wanted to burst out that her own poor husband was among them. But that would have had her breaking down and she had a duty not to upset the woman. Never bore your client with your own troubles: a lesson hammered into her by Mr Alfio Fichera. She was glad to see the back of Mrs Stokes so she could nurse her fears in private, giving her mind to Harry who had to be caught up in the bloody turmoil that must be going on over there.

Lost in misery in the seclusion of her front room, a brief glance out of the window meant she glimpsed through reddened eyes Harry's parents hurrying along the road. They usually came on Wednesdays, but this was Monday. It had to be today's news bringing them here. Not having bought a morning paper she'd not known until it came over the wireless.

Her tears got swept aside and she leapt up, rushing about the flat to hide away the evidence of her client's visit. On this warm day the open kitchen door had allowed the stench of heated tongs on unwashed hair to waft out and by the time her in-laws reached the foot of the stairs it had mostly if not completely gone, helped on its way by the frantic flapping of a teacloth.

Still sniffing the air, she waited, trying not to look out of breath as they came up the stairs. But they didn't notice as, gaining the landing, her mother-in-law rushed at her with open arms and surprised her by clasping her in a powerful embrace of grief, her face flushed and twisted with anguish.

'Oh, Brenda, our poor Harry!' she burst out. 'At the mercy of them Nazi brutes!' For once she was too devastated to huff. 'Honestly, coming up them stairs do get yer down!' as she never normally failed to comment when visiting.

Contradictory statements usually made Brenda smirk, but not this day. She too felt eaten up by concern. 'I'm sure he's all right,' she managed, suffering the embrace.

'What if he ain't? What if . . .'

'I don't want ter dwell on that prospect, Mum,' she cut in sternly. Extricating herself from the grip she ushered them through the kitchen to the living room. 'We 'ave ter think positive. Harry'll be all right.'

He had to be, she resolved as she followed close behind them. So long as she remained so he would be. Yet despite what she was telling herself, her whole body seemed to be quivering from the inside out.

Mr Hutton was already fumbling for his cigarette tin and papers while Brenda went to seek a much-needed cigarette of her own from a packet of Craven A on the sideboard. Only one out of its contents of five remained, and she had opened it fresh this morning.

Should have been Player's Weights – much cheaper – fags gone up to eightpence ha'penny a packet – she really couldn't afford it despite a recent increase in allowance for wives of servicemen. She was smoking too much.

These stupid disembodied thoughts surged through her brain when she should be thinking of her husband's predicament over there, maybe caught between an advancing German army and this place called Dunkirk, a name the newscaster had mentioned. To dispel them, she said inadequately through nervous puffs of cigarette smoke, 'We can only hope and pray.'

They nodded, so she hurried on animatedly, 'Look, sit down. I'll make a cup of tea, shall I? It'll do us all good.'

'Not much we can do about it, stuck 'ere at 'ome,' Sid Hutton said as if she had never mentioned tea. 'All we can do is 'ope and pray – like yer said – and wait.'

'Wait and pray,' Irene Hutton repeated, her words like a small echo.

With nervous energy Brenda hastily attempted to stub out her cigarette in a painted china ashtray shaped like a kitten lying on its back which Harry had bought from some stall or other just after they had got married.

She'd smoke the rest later. But the cigarette went on burning as she rushed off to make tea. She could hear them talking in low tones while she waited impatiently for the kettle to boil, pouring the hot water on to a couple of spoonfuls of tea leaves in the pot.

Armed with a tray of cups, saucers, sugar, milk, teapot and strainer, she hurried back to find Mrs Hutton sniffing the air.

'Funny smell in 'ere.'

Brenda sniffed, caught a trace of heated hair, looked desperately around the room and saw her cigarette still burning gently. Gratefully she pointed. 'Must be that. I only bought 'em yesterday. They must be stale.'

Mrs Hutton's nose continued to wrinkle. 'It don't smell like that to me. Smells more like yer've been ter the 'airdresser's or somethink.'

Brenda handed them their tea, relieved to note that the accusation only focused on her apparently spending too much, although her natural waves, these days grown slightly longer, needed no visits to a hairdresser. She merely swept back the sides and held them in place by two Bakelite combs.

To take her mother-in-law's mind off the faint odour, she turned back to the subject of Harry, letting her face crumple a little. It was no effort, her misery was real enough as his handsome face came to hover behind her eyes, the merest thought of him enough for tears to tremble on her eyelids.

'Oh Mum, he's got ter be all right,' she moaned, her voice letting her down. 'For Adele's sake, he has ter be.'

Putting her tea down, Irene Hutton got up and came forward, taking Brenda by surprise yet again by cuddling her close for a second time. Any censure or disapproval that might have lurked within her breast in the past melted away as she made an effort to soothe her, for a moment softened by her daughter-in-law's moment of weakness.

'I know, I know,' she murmured, looking to her husband for corroboration. 'I don't know what we'd do if anythink 'appened to him now.'

Those words were the last straw for Brenda who dissolved into a fit of weeping, leaning heavily against her mother-in-law, unable to do anything but draw on the comfort being offered.

Annie and David Wilson sat huddled by their wireless. He had come home as usual for his lunch; Vera would soon come in for hers. But eating was the last thing on their minds for the moment as the news was broken to every listener of the surrender of Belgium and Holland.

'What's goin' ter 'appen to our boys over there?' Annie whispered.

David shook his head. 'Thank Gawd our Davy's still stationed in this country.'

She looked at him. Yes, Davy was all right so far, up by Birmingham way, but for how much longer? 'But our Brenda's 'usband's over there,' she reminded. 'I 'ope he's orright. But what if he ain't? I wonder 'ow our Brenda is if she's listening ter this?'

A frantic rat-tat-tat-tat at the front door made Annie start as if caught doing something wrong. Jumping up from her chair she rushed to answer it.

Brenda almost fell into her arms, letting go of Adele's pram so that Annie had to catch at the handle to stop it rolling backwards towards the kerb. Dragging both her daughter and the pram bodily through the doorway, by no means an easy task with the passage so narrow, she helped Brenda to the back room where David still sat,

146

eyes staring at the door, ears still cocked to catch what was being said on the wireless.

'Dad, Brenda's here,' she announced unnecessarily. Then to Brenda, ''Ave yer eaten yet?'

It was a silly question given the circumstances but the only one that came to mind. Brenda shook her head as if she had completely lost control of her voice, and thinking better of her inane enquiry, Annie sat her in the armchair she had just vacated to answer the door.

'He's goin' ter be all right,' she interpreted in a stern whisper.

Brenda shook her head, at last finding the words. To her mother it sounded such a little voice, not at all like her normally bright one.

'I don't know, Mum,' she said. 'All I know is I'm so scared of what could be 'appening to him.'

All day Wednesday Brenda sat alone, half expecting Harry's parents to visit as usual and when they didn't, having assumed that Monday had made up for it, was glad that she didn't have to entertain them.

After her parents with their attentiveness to her plight, she couldn't have borne listening to his mother going on about her own anguish. Which was natural, she granted her that, Harry being her son. She'd have felt just the same in her place.

Her parents, being that much removed from a son-in-law, had been able to give all their attention to her, their daughter, and it had helped her beyond belief. She didn't want it spoiled by his mother coming round here.

She spent much of the day divided between seeing to Addie's needs and tidying the flat excessively, and hunched by the wireless devouring any item of news that might sustain the comfort her family had given her.

Dad had wisely left all the talking to Mum. When Vera had come in, her face full of sympathy and understanding (she too, being in love with Ron Parrish, feared for him even though he was still stationed in England) and had put her arm round her while Mum went to dish up their midday meal. A bit got taken off each plate for Brenda, though she'd had a job to eat it.

'I've been doin' a lot of praying lately,' Vera had said quietly so Dad wouldn't hear and maybe ridicule her. 'I never really believed in it before, Bren. But I'm sure it's what's kept my Ron from being sent across there. He could of been, yer know. But now I'm praying fer Harry and I really do know it'll work. I really do believe that.'

Vera's soft earnest tones had had her in quiet floods of tears which needed to be hurriedly wiped away before going to the table to eat the beans on toast Mum set before her. The toast was dry because of fat being rationed, though it wasn't that which made it an effort to masticate but her throat, which persisted in closing up with the weight of more threatening tears.

Now as Thursday dawned it seemed Vera's prayers were about to be answered. Early morning brought a little heartening news. British troops were being evacuated by naval ships. Eagerly she awaited that hurried letter to say Harry was among them. There, however, Vera's prayers began breaking down. Midday came and still no letter. She forced herself to look on the bright side. Why should she expect one this quickly?

Pushing it from her as too much wishful thinking, she determinedly tucked Adele in her pram that afternoon and in brilliant sunshine went off to the young wives' club.

Doris might be there. Maybe speaking to someone with a husband in the forces, even if it was the Air Force, would help bolster her courage and hope even more.

'You've got to 'ave faith, Brenda,' Doris said blithely if sorrowfully, and once again Brenda felt that small prick of injustice that Doris could speak this way, confident of her husband's safety while her own dwelt in the valley of the shadow as it were, if he still dwelt at all. She came away feeling how dare she? What did she know of anguish and fear for a loved one?

Friday arrived and still no letter. She made herself get on with everyday life, looking after Adele, getting their meals, washing out nappies, washing and trimming the grey head of another middle-aged woman who discussed the dire situation of their boys over there, and as often as possible listening for news over the wireless of the desperate rearguard action across the Channel. It felt like a sort of blasphemy to be here doing these everyday things while something like sixty miles away men under constant bombardment waited for rescue.

Shopping in the afternoon for her weekend bits and pieces had her hurrying so as not to miss too much of what the newscaster might have to say. Friday afternoon shopping was a habit left over from the days when Harry was here, making sure that he'd come home from work to find the larder well stocked for the weekend, a nice tea waiting for him, and Addie glowing from an hour or two in the open air. What lovely days they had been. Why hadn't she appreciated them more at the time?

149

Arriving home she met John Stebbings in the yard as sometimes did happen. Usually he greeted her with a passing hello, enquiring how she was. This time, he appeared to partially block her progress as she approached the foot of the stairs. His dark eyes surveyed her face.

'Are you all right, Mrs Hutton? You don't look at all well.'

Not wanting to push past him and strike him as rude, she leaned over the pram, adjusting Addie's cover so as not to have to look him directly in the eyes. 'I'm waiting for news of my husband. I think he must be at Dunkirk with the others.'

Why had she said that? It was none of his business.

He seemed to hesitate, then said, 'I was about to make a cup of tea. The shop's quiet now, almost time for me to close up and go home. I usually have one before leaving. I wonder if you'd like one.'

'Oh, I can't,' she said quickly. 'I 'ave to get Adele fed and ready for bed. And I don't want to be too long away from the wireless. In case we get some more news of them over there.'

'Yes, I know,' he mused, his offer of sharing a pot of tea apparently put aside. 'We're all hanging on news. It's a dreadful situation and I wish I could be of comfort to you, Mrs Hutton, at such a terrible time. All I can say is, I'm not far away if you need anyone to talk to. And I earnestly pray your husband will be home soon.'

'Thank you,' she managed, and picking Addie out of the pram, did as she always did, using one hand to manoeuvre the pram into the open shed Mr Stebbings still allowed her to use.

'Here! Let me help.' She stood back as he moved it deftly into place, thanking him yet again.

'No trouble,' he said, and paused once more. 'And remember, if you do need anyone to talk to.'

It was a kind offer. 'Yes,' she said, and hurried up the stairs with Addie in her arms. At the top she turned to look at him, but he had gone back into his shop.

With Saturday came the strangest item of news, *one* – so said one announcer – *to make the heart of every Briton swell with pride even in the midst of what might be seen by the rest of the world as defeat: the first of a veritable armada of four hundred or more tiny civilian craft of all kinds having voluntarily set out from coastal towns of south-east England for Dunkirk where our boys stand with their backs to the English Channel, at this very moment are returning with their human cargo plucked to safety . . . this is the determination of the ordinary man in the street to bring his fighting brother safely home. These survivors must be forever . . .*

The news reporter's usual monotone voice had risen with his flow of rhetoric and Brenda could visualise the man's breast swelling. She knew how he felt, had felt her own pride soar.

Until the voice mentioned the word survivors. He shouldn't have, it bringing her a vision of all those who'd not survived, of bodies lying still and silent on the churned-up sand, riddled and torn by the onslaught from the air and relentless gunfire – it was said people on the south coast could hear it quite plainly. And of those who still moved, injured, maimed, maybe dying – which of them could be Harry? Did he still move, twitch with pain, or was he by now forever beyond pain? No! She had to have faith. 'Please God let him still be alive. I don't care how. But alive. Please God!'

Soon though came news of the little ships themselves coming under merciless attack, being sunk along with their human cargo. Brenda held her breath, as did the entire nation, wondering if anyone could ever get through that terrible onslaught.

Sunday she spent with her parents. Monday she spent alone, hope fading. She preferred being alone, to nurse premature grief as she hugged the wireless, knowing that with no news of Harry he must be among those bodies lying still on some shattered beach.

There was nowhere from which to glean news, no one to answer her questions. By Tuesday it was announced with triumph that the evacuation of Dunkirk was complete. Three hundred and thirty-eight thousand men had landed back on British soil, safe if not completely unscathed, but home at last. Newspaper pictures showed helmeted soldiers coming off ships, women handing mugs of tea to men on their way home leaning from railway carriage windows, weary, begrimed, unshaven, their grinning faces designed to convey the message that they were unbowed, except that she felt those grins showed more relief than triumph.

How many hadn't made those boats, had been left behind waiting only to be taken prisoner? Of her own husband, nothing. Reading the news Brenda's heart refused to function properly as she waited for word of some sort, wondering if she'd ever hear, the thumping inside her chest making her feel continually sick.

Dead, hurt, captured, she had to be told some time. But the waiting could hardly be borne. And with it, a deep anger. All those others safe while her own dear beloved . . . it wasn't unreasonable, this anger. It was real. It tore at her, leaving little room for sorrow over others like her who still waited still not knowing what had happened to their loved ones.

When what she had been waiting for finally did come, it was early on Wednesday morning as workers were thinking about making their way to their jobs. Addie still lay asleep; Brenda sat at her window gazing down into Bow Road as it began to get busy. The wireless was off now, she had no wish to hear any more cheery news.

She saw the figure get off the bus and begin to walk across the road. A soldier without kit. The face that glanced up at her front window was that of a stranger though even from here she could see it was white and haggard, his gait that of someone utterly bone weary. She saw him glance up at her window and with a start she realised she didn't know the face. This . . . this messenger could only be the bearer of bad news. Oh, God! Harry! A comrade come to tell her . . .

She was out of the room, through the kitchen, bursting out through the door as the man reached the foot of the stairs.

153

Chapter Twelve

With her heart feeling as though it had lodged itself in her throat, Brenda was out of the front room, through the kitchen and out on the iron landing as the messenger reached the stairs. She saw him pause, his foot on the first step.

The early morning sunshine lit up his astonished expression at her sudden appearance and the shriek she let out, as with tears streaming down her face, she tore down the stairs towards him to fling herself into his arms.

'Harry! Oh, Harry . . . Oh, my darling!'

Steadying himself before the impact, she felt his arms encircle her as together they rocked in tight embrace, she crying on his shoulder, her cheek scoured by the stubble on his.

'It's orright, love,' she heard him murmur in her ear. 'Everythink's orright. I'm 'ome.'

'I didn't recognise you,' she sobbed. 'Oh, my love, I thought you was someone else. I thought it was someone come ter say you was . . . was . . .'

She couldn't finish. The dread word refused to form in case all this was only imagination. To make sure, she leaned away from him, gazing into the tired features, her eyes almost superstitiously searching the face.

'Are you all right? Are you hurt?' She saw the lovely, cheeky grin.

'Told yer I could look after meself. All I came out of it wiv was this.'

Holding up his right hand, palm downwards, he displayed the deeply scraped skin running from wrist to fingertips. The wound, if that was what it could be termed, had been cleaned, the raw flesh already drying over and darkening in the first stages of forming a crust, but to her eyes it looked sore and just a tiny bit angry.

'Gawd knows 'ow I did it,' he said still grinning, now at the aghast way she was staring at it. 'Must of scraped it on somethink. I don't know. Don't remember it 'appening. Prob'ly somethink soppy compared wiv what was goin' on all around me. Too much goin' on ter notice. Too much . . .'

The words tailed off. The grin faded. The face twisted suddenly, and Brenda thought he was going to be sick. She clutched him to her.

'Oh my darling, it must of been dreadful.'

Her hand came up to smooth the worn cheeks, feeling the stubble, she wanted to hold him like a baby, to cuddle away the terrible sights that were invading him.

But there was little chance. As though to avoid any mawkishness, he gave a shrug mighty enough to push her away, the grin returning, albeit betraying deep weariness. He looked thinner if that was possible, and taller.

'What matters is I'm 'ome all in one piece. An' now all I want is ter be in me own 'ome. Come on, Bren, 'elp me up these bloody stairs. What I want is a good long sit-down. In me own chair. Wiv a real cup of real 'ome-made Rosy Lee in me mitts.'

Tears still catching in her throat, Brenda put an arm under his and led him up the stairs. Even though he looked as though he had strength enough to climb them unaided, it was her way of conveying her feelings at that moment for the ordeal he'd gone through.

Helping him out of his dirty battle blouse, she tried not to notice the dark patches, long dried, ingrained into the khaki. Settling him in his chair, she knelt and undid the stained puttees, pulled off the boots that looked as though they'd not been off his feet in weeks. She dared not recoil before the stink that arose from unwashed feet as she pulled off socks, so threadbare they more resembled rag, and she wondered how long, how many days he'd been walking in that one pair for them to get like this.

She wondered why he hadn't found a fresh pair in his kit, but then he had probably been in too great a hurry to get home here to bother, or maybe he'd lost his other pairs, lost his whole kit, somewhere over there on his way to the coast. Surely he could have been given a change of footwear on landing in England? Allowed a brush-up? And why hadn't he sent her a quick note that he was safe? Why hadn't they given him rest before sending him home in this state? So many why's – not one that could be answered – maybe would never be answered. She had a feeling it would be a long time before he would refer to what had gone on over there, if ever.

'I'll make that tea,' she said, trying not to look distressed.

'Where's Addie?' he asked evenly, laying his head back with a sigh.

'Still asleep. I was going ter get her up in a few minutes when I saw you coming across the road from the bus stop.' It sounded odd exchanging such ordinary conversation, as if he'd never been away. 'I'll get her up,' she said.

'Get me tea first, luv. All I bin dreamin' of is a cuppa your tea, made at 'ome. Yer don't know what a lovely cuppa yer make, Bren.'

'And then I'll fill a bath of hot water for yer,' she added, filled with love at his appreciation of her. 'I'll boil every saucepan we've got in the place and yer can 'ave a lovely long soak fer as long as yer like.'

It didn't matter that her speech, which had improved while he'd been away, had reverted to the way he always spoke. She didn't care. All she knew was that he was home, he was unhurt, apart from his hand (and anyone could do that just building a fence) and he was alive. Beyond that she didn't want to go.

'And I'd better bandage that 'and of yours too. I wonder they didn't do it when yer came off the boat. I mean, it could of got infected, all raw like that, and I bet it wasn't clean 'alf the time, left open like that. Lord knows what germs could of got into it. Couldn't they of bandaged it for yer? It only needed a bit of bandage. I know there must of been a lot of chaps in need of attention more than you, but they could of spared you a bit of bandage. It wouldn't of hurt them.' She was talking too fast, gabbling, eager to find a reason to blame and a need to blame, not even knowing why blame should be present at all.

157

'I took it off,' he said quietly. 'The bandage was dirty anyway. As you said, there was too many ovvers worse orf. Anyway I don't want ter talk about it.'

'No, of course not, love,' she said, and went off to set about dragging indoors the galvanised tin bath they kept on a bent nail in the wall on the landing and filling it with hot water.

Brenda's first instinct had been to rush round to her parents to tell them the wonderful news, but Harry was more important than her at this moment and it was to his people that she went first.

Having woken Adele, she let Harry play with her while setting about filling up every saucepan she could find, putting them on the gas to boil. Adele could be washed, dressed and fed while he had his bath. She could hear him in their living room, the child giggling as he tickled her, then his deep voice calling towards the kitchen that she had grown like a mushroom even in the short while he'd been away and that one day she'd be a real stunner and break all the boys' hearts. Brenda called back in as even a voice as she could muster that you only had to take your eyes off kids that age for two seconds for them to shoot up an inch or so, and to herself repeated and repeated prayers of thanks for his safe return, still hardly able to believe he was here, and safe, after all her anguish.

With him luxuriating in steaming hot water enjoying the bar of Lux toilet soap she'd put aside for herself some time ago, the door of the kitchen wide open to let the warm summer sunshine play on his bare back, she was hard put to tear her gaze from that spare, tight-muscled body to concentrate on getting Adele dressed in order to hurry off to his parents.

'I'll see you later then,' was her casual parting shot, and he grinned.

'Don't start bringing 'em back wiv yer, will yer? I need a bit of time ter meself.'

'And I want a bit of time with you,' she called back happily as she carried Adele down the stairs to where she kept the pram.

Mr Stebbings came out and expressed his gladness that she had her husband back home.

'I saw him as he came into the backyard,' he said, 'but I thought it best to make myself scarce. I'm so very glad for you, Mrs Hutton.'

Did he see too her demonstration of utter joy and relief? She thanked him and hurried out, turning the pram in the direction of Grove Road where his parents lived in Frederick Place, just a short walk away.

She hoped Harry would be out of his bath and dressed in civvies by the time his mum rushed back here with her. She would, despite Harry's warning not to let her. Only natural she should, with her youngest son home from the war. But Brenda so wanted to have these first hours alone with him. And she knew too that all he wanted to do was to spend them with her and no one else.

'I'm too bloody worn out,' he had said, 'ter go traipsin' round there. I just want ter relax – 'ave a bit of a rest before I go back ter me unit.'

The implication that the leave he'd been given to recuperate would tick by quickly enough had upset her but she had put it aside.

His parents could come to them, and so could hers. And she could have bet her last farthing that it was just what his parents would do no sooner had she broken the news to them. So long as it was just his mum and dad and the rest of the family didn't come in hordes.

'Come round a bit later,' she managed to stall his mother. 'I left him having a bath and I expect he'll still be in it by the time I get back. He don't look as if he's 'ad one fer weeks.'

After a second of stunned silence when Mrs Hutton opened the door to hear her announce, 'I've just come to tell yer, Harry's 'ome and he's all right,' she'd grabbed at Brenda to embrace her in a show of abandonment quite out of character.

'Oh, thank Gawd!' had come the cry. Dragging Brenda indoors she'd given way to a tear or two of relief before controlling herself. 'Sid's at work. I'll 'ave ter let 'im know. We can stop at a phone box and phone his work.'

The word 'we', spoken through tears, conveyed the assumption that she would be accompanying Brenda back to her place. But before she could protest she found herself and Adele ushered down the passage and into the kitchen, there to be bombarded with questions. What time had Harry arrived? How did he look? Was he wounded in any way?

To all of them Brenda offered the briefest of information. Having done her errand all she wanted was to get back and be with Harry; to parry his mother, who was already making for her hat and coat, she said that he'd still be in his bath and no clothes on.

His mother stayed her hand in surprise. 'Good Gawd, I've seen 'im in 'is birthday suit more times than you 'ave, love. I don't take no notice of anything like that.'

160

'But he might, Mum,' Brenda said. 'He's a married man now. It's different.'

'We'll call up the stairs and he can put a towel round 'imself.'

'Why not wait till Dad gets 'ome at dinnertime?' Brenda put in desperately. 'And yer can come round together. Dad'll be upset, won't he, you not waiting for 'im? Dad can eat his sandwich at our place and I can make 'im a cuppa tea. Then he can get back to work from our place.'

'And I can stay on for the afternoon,' Mrs Hutton added, temporarily laying aside the need to get her hat and coat. But interpreting the look on her daughter-in-law's face, she gnawed her lower lip and her voice took on a less enthusiastic tone, tinged by disappointment and faint pique. 'Yes, well, I expect Harry could be a bit tired after his ordeal. We'll come round after his dad's finished work. We won't stay long, but we do need to see 'im.'

This last was said with such entreaty in her tone that Brenda burst out, 'Of course yer do, Mum. And stay as long as yer want.'

'But give 'im me love, won't yer, Bren?'

'Course I will,' Brenda assured her.

'Tell 'im, it's not because we don't care that we won't be round till later.'

'Course I will,' Brenda assured her again.

'Because we do. We've bin worried sick about 'im.'

'I know.'

'Gonna 'ave a cuppa?'

'No, I've got ter get back. Thanks. I don't want ter leave 'im too long.'

'Course not. Then we'll see yer ternight. Me and 'is dad.'

161

'Yes, see you tonight.'

Making a short detour on the way home, she called in to her own mum. The rest of the family were at work too; only Mum at home. Here her reception was quite different. Mum felt relieved for her and dragged her indoors. A cup of tea got poured out before she could say no, then Mum took Adele off her so she could drink it more easily. Over the tea she recounted all that had happened.

'I can't stay too long, Mum,' she warned eventually. But she wanted to stay, here where comfort was always on tap, where she did not feel ill at ease, could say what she liked. Except of course on this occasion she had to get back to Harry. 'I don't want to leave him on his own for long, Mum.'

'He can look after 'imself fer 'alf an hour or so, luv. He ain't a baby.'

'No, but you should of seen the state of 'im.'

'You must of gone through hell, luv. We didn't know what ter do for yer when yer was waiting fer news. I could of bled for yer.' She was rocking Addie as though she would have loved to do the same with her own daughter. 'But thank Gawd he's all right. Look love, we won't come round until termorrer or the next day now we know you're orright. Let you two 'ave this leave ter yerselves. 'Ope yer don't mind.'

'Of course not,' she said, but in a totally different tone from that she had used towards his mother, not loaded with protest but tripping easily off the tongue.

'I expect he'll be out of the bath by now,' she laughed, relieving Mum of Addie. 'I told 'im I wouldn't be long. He's probably wondering where I've got to.'

'You get along then. We'll see you in a couple of days. When's he go back? In a few days, I suppose. We'll be round before then. And I'm so blessed relieved, for your sake, Bren, he's orright. Go on, get along now.'

So it was that she returned to find Harry dead asleep on the unmade bed, in vest and pants, lying flat on his back as though he had fallen asleep at the exact second of throwing himself there, his arms flung wide, face turned a little to one side.

Tears filled Brenda's eyes as she studied him. He seemed so peaceful, his eyelashes forming dark semicircles against his lean cheeks, his lips gentle and his breathing slow and regular. Yet there was an odd ghost that might be seen as tension lying across those smooth narrow features that even sleep hadn't erased, rather an utterly worn-out look as if the very act of sleeping was draining every last ounce of energy from him.

She bent and gently kissed the lips, found them soft beneath hers, unaware of her caress. With a small sob of pain and gratitude, she covered his face with her kisses.

'I love you, Harry. I love you with all my heart,' she whispered against that face, but he didn't move.

All too quickly he was back in his uniform, cleaned and pressed by her own loving hand.

His parents had come every evening, his mother constantly gazing at him, touching his hand, brushing his cheek with a motherly kiss as if to keep him etched in her memory after he was gone, which made Brenda shudder as though it were an omen.

163

Her parents came. They made a social event of it, treating it all as a normal visit. 'Look after yerself,' was their parting shot.

Vera popped in one dinnertime, asked the inevitable question that was fast becoming ubiquitous: 'Lovely to see you home – when are you going back?'

She looked bright and happy and, of course, still very much in love with her Ron Parrish. She hardly stopped talking about him her entire dinner hour. She had grown her hair to shoulder-length and, refusing to cut it – 'Ron likes it that way' – wore it cradled in a snood which she crocheted herself from bright red or green silky thread, to keep the hair from getting caught up in machinery. She was doing war work now as one of the first to volunteer, at a local factory turning out something to do with smaller aeroplane parts, she said.

Harry's brother and his wife came, Daphne as frail-looking as ever, and he looked admiringly at Harry, saying, 'If this war goes on much longer I suppose we'll all be in it.' She gasped and said, 'Oh, no, Bob, what would I do if they took you?' at which he looked just a fraction irritated, saying just a little too sharply, 'Yer'd cope like uvver wives 'ave to. Look at Brenda – she don't go about moaning. She's getting on wiv her job of keeping 'ome and family tergether for when 'er man comes 'ome fer good.'

To Brenda's mind, Bob looked as though he couldn't wait to get in it.

As they did with all their callers, they sat out on the iron landing basking in the warm sunshine of the long summer evening until it was time to go home, chairs balanced on squares of wood to prevent the legs going through the holes between the iron. Brenda had got that off to a fine art this boiling hot summer after having nearly toppled off her chair when they'd first moved in.

Sitting there with her guests, with Addie squatting at her daddy's feet, Brenda would sometimes notice the curtains of her secretive neighbours twitch once or twice, but they had never come out and she always found it rankled, hating them unreasonably.

Joan Copeland had popped across while Mum and Dad were there, generously bringing a home-made cake which used her precious sugar ration for Harry to take back with him when he left.

'I don't suppose they feed yer all that well,' she had laughed. 'And don't yer go sharin' it wiv every Tom, Dick and 'Arry!'

That being his name, he'd quipped, 'Well, that leaves *me* out, don't it!' and they'd all laughed.

Now he was due to go back.

Brenda hadn't felt so low in all her life, not because of his going but because for her his leave had been spoiled. She had been struck down with her monthlies so all they could do was pet, she helping him out because he needed it so, while all the time she was aching for him. She had cancelled all the women whose hair she did, not because she was being underhanded but because she had needed him all to herself, but that leave had been spoiled by sodding nature! And now they were saying goodbye.

At least he was safely back in England. He'd endured his share of fighting for his country, even if there had been no victory apart from getting nearly all the men home. He'd done enough. Now perhaps he'd have a nice cushy little number not too far away, like Doris's husband in the RAF.

Harry deserved that after what he'd been through.

Chapter Thirteen

'Fancy popping off to the pictures termorrow sometime?'

Doris, nibbling at a fatless scone from a batch that one of the young wives' club members had brought in, eyed Brenda hopefully.

'I'm dying to see that *Gone With The Wind* film. But they say it gets packed, standing room only. But if we was to go early enough we might be near the front of the queue and get a proper seat. I know it means standing an hour or so outside but it's better than standing fer four hours inside.'

Brenda eyed her in return. She too wanted dearly to see *Gone With The Wind,* talked about in all the papers as the biggest and most colourful film ever. 'What about Addie?' she asked. 'She's too young to take. She'd play up.'

Addie was a handful now she was walking, her little fingers into everything. Brenda was constantly running after her, which was inconvenient when she was doing someone's hair. Her clientele had been building rapidly of late especially in the evenings when girls who still clung to their longer locks wanted hair put up into nice, professional rolls. To confine Addie to her cot while she worked was sheer murder, because her calls for attention quickly escalated into shrieks of fury if ignored. And because Brenda loved her and hated seeing her distressed, she would plead, 'Just a moment,' to her client and leave them to sigh and sit waiting with what patience they could muster until Addie had been calmed down with a kiss and a cuddle and a bit of bread reddened with a tiny smear of jam.

She could have lost a lot of customers, but surprisingly she didn't. She was too good at her job, doing wonders with curling tongs and pins, and her reputation was spreading. Her only fear was that it would spread to her mother-in-law.

Even so, Addie wasn't easy for a woman on her own to look after while she tried to hold down a small business as well. And Brenda was determined to hold down her little business no matter what. As for sitting quietly on her lap when Brenda went to see her parents or Harry's, it was nigh impossible with Addie forever wriggling to be on her feet, the novelty of going wherever she pleased still fresh.

'I'll ask me mum if she'd look after her,' she decided. 'I'll pop round there and ask her.' After all, she might as well take advantage of her mother's offers, and it was so seldom she could enjoy a little pleasure.

'All right,' said Doris with a brisk nod. Having no children she didn't understand the half of it. 'I'll come round to you and we can catch a bus up to the West End and see how the queues are.'

It had been a long time since she'd visited a West End cinema, and they got there early in the afternoon, but still had to queue for over an hour before being let in halfway through the big picture.

They stayed on until where they'd come in came round again; Doris, completely absorbed in it, whispered wickedly, 'Let's stay and watch the rest through again? The usherettes won't know.' But Brenda shook her head.

'I must get back and pick up Addie. I can't leave her with Mum all that time. It wouldn't be fair. And it wouldn't be fair to stay 'ere with people still standing in the queues outside.' At which Doris had to relent.

'I really enjoyed that,' she announced as they came out. 'We ought to go to the flicks more often. We could go once a week reg'lar.'

'I can't afford once a week.'

'Well, once a fortnight then, or every three weeks.'

But somehow they didn't. With July touching shoulders with August, Hitler finally decided to launch his delayed attacks on a now-isolated Britain. After Dunkirk, everyone had expected him to invade straight away. When he hadn't, they sat back with a sigh of relief. Now he had begun to send his Luftwaffe to bomb south coast towns and had ideas of reaching London itself, though that hope was thwarted by the RAF. By August Doris suddenly found her husband being thrown into the thick of it all.

She had told Brenda proudly that while her John had gone to just an ordinary school, he had passed all his exams to go on to a grammar school and joining the RAF had passed their tests with flying colours, as it were; Brenda's assumption that pilots came solely from public schools proved false, because Doris added that men found by the RAF to be as bright as her John were now pilots.

For a long time Brenda had felt the stigma of her own man being just a mere soldier, but now the boot was on the other foot. Now it was her friend whose face grew strained and fearful. Brenda would never have gloated over it yet there was a form of guilt in feeling for Doris, as if she really was gloating.

One day in mid-August Doris, who never missed a Thursday, didn't show up at the young wives' club.

'She sent me a note,' said the secretary, 'to say she wasn't well.'

'Will she be coming next week?' enquired Brenda.

'I don't know,' replied the secretary. 'She just said she wasn't well, and she didn't know if she'd be coming again. She'd see. That was all. Never even had the courtesy to say what was wrong with her.'

At the huffy tones Brenda allowed an apologetic smile on behalf of her friend. She knew Doris's address but had never gone to her house. Now she decided to pop round and see how she was. Probably she had a summer cold – they could be horrible, and she'd be feeling pretty down, the reason perhaps for saying she didn't know when she'd be back.

It might be that she hadn't wanted to go out after London had its first air raid last week. But it had been south of the river and didn't touch anywhere else in London, though the fact that over sixty people had been killed had had an effect and no doubt Doris was one who didn't want to venture far from home. After another couple of raids it had all gone quiet, thanks to the RAF doing such a marvellous job keeping the Luftwaffe at bay by shooting down huge numbers of German planes. It was said that people in Kent and Essex could stand

and watch dogfights going on high up in the blue summer skies just as if they were spectators at a game of football or a motor race.

For weeks Doris had told her proudly of her husband's part in it all. 'He flies Hurricanes,' she said. 'He's now stationed in Kent and he can't get home because he's so busy but he writes to me about it all.'

It was only these last few weeks that she'd begun to look worried and say less. At the time of Churchill's speech stating how never in the field of human conflict had so much been owed by so many to so few, Doris had appeared at the young wives' club with her face strained in the way Brenda remembered her own face feeling over Dunkirk.

'I know he'll be orright,' she'd said with determination that had all the look of being forced to its limit. Brenda prayed silently for her friend, knowing that she mustn't crow with her Harry safely stationed in this country having done his bit.

Now Doris said she was ill. Poor thing, on top of all her worry. With this in mind, Brenda put Addie in her pram and pushed her in the direction of Lincoln Street where Doris lived not far from Mile End Station.

Her knock on Doris's door went unanswered and she had to knock twice more before it was. What greeted her was the most haggard expression she had ever seen. She would never have thought in a million years that Doris could ever have looked paler than she always was. But now she did. The only colour visible was her eyes, bloodshot and red-rimmed as they stared out at her. Behind her gazed another pallid face like a ghost of the first. 'I said *I'd* open the door for yer, Doll.'

'It's orright, Mum.' There came a hesitation, then, 'It's me friend.'

'Are you orright?' was all Brenda could utter; thoroughly taken aback by the sight confronting her.

Doris nodded uncertainly, then shook her head, then nodded again as uncertainly as before. Before she could say anything, if indeed she had been going to, she was whisked aside and the older woman moved into her place.

'I'm sorry, we can't ask you in. We've 'ad a bit of a shock.' Turning to her daughter, she added, 'Go back in, Doll. I'll explain to yer friend for yer. Go on, now, I'll be in in a minute.'

As Doris seemed to half walk, half float back into the dimness of the passageway to disappear as though utterly engulfed by lack of light, Mrs Osborne turned back to Brenda.

'It's like this. My Doll's 'usband was killed four days ago. Shot down in a dogfight somewhere over Kent. We got the news next day – in the evenin'. We can't ask yer in. I 'ope yer don't mind. She ain't in no fit state ter see anyone. I know yer a friend but I 'ope you understand, we can't ask you in.'

Brenda found herself nodding her understanding, unable to find any word of comfort to say. Incapable of speech, she merely nodded again, automatically turning the pram round.

Seconds later the words came. 'Tell Doris I'm so terribly sorry . . .'

171

But when she turned her head to say them she found the door had already closed.

For a moment she thought to knock again, just so she could at least give her message, but wisdom prevailed and she merely carried on walking, tears filling her eyes.

'I didn't know what ter say,' she told her mother. 'I should of at least said something, but I didn't. If only I could of.'

For a time she had wandered, pushing Addie's pram blindly ahead of her, not sure where to go. Eventually she'd turned in the direction of her mother's in desperate need of company – someone to talk to, to share the turmoil that was going through her breast. All that resentment she had harboured against Doris because her husband had it so cushy while her own husband had been in the thick of fighting and bloodshed! Now she could hardly contain the burden of it all. She'd felt dreadful, totally unable to put into words how she felt, but if she got Mum alone she could pour her heart out to her. By the time she got there however Vera had come home from work.

Sitting now at the kitchen table wishing Vera wasn't hovering there listening in, she added, 'Who'd of thought it'd be her. It don't seem right, our boys being killed in our own country. It just don't seem right.'

'There's ordinary people bein' killed anyway,' Mum pointed out. 'Sixty-odd ordinary people went when South London was bombed the other day. All innocent people what 'ave nothink ter do with fighting. 'Ow long's it goin' ter be before it's our turn, I cringe ter think. Just a matter of time, it seems ter me. I wonder what's goin' ter 'appen to us all.'

Brenda chewed at her lip, angry at Vera. Because of her she hadn't got what she wanted off her chest at all, and there was Vera gawping, taking it all in while she buffed at her polished nails and added her two penn'orth, her thoughts only on herself, it seemed to Brenda.

'Glad my Ron ain't in the Air Force,' she remarked airily, her eyes trained on her nails.

'An' I just thank Gawd Davy weren't clever enough ter be taken into it either,' their mother added with more depth. 'Or I'd be worried out of me life for 'im. It's like what they say, ignorance is bliss. In 'is case I'd say it was a blessed sight safer too.'

Brenda picked at the edge of the tablecloth. 'I feel so sorry for Doris. I wish I'd of said something to 'er. I've a feeling I won't be seeing her again. She ain't likely to go to the young wives' club any more, is she? But come ter that, I'm not sure as I want ter go any more. Us making friends like we did, we didn't much mix with the others.'

Her mother looked at her in concern. 'You should keep on going, Bren. It'll keep yer mind orf things.'

'I've got me hairdressing.' The thought of her clients cheered her up a bit. She'd go and see Doris some time or other to show that she cared, perhaps to alleviate in some part this weight of guilt. 'I've got quite a few regulars now. I prefer them coming in the evening if they can. Addie's asleep then. I don't keep having to stop and see to her. That's the only problem, having to interrupt what I'm doing to sort her out. And it ain't fair leaving her to cry. Most don't mind coming in the evenings. Though I do worry in case Harry was to come 'ome unexpected. It could 'appen.'

She watched her mother get up from the table, going to the cupboard under the sink to collect potatoes ready for their evening meal. Dad would be home before long, and Brian too. She began peeling them on the draining board, her back to Brenda. Tonight by the look of it they would eat sausage and chips together with baked beans.

'You ought ter tell 'im, yer know,' murmured her mother, her back still to Brenda. 'Put yer cards on the table and be honest wiv 'im. He wouldn't thank yer fer being under'anded. Though he oughtn't start laying down the law about yer work when he ain't really living there.'

'It's still his home.'

'But he ain't there. Yer ain't got him ter run to for decisions. You left on yer own, you 'ave ter make yer own now. So he oughtn't to moan if yer do.'

'I know. But he was always so against me working.'

'So what yer going ter do? I think it's better ter tell him than tell lies. Yer might be surprised, he might be all for it.'

'Until his mother gets her say in.'

'It ain't nothink ter do with her.'

'She'd say I was neglecting Addie. And that'd put the cat among the pigeons straight away.'

'Well, if your 'Arry takes his mum's word against his wife's, he ain't much of a man in my estimation. And if somethink 'appened and you was left on yer own, yer'd 'ave ter work then and . . .'

'Mum!' Brenda was on her feet, a premonition racing through her. 'Don't say things like that. Nothing's goin' to happen to Harry.'

But things could happen right here. Enemy bombers had broken through the RAF's defence, bombs had fallen on south London suburbs, sixty people were dead. They could fall here as easily and it might not be her but Harry who could be grieving.

Mum was gazing at her, appalled by what she'd said 'I didn't mean that, Bren. I was just sayin' . . .'

'Then don't!'

'But he's safe in this country, like Davy is.'

Brenda shook her head wildly. 'You never know, Mum. None of us know what's in the future for us.' She knew her face had gone white, white as Vera's, who was standing there with her mouth wide open. 'I don't want you talkin' like that, Mum,' she ploughed on. 'Putting the mockers on us all.'

Mum was trying to make amends. 'All I'm trying ter say is, you've got yourself and Addie ter look after while Harry's away. He shouldn't 'ave no say in what yer do when he ain't here ter lay down the law. Yer should tell 'im. And if he cuts up rough, tell 'im 'is fortune. You're 'olding the fort now. You've got ter make yer own decisions. When he's 'ome fer good, that's a different matter when he's the breadwinner again. I mean, do he really want you and Addie ter live on the scrimpy little bit of wife's allowance they give yer? And you all on yer own night after night. What's he expect yer ter do? All the old values 'ave gorn out the winder. You're yer own mistress, Bren. Tell 'im and 'ave done wiv it. That's all I was tryin' ter say. I didn't mean nothink else.'

Brenda took a deep breath to calm herself. She nodded compliance, but left soon after, refusing a share of sausage, beans and chips. Mum's words concerning anything happening to Harry, even hypothetically, still hovered over her like some evil omen. Pushing little Addie's pram agitatedly before her, she decided to stay away from Mum's for a while. She wasn't angry, her feelings weren't hurt, there was just something she couldn't quite define that made her not want to be there, at least until she was over this.

'What the 'ell's that?' Annie started up, her eyes on her husband as sirens sounded in the distance, the far-off ominous wail quickly taken up by one much nearer, warning that they might be about to experience an air raid on their very own doorstep. 'Oh, my Gawd! Air raid. Bren's on 'er own wiv the baby.' A week had passed since Brenda had put a foot over her doorstep.

It was Sunday night. August's double summertime dusk had melted into the usual total blackout some time ago. Vera was at the table reading her *Film Goer*. Brian had come in, not having found his mates, not having found a girl either, sullenly taking off his coat with a dismal, 'Watcher all!' She and David were thinking of bed; he was about to turn off the wireless, she was going to wash up the cocoa cups. They paused at the approaching sound. Vera looked up, sat for a moment like a statue while Brian, equally stunned, stood in the doorway. Annie was first to come to life.

'I've got ter go round ter Bren!' She was already making for the passage where her coat hung on its stand and David had to catch her by the arm to stop her.

'Yer can't go out in that,' he snapped. 'Listen!'

There came the low, distant crump-crump of an explosion, whether bombs or anti-aircraft guns, it wasn't certain. It wasn't the first time they'd heard it; after the air raid warning that had sent families who had shelters scurrying down to them, they'd listened fearfully to that identical sound across the river a few days earlier. That time it hadn't come any closer. This time it was much nearer. Then to startle them all out of their wits, their local siren started up, almost defeaning them.

'Quick! Everyone down the shelter!' David roared. Everything seemed to happen at once. Opening the back door, all lights switched off, they stepped out into a warm night to the drone of enemy bombers almost overhead. Vera shrieked and fled down the path and down the two steps into the shelter, while Brian held back not to look cowardly by following with the same haste. Their mother stood rooted to the spot, looking up and around trying to pierce the darkness, glimpsing the fitful glimmer of an electric torch as the Johnstons scuttled down their own short garden path to their Anderson, their voices filled with fear as searchlights pierced the night sky. Over the opposite fence someone called out, 'You orright Mrs Wilson, Mr Wilson?' to which David answered that they were.

'Come on, gel!' he snapped at her. 'Get down there.'

'Brenda's on 'er own,' Annie reminded him. 'What's she gonna do?'

'We can't do nothink now. Get in! Oh, bloody Jesus!' This as guns cracked out, splitting the blackout with a flash of light. 'That's from bleedin' Victoria Park. Them bombers is right over'ead. Come on, Annie – inside!'

On her own as the sirens struck up, Brenda went and got Adele out of her cot. She fought to stay calm but her mind was a turmoil. They'd not had a Morrison shelter constructed. The flat was far too small. The thought of running through the streets with Adele to the nearest public shelter scared the living daylights out of her.

177

She did the next best thing. Dressing Adele as warmly as she could, because despite it being a warm night they could be spending it virtually in the open, and putting on her own coat, she hurriedly collected gas mask, the double eiderdown from her own bed, and two pillows. Then, loaded up, she carried Adele down the iron stairs as best she could. She was sure she'd drop something on the way, but somehow she managed not to. Each foot cautiously felt for the next step; it seemed to take ages to reach the shed against the wall of Mr Stebbings' shop where she kept the pram.

With half the eiderdown underneath to shield her from the concrete floor, the rest wrapped over them, and the pillows propped up behind her head, she sat with Addie in her arms, knees drawn up, the shed door closed tight with the pram between her and the door. With luck it would give some modicum of protection.

The drone overhead sounded as though it were inches from the shed roof as she prayed for the planes to go away, drop their bombs on someone else, to discover a lack of fuel and head back to Germany, anything. But it was apparent this was where they intended to be. She knew it as a sudden explosion jolted the floor and the shed door rattled. Moments later came an ugly tearing sound and an even nearer explosion.

Panting with terror, Brenda bent her body over her baby. If she was going to die, Addie mustn't. The iron stairs might offer protection. The safest place was said to be underneath a staircase in the absence of any other shelter and maybe these stairs might help.

Time became lost as the world outside dissolved in noise and havoc. The building shook with deafening explosions, and all the while Addie cried with a fear she couldn't understand, 'Mummy – don't like it – don't like it!' As if *she* could make it stop.

In any brief pause falling pieces of metal from burst shells tinkled and clashed as they struck the iron stairs, reminding her that to be out even during a lull was equally lethal. No one in their right mind would come nigh or by. She was the only one here. She had never felt so alone. The whole world was falling about her ears and not a soul to find her or come to her aid should something happen to her. If only she hadn't been so proud and gone to see Mum last week. Now it was too late. In this dark little hole she clutched Adele to her, her terrified heart yearning for the protection of her own mother's arms. If this building collapsed on her, trapping her, who would there be to rescue her? Mr Stebbings had gone home, her secretive neighbours had disappeared leaving their flat empty, Mr and Mrs Copeland had gone to relatives in Hemel Hempstead after that first raid on south London.

'It mightn't be for long,' Joan said. 'I know it looks like we're being cowards but we just want to be safe.'

She couldn't blame them. She'd have gone too if she'd had anyone to go to outside London. If only they had been able to move to Dagenham, came the thought, she wouldn't be in this predicament now. The thought made her bitter; she had no inkling of the temptation the docks there offered enemy bombers.

Through the hours their droning receded and returned in waves making it hard to ascertain if they'd left for good so she could venture out. At one time, realising that no more bombs had fallen for a while, she dared hope it might be over. If only Harry was here, she'd have felt less frightened even though common sense said he'd have no power to save her if there was a direct hit.

Gradually though, her fear blunted under the continuous onslaught; she sat merely listening to the high shrilling of ambulance and fire bells, and sometimes the sound of running feet and men's voices calling out in the road behind her which in one way consoled her, in another put her in a dilemma. Should she actually go out and seek help or not? There was an acrid smell of burning wood. Dust dislodged from the shed roof covered the eiderdown. Having forgotten her torch she sat listening in utter darkness. After crying for some time, Addie fell asleep, allowing her to shut her own eyes against their gritty feel.

She wasn't sure when the planes finally receded, but awoke with a start as the shed door was yanked open and sunlight flooded in, almost blinding her.

Blinking, she tried to make out the figure standing there against the light until the voice said, 'Mrs Hutton. Are you all right? Are you hurt?'

'Mr Stebbings!'

Pushing off the eiderdown and clutching the now-awake Adele to her, Brenda got shakily to her feet, already embarrassed at being found in such a situation.

'It's the only place I could think of to be safe,' she explained as she came out from behind the pram, taking the hand he held out to help steady her. 'We had a terrible air raid last night.'

'I thought of you and the baby. There was no way I could reach you.'

Why he should say that she didn't know. They weren't that close as neighbours, merely passing the time of day if they met. Now he was taking it upon himself to gather up her belongings, which he bundled up in his arms as he helped her up the stairs to her flat.

In her panic to find safety she hadn't locked the kitchen door, he opened it, guiding her inside. It was the first time he'd ever been in her flat since she and Harry moved in and she felt suddenly exposed. Not that it wasn't clean and tidy, just that she seemed to stand stripped of all privacy. Yet his eyes hadn't once wandered from her face to take in the place where she lived.

'Th-thank you, Mr Stebbings,' she stammered. 'I'll be all right now.' She'd become aware that everywhere was redolent of her hairdressing trade, different to the way most homes should smell. 'I can manage now it's over.'

'What about tomorrow night?' he asked, gazing at her standing in the kitchen with Adele complaining in her arms. 'And the next night and the next? Now it's started I reckon it will continue.'

She felt he was about to say, 'Until we give in.' She leapt.

'We won't do that. Never.' But she hadn't given any thought to any following night. 'I think I was safe enough,' she added. 'I wasn't hurt and neither was Adele, apart from being scared to death. I expect most people were last night.'

She tried to make a little joke of it, giving a small self-conscious titter. Perhaps he would go now. But he hesitated.

'It's Hitler's intention to try and beat us into submission, you know, and he won't stop now.'

'They're not goin' ter beat us,' she insisted, flaring defiantly. She saw his sensitive lips give a little quirk.

181

'Of course they won't. What I had in mind, apart from Adolf Hitler, was that you and Adele need somewhere other than an old store shed. Don't be offended, but the shop has a cellar and you'd be safe there. You wouldn't be disturbed as I go home at night. You could take all you need down with you and leave it there. Torch, bedding, food, flask of tea, toiletries. I can supply an oil stove and I keep stocks of old books down there, so you could have a read if you want.'

He chuckled then grew serious. 'You could make it cosy. A bed, table, chair. I'd give you a key so you could let yourself into the shop at night and let yourself out in the morning. What do you say? Safer than running to any public shelter. Safer than staying up here, and warmer than an old shed.'

How could she refuse such an offer? It was like a gift from the gods. Smiling, Brenda agreed and that very morning had him pressing a newly cut key into her hand.

Chapter Fourteen

It must have been an isolated raid for no bombers appeared the following night as everyone had expected them to, nor the next. People remained edgy and on alert, but after a week of peaceful sleep, began to relax. They sadly read of raids elsewhere in the country but thanked God it wasn't here.

Even so, for two nights Adele slept badly, startled from sleep by every slightest bang or bump outside. It kept Brenda sleepless too, having to get up to console her every time.

Hoping to divert her, she got a little kitten. It seemed instantly to do the trick and that night Adele slept soundly with it beside her, though even that small creature took up much-needed room. Adele was fast growing too big for her cot. All that mattered was that she was more content, allowing Brenda some sleep.

Her parents had come rushing round the very next morning to see if she was all right after that night's air raid, which people were starting to call the Blitz, in typical British fashion shortening it from the German word *Blitzkrieg,* meaning lightning war.

The look of relief on their faces at finding her safe and well turned to even more relief when she told them about how Mr Stebbings had given her a key so she could get into his basement through his shop if there were any more air raids.

'That's what I call a real Christian gesture,' her mother said. 'But I do wish yer lived nearer so as yer could use our shelter proper. Nothink can go wrong in them. Even in a basement, buildings could fall on top of yer.'

'That's it, Mum,' Brenda chuckled happily as she made a cup of tea, 'doom and gloom, eh? Be a Job's comforter ter make me feel better!'

She saw the instant change come over her mother's face as she recalled her last words of doom and gloom about Harry. Putting down the teapot she had been pouring from, Brenda put an arm about her mother's shoulder. 'Oh, Mum, it's orright. We're all goin' ter be orright.' Her mother smiled.

It was a wonderful morning having them here. Outside on this lovely warm sunny day some debris littering Bow Road was being cleared by council workers; a fire engine stood idle further down with the firemen coiling hoses from a smouldering, half-demolished shop some way off towards Mile End Station. No one had been hurt. The manager and his family who lived above it had gone to visit friends, she heard, and remained there during the raid. But Monday's papers did tell of civilian casualties, of considerable fires started in the City, of scattered bombing of East End suburbs – to Brenda, hiding alone in her shed, the air raid had sounded far worse than it was.

She went round to Harry's parents that afternoon to see how they had fared with the bombed shop that much nearer to them. She found they'd only lost a few tiles off the roof and suffered a few broken windows. These had been prevented from blowing in by the criss-cross strips of gummed paper the Huttons like most people had stuck on them to prevent injury from flying splinters. In the Huttons' case it showed that it worked.

Trying not to mark the contrast in warmth between her own parents and them, she stayed to tea at their insistence as they discussed their individual experiences last night.

Mrs Hutton grew tight-lipped when Brenda mentioned Mr Stebbings' offer. 'You hardly know the man, yer can't accept the key to his place.'

'I thought he was being generous, thoughtful.'

'It depends on what you mean by generosity and thoughtfulness. Your Harry wouldn't be all that 'appy ter know some strange man's offering yer a key to 'is premises.'

'I suppose Harry would be happier if I got killed or wounded in that rotten little shed,' Brenda snapped back, and saw the lips tighten still more.

'A basement 'as to be better'n that,' her father-in-law put in hastily, and to Brenda's immense satisfaction he returned his wife's glare with one of his own, shutting her up.

Hurriedly changing the subject, Brenda came out with her method of consoling Adele after the trauma of last night. Her mother-in-law, recovering from her husband's glare, looked at her as if she had admitted to voluntarily harbouring a horde of vermin.

185

'A cat! You're giving yerself trouble 'aving a cat, Brenda. Cats breed like rabbits. There's too many in London as it is. What d'yer want a cat for?'

'For Addie. She needed something ter take her mind off the other night. She's been terrified. And anyway, it's a kitten.'

'Kittens grow into cats.'

'I know. But Addie needed something to make her feel better.'

'You could of got 'er a little toy. Something furry.'

'You can't get toys that easily now.' Toys had all but disappeared from the shops. There had been an appeal earlier in the summer to everyone to surrender kitchenware and anything with aluminium in it to help make more planes. It was hardly the time to go out buying toys when it wasn't even Christmas or a birthday. And anyway she couldn't have afforded one. She wondered if Mrs Hutton might offer but she didn't. They were no more able to afford such things than she even if they could find anything other than from those who were turning to selling handmade items.

Instead she said darkly, 'Harry won't be pleased. He hates cats. And what you going to feed it on, all this rationing and everything?'

But it was her choice. She was doing a lot more of her own choosing lately. It was her home, like Mum had said. Harry was back there only occasionally.

Obviously it was not his fault; he couldn't help being away in the forces. He hadn't been given leave since coming back from Dunkirk, as if those few days had been considered adequate reward for what he'd gone through.

She wrote once a week to him and he wrote back as regularly, telling her to look after herself and how much he loathed not being with her at this terrible time, and he sent his love to her. She treasured his letters and sighed over his absence and longed for him to be here. But he wasn't and it was up to her to make the decisions now.

The week went on and still all was quiet. Churchill had sent their own bombers over Berlin as a reprisal. German bombers did reciprocate but they aimed at places like Merseyside and Liverpool. And while she sympathised with the people there, having had a taste of it herself, she couldn't help the feelings of relief that settled in her breast.

It was pure joy being able to leave Addie to her own devices safe in the other room happily playing with her kitten, which she had named Petty – her own interpretation of Brenda's description of its pretty tortoiseshell coat – while she put up a customer's hair for her.

Absently going along with all the young woman had to say about herself, Brenda allowed part of her mind to dwell on what Harry might have to say about the kitten, which in turn set her longing for him and wondering when his next leave would be.

A letter was due from him. She could rely on him telling her in it if he would be coming home, giving her time to clear away evidence of her work. The kitten would have to take its chances, but one day she would have to confront him with what she was doing.

As Mum said, she was her own mistress now. But it wouldn't make life pleasant having to tell him that this was her decision and he would have to like it or lump it. Easy for Mum to say; more easily said than done. And of course there'd be his mother putting in her two penn'orth, shoving a spanner in the works, voicing her opinions as if she personally owned the flat.

It must have been providence, thinking all this as she listened to her client, for next day Harry's letter dated the fifth of September came, a very brief one. In fact he wrote, 'I'll make this short, love,' after saying he was well, hoping she was too. 'Got ten days' leave but don't get too excited. Tell you why when I get home. All I'll say for now is we'll have to make the most of it because it might be a time before I get any more leave. Be home Saturday midday.'

In mad haste she cancelled all her hair appointments for the next ten days and settled herself down to wait.

He was home. He looked in much better health than when last she'd seen him. Naturally thin as he was, even so he had filled out a little, his cheeks less gaunt, his brown eyes all sparkling. It felt so good to have his arms round her, to touch him, to feel the warmth of him, his breath on her cheeks, the sound of his voice, so resonant for a slim man. She fell immediately to pampering him, hovering over him, seeing him put on his civvies which she had pressed and aired that morning, taking joy in seeing him play with Addie. Addie took it all in her stride, still knowing her daddy. There were times when Brenda feared Addie might forget him, with him being away from her so often. But not a bit of it.

To her relief he made no comment about the kitten, apart from brushing it away if it came near, accepting her explanation for getting it.

It was only as she dished up the dinner she'd cooked for him, a piece of scrag-end of lamb bought on her own ration book – he'd handed his to her on arrival and this she would use for another time – made into a delicious stew with carrots and onions, potatoes and an Oxo cube, that he set down his knife and fork and looked soberly at her.

'I'd better get this orf me chest, Bren. Yer know why I'm on leave – on such a long leave, don't yer?'

Something in his tone set her heart thumping heavily, sickeningly. So far she had managed not to question anything, only too glad to have him home. Now he didn't have to tell her: she knew. She'd known the moment he'd entered, but had refused to acknowledge the signs.

'Embarkation leave.' She whispered the words as though speaking any louder would have her dissolving in tears. Those tears were very close compounded since his arrival, held back only by the hope that what she was thinking had to be mere imagination.

She saw him nod dismally. 'Why d'they always spring it on yer like that? We 'ad an inklin' somethink was in the air. Signs, little fings yer notice, but there always is lots of bleedin' rumours flying about. Yer get so as not ter take too much notice of it or yer'd go barmy. Then, wham! Yer've got embarkation leave. Report back at so-and-so and off yer go. Ain't told where. But it's overseas and that's about all we know, me old love. It's a bugger!'

'Oh, Harry . . .'

Her appetite had left her. She watched as he bent his head to eat his food, eating quickly, and she knew

189

why – so that he wouldn't betray the feelings that would have choked him had he not used his gullet to stuff the food down.

She watched him clear his plate, push it away from him, sit back, pat his stomach and smile at her as if all he'd said a short while ago hadn't been. 'That was scrumptious, me old darlin', absolutely top hole. I always tell everyone what a bloody luv'ly cook you are. Yer should see some of the rubbish we're given . . .'

He broke off suddenly, and to avoid the desperate look on his face she leaned forward to put a spoonful of mashed potato into Addie's mouth.

'I'm sorry, luv. I didn't mean ter . . . It's a real bloody bugger!' he repeated with venom.

For the rest of the day they avoided speaking of all it implied. 'We'll make the most of it, eh?' he suggested cheerfully. 'Me mum an' dad'll 'ave Addie round their place and we'll go up West, see a show, or the pictures.'

She agreed that she'd like that, looking forward only to bedtime when she'd make the most of him, enough to last for whatever length of lonely time he would be away from her. Tonight and every night, until he was plucked from her by those wooden-faced, insensitive, heartless powers-that-be. Maybe from such intense love-making would come another baby. It would be such a consolation for his absence. Yes, she wanted another baby.

In the afternoon they made a dutiful visit to his parents. His mother hugged him as though this was the last she'd ever see of him, insisting they stay to tea, to which Brenda said they already had a tea waiting for them at home. So instead she plied him with cakes that she'd made, urging him and his father to smoke a cigar instead of their cigarettes, and clutching Adele to her with all the passion of someone expecting the child soon to be orphaned. Brenda found herself hard put to control herself and was glad when they finally came away.

His mother hugged him again in exactly the same way as they left, while his dad caught his hand in a prolonged grip and wished him well and to come back safe.

'Anyone'd think they'll never see me again,' Harry chuckled as they walked home. He was carrying Addie. 'We'll be round there again in a couple of days, 'cause they're goin' ter give eye to Addie. But that's me mum for yer. Always did wear 'er 'eart on 'er sleeve, me mum. She's the salt of the earf, me mum.'

At home around half five they sat down to an early tea of egg and chips. It had been a gorgeously warm sunny day. Addie was fed and ready for bed, Brenda was washing up and contemplating them being alone when from far away came the familiar wail.

'Oh, no . . .' The words dragged themselves from her lips. She uttered them half in irritation at the prospect of lovemaking being interrupted, half in alarm that London was possibly being targeted again after the deceptive lull it had enjoyed.

Harry was on his feet, staring about. This for him was his first experience since Dunkirk of an air attack and it revived memories that showed plainly on his face. Brenda had to take his arm and shake it a little for him to recover his wits.

'It's orright!' she burst out, but he'd already collected himself.

'We can make it ter the public shelter. We ain't sittin' in that bloody old shed of yours this time, now I'm 'ere.'

She'd written to him of her experience that night in the pram shed. What she hadn't told him about was the key Mr Stebbings had given her. In fact she had totally forgotten about it. Now she remembered it again.

'No need,' she said, hurriedly gathering up the paraphernalia she'd taken with her for that last air raid, plus a few more bits and pieces. Tomorrow they would make a corner of the basement more comfy ready for the next time, if there was a next time. Who knew whether this might not be another isolated attack? 'I've got a key to the downstairs shop's basement.'

He paused to stare at her. 'Where'd you get it from?'

'Mr Stebbings,' she said without thinking. 'He said me and Addie would be much safer there than the shed or a public shelter. They're only made of brick. Yer might as well be indoors as there.'

Harry was staring at her. 'Why'd he give yer a key?'

'He just felt concerned for me.'

'What's he doin' feelin' concerned fer you, me wife?'

A knot of anger made itself felt in her stomach. 'Oh, don't be stupid, Harry! Anyone would think we was 'aving an affair or something.'

'Are yer?'

'Harry!' Hurt, shock and indignation streaked through her. 'What d'yer think I am? How can you say something like that?'

He blinked, the tight features relaxing. 'I don't know why I said it. I didn't mean it, love.'

Her own tension dissolved, but the hurt remained as she said blankly, 'I know yer didn't.'

But as the room was pierced suddenly by the nearby siren, she put her hurt aside. 'Come on, let's get a move on! There ain't much down there except old books. Nothing to sit on, but we can use the eiderdown and pillows.'

'I'll get you and Addie settled down there then, and pop back up fer a couple of chairs or somethink. Give us the key.'

'No, I'll hang on to it,' she said quickly without thought and heard him draw in a short breath, but he said nothing more as they hurried down the iron stairs and round to the front of the shop.

It was quarter to six; the sun, having given the south-eastern counties such a beautiful hot day, was still well up in a cloudless sky, but that was all that was normal. Bow Road had come alive with people clutching belongings to their chests, carrying children, toting bags and cases, all set on getting to the nearest public air raid shelter. No one ran. They merely moved swiftly, taking no notice of anyone else.

Mr Stebbings had closed early as he often did on a Saturday evening, and had probably left only a few minutes ago. Just as well, Brenda thought, Harry standing silent still while she inserted the new key in the shop door.

They found the basement steps at the rear. A light switch at the bottom revealed a cluttered area in the fitful glow of a single naked sixty-watt bulb, with two narrow aisles formed by several racks half-filled with old books lying at angles or on their sides. Others lay piled on the floor, filling the place with their musty odour. High up in corners dark cobwebs gently undulated.

'Not much, is it?' Harry said in a tone that was very near to scoffing.

'But it's safe,' she told him in firm, stiff tones. Holding Addie's hand, she moved forward along one aisle. She'd never seen so many books.

'Come on, we'll find somewhere to—'

Her words broke off as reaching the end of the racks she saw a small truckle bed by a wall, a chair, a table, on it a small lamp, cups, saucers and plates, and several other items her amazed mind was unable at the moment to register. Mr Stebbings had set it all out in readiness for her. Turning to Harry, she saw his face, and blurted, 'I didn't know he'd do all this.'

For a moment he didn't speak. Finally he said slowly with an edge to his voice, 'No need fer me ter go up an' get them few bits I was goin' ter get, is there? Looks like he's taken it fer granted yer'd come down 'ere.'

She tried to smile. She wanted to say lightly, 'Don't be jealous, love.' But her better sense stopped her. He *was* jealous, no getting away from it. Wordlessly she sat on the one chair, acutely aware that there was only the one. Adele she deposited on the bed, feeling that in doing this she might eradicate the connotation the bed seemed to hold of some ulterior motive. Harry remained stubbornly on two feet, gazing about, coldly studying the preparations another man had made.

The sirens had died away. But now came the most dreaded of sounds: a low drone that was fast becoming a roar which even the basement could not muffle. It seemed to be vibrating the very walls.

'Stay here!' Harry commanded. 'I'm goin' up to 'ave a look.'

'No, Harry, don't go!' she pleaded as what sounded like every gun ringing the City opened up in a deafening barrage.

But he was already up the stairs. Seconds later he was down again, eyes wide with awe. 'Bren, yer should see it. There must be 'undreds of 'em. Like a bloody great black cloud, right over'ead . . .'

To prove his words, they were almost thrown to the floor by a series of high-pitched squealing sounds and terrific explosions, one sounding so near as to have landed almost on top of them. Brenda shrieked and threw herself on Adele who broke into terrified crying at being so roughly treated.

As more poured down, she leapt up to seek Harry's arms. He in turn dragged Adele off the bed, pulling all three of them down to crouch together close to the floor. Compared to this, that night two weeks earlier had been a mild few hours of inconvenience. Her mind felt numbed by the awful din, her nerve endings seeming to jerk with each detonation.

'We're going ter be killed,' she sobbed and felt Harry's arms tighten still more round her.

'No we ain't,' he muttered firmly, though it was impossible to believe as the uproar continued. But after a while the raiders began to depart.

Coming upright like hedgehogs uncurling after a predator has lost interest, they stood up, looked around. Brenda consoled her still-sobbing, still-terrified child.

'She orright?' Harry asked in a sort of monotone. Brenda nodded.

'You?' she asked and had him ask the same of her, to which she again nodded.

'I'm going up ter see what's what.'

'No, Harry.'

'It's OK. They've left. Better see what damage they've left be'ind. Might be able to 'elp in some way, if 'elp's needed.'

All she could say was, 'Be careful.' She filled with pride for his conduct.

But after a while when he didn't return she followed, clutching Addie to her, glad to give the child a bit of air and to see the sun still there, though now it had become reddened behind one vast rolling billow of smoke.

She found Harry gazing up at it and towards where it all was coming from, which seemed to be the whole of the souther parts with more to the east.

'They've got the docks,' he said quietly. 'All along the river. Gawd 'elp them poor buggers what live there.'

From all over came the shrill ringing of fire and ambulance bells. Bow Road and the surrounding area appeared to have escaped any direct hits, but it was littered with tiny bits of charred wood, still smouldering, road and pavement blackened by burnt paper and sparks that had drifted over. The air hung thick with a stench of burning rubber, sugar, timber and leather, all of which combined to make her put her hand over her nose and mouth and almost gag.

Seeing her action Harry took her arm gently. 'Take Addie back down. The air's cleaner down there. I'll be down in a minute. Just want ter make sure. Anyway I don't fink it's all over yet.'

The raid had lasted under an hour, but she was conscious that no all clear had sounded. A heavy foreboding lying inside her chest, she did as he said, feeling now that he could be right. And he was.

Shortly after seven came the now-familiar drone growing into a deep, inexorable, throaty roar that had the little family in Stebbings' basement scuttling into what they hoped was the safer cubby hole under the stairs. There, as the multiple whistles and deafening crashes of one after another stick of falling bombs merged with a constant pounding of anti-aircraft guns trying to protect the city, the family crouched the rest of the night. In wave after wave came the Luftwaffe with hardly a let-up until Brenda began to wonder if anything at all would be left standing by morning.

Time after time her thoughts flew to her family in their air-raid shelter at the end of their little garden as all this death and destruction rained down. Dad had sounded so certain that nothing could collapse on top of a shelter at the bottom of a garden. If they didn't receive a direct hit, that was. But with so much stuff being dropped, it could just happen.

With Harry's protective arms about her and Addie, in the same breath as she prayed for each explosion to miss her, she prayed for them in that air raid shelter not to be harmed.

Somehow the hours passed. Somehow the brain became numbed if not quite inured to a din muffled only slightly by the basement, even to the terrifying vibration of its walls at each explosion. The bombers finally left as dawn came, around five o'clock as Brenda, creeping out from under the stairs, discovered from a little clock Mr Stebbings had thoughtfully left. It was the first time she'd noticed it. It was lying face up, having been tipped over by all the explosions, but still ticking.

The sweet sound of the all clear greeted them as they emerged to behold a pall of smoke and dust, smell the nose-stinging stench of smouldering wood, see Bow Road strewn with grit, broken glass, bricks, tiles, splintered wood and household possessions.

Further along across the wide road Civil Defence workers in dark, plaster-streaked dungarees and dirt-spattered tin helmets were searching a pile of debris which had been a shop and dwellings above, and again Brenda breathed a prayer of relief to a silent God that what had dropped there had avoided her and her family.

Ambulance bells rang wildly as their vehicles dashed by towards the London Hospital. Water ran in the gutters from the night's fire hoses. People were going back to their homes from the public shelters, each hoping they would find them still standing, none needing the Civil Defence men to send them on their way rather than hover to view the bombed shop. They walked past as if it wasn't there or with just a glance of sympathy. They had their own homes to view: the shattered glass, the lost tiles, the door that hung on its hinges, if they'd been lucky. If they weren't, a heap of bricks and broken beams would pronounce them homeless.

It was to be like this for the whole time Harry was on leave. Of John Stebbings there was no sign; he took to closing early to be home before the air raids started with the sun going down.

One time Harry made a point of going into his shop to thank him for his generous gesture. But Brenda knew it was to assess him. He came back upstairs, his face set and thoughtful.

'A bit of a charmer, ain't he?' was all he said, and after that refrained from mentioning him again. Brenda deemed it prudent to keep quiet as they went about using up Harry's leave as best they could under the present circumstances with London now in the front line, by day going out and making the most of the continuing lovely weather for Addie's sake as well as for their own. Most of the time though was taken up in visiting her parents and his, and making dutiful farewells to further-flung members of his family who had seen him grow up, for he would never be forgiven for not presenting himself prior to leaving home for some godforsaken part of the world. Each in turn embraced him, uncles and aunts respectively wrung his hand and wept over him while his cousins could not care less. Grandparents remembered earlier wars and, dry-eyed, solemnly bade him safe return with honour.

Three of their precious days had to be used up seeing his parents at his mum's weepy insistence. Brenda weathered it as stoically as she could. After all one day had been to take Addie round there to be looked after while the two of them went off on their own, needing to be together before being torn apart for God knows how long. But it was hard to witness those endless cuddles, pecks on the cheek, an emotional hand laid on his arm when he came within touching distance. His dad was less demonstrative and his grandmother less still, deaf and in a world of her own these days.

'Here's Harry ter see yer, Mum,' received an absent nod, and 'Harry's going overseas, Mum, might be years before he's back,' reaped a mumbled, 'Yes, nice – cup o'tea, then?'

At each visit Brenda felt stifled. As well as behaving as if every visit was his last day on earth, his mum hardly ceased to bewail the battering they were all taking from these air raids. 'We'll all be dead soon, I'm sure.'

Her own parents, thank heaven, were more the stoic, down-to-earth East Londoners whom announcers and newspapers took joy in raving about to the rest of the free world. But after nights of intense bombardment, Vera's face had been chalk-white and Mum had pressed Brenda to maybe move in with them while it all lasted.

'The Anderson's one of the safest places yer could 'ave,' she said, but Brenda shook her head.

'There ain't no room, Mum.'

'Of course there's room. There's only me, Dad, an' Vera, now that Brian's gone.' Brian had been called up in the summer, now he was stationed somewhere up in Yorkshire. 'Plenty of room. An' I'd feel better knowing yer safe.'

Explaining that she was safe as houses in Mr Stebbings' basement brought a tight expression to Harry's face and she said no more on the subject. Mum noticed it too, giving them both a searching look, but wisely she refrained from pressing it.

Brenda and Harry popped in to see her parents only twice, mostly to make sure they were still OK after yet more nights of air raids, the neighbours who should have had more sense asking the now-inevitable but exasperating question 'When yer going back then?' as if leave wasn't already speeding by.

By night they cowered in Stebbings' basement, trying to harden themselves to the havoc going on above with flasks of tea and jam sandwiches which Brenda automatically made up each evening. She saw this leave filtering away; her hope of conceiving another child to help fill the lonely gap Harry would leave had gone by the board. No chance of making love with so much going on around them and Addie sleeping close by them. By the time Harry's leave was up, his only thoughts were for her and Addie's safety while he was away.

'I can't bear leaving yer like this,' he muttered as, back in uniform, small kit ready to be heaved on to his shoulders, he hugged her so tightly that she thought he would crush her ribs, at least stop the aching heart below. But it continued to ache on, thudding with misery.

'We'll be orright,' she told him. 'You just be orright too.'

It was the worst feeling she'd ever known to see him go off down the road towards Mile End Station, going all through the same ritual of waving and waving as before. This time she knew that he had nearly not come back the time before. How easily a soldier could lose his life. Forget all the glory of wars through the ages, the proud wife waving the flag, sure of her husband's return. Fear tore at her heart.

Again he'd refused to let her go with him to the main railway station, and in a way she was relieved. Of course she longed to be with him for as long as she possibly could but it would only have dragged out the inevitable, her throat hurting from the tears she would have had to suppress on a busy station. Now would come the waiting for that first letter saying where he had landed up, God willing safely. She would only know once it came. For now she must settle down and endure these nightly raids along with everyone in basements, shelters and tube stations.

Chapter Fifteen

Brian had been called up into the RAF, of all the services. Mum was fiercely proud, feeling he'd achieved something remarkable and making sure everyone knew it. Only ground crew, but he was safe, she made a point of saying, not up there in the air to be shot down as Brenda's friend Doris's husband had been. And in his nice air-force blue uniform he had all the girls around here dying to be asked out on a date by him.

'One of these days,' Vera countered darkly, knowing even if her mum didn't what he had in mind with every single one of them, 'my brother's going ter come a cropper and get one of 'em in the family way. Then he won't be crowing so 'ard.'

Brenda, having popped in to see if everyone was still all in one piece after another night-long blitz, laughed, but Mum bridled. 'Oh, don't Vera. Brian's a good boy really. This war. The youngsters 'ave ter let orf steam.'

Vera said, 'Humph!' and went on thinking her own thoughts about Brian, about boys in general, about Ron Parrish in particular.

It wasn't fair on her. You get yourself a bloke then he gets called up, leaving you to sit at home as if you was married or something. Well she was not married, not even engaged.

He was hardly ever home, stationed up in the Orkneys of all places. What good was a bloke up in the Orkneys – to her or the country? Might as well be on the other side of the world. Might as well be a sailor for all she saw of him. A photo or two to look at and a letter every fortnight, that's all she had, and having to reply to the letters. She hated letter-writing. It took so long, keeping her indoors to do it. It was like she said to Brenda:

'After all, I should be seeing a bit of life. He wouldn't expect me to stay in all the time wasting me life away, would he? It don't do no harm goin' out sometimes, just up the West End with a few friends from work.'

She usually went up the West End with them on a Saturday, though Mum wasn't too happy about that.

'I don't like yer going there when there's air raids going on, luv.'

'I get home before they start, don't I?' she challenged. 'I make sure of that. And I need ter get out, Mum. I'm sick of being stuck in a factory doing rotten war work. If you was doing it, yer'd understand. You don't get no let up. It's go, go, go, till yer want to drop. I 'ave to get out or I'll wither away!'

Anyway, raids had become more spasmodic lately. Like they'd been prior to Christmas, when the Luftwaffe had been kept away by the bad weather. True, they hadn't really stopped. A terrible one had taken place on the Sunday after Christmas just as people had begun to think the worst was over. Then bang! the most horrendous raid of all.

She recalled peeping out from the door of the shelter sometime in the early hours after cowering there for hours with her family while explosions rocked the ground all around. Before being quickly dragged back into it by Mum, what she had seen had appeared to be the whole of London going up in flames, the sky in every direction lurid red like a dozen sunrises all at once, the tinsel freckling of exploding shells and the greenish light of parachute flares lighting everything up even above the fires, white cascades of incendiaries coming down creating more fires. Some lay burning in gardens, some landed on nearby homes – she'd heard them, as always, rattling on the tiles, some going through into the attic to be dealt with by whoever could get up there in time to save their house. And all the time searchlights were crossing and recrossing in long stiff fingers.

With a shriek of, 'Whatyer fink yer doing?' Mum had dragged her bodily backwards into the shelter before the lethal blast of a high explosive bomb coming down too close for comfort with a tremendous roar could reach her, though not before she'd seen the upward surge of white flame from the gasholder it had struck.

Later that night it had been Dad's turn to rush out and into their house as incendiaries landed on their roof. Dad had stood outside watching for them despite bombs and shrapnel. Mum had been silent with terror on being told to stay where she was, praying the house wouldn't be hit as he dealt with the thing. He'd come back shortly after, almost falling into the shelter out of the noise and chaos, to say the bloody thing was out, covered in sand. Fortunately it had been one of the nights he wasn't fire-watching for his employers, or helping the local warden as he sometimes did.

After that, for a lot of January and this month the weather had again been too foul for the Luftwaffe, which targeted other cities like Birmingham and Bristol instead. But there was always the certainty of clearing skies and a bomber's moon during the middle of the month, attracting them back to the capital. Hence Mum's worry about Vera being out too late.

But sometimes she and her friends couldn't help meeting a few boys, usually in uniform of one kind or another, and did leave it a bit late. Then they'd have to scamper like mad for the tube, or a bus, the rest of the way home having to be covered on foot. They would stop in shop doorways when shrapnel came down, being warned by an air-raid warden or Civil Defence bloke to get under cover quick!

Vera preferred the bus even if it was slower. The underground always stank of people sheltering. Even though it was better organised than it had first been, now with proper bunks and proper sanitation, that nasty fetid odour of close-packed bodies lingered. It was so depressing seeing them preparing for the night, wrapped up in overcoats and scarves and sorting out bedding and belongings, even though there was music and they made their own lively entertainment.

They'd arrive well in advance of the warning, and the queues to get down there could be seen growing longer and longer during the day to stake their claim. Vera was glad of her own Anderson and thought of Brenda all on her own in that basement with just little Addie for company and that cat she'd got her.

Brenda should have accepted Mum's offer to stay with them while all this was going on. With both Brian and Davy away now, there was enough room. But she'd always been independent and stubborn. One day though she'd rue it.

On the bus coming home this Saturday after seeing *Only Angels Have Wings* at the Regal, Marble Arch, she and the two friends she'd gone there with mooning over the suave and sophisticated Cary Grant, and all wishing they had the same husky, seductive tones as his co-star Jean Arthur, Vera thought momentarily of her independent sister, then put her aside. It had been a wonderful film. They'd sat through it twice and the time had gone on.

If only Mum wouldn't be so concerned at her being up West. There had been a bit of bombing but it was still safer than her end, where the docks and industry attracted raids, in the process devastating the poor people who lived there.

Vera gazed dismally at the bombed and gutted buildings growing more and more numerous as they approached her part of London. February 1941 and still no sign of the Blitz letting up. As dusk began to creep down she just hoped she'd be home before the warning struck up, not relishing being in some strange shelter during an air raid usually lasting all night. She should have kept an eye on the time and not sat through the film again, even though the other two had wanted to.

She turned in her seat and raised her voice to them over the rattling of the bus. 'My mum's gonna be ever so worried,' she said in a sort of reprimand.

Buses would sometimes stop if things got too hot; then passengers were obliged to get off to seek immediate shelter. It had happened before. Nothing worried Mum more than her not being home during an air raid. 'I'd rather us all be tergether,' she'd say as if that made all the difference to a direct hit if there was one.

The two girls paused in their conversation, from which Vera had been partially excluded. Madge leaned forward briefly to concur that all their mums would be worried, then went back to what she'd been saying to Gladys.

Isolated from their chatter by her seat's high back-rest, Vera extricated Ron's latest letter, somewhat crumpled, from her handbag. The joggling bus and the gloom made it difficult to read, the unlit interior growing darker by the second with the fading of a glorious sunset that promised a clear, frosty night, perfect for bombers, when a full moon would light up the Thames like a silver ribbon, guiding them to their targets.

Vera held the letter as steady as she could, peering at it closely. No good, the words remained a blur. His letters had become boring anyway. So little to say, she supposed, stuck up there in the Orkneys. Not that she had much to say herself either these days. She no longer felt any eagerness about his mail, in fact a sigh of apathy came from her when a letter did land on the mat because it meant having to write back. She had never much enjoyed letter-writing.

Giving up, she stuffed the letter back into the handbag and twisted round to the two girls. 'Nearly home.' But neither of them heard her.

They'd both found dates for tomorrow. She too could have had one – the tall, loose-limbed matelot with his hat set at a jaunty angle on his fair hair. But she'd hesitated, half shaken her head, not wanting to be disloyal to Ron. To her horror the matelot had shrugged and placed an arm about Madge instead. Now he and Madge would see each other tomorrow. Damn all this loyalty! She should have taken the offer up there and then instead of thinking of Ron. She could bet he wouldn't have given her a second thought if some girl had nodded to him. She'd been a silly fool.

'That was gorgeous, Mum,' Brenda sighed, pushing away her empty plate.

She went to Mum's for dinner every other Sunday, seeing Harry's parents on the alternate ones. She'd have offered to have them come to her on occasion but she was only one mouth to feed – Addie at two years old did not count – and having to feed several wasn't easy in these days of rationing. She couldn't very well ask them to bring along their own food. It was all very awkward. Better going to them instead, armed of course with a bit of meat from her rations though Mum always insisted on her taking it back home.

'If I can't feed me own daughter wiv a couple of slices of meat, what sort of mother am I? Take it back 'ome an' make a stew for Addie.'

Harry's mum was often the same, though now and again would look embarrassed and accept the offering, saying, 'We 'ave been a bit short this week. Harry's grandma do like 'er food. I can't keep up with 'er and she's got no idea of rationing. She'd 'ave our share too if we let 'er, poor ole thing.'

These Sunday visits did at least get Brenda out of herself. She saw so few people, save on occasion John Stebbings, who had said to call him by his first name – 'Mr Stebbings sounds so formal, and we do know each other by now' – and of course her regulars coming to have their hair done.

Dinner at Mum's this week had been liver, off ration, and for which Mum had queued for at the butcher's for half an hour, she said. The word going round that he'd got offal, she'd been off like a shot, streaking ahead of her neighbours, she said proudly. But she'd still found a sizeable queue there already.

'I'm sure some of 'em are up at dawn just in case there's anything. I think I was the last but four to get any,' she said as she cleared away the dinner plates ready to dish up date pudding with custard. 'I felt sorry for them what had stood all that time queuing up to have him run out of the stuff just as they get there. Still, that's 'ow it goes, don' it?'

After they'd washed up she asked if Brenda fancied staying over. 'You ain't got nowhere to rush orf to termorrer. Looks like it's goin' ter be another moonlit night an' them buggers'll be coming back ternight fer sure. Sunday night – why can't they give it a rest on Sunday? Yer'll be safe in our shelter, love.'

But on Monday morning Brenda had a woman coming at nine, a new lady who'd heard of her. She told Mum. 'So I've got ter go home.' She was also worried about the cat. It would need feeding. Also the guns terrified it even down in the cellar, crawling under the bed cover to lie shivering.

'Yer can still make it in time termorrer,' Mum protested, backed up by Dad, with Vera chipping in that she never saw her for all that long these days and it would be nice to have a nice long talk.

'I don't like thinking of you down there in that cellar all on yer own.'

But she wouldn't be alone. Over the months she had settled herself in quite nicely, like everyone else now in the habit of taking shelter whether the Luftwaffe came or not, because you never knew if it would, and she had John Stebbings for company. He now did ARP duty in the area, saying he had little to rush off home for.

If things were quiet, and during bad weather they often were, he'd pop down there to see if she was all right. The warden's post only stood just a hundred yards down on the corner, and they'd talk or play draughts; he would leave them set up if he did have to hurry off.

He was teaching her to play chess as well. She had begun to look forward to his company and if a raid was heavy, he'd make it his business to look in briefly to see how she was. It left her feeling safe even when he had to leave during a raid.

It was best not to say too much about it though. Even Mum might get the wrong end of the stick.

One good thing was that not that many bombs had fallen too close. Mile End Road for some reason lay slightly outside what had become known as Bomb Alley, the susceptible corridor either side of the bright guiding ribbon of the Thames in moonlight with wharves and docks and industry the target.

Sometimes there was a near one. One on the corner of Burdett Road, demolished the La Boheme cinema where she had so often gone with girls from work or a boyfriend, and then of course with Harry. Its name had changed only this year to the Vogue; it was now rubble. It was as if her youthful years had been obliterated along with the beautiful decor, plush seating, romantic atmosphere, the ice creams steadily licked and the sweets steadily munched through Walt Disney cartoons, short second features and thrilling main films. The cinema looked so sad, all wrecked, its once glorious facade and hoarding flattened like a badly tossed pancake.

She wrote and told Harry all about it. He was in North Africa, his air letters bearing name, number, unit and area, giving her very little idea as to exactly where he was. Her own address on one quarter of the single folded flimsy blue sheet, as ever, bore the censor's black stamp and the words ON ACTIVE SERVICE.

She awaited each letter with eagerness, with fear too when reading in January that he'd seen a bit of fighting early in that month, and then that he was in hospital in Alexandria having gone down with sandfly fever. Their separation had been more than she could bear. But his next one had again bucked her up because he was hoping to go to a convalescent camp.

She had even hoped in her innocence that he might be sent home but that was soon scotched. His next letter, bright and cheerful, said he was in good health again and ready to be sent back to his battalion. He would write again as soon as he could, leaving her to stew for his safety all over again.

He seemed to be viewing it all as a sort of game as he told of all the Italians they were capturing. She felt torn between seeing him as her hero and experiencing twinges of irritation that he appeared to have no notion of what she was going through back home with the Blitz and rationing, though he did mention his concern here and there in between referring to the pleasant way his

Christmas had passed with double rations, flowing beer and plenty of singsong. He said he'd been given some leave and had spent it in Cairo, taking a train there.

Her own Christmas had been miserably got through with no respite from the Luftwaffe. It was horrible to think of those buried, injured, or killed during what should normally be a festive season.

The world of course was being made alive to the fact that Britain could take it. But for ordinary people it was becoming an endurance test many felt would see them go under if it went on for much longer. That was her view as she traipsed round to her parents after a particularly bad raid to let them know she was all right and to be sure they were too. She had become thin and edgy. If it hadn't been for her hairdressing, she sometimes felt she would have gone mad.

She had regulars with a few new ones besides. Signor Alfio Fichera had been interned the moment Italy came into the war, his salon had closed and with a wartime shortage of hairdressing materials no one had opened another in its place. It now sold second-hand clothes. Although Brenda felt sorry for the inoffensive little man his going had been a boon; some of the old customers who had known her heard from one or two old colleagues what she was doing, and now came to her.

Her only worry was that if any should happen to know her in-laws, her secret would be out. Lately she wasn't quite so worried about them as about how she was going to keep her little business going. Shortages of what were termed luxury materials made it hard enough for large hairdressers to keep going let alone a woman on her own trying to subsidise her allowance. By making do and mending and not getting too ambitious, she struggled on.

She thanked heaven for John Stebbings, who had become quite a friend, a tower of strength and generosity. When blast blew out some of the windows of her flat and shattered some of its roof tiles he had got an elderly man and a young lad he knew to replace them, not waiting for the landlord or the council to sort it out.

Leased though his shop was, he no doubt had an interest in that books could suffer if water came through in a heavy downpour. Of course, nature being as bloody-minded as ever, weather liable to keep enemy planes from doing their job never occurred. But it was still generous of him in refusing her offer to pay for the repairs. The trouble was the stab of guilt she felt in thanking him, of rebellion too, recalling that bit tagged on to the end of Harry's first letter after he'd gone back off embarkation leave:

> . . . *And Bren, just one more thing. Better not to get too familiar with that Stebbings bloke. You don't know what he's got in mind, offering you his basement like that. Bit too generous for my liking. I know you won't let yourself get involved or anythink, but I'm not there to protect you. Men like that can prey on a woman under a cloak of being kind-hearted. There's never no smoke without fire. So I'm just saying be careful* . . .

The rest had been filled with longing to be home with her, and how he hated the heat and the flies, the awful food, the feeling of being on the edge of nowhere; sending his love and hoping she was all right with the bloody

213

blitz still going on. But she couldn't get out of her mind what seemed to her his lack of trust. It made her angry and hurt, and uncomfortable too, that by writing to say he could trust her implicitly, the mere fact that he needed to only made it seem otherwise.

Even so, for a while she found herself backing away from Stebbings' obvious good intentions, guilty about that as well. 'I hate this bloody war!' she said to herself again and again as the February days crept into double figures with raids continuing with what often seemed mounting ferocity, and Harry's letters arrived all bright and cheerful again, seeming to have lost a little of his concern for what she was going through at home.

Even his news that he was now guarding a prisoner of war camp full of thousands of cheerful Italian prisoners of war who all seemed quite nice blokes really, made it appear that he was seeing his war as a kind of game. Though she wouldn't have wished it otherwise.

Chapter Sixteen

'I wonder this Mr Stebbings ain't been called up,' Mrs Hutton said darkly after Brenda, over Sunday dinner, had mentioned how she and Addie always felt so much safer in the basement under his shop during the nightly air raids.

She had only mentioned it because Mrs Hutton had expressed surprise that she had never availed herself of her parents' air raid shelter. Brenda found herself having to defend them in that there wouldn't be time to run round there if the bombers arrived as soon as the sirens had gone off; again making excuses for the intimation that it was a wonder they hadn't invited her to stay there permanently. 'All by yourself in that flat,' Mrs Hutton had remarked. 'I'd of thought they'd of been more worried for yer.'

No amount of insistence that of course they were worried and it was her decision would alter her mother-in-law's conviction that they were neglecting their own daughter. 'Not as if they ain't got room, now yer two brothers ain't there,' she had once said.

Brenda shrugged at her mother-in-law's latest remark, this time on the verge of retorting that what Mr Stebbings did or did not do was no concern of hers. Her father-in-law came to her aid.

'It's probably somethink medical, like flat feet or a weak chest.'

'He looks healthy enough to me whenever I see 'im.'

Which was all of twice, Brenda thought, hugging vexation.

'And, if you ask me—' Mrs Hutton went on, to be cut short by her husband.

'If it's medical,' he said as he munched reflectively on a hard bit of the Sunday meat, 'I don't s'pose he'd want ter bandy it about. I don't s'pose he'd confide it to our Brenda. Nice that he lets 'er use the basement. Some wouldn't.'

Daphne was having dinner here too today. Bob was stationed somewhere up near Birmingham. 'He could be a conscientious objector, this Stebbings chap. The government do let them off, though I sometimes think it's just a cover for being too scared to fight.'

She said it with a bitter ring to her tone. At any moment her husband could be sent into some battle. Brenda leapt in fiercely. Anyone would think she was the only one.

'I don't think so. He does ARP and fire-watching. That can be just as dangerous, stuck up on some flat roof with incendiaries falling all around, running to people's aid through a rain of shrapnel. He could get blown up any time. I don't think that's being cowardly. I don't think there's a cowardly bone in his body when he volunteers ter do things like that.'

Immediately she knew she had spoken out of turn as Daphne, potato and cabbage pronged on a fork suspended halfway between her plate and her mouth, gave Brenda a curious glance.

'Sounds like you're quite familiar with what he does.'

'Familiar!' Brenda shot at her, already fearing that the stab of guilt that propelled her upright had revealed itself in her eyes. She fought to brazen it out, her voice going up one tone. 'All I know is that people what go out during a raid to look out and watch over other people can't be cowards.'

Daphne wilted. 'You know what I mean. Him letting you use his basement, I thought he might of confided in you why he ain't in the forces.'

'Well, he hasn't. And he doesn't.' That sounded too hasty for comfort. The truth was, he had.

'When I did try to enlist,' he told her once, 'and they found I had asthma as a youngster. They rejected me. So here I am. It can be most embarrassing, trying to explain why you're not in the forces and feeling you're not being believed. It's not as if I were exempted on some essential public service.'

She had felt so sorry for him. He was doing his bit. He was every bit as needed as anyone in the front line, ironically much of the front line being right here at home. And here she was getting letters from Harry who *was* in the forces and writing of the great time he was having! When he had fought it had been against an enemy with no real interest in combat, easy-going Italians who seemed happier being captured than fighting, according to the pictures in all the newspapers of them with their hands in the air, faces wreathed in smiles.

His letters to her during March were still describing the marvels of Egypt with just a passing concern here and there at how was she faring. She wondered if she was plaguing him too much telling of the continuing blitz, how exhausted she was from loss of sleep and oppressive rationing, where some bomb had dropped locally, and her fear for Addie.

Perhaps in an effort not to worry him, in her last letter she had tried to make light of its ferocity, but had been angered by his blithe reply that he was glad she was weathering it. 'I know you, Brenda, you're made of strong stuff. You won't let them get you down.'

Had he been here she'd have aimed a saucepan at him!

That night, as bombs fell and the abrasive jangling of fire engine and ambulance bells split the lurid, dust-filled air that stank of the burning contents of warehouse after warehouse along the Thames, she poured it all out to John Stebbings when he popped into the basement during a brief lull to see if she and Addie were still in one piece.

Taking her tight expression for fear, he soothed, 'You mustn't give way,' and had her look up at him from where she sat on the bottom edge of the bed, fury in her eyes.

'I don't care about the bloody bombing!' she burst out.

Addie, fast asleep on the narrow camp bed, didn't stir as Brenda raised her voice in pent-up indignation.

'It's Harry and his bloody happy letters. He don't have any idea what I'm going through and cares even less.'

John Stebbings came and sat on the edge of the bed beside her. His arm came about her shoulder. 'Now, that's not true,' he murmured slowly. 'Of course he cares. He's worried being so far away from you, but how can he keep on saying the same thing in letter after letter?'

The arm was comforting, offering safety from all that went on outside. She let herself lean against him and despite the harsh ARP dungarees and jacket he wore felt his warmth begin to transmit itself to her own body. All at once it emphasised how alone she was. She had Mum. But Mum had her own worries and she was a grown woman with a child of her own. The wish to be a child herself in her mother's arms only drove her to fiercer independence even if Mum had attempted to cuddle her.

Now a man was offering his protection, something she'd not had in over six months, and she missed it so. In the chill basement, Addie asleep, above their heads the ringing of fire and ambulance bells, and in the brief lull in the bombing the low crump-crump of some distant ack-ack gunfire where bombers still played havoc, Brenda lay against the strong, comforting body of John Stebbings.

A well-known fluttering had begun to make itself known deep in the pit of her stomach. And maybe it was the way she had taken a deep breath, maybe it was the way she had moved, but its message was clear enough to him and maybe he was feeling the same way himself. His arm tightened and as she looked up at him, he lowered his face to hers so that their lips touched. It may have been that he was trying to comfort her, no more, but she felt the hunger there, and her lips too had grown hungry.

She felt her muscles grow taut against the terrible desire that had come over her, heard herself whisper, 'We mustn't . . . I'm married . . .' but the wonderful feel of those lips, the warmth coming from them, the need not to be alone, stopped all further protest. As if she was floating, the world rolled away and with it all need to be responsible, to think, to consider what must come afterwards.

Addie's little body twitched irritably, her voice protesting briefly at the disturbance from two lonely people seeking respite from their lonely lives before resuming sleep. Accustomed as she was to noise and disturbance, this was nothing by comparison. She neither knew nor cared when the two people finally lay still, not speaking, each wrapped in thought. Each now knew that they had been taken over and already they regretted it. They felt awkward with each other, and did not exchange any look as, getting up from the narrow bed while the ack-ack grew from a low grumble to sharper cracks announcing an end to the lull, he adjusted his dress and murmured, 'I must get back.'

Brenda didn't answer. Hating herself for what she had let happen, she watched him start up the short flight of stone stairs that led up to the shop, one hand clutching the thin iron rail.

Two steps up he stopped to look down at her. No doubt he saw the way her teeth had lightly caught at her lower lip, probably interpreting the mute appeal on her face as love, or more correctly as shame, she couldn't tell. His voice was barely audible. 'I'm sorry, Brenda. I shouldn't have . . .'

'John!' She came to life as he made to ascend the rest of the stairs, as his face began to be hidden from her by the floor of the shop above. He bent his long body, his features coming into view again, his expression enquiring, eager.

'John, I'm not sorry,' she burst out.

No, she wasn't . . . yes, she was . . . but only for some things. For the fact that she still loved Harry but that a war had torn . . . no, was tearing them apart – that his

220

letters never seemed to convey a deep enough concern for her, only told of the unexpected good life and fine adventure he was experiencing while she, stuck in a humdrum existence, must battle on against food rationing, bombing, loneliness . . . oh, such loneliness and longing. And now it had led to this. Yes, she was sorry, but not because of what had just occurred. She felt alive, real, wanted, a person again.

She saw him nod and could not say whether it translated into regret or reassurance. Then he'd gone, the door above her closing quietly while the noise of anti-aircraft gunfire grew louder and the low menacing drone of the searching bombers grew in volume. Soon came the tearing sound of falling bombs, the explosions, the fine dust of ages trickling down from the wooden ceiling, the shuddering of the old bookshelves as yet a few more books tumbled to the floor. She was alone, guarding her child. It was as if the love she and John Stebbings had made had never been.

One particular huge explosion that rocked the cellar made her cry out and throw herself across Addie, waking the child enough to protest with her little fists and arms flailing before turning over in sleep. Brenda too fell asleep as the bombers finally departed with the first glimmer of dawn. But when she awoke she had a distinct feeling that during that time John Stebbings had peeked down at her and had gone away again without waking her. It was just a feeling, but a warm and comforting one.

At first light she crept out to a grey day to survey the wide Mile End Road. It was never possible to do this without a strange sense of being in some primeval time as she gazed around at the result of the previous night's bombing. Oddly deserted, yet there were people. Unnaturally quiet, yet with London making its own sounds. Probably early morning had always been like this, but in these unnatural times, yes, it felt different. The pavements were all littered with shards of glass, broken slates, pieces of wooden railings, and bits of grotesquely twisted exploded metal, shrapnel with edges sharp enough to cut the careless hands of young children snapping up the most interesting examples as souvenirs, to their harassed mothers' disgust.

John Stebbings had gone, no doubt to see if his own home was still in one piece. He would come back later to take stock of the shop's front windowpane that now lay in smithereens on the pavement, already being swept back into the kerb by a thoughtful warden who said 'Mornin'!' to Brenda as she appeared, as though it were the morning of any day before the Blitz.

More windows to be replaced in her flat, she thought distractedly, returning the man's salutation with a sociable smile, or if not, they'd have to be boarded up with old cardboard if she could find any, anything to keep out the early March winds. More, she thought about how she was going to face John this morning. How would they greet each other? Would they smile like friends? Avoid each other, ashamed? Would he not look at her or would he approach her with that usual directness of his, put an arm round her, behave as though he belonged now?

How would she react to whatever it would be? It was best not to be there when he did return. Hurrying up the back stairs with Addie in her arms, Brenda set about her normal daily tasks, first feeding Addie and then herself. She got a little angry when Addie seemed not to want her breakfast, as often happened, unsettled as the child was by all the to-ing and fro-ing. Then scrupulously and furiously, before Addie hurt herself, she swept up the bits of broken glass from yet another small windowpane which had taken the brunt of one blast or other from last night. Dust lay everywhere, veils of it as though she hadn't dusted for years. Hurriedly she went over everything with a wet cloth, the only way to deal with it, then a dry one. A woman was coming to have her hair done this morning, unless she had more important things to deal with like a wrecked home, or had been taken to hospital injured, or was even dead.

Then she must write to Harry, the only way to rid herself of the guilt that last night had gripped her. Where had her mind been? How could she have let such a thing happen? And yet, as the thought brought the face of John Stebbings before her, there came fresh flutterings in her stomach. How could one be in love with two people at the same time? Harry was her husband, she loved him – it was just that she had been so lonely, lonely and afraid.

Glad of an anaesthetising burst of energy, she methodically set herself to giving the flat a thorough if hurried tidy-up in readiness for her client, and to dealing with Adele's needs.

It was best to keep John at arm's length if she possibly could. Keep away from temptation, common sense shouted at her. But how? He'd never let it go at that. It was Mum who came to her rescue without realising it.

'Them raids is gettin' worse an' worse,' she said, gazing in distress at Brenda when she popped round there that afternoon with the usual need to find out if

223

they were all right. She'd have known soon enough if they weren't – Mum had enough good neighbours to come hurrying round to convey the bad news if they'd been hurt or . . . She dared not think of anything worse. Mum had come out with the right solution to the need to stay clear of the shop basement for a while.

'I do wish yer'd stay 'ere with us while things are so bad. It can't go on forever. They've got ter stop some time or we'll all be six feet under or in some bloomin' lunatic asylum. I do worry about yer, yer know, Bren.'

'And I worry about you, Mum. All of you.'

'I say, if we 'ave ter go, we all go tergether.'

Brenda pursed her lips in assumed contemplation, gazing down at Addie sitting on the floor with a biscuit Mum had given her. Addie had been upset when her cat had failed to come home after a raid and had never been seen again. How could she explain to a child? Being here would make Addie get over it.

'Well look, Mum,' she said. 'If that's how you feel about it, p'haps I could stay with you for a while, see how it goes.'

Mum's eyes lit up, and before much more could be said, it was all settled. 'Bring what yer need with yer this evening, I'll supply whatever else yer need. Oh, Bren, it won't 'alf take a weight off me mind, you bein' 'ere.'

Waiting until John closed up to go home no doubt to return later to go on duty, Brenda left him a note on the little bedside table in the cellar to say she'd had to go and see her parents. Later she would explain to him when she saw him tomorrow that with her mother being so concerned for her she had agreed to go there each evening for a while, coming home in the morning. 'Just for a little while,' she wrote. Then packing a few things for the night she hurried off, her mind in a turmoil as she pushed Addie in her pram across Bow Road and through the streets to Trellis Street, her parents' home a quarter-mile walk away.

How would he take it? She didn't want him to think she was spurning him. She didn't want to upset him, give him to believe he had gone too far. She was as guilty as he in that respect. It was her head telling her they must stay away from each other, but it was her heart that with each step she took wanted to turn back, to go down into the cellar and hope he would come to her again tonight.

Sternly she put the thought out of her mind and strode on. It wouldn't do. She had a husband. How would he feel if this grew into an affair while he was thousands of miles away? It had been bad enough losing control that once. It mustn't happen again. It wouldn't happen again.

She'd have to come back tomorrow morning of course. There was her hairdressing business, that couldn't be let go to pot. In the evening she'd go back to Mum and Dad's for yet another night huddled in the shelter. A real blessed chore, but it avoided the temptation that no matter what she did or thought continued to lurk at the back of her brain: that she wanted more.

Three weeks later found her still trundling round to her parents. It was hard to tell them that she'd had enough of huddling in the cramped air raid shelter night after night, with just enough room for the four hard, eighteen-inch-wide wooden bunks. Mum and Dad had one each, she and Vera took the other two, with Addie squashed in beside her unable to stretch her small limbs so that her whining woke everyone from what fitful sleep they were able to get.

Every night spent there where even to turn over disturbed the others, set her thinking of the comfy if makeshift little bed in John's cellar, of the warm halo glow from the small table lamp, or candlelight when electricity got cut off. It was shared by only herself and Addie, and it provided the pure luxury of being able to get up when she wanted, stretch her legs and walk around the dusty bookshelves. Before long she was making excuses about it being inconvenient traipsing round there every evening and home again every morning.

'It do disrupt Addie's routine, Mum.'

'Better disrupt that than 'er little body buried under a pile of bricks. I never thought basements safe. Look at them as what's been buried under there fer days and 'ave ter be dug out. No, love, yer better orf 'ere.'

But how nice to go straight on upstairs as dawn broke rather than walk through rubble-strewn streets in the cold early dawn, depressed by the sight of a couple of dwellings blasted to the ground, the gap they left like a tooth pulled from a previous complete row, wondering if people were underneath as men in boiler suits and tin helmets dug in the pile of pulverised plaster, shattered furniture, splintered wood and blackened bricks that constituted the remnants of someone's home. Wallpaper could still be seen on one exposed wall.

There had been people under there, she learned later, two, a middle-aged couple, and only the woman had been dug out alive. Each time she passed the place after that she thought of the man, whoever he was, of his widow, how they'd gone about their daily lives the day before a bomb claimed one of them. It broke her heart and made her think that it could one night be her and Addie under a pile of rubble. What an irony if Harry, a soldier, got made a widower. It almost made her think twice about going down into that cellar again.

Yet it was so depressing pushing Addie's pram through an acrid stink of burning hanging on the chill morning air, seeing the expressionless faces of those she passed. All this propaganda about how Londoners '*could take it*', with pictures of them grinning through soot-grimed faces, the thumbs-up sign and the ubiquitous mug of steaming char, was a fiction. The real truth was there in those faces that she passed, betraying nothing to outside eyes of whether a loved one lay in some hospital ward or hospital morgue, of whether house and belongings had gone or where they were going to stay now, if they needed new ration books and identity cards. Mum had always taken these essentials in a little American cloth satchel down into the shelter with her. 'Yer never know,' she'd say, as if they were worth more to her than her life.

Gas masks sometimes appeared to be the only remaining possession as a couple poked through the ruins of what had once been a home, faces plastered with grey dust making them look inscrutable. Now and again one would clamber down from the rubble with a piece of furniture while other members of the family continued to pick through the debris.

Trying to avert her eyes for fear of being thought to be staring, she always felt glad to reach home. Into her third week of this, the arrangement had become impossible. Tomorrow she would explain how hard it was getting to keep her business running and that she must take her chances in her own place. This was true. It was hard enough trying to get the hairdressing stuff that wartime had made scarce, let alone having to rush back almost too weary from lack of sleep to give proper attention to her ladies.

There was John Stebbings too. He had nodded silently when she had seen him that first week with her excuses ready. His apology for what had happened had been abject, taking all the blame upon himself.

She'd burst out, 'No, it was me, my fault, I shouldn't ever have let it go that far.'

'And that is the reason why you're staying with your parents,' he had stated.

For all her protests that it wasn't, he knew. Then, a couple of days ago, seeing her returning that morning as he was clearing up bits of debris from the backyard after ARP duty that night, he asked how she was, commenting that she looked tired and drawn.

'I am tired,' she told him flatly as she lifted Adele from the pram and began putting the pram in the shed. That done, she made to hoist the child in her arms to take her up the stairs.

'Here, let me,' he said, taking Addie from her.

'No, John, it's all right – really it is.' Using only his first name came quite naturally to her lips. So far she'd always tagged on his surname when thinking of him but knowing what had happened between them, unplanned or not, it now seemed silly. The times she had raged at

228

herself for letting it go that far, yet the times the yearning returned to be with him again.

Using his first name made her look at him. She found him regarding her with a light in those dark eyes that seemed to probe her soul so deeply that she could actually feel it.

'I've decided not to go round my mother's any more,' she said, trying to keep her voice steady. 'I've missed . . .' She caught herself in time and stammered inadequately, '. . . being down in the basement.'

Her voice had quavered and the expression on his face told her that he knew it was he whom she was missing. Before she could stop herself, her face crumpled and seconds later she was committing herself utterly. 'And I missed you as well.'

All that resolve to be friendly but distant, blown to the wind. Those silly butterflies had started up in her stomach all over again, no matter how she commanded them to be still. They still fluttered at each thought of him, no matter how she told herself to be firm and think of Harry, to concentrate her mind on him. It was in fact already being concentrated by the news of the North African campaign, as was everyone else's.

Chapter Seventeen

After the easy-going Italians whom the Eighth Army had so easily overrun, Rommel's Afrika Korps, specially trained for desert warfare, had recaptured Benghazi. To the despair of everyone at home, British and Australian forces had had to fall back and were now being besieged at Tobruk.

Harry's next letter too was different. Written around mid-April, it told of an end to those good times in Cairo with booze and belly-dancers which Brenda swore had been the initial cause of her being practically thrown into the arms of John Stebbings. But she'd been lonely and in a way angered by the wonderful time Harry kept describing to her while here at home she had been enduring all the violence the blitz could throw at her. Now she regretted her impulsive behaviour.

This letter, after having hoped she was OK, had gone on to tell of a night patrol he'd done, of freezing desert nights, the dark so absolute that the stars seemed, 'only an arm's length above your head', and to give a graphic description of his platoon's silent, stealthy advance, rifles held ready, how they'd sink down on one knee at some hostile shadow or movement, mostly imagined with their eyes hardly able to probe two feet ahead 'playing tricks on us all', then the inky darkness suddenly rent by a Very light telling everyone that there really was an enemy not all that far ahead.

How it had ever been passed by the censor was beyond her as her skin prickled into goosebumps on reading it. Could the blitz ever compare to what he described, the ordeal of creeping ever nearer a living yet unseen enemy, knowing that the crack of a rifle could send a bullet straight into your chest, your last glimpse of the world a crack, a flash, before oblivion darker than any desert night blotted out all things?

She felt humbled and frightened, and vowed to put a stop to her association with John, until another letter came almost on top of the last one, once again joyful and full of well-being. Not that she didn't feel relieved.

. . . We've had a crack at the buggers at last. Went on a patrol and hit a German position. All hell broke loose and you wouldn't believe the mayhem, Bren, us surrounded by machine gun-fire. I just can't describe how them flashes coming out of the total darkness hurts your eyes and after the silence just before, how the noise of gunfire deafens you. Anyway, we done our job. We got back to our company position just as it was coming up to dawn. That's where I'm writing this from now. We're smoking ourselves silly and tearing into our water ration to make endless cups of char. I think we needed it. I don't suppose we'll be going forward again for a couple of days.

231

The rest of the letter was about how he missed her, how he wished he was home lying in bed beside her, asked how Addie was, again as he always did, said that she must be growing fast and probably wouldn't know him when he finally came home. 'God knows when that will be, this bloody war looks like it's going to go on forever.'

He asked how she was, how she was bearing up under the air raids, expressed his concern for her, wished he could be there to protect her, then returned once more to the patrol he'd been sent on. No doubt it seemed different in retrospect, but he wrote as if it had all been a great game. Didn't he realise how easily he might have been wounded, or killed? At one and the same time it terrified her and angered her. Didn't it occur to him that she could be made a widow, Addie made fatherless? If only he had told her that it did instead of writing like a small boy scoring his first goal in a school football team.

Harry wrote of his conviction of war going on forever, and it seemed the Blitz would go on forever too, not letting up until every last home was flattened, at least in East London. If anything, with the coming of April, raids had got worse with fewer and shorter lulls between each onslaught which meant fewer chances for John to come and find out how she and Addie were doing. Since her return to shelter in the basement, the opportunity to be together for any length of time had occurred three times, and probably just as well. It didn't do, this longing to be with another man when being a dutiful wife to her own man away fighting was what she should be. It was unhealthy. It was wrong.

Yet at the first sound of the door opening at the top of the stairs, she would leap up in her bed, leaving Addie still fast asleep, and as the tall slim figure in its dark boiler suit, tin hat and respirator pack appeared, she'd sit there tense and expectant, knowing what the outcome of this visit would be, hating it yet with heart thumping heavily and stomach all a-churn wanting him to come to her, have their lips meet, have the guilt melt in a need to be held, to be loved, to touch and be touched, to know that he wanted her as much as she wanted him.

Ironically it was when an attack was at its height that she most needed him with her and then of course he was given no time to come to her.

All through April they had become increasingly severe. The sixteenth had been the worst so far, with no let-up all night. A hundred thousand tons of high explosive had been dropped, she learned next morning. John had dashed down in panic to see if she and Addie were all right seconds after something fell very near; the whole building had shaken, Addie had awoken screaming, both of them as well as the bed had got showered in dust from the roof, several book shelves toppling at once with a resounding crash scattering their contents everywhere.

Holding Addie to her, her own heart racing and her face so blenched that it felt cold, she broke out with a cry of relief as minutes later John's head appeared through the door gazing down at them in concern.

'Are you OK? Are you hurt?'

She shook her head, too stunned to speak. He'd withdrawn, calling back, 'Must go! It's chaos down the road!' leaving her feeling forsaken for all she knew it was wrong to feel that way. He was needed elsewhere this night. Full of fear that he could get hurt, even killed, she found herself unable to think beyond the fact that she might never see him again.

Sitting there, praying he'd stay safe, praying for herself and Addie as with every explosion her body leapt, cowering protectively over her daughter as more dust showered down and around the two of them, it was the longest night of her life. But then it must have felt like the longest night of everyone's life as savage attack after savage attack ripped East London to shreds until it seemed nothing could possibly be left standing when she finally emerged in daylight – if she emerged at all.

Somehow, in her basement surrounded by splintered bookcases and scattered books, when finally the raiders departed and the sweet single note of the all-clear filtered down to her, the heaviest debris to have fallen on her and Addie had been only the age-blackened dust from the wood beams.

Since Addie had dropped off into exhausted sleep, her little face streaked with dirt and tears, Brenda chose to sit on beside her rather than go up and see what damage had been done. At that moment she did not want to set eyes on another piece of splintered wood, broken tile, smashed window and, by the way it sounded last night, flattened homes. She even wondered if her own flat still stood above her. Or had the entire top part gone, leaving her no roof at all over her head?

If the worst came to the worst, she could somehow live down here in the basement, like a sewer rat perhaps, with no daylight. Depressing but, it appeared after last night, safe. She was, but was he? All night she had felt sure he was, yet underneath convinced that something might have happened to him, that later would come someone to say he was dead.

Sitting on the edge of her bed, one hand smoothing the fair hair of the sleeping Adele, Brenda experienced a surge of terror as the door to the basement opened, followed immediately by utter relief as John in a begrimed boiler suit came wearily down the stairs.

Perhaps it was that very leap from terror to relief that stayed her from jumping up to greet him, as though it had drained every vestige of energy from her. She watched him take off his tin hat, ease off his respirator pack, and come to sit on the edge of the bed beside her, her only response then being to automatically shift along a little to make room.

'Are you all right?'

She nodded.

'Sorry I couldn't . . .'

'You weren't able to, I know,' she said, finding her voice.

He drew her to him, taking her in his arms so gently that she burst into tears.

He was rocking her, his voice soothing, saying over and over, 'There now, darling, there now, it's all over,' patiently waiting until she was finally able to pull herself together.

'I needed you so much,' she said finally.

'I know,' he said. 'But so much was going on . . .'

'I know,' she replied wearily and lifting her face had him kiss her tenderly.

As on every time before, making love was not a comfortable thing, more a frantic desire to satisfy a craving; no laughter, no real joy, indeed no light-heartedness and quiet pleasure as there would have been with Harry. The whole thing remained fraught by guilt after they finally parted in silence, each with their own thoughts that could not be shared. It was disquieting, and as with every other time, Brenda told herself that it must cease – she couldn't go on like this, being disloyal to Harry.

Harry's next letter helped in making up her mind. Arriving several days into May, it again told of being sent into combat.

A short, grubby note, that's all it was. Full of his misery in being in the desert half-suffocated by the heat and stinging sand of what he called the *khamsin,* a wind that blew for days, sometimes weeks, without a break, robbing every man of the desire even to think.

> *But it don't matter to them – we've bin ordered forward and I dread to think what the outcome's going to be. All I want is to come home and be with you, Bren. I love you, Bren, and I don't want not to ever see you again. Kiss Addie for me. Tell her about her dad.*

Was it her imagination or was there a ring of finality in what he'd written? Had he some premonition? Fear for him gripped her as she read and reread, hardly able to see for tears. Here she was concerned over the safety of a man she'd so foolishly allowed herself to become infatuated by when the very man she'd married out of pure love was himself in such immediate danger that she might never see him again.

How had she got to this – a grubby affair with someone else? All of a sudden that was how it felt. She felt ashamed.

But this was it. No more. She would put her cards on the table, say to John that it couldn't continue. If need be she'd sleep upstairs in her flat and take a chance on the ceiling collapsing on top of her. She rejected the idea of going back to sharing her family's shelter; the thought of again being cramped together all night was as awful as was now using the basement. No, she would take her chances up here in her flat. If John came up asking what she was doing and if she was all right, she would not open the door to him, would call out that, thank you, she knew what she was doing and was all right and to go away.

Four days later on the Saturday night she was to regret her decision. The raids were just as bad during those four days, the flat was shaken by one explosion after another, but nothing fell too close, thank God.

She devised a safety measure of sorts with the legs of the bed raised on several bricks she'd brought up from the yard, the bedding arranged on the floor underneath the bed for her and Addie to sleep on. At least if the roof fell down, it would fall on the bedsprings and not on her and Addie. It could be that the whole building could be hit, but then it would make no odds if they were up here or buried in the basement by tons of rubble.

She did leave the back door unlocked though, for easy access should they need to be rescued. Always better safe than sorry. It was taking a chance on John coming up to persuade her down into the cellar, but those times were gone forever.

She hadn't the courage to venture into his shop to tell him of her decision, but left a note for him in the basement. The moment he found it he came hurrying upstairs to ask what was the matter.

Though the kitchen door was unlocked, he tapped lightly on it that first night.

'Brenda, darling, are you in there?' His cultured voice was faintly panicky. 'Darling, come to the door. I need to talk to you.' And when she didn't reply, continued, 'I know how you feel, but I love you.'

Now she replied. 'John, go away. We can't carry on that way.'

'But you can't stay up here.' His mouth close to the door, he sounded as though he were in the flat. 'You're putting yourself and Adele in terrible danger. I promise, darling, I won't go near you if that's what you want, but you must come down.'

But she knew she couldn't trust him to keep that promise, nor would she be able to trust herself if he came near her. Already, hearing his voice, her insides had begun to flutter. Concentrating her whole mind on Harry's letter, its dire contents, his words of love and the terrible loss of hope that seemed to penetrate every word, Brenda tightened every muscle in her body to stop their inane fluttering.

'I can't, John. Please go away.'

'But you could be killed up here. It's silly.'

Maybe it was. Maybe she was putting herself and Harry's daughter in needless danger. Perhaps he could come home to find them both dead. The basement was the only safe place. She almost succumbed. But surely it was worse if Harry came home to find that she'd been carrying on with another man all the time he'd been away. She felt suddenly ashamed. Her words burst from her as though she were speaking to a hated enemy.

'Go away! It's over, John. So go away – sod off!'

There was silence. The silence went on and on, leaving her regretting the outburst. He didn't deserve that. He had been kind and helpful and it wasn't his fault that circumstances had made him love her, and she him. It wasn't his fault. In a welter of remorse, she ran to the door. But he'd gone.

All that week he did not come nigh or by. She in turn avoided him, peeping out of her kitchen door to make sure he wasn't in the yard if she needed to go out, hurrying down to get Addie in her pram. Her heart would be in her mouth on returning in case she should bump into him. It was the same ritual in going down to use the toilet, peeping out of that door too to make sure the coast was clear when ready to go back upstairs. It was hateful.

Even more hateful was during a raid, cowering under her bed cursing herself for a fool being up here when there was a safe basement there for her. Yet the next morning emerging all in one piece, she was glad she had resisted temptation. At least John couldn't decently invade her flat without her sanction whereas he was free to enter his own cellar at any time. Even so, she missed him and a great void seemed to encircle her heart each time he crept into her thoughts.

As time went by, though, she would overcome that, grow stronger in will, become braver and slowly more inured to sleeping up here in a raid. In an odd way, if only imaginary, it even felt safer with just a roof to fall on her, whereas in a cellar, she'd be buried alive by tons of masonry, waiting to be dug out – if she wasn't killed . . .

Over those four nights she told herself that she'd done the right thing. Then came Saturday night, the tenth of

May. She had thought the raid in mid-April had been the very worst – it was nothing compared to this night.

Beneath the bed, curled about a screaming Adele, her mouth dry with abject terror, her body quaking, the noise sounded unbelievable with no basement wall to muffle it. Every second felt that it would be her last as blast after blast shook the floor beneath her until she was sure it would collapse with them along with it, buried despite that earlier attempt at reassurance that there was only a roof above her.

More and more came the now familiar, horrible sound as of a sheet being ripped as a bomb fell close by to land with an explosion that showered glass and ceiling plaster over the room, blowing tattered blackout curtains inward on a Shockwave capable of lifting a full-grown man off his feet and tossing him twenty feet or more, of stripping off clothing and ripping flesh.

How anyone could endure it for hours on end, powerless to do a thing about it? Out there in the desert Harry at least had a gun to defend himself with. She had nothing, could do nothing but cower here under a flimsy bed, her hope of its protection all gone as what sounded like tons of shrapnel tinkled and crashed down on the tiles above her, taking them off not one at a time but in their dozens. Soon there'd be nothing left, her room open to the sky, the ring of fire set by incendiaries now sending its lurid, wavering, orange glow into the room through the broken windows, searing her with its heat, she and her child at the mercy of shrapnel that with no roof left would tear through the bedsprings and into their flesh, cutting and piercing and killing.

In one moment of panic, she almost leapt up to run out with Addie in her arms and down the staircase to the basement, but common sense stayed her. To set one foot outside now would be asking to be killed.

There was no sleep that night. No John to come and soothe her; his time was completely taken up with ministering to those who needed it most. It seemed dawn would never come, that this would go on forever and ever.

But dawn did come. The raiders did depart, leaving behind them the stink of still-burning buildings, warehouses, and their variety of contents. The air had become acrid enough to sting the nose; quantities of charred paper and cloth floated weightlessly on a fire-induced breeze, and billowing clouds of thick, black and sulphur-coloured smoke covered the whole of London.

With a sinking heart she looked out at it through the broken window of her bedroom after having crept out from beneath her bed, window glass crackling underfoot, careful to find her shoes before making her way across a debris-strewn room, Addie in her arms. Her mind flew to her parents, as it had done countless times that fearful night. She must go and find out if they were all right. But first, it was essential to clear up all this glass. Addie might hurt herself. Dragging the bedding back on to the bed, she put her in the centre of it all.

'Now, you stay there,' she commanded tersely, the child's blue eyes returning her stern gaze and seeing trouble if she didn't. 'I've got ter sweep up. If you get down you'll cut yerself and I'll give you such a smacking.'

Running to the kitchen, the glass everywhere, she seized the broom, then nearly leapt out of her skin as

John's face peered through the broken window at her. 'Oh, my God!'

'Didn't mean to make you jump, Brenda.' He came on in as if the havoc of last night gave him every right to do so. 'What damage has been done?' But a glance was enough and he let out an exasperated growl.

'You're lucky not to have been killed up here.'

'It is a bit of a mess,' she conceded, starting to sweep without much purpose. 'But I can soon clear it up.' What she really wanted was for him to leave her in peace. 'Look, I can't talk now. I've left Adele on the bed. I'm worried she'll get down and cut herself.'

He went straight past her and, following him, she saw him lift Addie in his arms. He handed the child to her. 'You take her down to the shop. Go into the back kitchen. The electric's off and so is the gas, but there's a primus stove. I've lit it and put a kettle on it. Make yourself a cup of tea. You'll find everything on a shelf out there. There's milk for Adele. I nailed wood up over the back door window so it will be dark, and now of course there's no electricity, but there are matches and candles.'

She didn't want to go downstairs, didn't want to be dependent upon him, in danger of starting it all up again. She needed to clear up here. This morning she had two hair appointments, though whether either would turn up was unlikely after a night like they'd had. Everyday life had more or less come to a standstill, apart from rescue work, fire-fighting and trying to get the services back on. It was chaos.

'I have to clear up,' she said lamely, holding Addie.

'No, you go downstairs. I'll clear this lot up. You could cut yourself badly. I can start boarding up your windows with cardboard and make the place habitable again, or at least some way towards it.'

He was surveying the damaged ceiling. 'I expect you've lost quite a few tiles. It could have been worse after seeing what's out there. Thank God it's May and not likely to rain. You won't have that coming through. By the way, the water mains are broken down the road. They're turning it off in order to repair it. I filled a couple of buckets downstairs with what there was. We can make tea with it and have a wash.'

He'd thought of everything, was being very efficient, and in a way she felt grateful. What would she have done here alone, with no water, no means of heating a kettle or cooking or washing?

'I've got to go and see if me family's all right,' she said as lamely as before. 'See nothing's 'appened to 'em.' After a night such as she'd had, she had no energy to concentrate on talking nicely.

He was regarding her with a slight frown as if realising that she was indeed trying to avoid him. 'Yes,' he said slowly, 'you go. I'll carry on here. You can't do all this by yourself. It'll only take me an hour or so. By the time you get back, it'll be done.'

If I get back, came the awful thought. What if Mum and Dad and Vera had got a direct hit and what if . . .? She wouldn't let herself think of that. But if they'd been injured, taken to hospital, she would have to go on there. There were Harry's people too – were they all right? If they weren't, Harry must be told. Would he be sent home on compassionate leave? And there were her two hair appointments today, how to let them know she wouldn't be here? Her head began to reel from all the questions.

There was a buzzing in her ears and her face was feeling flaccid, her brow coldly sweaty.

She had just enough time and presence of mind to thrust Addie back into John's arms before the ground which had gone a funny dark colour began to come up to meet her.

She came to, finding herself slumped forward on a chair.

Someone was holding her shoulder to stop her falling. Addie was whimpering. She knew she must console her, reassure her that her mummy was all right. Drawing in a deep breath she opened her eyes and saw the face, filled with concern, gazing into hers – John crouched on his haunches in front of her.

'I must of 'ad a bit of a fainting fit,' she managed feebly.

He pressed down on her again as she tried to get up. 'Stay quiet now. Rest. You've been through a lot. I wish you had gone down to the basement. I wouldn't have disturbed you. Not after . . .' He let the words die away then asked gently, 'Can you manage to lie back on your bed? I'll go down and make you a cup of tea. With plenty of sugar in it. You probably need it.'

She did as he asked, lay down gratefully, had him cover her with the eiderdown which he first shook free of plaster and glass.

'Where's Addie?' she asked and hearing her name spoken there came an answering call right next to her. 'Mummy-Mummy!'

'Oh, darling!' Brenda's voice broke. Pulling her daughter to her, she held her so tightly that the child squirmed and cried out in protest.

'Mummy! I can't breave – can't breave!'

'Oh, sorry, love,' Brenda burst out. 'I couldn't 'elp it.'

'I'll go and make you that cup of tea.' John moved away, leaving mother and daughter to weep away the anguish of those long hours of bombing and mayhem.

He was back in a few minutes, placing the steaming cup into her hands to drink, Addie, now over her trauma, rolled around the bed.

He watched while she sipped the hot sweet brew, the heat through the thin china almost burning the palms of her hands, until it was all gone.

Revived, she smiled up at him in an impromptu gesture of gratitude, and in response he sat himself on the edge of the bed beside her. For a second Brenda felt herself stiffen, but he was being so attentive, seemed so concerned for her, that her body relaxed and she let herself remember all she had gone through last night here all on her own. She'd been thoroughly stupid. She told him so.

'No,' he disagreed, his arm falling comfortingly across her shoulders. 'I understand. We should never have let it go so far.'

The sadness in his voice wrenched at her. 'John, I do love you, I can't help myself, but it *is* wrong and it has to stop.'

'I know. I wish you weren't married. You're very precious to me.'

She sat silent. On the other side of the bed next to the wall where she couldn't fall, Addie played on, rolling her small body in and out of the pillow case and prattling away to herself in some game of her own. Brenda allowed herself the comfort of leaning against the man beside her, his body warmth penetrating the dress and cardigan she had spent all night in.

Automatically she felt his face lower to hers, lifted her own to receive his kiss. His lips warm on hers, the clean fragrance of freshly shaved cheeks and lightly brilliantined hair, stirred her loins for a moment. She should be pushing him away. Could she? She felt her body melt against his, his hand come up to her chin to hold her mouth to his . . . A frantic bashing at the kitchen door, the sound of it opening, practically bounced them apart.

Chapter Eighteen

'Bren! Yer there?' The voice held a note of rasping urgency.

Brenda leapt up. 'Oh, God, me dad!'

John too was on his feet. A man she had always thought of as in total command of himself looked like a small boy caught stealing sweets. But she had no care how he appeared, the only thought flooding her mind was the fear of being discovered here together.

One look passed between them and each knew their next move with no need to discuss it. By the time what struck her as a horde of people had piled into the kitchen, though they were only three, she was there to meet them. John had already stationed himself by the bedroom window, broom in hand as though in the process of sweeping up glass and plaster, the good Samaritan. Adele thank God, played happily on the bed, making his presence in the flat innocuous enough.

Brenda was still trembling as she halted her family at the door to the rest of the flat. 'Mum, Dad!' But the sight of them told her everything.

Mum was hatless – she never went out without one on. Vera was crying. Dad looked grim-faced, that face streaked with soot. Each carried a bundle of clothing. Each carried their gas mask in its box over their shoulder. Mum clutched the bag she religiously took down into the shelter with her each night. It held their ration books, identity cards, savings, spare back door key and it never went shopping or visiting with her. That bag was special. 'Me night bag,' she was fond of calling it.

But it was the appearance of each of them that shook Brenda, banishing all else from her mind: Mum, coat dusty, hair dishevelled, face pale and drawn into lines around a set mouth and between her eyebrows. And Vera, Vera without make-up, fair pageboy hair still in curlers beneath a triangular headscarf, her half-open coat revealing the top of a nightie over which she'd dragged a pair of slacks. Dad, he looked the worst, his once blue-striped shirt filthy and collarless, his face and neck, hands and wrists covered in soot, his jacket scorched, his hair singed, his eyes red-rimmed and bloodshot.

'Dear God! What's happened?' Brenda burst out, staring at each in turn. It was her mother who spoke.

'We've bin bombed out.'

Vera began to cry again.

'Burnt out,' corrected Dad. 'Bleedin' incendiary. It went through the bloody ceiling into our bedroom before I could get at it. Gutted the 'ole of our bloody 'ouse. Three doors down got a direct hit. Luckily they was down their shelter, like us, but they got buried. Civil Defence workers was gettin' 'em out when we left. I expect bloody Jerry was aimin' fer the railway. Half the street's 'ad it.'

Brenda ushered them through to the living room, that too littered with broken glass and ceiling plaster, one small corner of ceiling hanging down like a sheet on a washing line. She ignored it. 'But what about you? Are *you* all right?'

'We're orright,' sighed her mother, brushing away shards of glass from the settee with a handkerchief so as to sit on the few cleared inches. 'Yer dad could of got killed trying ter douse the fire, but he couldn't save it. So we just lorst all our 'ome, that's all.'

As Vera's crying rose, she turned on her angrily. 'Oh, shut up, Vera, yer silly cow! You ain't even scratched.'

'But all me dresses gone. All me make-up gone. I ain't got one thing left. What'm I gonna wear? I'm gonna look a right sight. 'Ow can I . . .'

'Yer'd look a bleedin' worse sight if yer'd bin in the 'ouse. Yer'd of bin dead!'

'Oh, M-u-m!'

'Well, it's true. Thank yer lucky stars we never got a direct one. Thank yer lucky stars we was in the shelter.'

'But Dad wasn't. He went and tackled that rotten incendiary bomb. He could of bin burnt to a crisp.'

'Well, he wasn't – so shut up!'

Brenda's mind was in a whirl. John was in the bedroom. Two clients were coming this morning to have their hair cut – that's if they came at all after last night, though people went on with their lives, blitz or no blitz. How was she going to cope with them, with all this, house her family, feed them, sleep them and carry on with hairdressing?

'I don't know where I'm going ter put you all,' she began.

'They said they'd put us up in one of them community places until they find us somewhere,' Mum said, looking round at the mess. 'You took a bit of a walloping too by the looks of it. I was just 'oping you could put us up fer a while 'til they find us somethink. I don't fancy sleeping in one of them community places, all of us crammed in with a lot of other people, listening to 'em doing what should be done in private.'

'Like farting,' her husband put in. 'Yer mum never could abide anyone fartin' outright.'

'Dave! I don't 'old with that kind of talk in front of everyone. Anyway, it don't seem ter worry you. You go ahead and do it whenever yer feel like it. Don't matter what I like.'

'I'm yer 'usband,' he shot back at her, a grin forming a white line in his sooty features. 'I'm allowed.'

'P'haps. But I don't want ter 'ear strangers doin' it in me face. And nor d'yer know 'ow clean they are in their everyday 'abits. Strangers – I don't want ter 'ave ter sleep on a floor next to 'em.' She turned back to Brenda. 'Would yer mind us stayin' 'ere, Bren? Only be fer a little while, I'm sure.'

How could she say no? 'I'll be only too glad to 'ave yer, Mum.'

She looked up as John appeared in the front room doorway. His eyebrows were raised in an almost comical fashion and it occurred to her how expressive they could be.

'I've swept your bedroom, Brenda, Adele is quite happy playing on your bed, but the floor is clear of glass and she can get down now.'

'Oh, thank you.' She adopted a gushing tone, perhaps too much so. 'It was so good of you. I can carry on from there. And thank you again.'

'I'll pop up later with some cardboard for your windows until I can get a glazier. My shop window was blown out too, so I'll get him to have a look at yours when he can get round to doing something about mine. He'll most likely board the thing up and leave just a small aperture for a bit of glass. That's all you can do these days. I'll put your broom away for you.'

As he disappeared from the doorway, her mother turned to her. 'Do he always call yer Brenda?'

'Well, I do use his basement and we do have a few talks – to keep me company when there's a raid on. Of course he calls me Brenda.'

'And what d'yer call 'im?'

She felt her insides squirm as though Mum had detected something more than mere neighbourly familiarity. 'I s'pose I call him Mr Stebbings.'

'Yer do?'

'Sometimes I've said his first name. It do seem a bit unsociable not to really. Do it matter?'

Hurriedly she changed the subject. 'Look, Mum, the water's off so I can't make a cuppa until it's back on again. But J . . . Mr Stebbings filled a couple of buckets with water. He's a warden so he knew in advance. He said he had a primus stove which he can boil a kettle on. You try and make yourselves comfortable. I'll run down and see if I can make us a pot of tea.'

Mum's coat had come off. She was rolling up her sleeves. 'I'll sweep this lot up in 'ere and in the kitchen while yer gone, and sort Addie out,' she said briskly, adding, 'I don't suppose yer'll be too long down there, will yer? Now we're 'ere?'

Which to Brenda's suddenly over-sensitive comprehension came as a somewhat pointed remark as she hurried off.

'Thank Gawd it's summer so we don't need lights on all the time, and warm enough not ter get draughts from them blessed windows.'

The windows had never been properly replaced. John had used all his persuasion on his middle-aged glazier, but materials were needed for more urgent cases. Dad knocked up proper solid blackout frames for the windows from pieces of wood scrounged from bomb sites, making sure of a good fit so that no chink of light showed, each morning to be taken down and stood against the wall. Cardboard took the place of many of the missing panes so there wasn't too much fresh air coming in that could be termed a draught.

Dad had stood proudly back having fitted the final one, announcing, 'Better job'n 'im downstairs could of done, I bet. Yer don't want a strange neighbour buggering about in yer place, do yer, Bren?'

She could only smile, letting it go at that.

What had promised to be a couple of weeks of them staying with her was running into months. There had been such extensive damage from that night in May on top of all the other raids preceding it for months that more urgent rebuilding was taking precedence over work on gutted private homes and there were few places for her family to go other than community centres.

A lot of bombed-out Londoners had been found places in the country, often empty, practically derelict cottages on the edge of a village, miles from shops and unreachable but by a local bus once a week. The locals, digging for victory with their smallholdings or large kitchen gardens, their pigs and ducks and chickens and eggs, bartered purely among themselves regarded strangers from London with deep suspicion.

'I ain't goin' ter be fobbed off with some flea- and bug-ridden, antiquated old cottage,' Mum announced when a letter from the authorities arrived two months after coming to live with Brenda. 'No runnin' water, no roads, outside toilet . . .'

For a moment it didn't occur to her that her daughter's was itself an outside one, but recalling that it at least had a flush, she hurriedly went on, '. . . all yer doings droppin' straight into some stream.' She had made a small sound of revulsion. 'I've 'eard about it. Mrs Calvin – yer remember Mrs Calvin an' 'er lot – lived a few doors down? They was given an old farm'ouse of sorts, Lord knows where, somewhere in blinking Wiltshire. They 'ad ter fumigate the 'ole place. 'ad no curtains, or bedding, no rugs nor nothink. The bedding they did get 'old of was runnin' alive. They all got bites from bed bugs. After four weeks they'd 'ad enough – came back 'ere ter live with her daughter-in-law. Yer won't get me bein' sent away an' going through all that. I'd rather be killed in me bed 'ere.'

It was easy to say that now. There'd been no more raids since that night in May, the raids ceasing as abruptly as if a tap had been turned off. For the next few nights, Brenda and her visitors crowded down into the basement, which John was generous enough to allow though he no longer showed himself, and like everybody else they waited. But nothing happened. The night sky of early summer remained clear and starry, a perfect bomber's moon lighting up the gaunt outline of wrecked and gutted buildings, many of which took a week of hosing before finally ceasing to smoulder, and still no bombers appeared.

People had sat in their shelters waiting with bated breath. Rumours had flown far and wide. Had Hitler some secret weapon, biding his time to release it on London? Other cities had still been bombed, but to have ceased so suddenly just when poor old London had been on the brink of despair – it had been uncanny, it hadn't made sense, but it had been welcomed with a sigh of relief.

Slowly they had breathed again, clinging to every minute fragment of good news that might boost morale: Hess landing in Scotland at the beginning of May – were Hitler's henchmen forsaking him? Did it mean the end of the war was near? The sinking of the *Bismarck* – perhaps that had made him realise Britain wasn't yet finished? Obviously bombing London wasn't the answer, and he'd turned his sights elsewhere. It seemed likely. Greece already lay in his clutches; by the beginning of June Crete had been overrun, and now he had broken his pact with Russia, was massing troops on its borders ready to strike.

It at least gave everyone at home respite from air attacks, but it didn't help those with homeless relatives living in with them nor those fearing for their men's lives in North Africa. Brenda suffered the one and dreaded the other as she tried to keep the peace in an overcrowded flat (made even more so by Brian or Davy each coming home on separate weekend leaves during early June) and carry on with her hairdressing.

'You ought ter give it up fer a while,' advised her mother. 'At least until we've bin rehoused.'

'And lose the clients I've got? No, Mum, I've got to carry on somehow.'

'It must make it awkward, Bren, us all being 'ere.'

'I'll manage. So long as I can use the kitchen and me bedroom.'

She was now working in her bedroom, taking her ladies out to the kitchen to wash their hair at the sink, a kettle and saucepans forever on the boil. She thanked heaven for the good summer which meant she could leave the door open so that steam could escape. What would it be like when winter came if the family was still here?

Yes, it was awkward. Often she had to move a lady closer to the sink for Mum or Vera to get by for the toilet. Dad, working all day, spent most of his weekends on an allotment he'd acquired; what he produced would come free at least. It also meant having to move Mum and Vera's things off the bed and the old chair (all three women now slept in her bed, Dad on a palliasse in Addie's room) to make room for a client to sit.

The conditions under which they were having their hair done were enough to brown customers off forever, yet they still came, and Brenda felt proud that they had no wish to go elsewhere. Of course she was cheap, and that probably accounted for it, and she still managed to make do and mend despite the shortage of supplies that had already closed down many a salon.

'I wish I had your talent,' Vera said in July, gazing enviously after yet another satisfied customer leaving with her new set smelling of the shampoo which Brenda skilfully made up herself with shredded Knight's Castile soap and boiling water. She used a lemon rinse on fair hair or vinegar on dark with a touch of perfumed glycerine.

'It's not a talent,' Brenda told her, washing her hands free of the cloying smell of home-made setting lotion. 'I had to learn it.'

'I 'ate working in a factory doing war work, clocking on and clocking off, 'aving to do overtime. I don't get no chance to go out of an evening.'

In fact Vera was out most weekends with girlfriends, looking for boys. And on the odd occasion she'd gone with Brenda to see a film together. Brenda was hardly able to get out of the house and got no chance to find any friends of her own. She felt awkward asking Mum to give eye to Addie, though Mum was always willing. 'Yer don't get out 'alf enough,' she would urge.

'I'm sure I could of made a decent fist of hairdressing if I'd of bin given your chances,' Vera went on. 'Couldn't you teach me?'

'Vera, it takes more than just "couldn't you teach me". It took me a few years of apprenticeship.' She hesitated before Vera's pleading look. 'I suppose I could show you how to do a simple, straight trim. But you'd have to follow me very carefully.'

Vera's face was a delight to behold. 'Would yer? Would yer really?'

'But yer'll have to stay in of an evening when someone comes, not go galivanting off out.' She saw the doubt creep into the blue eyes. 'If yer not serious about it.'

Vera livened, already seeing herself one day owning her own salon, pots of money pouring in. Brenda could read her sister like a book. 'Of course I'm serious. I want ter learn.'

'Right then. And not just the odd night when it suits you. You might have to give up a couple of Saturday nights, if I get any clients on that evening. I don't want yer playin' around, Vera.'

'Of course not.'

Vera spoke in all earnestness at this very moment. But how long would that last? Until the next boy came along? She'd finished with her Ron Parrish. Where he was now she didn't know or care. Since then she'd had other boys – and one big scare last month due to a late period. She'd asked Brenda in confidence what she should do.

'You let him?' Brenda had exclaimed, and Vera, near to tears, had nodded dismally. 'You silly fool, Vera!' was all she'd been able to say. Brenda had no idea of how one brings on a period or gets rid of an unwanted pregnancy, so Vera would have to seek her own salvation. But her condemnation of her sister renewed her guilt over her affair with John. They'd always taken precautions but there could be a slip-up one day. Vera's trouble was a warning that it could happen to anyone and even as Brenda bit back her censure of her to console her instead, it made her think about being so free with herself.

A week later, Vera had come to her all smiles. 'False alarm,' she had trilled and gone merrily off to a date she had made with someone different.

It had been such a scare and it had all come about so innocently. Going up West that Saturday with three girlfriends to a nice dance hall they knew, for Vera the evening had followed its usual lively routine, dancing with this one and that until finally ending up with the boy of her choice to take her home.

There was so much choice these days for a single girl. Servicemen of all sorts, soldiers, sailors, airmen (boys in civvies didn't stand a chance, too drab and too immature) and servicemen from other countries, flamboyant Canadians, smooth Free French – in fact she was having a lovely war.

When she said this to Brenda, her sister had been shocked. 'How can yer talk like that after what we've all been through with the Blitz – people being killed all over the place? People being made homeless. And there's my Harry fighting in North Africa, and yer own brothers, and Harry's brother – how can yer say that, Vera?'

But she hadn't meant it in that way. What she had meant was that the war had allowed a single girl so much scope with all these uniforms to choose from.

It was more usually a British boy she picked to walk her to her bus to take her home. They were her sort, her countrymen, she'd always felt safer with them. That was until that night.

It had been a British boy, a quiet lad from Northumberland, who had proved the exception. His accent had intrigued her; his shy request for a kiss couldn't be refused. His hands on her shoulders as they stood in a dark shop doorway had been gentle, as had his lips. But when he had tried it on, fumbling up her skirt, she'd yelled at him and walked off.

He had followed her. Almost in tears he had begged her pardon, telling her he was the only one in his unit who hadn't had it off properly with a girl and that he had become the laughing stock of his mates. He hadn't meant to upset her. He had seemed gauche and she'd felt so sorry for him. Finally she had stopped marching ahead, had let him slip into another dark doorway with her and kiss her again.

That second kiss had been passionate, and what harm if his hands did happen to wander a little? It was wartime, everyone gave themselves a little licence. Her friends did, judging by their tales. So long as he didn't go all the way.

He hadn't seemed the type who would, but then his grip had become fierce and when she started to fight against him he had murmured, 'No, no, it'll be all right, I won't go that far.' But he had and she'd been mortified.

It was the first time she'd ever let anyone do more than kiss her. As a rule at the first sign of anything more, she'd shrug them off with plenty of light banter and usually they got the message. She hardly felt able to believe that she'd let it go this far; it wouldn't have done any good having a go at him – she should have fought him off more determinedly.

She did tell him what she thought of him. He'd said he didn't know what came over him and she'd snapped back through stifled tears that now he could tell his mates he'd had a girl, couldn't he. He hadn't replied to that; in silence they'd adjusted their clothing and he walked her to her bus stop because she didn't want to walk there on her own.

He'd asked to see her again and for her address so he could write to her, but after what happened she wanted no more to do with him. He wasn't even her type. She told him she never wanted to see him again and he left her at the bus stop.

Then had come the counting, the waiting for her next period to show itself, panic when it hadn't. It was all right now, but she had been taught a lesson and wouldn't be so silly with her favours ever again.

One thing she did wish, that she hadn't been so quick confiding in her sister. Brenda now knew her little secret. But she trusted Brenda. She wouldn't tell Mum. She wasn't that sort.

Brenda's tone was downcast. 'John, I don't think we should go on like this.'

In the poor light of the tiny back kitchen, despite a brilliant if narrow shaft of July sunlight squeezing between two pieces of cardboard that took the place of a windowpane, she saw his thin face become taut, his dark brows draw together.

The shop had closed for the evening; he would soon be leaving for his own home in Leytonstone. A couple of times a week here with him was the only chance they had these days with her family breathing down her neck. She'd make the excuse that she had to change a book, John having begun a small private lending library a few months ago since so few people now actually bought books. She'd return upstairs, her book changed, making it all look right and proper. Of course it was foolish. She hated it, vowed that each time must be the last. But the ache to be with him would grow and grow until, unable to help herself, she would hurry down to the back kitchen moments after his shop had closed. Often they would merely talk. But other times . . . Then she'd come away ashamed and guilty.

Today, she vowed, would be the last. What Vera had confided in her had changed her whole outlook. One day she and her lover would be found out. One day Mum or Vera on their way to the toilet would hear voices and peep through the narrow aperture in the boarded-up window that looked out on to the yard. With bright sunlight streaming in they would see her and John, even catch him kissing her.

It was only a moment ago that he had leaned forward and kissed her. They had made love before in this confined space and somehow it gave it the feeling of spontaneity. Once he'd suggested the basement but knowing the bed was still there, to follow him down there made her feel that it would be changed into something planned and thus sordid. She had refused and he hadn't mentioned it again. But today even his kiss had her pulling away.

'No, don't!'

He too drew back. 'What's the matter?'

'I don't want you to, that's all.'

Not only had Vera's revelation several days ago put her on guard but this morning a letter from Harry had strengthened her resolve that this business with John Stebbings had to end.

Harry's letter had come from a hospital bed. He had been wounded. Not too badly, he'd said – a lump of shrapnel had shattered his shoulder. He'd be in hospital for a while and when mended return to his unit. 'Just a pity it weren't a Blighty one,' he quipped, using the old First World War term.

She was glad it hadn't been. He could have come back crippled for life. In another way she wished it had, at least enough to have got him sent home. Either way it had shaken her, terrified her, and it was why she was facing John. How could this go on with Harry away fighting, wounded, and all the time so certain of her, his constant and loving wife. She did love him, so she must stop all this, stay true to him. He deserved nothing less from her.

And now she was pleading, 'I don't think we should go on like this.'

She'd said this so many times before that he must have become inured to it. But it always brought a look of fear to his face and he would catch her hands between his, melting her resolve. He caught them now.

'Darling, don't say that!'

'This time I meant it, John.' Forcing herself to be strong she told him of Harry's letter. 'I can't carry on knowing he's been hurt. I feel terrible for him. Please, please understand. It was hard enough for me before, but now, every time we kiss I'll think of what I'm doing to him. He trusts me.'

'But you love me, Brenda. You must do, to be doing what we do.'

'I don't know. Perhaps it's just that I've felt so lonely.'

She had never said this before and she saw his face go bleak. 'Is that all I am to you?' he said slowly after a small pause. 'Merely someone to fill your loneliness?'

'No. Of course I was lonely. But once it happened I couldn't let go of you. And it was wrong. I knew how wrong it was but I wanted you.'

'Though not enough.'

Tears clouded her eyes. 'I still do, darling. It's just that—'

'He's your husband,' he interrupted. 'And I'm merely...'

'Don't say that. You're not *merely*. It's just that I can't anymore.'

There was silence between them, then he said, 'Well, if that is what you want, Brenda, I shan't spoil things for you. I only want to say that I am in love with you. I'll always be in love with you. I wish things were different, but I can't make you love me, not the way I'd like you to, with no one else in the way. Maybe it's best. There is only one thing – if you ever need anything, anyone . . . I'd like to remain a friend.'

'I know,' she said miserably. 'And I'm so sorry.'

He did not reply but got up and opened the kitchen door to the yard for her. 'Just remember me,' he said simply as she got up, head bowed to hide the tears, and went past him into the brilliant July evening sunshine, his words echoing in her head. '*Just remember me.*'

She almost turned to run back, throw herself into his arms and cry out that she wanted to be with him always. Instead, one hand on the rail of the stairs with their rusting cast-iron treads, she hoisted herself upward as if her body was as heavy as the very iron itself.

She knew he'd already gone back inside so as to avoid any glimpse of her exposed legs through the open treads. And all she could think of as she climbed was that those upstairs mustn't see one hint of distress on her face.

Chapter Nineteen

Trying to read between the lines of Harry's letter she searched for the truth about his injury. Was he hiding something? He seemed to be making light of his wounds, but was it worse than he said? Was the shattered shoulder really an arm about to be amputated? The handwriting was shaky, he was in pain – were they giving him enough care? What if he died of gangrene? The simplest of wounds could erupt into fearful things under certain conditions.

Mum, dishing up the tea, was calling everyone to the table. Chaos reigned with Davy and Brian home together. The pair, both well built, in khaki trousers and shirts, seemed to fill the room; Dad, collarless, in his shirt-sleeves, was dwarfed by them; Vera's high voice rent the air as Mum asked if she'd be going out tonight, Friday; Addie was banging her beaker on the tray of her high chair.

Brenda hung back from coming to the table. John Stebbings faded from mind as she scanned the letter yet again. Its contents veered so much from one thing to another it made her wonder what he was keeping from her.

> *. . . ain't like the last war. No front line. Skirmishes going on miles apart. You pull back but it ain't a defeat because somewhere else they're going forward. Fighting stops for sand storms or Jerry's moved off. We don't know who's winning and who ain't. Expect the top brass knows but they ain't telling us buggers nothink. Well, I'm out of it for a while. No more scorpions, no more sand in your nose and mouth, no more strafing, no more shortage of water, baking up all day, freezing at night. Mind it weren't no picnic being dumped in a truck with me shoulder all busted up and ridden back . . .*

'If yer look at that blessed letter any more, it's goin' ter disintegrate in yer 'ands,' her mum interrupted her. 'Put it down, love. Come an' 'ave yer tea. Keepin' on reading ain't goin' ter make him better any quicker.'

'Let 'er do what she likes,' her dad said understandingly. 'Bet you was the same with my letters in the last lot.'

Dad had been in the last war. He and Mum met in 1914, then married almost immediately just before he enlisted.

'Even so,' her mother went on, returning to her daughter. 'Come and sit up and 'ave yer tea.'

'I don't feel like eating at the moment, Mum.'

'Understandable,' agreed her father tucking into the plate of egg, luncheon meat, beans and chips she put before him. Going off on his own train of thought he looked towards Davy.

265

'D'yer get a decent issue of razor blades in your lot, son? Yer can't get 'old of a bloody single one in our shop. I know the country needs the steel, but what we s'posed ter do, all grow bloody beards?'

Mum, giving Addie a beaker of government orange juice, shot him a look. 'If that's all yer got ter moan about.'

'I've got some spare in me kit yer can 'ave,' Davy was saying.

Brian was talking to Vera about where he was going this Friday night, and she was saying how she was hoping to go out too, with some friends.

'Yer don't mind, Brenda, do yer, just this once? I know you've got a lady coming this evenin' but . . .'

'It's just a set,' Brenda said without enthusiasm, not caring whether Vera stayed in or not.

Vera was not a willing learner for all she'd asked to be taught. The gilt soon came off the gingerbread when she had to wash hair that might not be quite as wholesome as it should be in these days of shortages. Vera would often pull a face, accompanied by small sounds of revulsion and a strand of hair held fastidiously by the very fingertips so that, embarrassed, Brenda would hurriedly move Vera aside to take over herself and restore the woman's peace of mind. Anyway, she had been pulled through the hoop enough this afternoon. If the whole world fell apart now, she felt she wouldn't have given two hoots.

'I'm going to me room,' she snapped.

'What about yer tea? It'll get cold. Eggs are rationed, y'know, Bren.'

'I'll 'ave it later.'

'It'll get spoilt. Yer can't go wasting stuff like that, Bren.'

'Let 'er go, Mum.' Davy's gaze was trained on his sister and she gave him a grateful look as she left them at the table. He understood.

In the bedroom that had once been hers alone, she closed the door and in relative peace for the moment unfolded Harry's letter again, focusing her whole attention on it so as to erase this afternoon from her mind. If he were to die, it would be retribution on her. She bent her head to pick up where she had left off though she'd read it several times since getting it.

. . . *Bloody awful ride back, us wounded piled in together any old how. Then in an ambulance what got hit and I got a bullet in me foot on top of me perishing bad shoulder. Casualty clearing station was a nightmare. That got bombed too. Finally put on a ship. Writing this from Alexandria. Peace at last. Looked after by nurses all lovely and fresh-smelling. Me wounds still giving me gip, but not as bloody much as getting here with no proper medical treatment. You can't believe how filthy I was. Nurses none too gentle cos there's hundreds of us blokes to be patched up. It don't do to make too much fuss though. I ain't having no nurse tell me I'm being a baby and there's lots worse off than me. Some of these Alexander nurses are really pretty but I wish I was home with you, Bren, have you looking after me . . .*

'Yer comin' out now for yer tea?' Her mother popped her head round the door and startled her. 'Sorry, love, didn't mean ter make yer jump. But Addie's gettin' tired and I think she ought ter go ter bed.'

'Yes, of course, Mum.'

Why was she letting her mother do all the dictating? Maybe because she herself had lost heart, had allowed her home to be taken over. Her mind felt buffeted by this longing to see John even as she swore to end it, life seemed utterly empty. After tea a young woman was coming to have her hair set for the weekend. A chatty young thing. Brenda felt far from chatty as she struggled to make something of the straight, dark strands while the family did its best to keep out of the way. Oh, to have this place to herself. Would it ever again be hers alone?

She felt sick, without appetite. But Mum had put herself out to do the cooking this evening. She must try to eat.

'Yer egg's gorn all cold an' congealed, of course.' Mum said, faintly huffy, as Brenda got up from the bed. 'Couldn't eat it like that. Brian 'ad it – in a san'wich. Couldn't let it go ter waste wiv eggs in short supply. The rest is all right though, warmed it up, barrin' the luncheon meat of course. That can be quite nice hotted up sometimes as well.'

Tucking the letter away in the old chest of drawers that almost filled the room, Brenda thought of the days when her flat had been all hers as she followed her mother out, regretting how many times she had pined at being alone. She had no room to move now, no secrets could easily be kept. What if Mum guessed what she and John had been up to downstairs?

Still, that was over. Being a good wife to Harry was important now, even if he was miles away. John could plead all he liked, she and John were finished, and that was that. From now on she would be a good wife.

*

'Coo-ee! Orright ter come in? Yer back door's open.'

The kitchen door, ajar to let out the odour of home-made setting lotion, was being tentatively eased further open.

Brenda looked up sharply from the hair she was skilfully moulding into a series of bangs, as the bouffant rolls were termed, to see the face of her mother-in-law peeping round the door's edge, and behind her the angular face of Harry's dad.

Seeing Brenda with comb poised over the head of a strange young woman seated on a stool with a towel around her shoulders, Mrs Hutton came to an abrupt halt, her square face a picture of what could only be called embarrassment.

'Oh, we intruding? I didn't realise yer was doing a friend's 'air. And yer've got all yer family staying 'ere as well.'

Brenda stood rooted to the spot, comb still poised. Her lady gave a little giggle at the term 'friend'.

'I ain't exactly a friend,' she offered sociably. 'Though Brenda does do me hair once a week every Friday, all nice and ready for the weekend. She's so good at it and don't charge as much as other 'airdressers do.'

Mrs Hutton was staring at Brenda in confusion. 'You charge? You mean you do this as a business?'

Brenda wanted to ask what concern was it of hers? It helped to supplement her meagre wife's allowance and she was a free agent. Harry was not here and most wives were working these days at war work or outdoor work, all trying to grub up an extra few bob while stuck on their own with their men away fighting.

But she merely smiled ineffectually and said, 'You two go through. The others are in the front room. I'll be finished here in a few minutes and then I'll make a cup of tea.'

It would take longer than a few minutes to get this hair right. Heavy, naturally greasy hair with a will of its own didn't lend itself to these modern bangs. Any other head would have turned out gorgeous. She had done Vera's hair this way sometimes. Her own too, though why she bothered with only John to see it, she couldn't be sure. And now she had sent him packing. Then what? No more excitement, no anticipation of the secret tryst, just this dismal round of doing other people's hair, trying to keep herself together with the family living here, bringing up Addie. What a future. She almost envied Vera her freedom, going dancing, dating boys, having a high old time.

'We'll go on in then.' Mrs Hutton was giving the client a scrutinising look. 'We'll try not ter get in yer way.'

You're all in my way, came the infuriated thought. I'm sick of being expected to sit idle like a sweet little wife, told what to do, everyone judging, judging, ready to see the worst but happy enough to make use of me. I've no life of my own. But she continued to look as pleasant as possible as the two people eased past her. Now she must make excuses, explain, defend herself for doing what she did best.

Why should she defend herself? Yet she knew she would. It was unfortunate, them coming round here this evening. But she knew why. They too had got a letter from Harry, and had come to see if she was all right. She must be charitable, they were only thinking of her. And perhaps he'd told them more than he'd told her concerning his injuries. It was worrying the life out of her that he appeared to be making too light of his wounds.

She could hardly wait to be rid of her client so that she could go and ask them.

They were all talking together in the front room when she came in with a tray full of tea.

'Oh, there you are, love,' said her mother. 'I was just telling Harry's mother how well yer doin' at the 'airdressing. I said it was a pity you 'ad ter use this place ter do it in. An' all us 'ere as well. Though of course, it ain't usually this crowded – Brian and Davy'll be going back off leave in a few days and then there'll only be us and Vera, but usually there's only me and 'er with Vera and 'er dad at work, so it ain't so bad, is it, Bren?'

Chatting away nineteen to the dozen, she didn't appear to be aware of Mrs Hutton's continuing tension. Mum seldom if ever noticed an atmosphere – she saw others as chummy and sociable, and if ever snubbed, would remark, 'Silly cow – must be suffering from somethink or other,' and get on with her life. She'd certainly not noticed anything amiss this evening, though Brenda had felt it immediately on entering the room.

Mum continued chattering away about this and that, about being bombed out, about waiting and wondering when they would finally be rehoused. 'Takin' their time about it, I must say'; about how fortunate the Huttons had been, 'not to've had any damage, or not too much anyway'; about rationing; about Harry, 'gettin' 'imself wounded like that,' and hoping he'd be 'orright'.

Brian was in and out getting himself ready to go out, as was Vera, while Davy seemed content joining in with his dad and Mr Hutton's conversations. Mrs Hutton said nothing, so Mum took it that she was merely listening.

271

Brenda, with little to say herself, knew different. When her mother-in-law turned to her in the middle of Mum's conversation and asked stiffly, 'What about this thing you're doing, Brenda – this hairdressing thing?' she wasn't a bit surprised, was ready for her.

She smiled sweetly. There was no point hedging; in fact she experienced a tiny surge of pleasure in affecting nonchalance even as a warning voice in her head said 'careful'.

'Oh, I've been doing that for ages. It brings in a bit extra so Addie can benefit. No one can live on what the government gives us. It don't make a lot, but it's something.'

Mrs Hutton was ruffled. Her voice trembled. 'No one told us. You've never mentioned a thing about it, almost like you was keeping it a secret from us. Underhanded if you ask me. Harry wouldn't be pleased. You know how he felt about a wife going out to work. A wife's place is looking after her 'usband. It's an 'usband's place ter go out and earn the money, not you.'

Her voice sounded so loud and rapid that the others stopped talking, while Mr Hutton coughed, ready to intervene. But Brenda got in first.

'Harry's not here, is he?' There was an angry edge to her voice which she couldn't avoid. 'He's away fighting, and I have to keep Addie decently clothed and fed and I'm doing that the best way I know. Anyone'd think I was earning it by being a prostitute or somethink.'

'Bully fer you,' came the barely audible whisper from Davy and Vera tittered. Brian gave a short, explosive laugh. Mrs Hutton gave a gasp.

'Well, I never . . .'

'Brenda!' This from her own mother. But she ploughed on.

'I'm earning doing perfectly respectable work and until Harry comes home I'll keep on doing it. I've got a good talent and I don't see why I should let it all go to waste just because Harry didn't approve at one time. Things've changed, Mum. We're all 'aving ter do things we didn't dream we'd ever do. And when Harry comes 'ome, then we'll see what 'e 'as ter say about it.'

Mrs Hutton was searching in her handbag for a handkerchief. Finding it, she clapped it to her mouth and nose. '*If* he comes home!'

'Now, there, 'Rene,' mumbled her husband, getting up to touch her arm tentatively. 'Don't come over all unnecessary. He's gonna be orright.'

'And what if he ain't? What if his wounds turn septic and he dies, out there in North Africa, and no one of his own with 'im.'

This was Brenda's feeling, and impulsively she got up to crouch in front of her mother-in-law, putting her arms round her and drawing her close. 'Don't cry, Mum. He's goin' ter be orright. He's strong and wiry and he wants to come back to us all – you and Dad, me and Addie – and he's got a lot to live for. I keep telling meself that, and I know he'll come 'ome.'

She felt her mother-in-law's arm embrace her in a kind of reflex action, the hand patting at her back, until the woman broke away and sat back in the armchair to energetically blow her nose.

'I s'pose I'm being a silly old fool.'

'No.'

'Yes I am. We've got ter be strong these days. I know you are, Brenda. But you mustn't be too strong so when he do come 'ome, you won't let go an' let 'im take up 'is rightful place as an 'usband an' father. A man 'as 'is pride, Brenda. It wouldn't be fair on 'im otherwise, after 'im fighting for 'is country like he's doing. Yer should let 'im feel he's goin' ter come back ter being 'ead an' breadwinner in his family.'

We will see, went the thought through her head, but Brenda nodded in apparent agreement and let it go at that.

No more was said about her hairdressing. Talk turned to how Harry was, how soon he'd recover, whether he'd be patched up and sent back into battle or sent home if he had been permanently put out of action which would be tantamount to declaring him crippled; and though she hadn't engineered it that way, Brenda was glad her gesture of sympathy for her mother-in-law had turned aside the woman's self-righteous disapproval.

Whether or not Mrs Hutton disapproved, Brenda wasn't going to be put off doing her hairdressing. Having ended her association (her mind avoided the word 'affair') with John Stebbings, it was all she had to lighten the humdrum life she led.

Chapter Twenty

'Take a look at this!' David Wilson held up the letter he had just opened, his blue eyes glaring at it as though it had done him physical harm.

His initial reaction to seeing the recycled wartime envelope with its adhesive address label and official lettering had been alarm. Perhaps it contained more bad news of Brenda's husband. Harry had long since been returned to the fighting as apparently fit, but could cop another one. His letters had been irregular and Brenda said he complained of getting hardly any of hers.

Sighing with relief, he saw it was from the housing department. Another reply to his endless requests for rehousing, probably to say that he must carry on waiting his turn in the lengthy queue, that his family at least had a roof over their heads in Brenda's home while others were still having to make do in centres.

He'd slit the envelope, already guessing its contents. He had read it all before: the Directorate of Emergency Works was repairing houses as fast as they could, it took time and some had been rehoused in the suburbs only

275

to be bombed out again. Delays. They'd get around to him as soon as they could. And no, they couldn't say where his family would end up if their old house was beyond repair. And please be patient.

He'd been patient for six months. It was now November; air raids had mostly become a thing of the past, but still nothing came from the Housing people. How much bloody longer would they take? He was heartily sick of it.

Not that he'd sat on his backside here. Over the months he'd done a good job on Brenda's flat, patching it up with a few panes of glass here, a few there. Same with roof tiles, in spite of Annie's fear for his safety he got up there himself to replace them. Silly woman, he'd done his stint of fire-watching for his firm during the Blitz and had scrambled over many a roof. And if he could get his finger out doing this place, why couldn't the authorities with their hordes of workers get theirs out? He felt he'd pulled his weight while staying at Brenda's, but of course it never quite made up for this intrusion into her life.

Though maybe it wasn't so bad a life for her. She and her mum would go shopping together quite a bit with Addie. They'd go to the pictures one or two afternoons a week while he was at work, and in the evenings they'd listen to the wireless, all nice and cosy.

Brenda never complained of having no privacy, but Vera did. Having to sleep with Brenda and their mother, she'd often keep out late and next morning they'd find her snuggled under a blanket on the settee. It didn't matter what he said about her being out late, there wasn't much he could do about it, being in someone else's home, no longer boss of his own.

Before long, though, there might only be the two of them for Brenda to cope with. For a while Vera had been in constant fear of being called up. She'd had to register even though doing war work. But she was single, and single girls of her age were now liable for call-up in the forces. Last week her fears were realised. But rather than loathe the idea, she said she was rather looking forward to a life of her own after being stuck here in the flat with them all. He couldn't see it really. What was the difference between sharing this flat and sharing a hut crowded with several dozen other girls? Well, maybe it was different.

So there would soon be just him and Brenda's mother here. Brenda appeared to have got used to them living with her, and in fact it provided company for her and helped her work too, with her mother to do for her and give eye to an increasingly energetic Addie. He could do all the repairs instead of her having to ask that slimy Stebbings bloke. He'd never thought much of that. The man's dark eyes, he'd noted, had seldom been off Brenda when he had been around. He didn't trust that one no more than he could throw him, but perhaps as a father he was being just a bit too protective. Brenda could look after herself well enough. She was a good girl and he wondered why Harry's mother tended to act as if she wasn't.

David Wilson stopped thinking, and, holding out the grey notepaper to his wife, growled, 'So much for bloody re-'ousing. There's us bloody waiting an' 'oping we'd get somethink decent, and this is what we get told.'

'The Glovers did all right,' Annie remarked absently as she read on. 'Nice little 'ouse in Dagenham they was given.'

277

'I thought we'd get the same,' he raged on. 'But no bloody fear. All we get is our own 'ouse ter be patched up an' made wind- and weatherproof they say. What's that s'posed ter mean? Like what I've seen bein' done wiv ovver places, I s'pose. Bleedin' tarpaulin fixed on the roof. Winders boarded up wiv wood. Wiv only us two livin' there, they say we only need the downstairs. It was only burnt, they say, not blasted. It can be renovated, they say. Not like some 'ouses what are just shells an' can't be rebuilt while the war's still on, they say. Well, bugger 'em! I ain't goin' ter live in no 'alf 'abitable 'ouse – not wiv winter comin' on.'

Annie, who had stood blankly gazing at him in silence while he raged, shrugged and handed back the letter, 'It's really up to Brenda, Dave. It's up to 'er what she thinks about us carryin' on stayin' 'ere.'

As far as she could Brenda had managed to avoid John Stebbings for nearly four months. With her parents still here and work now so busy she'd had little time to see him even if she'd let herself succumb to temptation.

So many times she nearly did. It hadn't been easy. Seldom did a day go by without remembering those tender little caresses of his with such a longing she could hardly bear it. The way he'd lean forward as they talked, smooth her hair, caress her hands, touch her cheek, her chin. Little touches full of love, soft and gentle. He'd always been gentle. That was one thing she adored about him, the way he cared for her, considered her, the feel of those hands sending little thrills through her, making her feel so very wanted.

She hated it when they did bump into each other. He'd be formal and she'd be formal too, striving to keep him at arm's length. Now and again she'd feel her defences breaking down. He would sense it, move nearer while she stood mute. He would murmur how much he missed her, how often he remembered their being together. Always she would be the first to step back, mumble something about being sorry and hurry on through the gate into the Mile End Road off to wherever she was going, her heart thudding to an empty ache and hardly able to see for the misting up of her sight.

It was Saturday evening. The short November day had long since faded, and most shops were closed. Why stay open with the job of putting up blackout? Dad had gone down the pub. Vera had gone straight from work for a farewell drink with her friends. She would be leaving tomorrow to report to her unit by Monday morning. Addie would soon to be put to bed, then she and Mum would sit and listen to the wireless, Mum knitting a jumper from two old ones she'd unravelled.

Brenda put Addie into her nightie. 'I'd better pop down to the lav, before I settle her down,' she informed her mother. Then she'd be settled for the evening. She grabbed the torch that she kept by the kitchen door. Its light was shielded by a black paper mask with a slit just big enough to allow the tiniest glimmer, and she felt her way down the stairs to the yard. About to negotiate the Stygian darkness between her and the lavatory, she collided suddenly with something that yielded.

There came the sound of a falling cardboard box as, nearly losing her balance, she let out a small cry of alarm.

A hand caught at her arm. Someone said, 'I didn't see you.' It was John's voice. 'Brenda, have you hurt yourself?'

'No, I didn't know what it was.'

She let her voice die away, disturbed by the faint but familiar and fascinating mixture of tobacco and brilliantine that in her mind belonged essentially to him and no one else.

He had stepped closer, so that her nostrils filled with the scent of him. She tried to break away but her own lack of will prevented her from doing so.

'I was just popping down to the . . .' She couldn't say it. 'I've got to go back upstairs,' she said instead. 'I've got to get Addie ready for bed.'

'I've not seen you in weeks,' he told her.

'I know, I've been busy.'

'I miss you, Brenda.'

'It had to end eventually. Now it has, I—'

'Has it?' he cut across her words, but softly. 'There's not a day goes by but I think of you, Brenda. I've tried to do it your way, but it's destroying me.'

'I'm sorry,' was all she could think to say. She wanted desperately to be away from him, his closeness reawakening the longing inside her which she was so sure at times she had succeeded in stifling.

'There's something I need to tell you,' he said now. 'But before I say it, I want to be made certain that your feelings for me have died. Have they?' he pressed when she didn't reply.

In the darkness, Brenda shook her head, but her voice spoke. 'John, you've got to understand, it couldn't . . .

can't go on. I have to be fair to my husband. I couldn't let him down, not like that, him all that way away and trusting me. I've got to wait for 'im. Please, John, you 'ave to understand.'

'I understand,' he said gently. 'I realise you want to stay faithful, but you can't turn away from what you really feel.'

'I've got to get back upstairs.'

'What do you really feel?' he persisted, ignoring her plea. 'I know you love me. Still love me. That's something you can't just turn off.'

Again there were no words to say against that as he paused. Then, with her silence obviously proving to him that she still did love him, he went on, 'I love you, Brenda. I'll love you to the day I die.'

There came a long pause; in the silence she could hear distant traffic.

He seemed to wilt. And when he spoke again his voice trembled with despair. 'There's hope for me, is there?'

In the darkness she shook her head again, a little desperately, but this time her voice echoed the negative movement of her head. This time it had strengthened. 'It's over, John. It 'as to be. I'm married to Harry and I don't want to spoil that. I'm sorry it's had to end this way. I do love you, John, but I'm not going to let it destroy my marriage. Before it all comes out and someone finds out what went on between us, it's finished.'

'Termination of contract.' The words, almost inaudible, were laced with bitterness.

'No! It's not like that!' she cried out. 'How can I make you see?'

More silence as her voice died away. Then he spoke again, his hold on her arm loosening a fraction.

'I know what I have to do now,' he said slowly as though talking to himself. 'Last month, when I sensed this is what you'd eventually tell me, I tried again to get into the forces but it's still the same. Grade F4. Asthma. I would get it quite badly when I was young. It still counts against me.'

She'd known of it for some time. The time when Harry's mother had queried why he wasn't in the forces and his dad had mentioned flat feet and a few other reasons, she had preferred to let them think what they liked, for why broadcast a man's private business. He'd never had an attack when she had been with him. But the armed forces were finicky, registering him as unfit.

'So I made enquiries about going into the merchant navy,' he was saying. 'There seems to be no trouble there. I shall be leaving very soon. But before I go, there's something I need to tell you about the shop. I'm changing the name on the lease rather than terminate it. I'm putting your name on it.'

She had been fighting with devastation at his news, but this piece of information dashed it from her. 'My name?'

'The place is yours, Brenda. I won't want it. You've always needed a salon. So that's what I've done. A buyer will be taking the books. What's left can go down in the cellar. The business was going down anyway with this war, and I've had enough.'

'But you can't go!' Her voice echoed in the dark yard. 'John . . .'

'Ask me to stay, Brenda.' His tone was even, almost harsh. 'Say you love me and you want me.'

She dared not answer that, could only trust herself to say, 'I don't want your place. I can't take it.'

'It'll be in your name,' he said softly. 'And I've laid down six months rent for the time being so that you don't have any worries on that score. When the war is over and your Harry comes home, all you need tell him is that it fell vacant and you took it over. You can even give it up if you wish.'

There was indifference in his voice and she felt him move away from her; his features, which had slowly been growing more distinguishable as her eyes accustomed themselves to the darkness, began to recede in the direction of the gate to the main road.

'I don't suppose I shall see you again, Brenda. Maybe it's all for the best. I'll never forget you, my darling. And I'll always love you.'

'John, no!' She made to follow as he retreated, but the fallen cardboard box impeded her progress. By the time she'd kicked it to one side and run out to the road, there was no sign of him. The blackout had swallowed him up and she dared not call out his name in the street.

Was this it, all the love they'd exchanged, the moments they'd shared, cut off without once seeing each other's face in this total darkness, without one last clinging kiss? But for months there'd been no contact between them so what difference did it make? In reality tears welled up inside her without any hope of escape as she turned and went back through the gate into the yard, stifling that weight inside her with deep breaths as she made her way back up the iron stairs.

He must have returned the next day and maybe the day after too, to clear up the business, but she didn't see him at all.

Three days later, during which time she did all she could to appear normal, avoiding her mother's enquiring gaze, forcing herself to smile, eat, chat naturally, came a letter from the landlord confirming her as tenant of the premises downstairs.

'I've bin saving up,' she told her mother. 'I'll get a lot more clients and run a proper business.'

'What about insurance and stuff and all the things yer need to run a proper 'airdresser's? Yer'll need more equipment ter make a go of it. Oh, love, yer throwin' yer money away. Yer bein' a silly fool. Yer bein' too rash. Write an' tell the landlord yer've changed yer mind and can't afford it after all.'

How could she tell her the truth? And Dad when he heard showed his anger, said he couldn't understand her thinking. 'And yer didn't even tell us what was on yer mind. If you 'ad, I'd of told yer not ter be such a silly little cow, slinging money abart – wartime an' all. It's one fing doing a spot of 'airdressin' up 'ere. But a shop. Yer must be orf yer bloomin' chump!'

But there wasn't much they, or she, could do about it.

The following week a letter came for her. Fortunately she was alone when she opened it. Mum had gone shopping while she was doing a woman's hair. In it lay six large, white, five-pound notes. Thirty pounds! She'd never held thirty pounds in one go in her whole life. The letter merely said 'To buy whatever you need to start up with. All the luck in the world. John.'

Nothing more, no forwarding address, no word of endearment. But she knew those few words concealed all the love that lay within him for her. And she knew what he meant for her to do with his letter, as gently, almost with reverence, she laid it on the fire and watched it slowly turn dark, curl and blacken, disintegrating among the coals. The large white banknotes of the sort she had never seen in her whole life, much less held in her hand, felt as though they too had grown scorching hot in her tight-curled fist. Even the tears that flowed down her cheeks seemed to burn; wiping them fiercely away she knew that she was never going to see John Stebbings ever again.

Chapter Twenty-one

Annie and Dave Wilson went back to their patched-up home around the beginning of December.

A lot had happened since summer. Hitler had invaded Russia, reaching the gates of Moscow; now the Germans were being repelled by the people and their winter. There was still fighting in North Africa. Harry had been patched up and sent back into it. HMS *Ark Royal* had been sunk by an Italian torpedo. The RAF was giving Germany what for. Clothing was now on coupons. And on the seventh of December, Pearl Harbor was bombed, so that America, to the satisfaction of all Britons who had all this time stood alone, got drawn into the war.

But all this and more paled beside the most important event in Annie Wilson's life: going back home. Dad went under protest, feeling they should have been properly rehoused, but she felt only too glad to be back in her own neighbourhood with people she knew. Though several were no longer there, with homes at the far end of the street razed to the ground, and one couple killed, it was nice having a good gossip at the door again with those who remained.

The place wasn't much. Upstairs of course had been gutted though there was no real structural damage apart from the lack of ceilings and great holes in the floors where they'd been burnt through. Downstairs the ceilings had been replaced so that the occupants wouldn't have to suffer an uninterrupted view of charred rafters. The doors upstairs, burnt and blackened, had been taken out and the apertures boarded up, so they couldn't have gone up there if they'd wanted to. The upstairs furniture was reduced to ash, and this was what upset Annie the most.

'All me best stuff, all the stuff what was me muvver's, and ter think I dusted and polished it every day. Now look at it. I tell yer one thing – I put me 'ands tergevver every time our boys fly over there ter give 'em a bit of what they give us. I ain't a bit sorry for that lot. They weren't sorry fer us when they bombed us out of 'ouse and 'ome.'

In the run-up to Christmas she had made a little haven from the renovated downstairs even though there was no getting rid of the smell of burnt fabric and wood. Lino now lay over scorched floorboards, doors had been replaced – though no two were the same design, they fitted and kept out the cold – and the walls had been distempered a dispirited cream by the authorities. Dave did a pattern on them with an old sock dipped in contrasting beige distemper; actually it looked quite nice.

The windows had been boarded up, but he had salvaged more glass and after sawing a hole in each board inserted small panes, cut to fit, to at least give some daylight. Her sister had given her some old curtaining which she made to fit each window, enough to be able to draw at

287

night after fitting up the blackout board from pieces Dave had cut out to put in the glass. In spite of the lingering redolence of charred wood it was quite cosy.

Once the gas was restored, she cleaned the gas stove and went back to making good hot meals while he, working in December cold, cleared the garden of rubble that had been blasted into it from bombed neighbouring houses.

That done, he went and bought six chickens off a workmate who had been bombed out, had got sick of going back to his devastated house and garden to feed them and was now being rehoused in Becontree Heath, much to Dave's chagrin. The buy comprised two hens well past laying but good boilers at a pinch, one cockerel, the rest of them already having provided a few dinners for his workmate, and three younger hens. 'Ain't seen one egg orf 'em fer weeks so I won't charge yer much for 'em,' said the workmate, but when their new owner got them home they excelled themselves by beginning to lay straight away.

'Prob'ly a change of scene,' he said.

'More like a bit more better grub,' Annie told him. 'Poor things was 'alf starved, 'im only going round there when it suited 'im. Don't you tell 'im though or 'e'll be askin' fer 'em back.'

From bits of wood lying about he constructed a chicken coop almost overnight and a small run at the bottom of the garden next to the air raid shelter.

By Christmas, with the hens laying regularly, the cockerel's neck having been wrung to make a proper Christmas dinner, together with the vegetables stored from Dave's allotment during the summer, the Wilsons felt thoroughly self-sufficient.

Once the light was on, it all looked quite festive. The roast chicken was on the table, and a Christmas pudding made with dried dates, prunes, their own eggs, a bit of suet begged from the butcher's and put in flour to keep it, plus sugar and black treacle hoarded bit by bit from the ration.

''Elps yer forget there's a war on, don't it?' Mum, still in her wraparound apron, said as she tucked into her homegrown Christmas dinner.

Brenda, delving into the food on her own plate, gazed round the assembly. It was a squash in such a small space. Brian, Davy and Vera had all managed to get leave. As if that wasn't enough there were her aunts Grace and Kath and uncles Herbert and Norman and their kids. Her gran sat wrinkling her nose from time to time at the persistent taint of burnt wood, of which she had complained the minute they got her in the house. Mum said testily, 'If yer don't like it, Mum, yer can always go 'ome.'

But of course that wouldn't have happened. Gran now lived in with Aunt Kath who didn't want to see her mother fetching for herself. Everyone seemed to be living in with other members of their families these days, except Brenda, who was alone again.

Mum had been concerned for her. 'I don't like leavin' yer all on yer own, love. Yer've put up with us all this time and it feels like we're walking out on yer.'

'You mustn't feel that way, Mum,' Brenda told her. 'You had to go back 'ome some time. Nothing like yer own 'ome.'

'S'pose not,' Mum had admitted. 'But not even someone down there in the shop. I can't 'elp thinking it won't 'alf feel strange to yer. Yer goin' ter feel lonely?'

Brenda had put on a brave face. 'I'll be fine, Mum. An empty shop ain't going ter worry me. And you ain't far away, are yer?'

But she hadn't felt fine. She had thought she'd be able to cope after they'd left, but the flat felt all the more empty after those months of crowding. And every so often it would idly cross her mind to pop down to John only to realise he was no longer there, the knowledge leaving a great hole inside her which even people coming to have their hair done couldn't fill. In the same way, it was hard to venture down into what was a shop in her name now. When Christmas was over, she'd have to pull herself together and face it. At the moment it was hard to know where to start, so terribly strange to adjust to the idea that the premises were hers.

Meanwhile she intended to enjoy her Christmas Day among her own family, except of course that Harry wasn't there. He was still in North Africa and the way things were going out there, no sign of his coming home.

She would be going to his parents for Boxing Day, still loyally keeping up the tradition of one day with one family and one with the other. She was not looking forward to facing the inquisition about the shop being put in her name. She had all her lies prepared, and hoped to convince them of having saved up enough for rent and stuff. Even so, she wondered how her mother-in-law would take it. The woman seemed prepared to see ill in anything her son's wife did without his say-so.

So far she'd done nothing to the place. Before John left she'd heard lots of hammering and from her window saw men taking out dismantled bookcases and shelves and dumping them in a horse-drawn cart as if valueless.

The books must have gone when she wasn't watching for she saw none of them go out. Then suddenly the shop was closed.

She had not gone down immediately in case he had lingered behind. To meet would have caused all sort of complications. They had said their goodbyes at that final meeting, in the total darkness of the blackout, keeping their distance from each other, each wary of even a last kiss. Why hadn't she made the first move? Why hadn't he? What fools lovers were, hating to be parted yet fearing to be together for what the world might say. Had he kissed her at that crucial moment she'd have begged him to stay, promising herself to him forever. But it hadn't happened.

When she ventured down after the men had gone, knowing he would not be there, yet wanting him to be, she had gone into the old shed, just as a postscript to the note that had held the thirty pounds, 'keys in shed', brief as the rest of it, had directed.

Finding them, she'd held them in both hands against her breast and there all alone in the shed had bent her head and wept over them as though they represented part of him.

It had been strange and painful venturing into the shop by the back kitchen door. The kitchen was left exactly as she remembered, all for her she imagined, even to the kettle, teapot and crockery, conjuring up those times when he would reach out and touch her hair, her face, would lean forward to lay his lips on hers, his hand stealing between her blouse buttons to touch her, she responding until their love became satisfied. It seemed so long ago and so unreal. Stealing on into the empty shop, she'd been surprised by its smallness. With the books and bookshelves there it had always appeared to be far more spacious. What had greeted her had been a few bits of paper and the lingering, ever-intriguing musty taint of old books. Venturing downstairs, she saw that the old narrow bed and square of carpet were still there, and the little table still with its lamp, reawakening her memory of the Blitz and lovemaking. She even thought she could detect that special essence of him, but it had only been imagination. She'd come away, locking the door carefully behind her.

She hadn't been down there since. With no one downstairs now and her parents gone back to their patched-up home, there descended on her a vaguely unnerving awareness of being totally alone in a vacant building. The small sounds that had once filtered up from the shop beneath her, of customers entering and leaving, the comforting knowledge of someone there, all were gone. Even when she'd been on her own before Mum and Dad came, when John locked up for the night and went home, she had not felt quite so unnerved. Now it was eerie and she was glad not to be there over the Christmas.

'How yer coping, with yer parents gone back 'ome? That shop downstairs empty too – it must feel a bit strange.'

'It does a bit,' Brenda ventured.

'Anyway, yer was at yer mum's yesterday, and now yer 'ere with us fer Boxing Day, that must take it off a bit.'

'Yes, I s'pose it does.'

Sitting at her in-laws' dining table with Daphne and Harry's brother Bob, on Christmas leave, Brenda felt the weight of her own husband's absence all the more. Everyone else appeared to be on leave this festive season, though she knew that wasn't true, but being here did help compensate for the loneliness she'd been feeling.

Also present were Harry's grandmother and his mother's widowed sister Carrie. His sisters and other relatives were spending Boxing Day with their own families. Brenda wished they were here – it would have taken some of the limelight off her.

'I wonder what sort of people will take it over,' Mrs Hutton said as she got up to collect the used dinner plates, Daphne leaping up to help her while Brenda did her best to dissuade her almost three-year-old daughter from trying to leave the table with afters still to be dished up. 'I 'ope they won't be too noisy. You said that Mr Stebbings bloke was a very quiet man. But I s'pose book shops are, aren't they?'

Brenda nodded, holding a protesting Addie on to her chair.

'Did he say cheerio to yer before 'e left?'

'Oh yes.'

'Yer'll miss 'im. He did a lot in your flat for yer, didn't he?'

Again Brenda nodded, her heart beginning to thump at what sounded like a broad allusion to something slightly suspect. If her mother-in-law did but know.

'Joined up, didn't he?'

'Yes.' She wasn't prepared to enlarge on it.

'Not before time. I s'pose in the end he thought he ought ter. We'll use that tinned fruit yer brought me, Brenda, fer afters, with custard. I couldn't do Christmas pud this year. Blessed rationing! Thanks for bringing the tin of fruit though. It was a godsend, dear, and the couple of eggs.'

'They was from me dad's chickens,' Brenda said, relieved to have the subject of the downstairs shop put aside. Harry's mother had no idea as yet that it was in fact hers. She'd already spent quite a few sleepless nights in a dilemma as to how to break the news, which she'd have to sooner or later.

'We thought of keeping chickens, didn't we, Sid,' Mrs Hutton called over her shoulder as she went out of the room with the dirty plates, Daphne following close behind.

'You ought to, Dad,' Bob put in, leaning back to light a cigarette.

His father nodded slowly, thinking for a while. 'It's getting the blessed thing built. I ain't much of a builder. Never was.'

'It's only a matter of sticking up four walls and a roof, with a couple of planks for 'em ter roost on at night. Yer'll have a few free dinners off yer cocks, and a nice lot of eggs off yer 'ens.'

'It's not as simple as that.' Brenda began to explain that egg rations got cancelled, replaced by chicken feed, but his mother, returning with the tinned fruit in a glass dish and a jug of custard, followed by Daphne with the glass dessert dishes, interrupted her.

''Eard from Harry lately, Brenda? It's been ages since we 'ad a letter. The silence worries me out of me mind, 'im out there fightin'.'

'It can't be easy writing, being in the thick of it,' Brenda said as the dessert was ladled out. Addie had gone quiet, anticipating lovely custard.

'Not too much for me,' Carrie was saying, waving a thin hand in the air. 'Too much pineapple gives me indigestion.'

'What about you, Mum?'

Mrs Hutton leaned attentively over her mother who gave a little giggle and said, 'Only custard fer me, luv. The old teeth just won't get round that fibrey stuff, an' pineapples is a bit too sour fer me.'

'Right you are, Mum. So when did yer last get a letter from Harry?'

'A good three weeks ago,' Brenda obliged as Mrs Hutton returned her attention to her.

Her parents had only just left to go back in their own home when his letter had come. It was very short, saying little apart from hoping she and Addie were in good health, that her parents being with her wasn't too much for her, that she was continuing to talk about him to Addie so that she'd remember him when he eventually came home, that he was always thinking of them and loved her and wished he could be home with her and once they were together again he'd make up for all this lost time; to write back as soon as she could because he looked for her letters constantly in these days with mail coming so erratically and sometimes not at all.

Since then, with not even a letter at Christmas, she too had begun to worry for his well-being, having constantly to remind herself that no news had to be good news. If anything had happened she'd have been informed immediately. Bad news always travelled fast, the authorities made sure of that. She'd spoken to Vera about it yesterday after Christmas dinner while Dad was digesting his large meal with a well-earned nap, Mum snoozing in the other room she and Dad now used as a bedroom. Davy had gone off out to look up an old mate, and Brian to see if a girl he'd once gone around with was still in the area.

Vera had been concerned for her but had soon gone on to talk of her exciting life in the ATS. 'They've got a lot of American boys stationed near us and when we can get into town we go fer them straight away. They've come over 'ere with pots of money and they don't half know how ter spend it. So far I've had chocolates off ration and a pair of lovely sheer stockings. They call 'em nylons. Trouble is you have to learn to keep 'em at arm's length 'cos if you give 'em an inch they'll take a yard! But they're great boys.'

'It makes yer worried, don't it, not hearing nothing?' Daphne said as she and Brenda sat together by the fire. But Daphne had her husband here today. What worries did she have? 'Me an' Bob'll pop over and see you before he goes back,' she continued. 'He's got a whole week.'

'That's nice, though I'll probably be busy,' Brenda said, without thinking until her mother-in-law chimed in.

'Oh, yes, yer 'airdressin' business. 'Ow d'yer manage with Addie now yer mother's not there to give eye while yer occupied with people's 'air?'

Brenda clenched her teeth but smiled, so bent on proving that she wasn't neglecting Addie the least bit that before she knew what she was about, she had retorted, 'She's older now and not so much trouble. And when I move downstairs, she'll have plenty to keep her—'

Too late she pulled herself up, seeing her mother-in-law staring at her while the others, taking their cue from her, stared in their turn.

'Downstairs?' echoed Mrs Hutton. 'What d'yer mean, downstairs?'

'Oh . . .' There was no brazening it out. She would have to tell her. Brenda took a deep fortifying breath. 'I'm going ter take over the downstairs shop. It's not too big and the rent's not too bad.'

'Taking over the shop? You?'

She made it sound as if such a thing had to be the most ridiculous idea she'd ever heard and Brenda's back went up.

'The shop's to let,' she blurted indignantly, 'and I've saved enough up and I don't see why I shouldn't have a proper place to do hairdressing.'

'Harry ain't goin' ter be pleased about that, you going off and getting a thing like that without even consulting 'im.'

'And how'm I going to consult 'im,' Brenda demanded hotly, 'with 'im all them miles away?'

'By *writing* and *telling* 'im what yer up to. Keeping 'im in the dark like that!' Anger was beginning to darken Mrs Hutton's face.

But Brenda was also angry. 'By the time he got me letter, the shop would of gone, and I won't get another snip like that so easy. We ain't 'ad no letters from 'im fer three weeks and he says ours ain't getting through all that quick. So *how* am I goin' ter let 'im know?'

Mrs Hutton's lips had become a thin line. She and Brenda glared at each other while Harry's father sat forward ready to intervene. Bob, though, had sat back, having finished his dessert, and was now lighting a cigarette.

'If you ask me, Mum,' he said slowly, puffing a cloud of white smoke across the table like a sort of

297

smokescreen, 'I think she's doing a grand job. I think our 'Arry ought ter be damned proud of 'er when he does come 'ome and sees what she's done. Not many wives'd do what she's doin'. And if he don't appreciate 'er, then I think he's a bloody fool!'

'I think we've more to worry about,' Brenda added, encouraged by her brother-in-law's support, 'than what he thinks, with us not even 'aving a letter from him at Christmas.'

At the significance of the statement a silence descended, through which Mrs Hutton's mother could be heard slurping her custard without a care in the world.

No more was said about the shop though Brenda could tell her mother-in-law was aching for another go at her by the several small hints she dropped during the remainder of the day when she spoke to her at all. Most of the time she managed to distance herself from Brenda by indulging in close conversations with her sister Carrie, leaving Brenda mostly with Daphne, while Bob and his dad chatted together like two old long-lost friends.

It was New Year when she finally had a letter from Harry, a Christmas postcard with it, a strange foreign-looking card with angels in what looked like caftans and circlets around a sort of headshawl as well as the accepted shining halo while a camel train passed in the background, all in lurid reds, greens and golds.

'All I could find at our depot in Benghazi, time I got back there,' he wrote, though what he meant wasn't enlarged on as he continued, 'Got your letters at last, and the Christmas card, and the photo of you and

Addie . . .' She'd had that done several weeks ago for him for Christmas, not knowing what else to send him. 'And Addie's drawing. It made my eyes water. She's growing up so fast. Almost three! Anyway, thanks, love, everythink was all lovely, a real breath of home. Got a card from Mum and Dad as well, and from my sisters. All a bit too late for Xmas, but that's the bloody army for you.'

Devouring every word, she went on to read that his battalion was being taken out of battle, and her relief at reading it was beyond all measure. Her need to have Harry's arms about her was so strong she could almost feel them, and she went to bed that second day of 1942 to weep away her longing.

Strange, it occurred to her, just before her eyes closed, how she had got over John Stebbings so soon after his departure. She almost felt guilty now at taking advantage of his generosity in paying the six months' rent for the shop in her name. He had truly been in love with her, but had she ever really been in love with him, or had she merely needed to fill a deep loneliness? She should never have let it go that far. It was a shabby way to have treated a man, wasn't it?

Chapter Twenty-two

It took a while to get back into a routine with Mum no longer living at the flat giving eye to Addie. But Addie was no trouble these days. She would play to her heart's content in the shop while Brenda set about using her treasured thirty pounds turning it into the suitable place she wanted. She started by distempering the walls a pretty pink and the ceiling a paler pink by adding white.

With some of the money she attended a sale in February at a salon in Shenfield in Essex which she had seen advertised in the *Hairdressers' Weekly Journal.* The salon was closing down. It seemed a long way to travel but everything was apparently going cheap and there might never be another chance of a better bargain anywhere nearer.

Leaving Addie with Mum for the day, she caught a train. The journey, straightforward enough with no changes, took nearly all morning, the train dawdling, as people had grown to expect these days. Not one soul complained while it stopped for nearly twenty minutes to let another train come through carrying troops or arms or something, starting up again with jerks and jolts only to stop further up the line for more or less the same thing.

Passengers suffered it all with resignation, every carriage thick with tobacco smoke, and as ever, filled by servicemen and women with their packs and kitbags taking up loads of space allowing standing room only. She too had been compelled to stand; no one was about to give up a hard-won seat if they could help it. But she was young, so her only concern was to reach her destination by two o'clock. She wished she'd started off earlier than ten o'clock.

Managing to get there just in time she came away later that afternoon having bought at bargain prices three chairs, two upright hairdryers, an electric perming machine with its tangle of wires and metal rods, two oval mirrors and some framed posters fitting to a hairdressing salon, as well as sundry items like tins of hairpins, curling tongs, metal rollers and scissors, which she packed into a large holdall. The rest would be delivered by Carter Patterson – expensive, but she could now afford it.

A sink she would get in a local plumber's yard and have him plumb it in, with a carpenter to build shelves and an electrician. Luckily she didn't need to buy any floor covering, which was hard to come by in wartime. Her only problem now: would her little business pay for itself or go the way of that salon ruined by the war, from where she'd bought all this equipment? It was well into March though and, war or no war, with luck women would put the winter with its need for headscarves behind them and look towards spring and nice hair.

'It looks ever so nice,' said her sister-in-law, Daphne, when she and their mother-in-law came round to view the results. 'The pink is so pretty.'

Daphne was more often at her husband's mother's than in their own home. Pliable, easy-going and, in Brenda's eyes, far too easily manipulated, she seemed sometimes mystified by the way Brenda distanced herself from the woman. 'She's always bin so sweet and helpful to me,' she'd say, but then what she might see as helpful, Brenda would have called interfering, though it was probably better to keep silent as to who might be right or who wrong, particularly as she herself couldn't have said which.

Daphne, now three months pregnant with Bob away in the forces, had drawn even closer to Mrs Hutton. Before that she had paled at the possibility of being forced into doing war work, but that threat had been lifted. Whether or not that was the main reason to have let herself get pregnant with Bob not there to protect her, Brenda had to smile, for Daphne had always struck her as not being capable of taking on the responsibility of motherhood. But she was over the moon, perhaps for reasons other than just starting a family.

'I think yer ever so brave, doing all this,' she said with a tiny ring of envy in her voice. The senior Mrs Hutton wasn't so forthcoming.

'I think yer must be mad,' she said, fingering this and fingering that, picking something up to scrutinise it, leaning forward to stare at herself in one of the oval mirrors, studying the framed posters of the latest or nearly latest hair fashions, looking the wires of the perming machine up and down and grimacing at the idea of being hooked up to it. ('What if yer was tied up on this thing,' she'd said, 'and there was an air raid – 'ow would yer get out of it to take shelter?')

'Spendin' out on all this.' She fingered a newly washed hairbrush. 'Tryin' ter start up business like this in wartime. Yer just throwin' yer money away. Yer was orright when yer was upstairs, but ter take on a shop – yer could go broke quick as anythink. Yer bein' a fool, Brenda. The cost of all this, yer'd of bin better savin' it fer when Harry comes 'ome an' using it ter furnish a nice little rented 'ouse. He ain't goin' ter be pleased ter know yer've squandered away all yer've saved.'

Always what Harry might think. Her precious son, King Harry! Well, King blooming Harry could think what he liked. She was going to make a go of this business whether he liked it or not, she'd make him proud of her when he finally came home, whenever that might be the way the war was going in North Africa. But what would his mother say if she knew that not one penny that had gone on this place had been from savings of any sort?

She had written to him about the shop soon after the New Year. His mother wasn't going to get in before she did. It would have been just asking for trouble, him hearing it all from his mum first and thinking she was being secretive. She tried to make her letter sound pleasing, laying emphasis on how hard she had saved from the money her hairdressing had brought in though not so much as to make him feel superfluous as a husband, telling him she knew he would have told her to go ahead with the idea.

It had been a hard letter to write. His reply hadn't been what she had hoped though she'd not been that surprised: he was a bit taken aback; she should have asked his opinion before doing such a rash thing and he'd have advised her against it had she done so; that from now on he'd be spending his time worrying about her; could see the money she'd saved being blown up the wall in this stupid idea of hers; that he only wished he was there to put her right and what did she think she was doing going off half cocked like that. It was almost a telling off, her enthusiasm for their future ignored.

Tightening her lips, she folded the letter firmly, running her thumb nail viciously along the creases, and stuffed it behind the clock. Silly fool! Who did he think he was? Perhaps his mother had got in first. She vowed to write no more to him about the shop.

It was May before the place was really ready to open, but it caused no big concern, the rent having been paid by John Stebbings. By the time that gave out, she'd be raking the money in. She would wonder from time to time how and where he was. She'd at least expected a letter from him but there'd been none. He seemed to have totally vanished from her life. There were times when she still missed him. But there was so much to do trying not to delay too long in getting the place ready that her mind was mostly taken up elsewhere.

She had posters put up on the boarded part of the shop's frontage, leaving the small glazed area to display the framed photos of 1942 fashions she'd bought at the sale. It certainly drew attention. She would see women pausing as they walked by, to backtrack a few paces for a better look. They would come as soon as she opened, she was sure of it. The clients she did upstairs were all asking about it.

'Be nice to 'ave a real place ter be done in, luv. I'm lookin' forward to it. Bet you are too. When d'yer open?'

'May,' she told them. 'Got to get it all ready first. But, yes, May.'

Now was the grand opening, the fifteenth of May, Friday, right in time for the weekend.

Standing there at nine o'clock clad in a pink overall made of material bought with her own precious clothing coupons, her heart beating heavily in the hope that customers wouldn't be disappointed with all she'd done, the fact that she was having to charge a few pence more because of overheads worried her.

Beside her was her little assistant, fourteen-year-old Joan, daughter of one of Mum's friends, who would earn a few pence for sweeping hair up from the floor, cleaning the basin, washing brushes and combs, tidying the hair-pins away in their containers, polishing, and making tea for clients when necessary. Later she might teach her to wash hair. The girl appeared bright enough and very enthusiastic on this first day.

She stood there, her blouse and short utility skirt well hidden under another skimpy pink overall Brenda had managed to squeeze out for her from what had been left of the material she'd bought. The girl's legs were bare but for gravy-browning staining to make it seem as though she wore stockings and thus appear presentable. Her dark shoulder-length hair was swept up with pins towards the back of her head by Brenda herself; a dusting of Brenda's own precious face powder on her pert little nose and just a touch of beetroot juice on her lips all made her seem less of a child.

'I can't wait ter start,' she said, broom in hand, until Brenda told her she had no need to sweep till much later on.

305

'Let's get my customers in first,' she said. But three were coming this morning, booked last week, and quite a few more this afternoon, and for the next few days her book was beginning to fill.

The doorbell tinkled – her first customer, wash, trim and tong-wave.

Vera was home on leave. Vera was over the moon about an American boy she had met and was writing to. Even when scarcely inside the house she was telling her mother all about him, hardly giving herself time to draw breath as she dragged off her khaki ATS hat, not caring how she tousled her short fair curls. She threw herself at her mother to embrace her.

'Oh, Mum! He's gorgeous! He's in love with me and I'm in love too.'

Told to calm down and not be so silly and to come into the living room before she went off half-cocked, she was made to say hello to her dad in the proper manner, sit down and tell them how she was and how long she had before going back.

'It's only a weekend leave,' she told them impatiently, and embarked once more on her main topic of news.

'I 'ave ter tell yer about Hank. He's an American. He's in the army and he's ever so nice, Mum. We met in April at a dance and we've been writing to each other for three months now. I didn't write to you about him because I wasn't sure, but now I am. His family are nice people – he's showed me photos, and he's told his mum about me. She wrote to me and told me what a good boy he was to her and how she missed him so and how she hoped that one day he'd find a really nice girl, and he told me that as far as he was concerned *I* was that nice girl. We've met three times since, and he's lovely, Mum. Ever so handsome. He's about six foot tall, and blond, and ever so athletic. He runs for his outfit. Look, here's a photo of him.'

The photo dug from her breast pocket was pushed at her somewhat stunned parents.

'I want you to meet him as soon as we get leave together and I can bring 'im home here. He's never been in with a real English family and he's dying to meet you.'

'But he's an American.' Mum at last got a word in, her tone stopping Vera in her tracks, and Vera's happy face fell.

'What difference do that make?'

'Well, when the war's over he'll be goin' back to 'is own country and yer won't ever see 'im again.'

'Mum, he's said he's bin told that American servicemen can apply for their wives to go back with them if they marry an English girl.'

'Oh, Vera! You ain't thinking of marrying him?'

'Not yet. We ain't even engaged.'

'Then what's all the fuss about, gettin' all excited? By this time next year yer'll of gorn orf 'im and got someone else – a nice English boy.' She knew her daughter, who was a bit like her brother Brian, so sure that this was the one, then next minute off them as someone even more exciting loomed on the horizon. 'Anyway, I ain't all that keen on you inviting some strange American inter me 'ome.'

'Americans ain't bloomin' foreigners, Mum!' Vera shot out, and pouting, fell silent, becoming very distant to her parents for the rest of the weekend.

And when her mother was out of the room, her father, making himself busy by filling his pipe so he wouldn't have to look at his daughter, said as though he had taken her to one side, 'Them Americans, Vera, they're just as much foreigners as French or Greek or Polish. We've got different ways of goin' on even though we both speak the same language. You take my advice, Vera, do as yer muvver says and find a boy like ourselves. Yer know where you are wiv boys of yer own sort.'

Which only went to upset Vera all the more.

'I wish I hadn't told them!' she said vehemently to Brenda, having gone to her flat on the Saturday afternoon to ask if she'd like to go to the pictures. Anything to get out of the house. 'I wish I 'adn't come 'ome. I'll be glad to go back tomorrow.'

Brenda had been happy to go to the pictures with her, leaving Addie with Mum who, as always, was only too happy to have her grandchild there. And Brenda was somewhat more forthcoming than their mother, far more interested in the relationship, and far more sympathetic.

'So how long did you say you've known him?' she asked as she got tea for her and Vera after the pictures.

'Three months.' Vera pulled a face. 'Mum said we've only just met and it's not long enough fer me ter get ter know 'im properly. She said he'll probably not be the same man at 'ome to what he is here, and she said I'm seeing 'im through rose-coloured spectacles and she'd rather not meet 'im because in time I'll probably get over 'im and it wouldn't be worth it.'

Brenda smiled. 'I don't think there's a lot of danger of Mum meeting him, him in the American forces and you in ours. I shouldn't think it'd be easy for you both to get leave at the same time.'

'Oh, he can get leave easier than our boys,' Vera put in, biting into one of the Spam sandwiches Brenda had made them. 'Their officers are a lot more lenient than ours and they get lots more privileges than what our boys get. If he explained to his commanding officer why he wanted leave, I'm sure they'd give 'im it.'

'Maybe. But I'd wait until he starts talking about marriage before you start bringing him home, the way Mum and Dad are. Just make sure he's as much in love with you as you say you are with 'im, that's all.'

But Vera saw no problems on that score. There was only one doubt that she had. 'Mum says I'm being silly. You don't think I am, do yer, falling for a guy from so far away, like the States? I just know I love 'im ter bits. I get tingles all down my spine even getting a letter from 'im. That 'as ter be love. The thing is, yer can't ask love to discriminate once it gets its teeth in yer.'

Brenda's mind flew instantly to John Stebbings as she put her half-eaten sandwich back down on the plate. Her heart still ached whenever she thought of him. Where was he now? She had not heard a word since he left.

'You can't,' she admitted slowly. 'Just don't go overboard all at once. Let things take their time.'

It was the best advice she could give, but it must have hit some spot inside Vera. She put down her teacup and, getting up, came round the table to cuddle Brenda to her as if she were some generous benefactor.

'I knew yer'd understand. And I know he's gonna ask me to marry 'im, eventually. He keeps saying in all his letters that he can't wait till we see each other again and that he can't live without me and that when we're not together the days go by slow and he longs fer when we can both be together, always. Oh, Bren, I'm so happy! I know he loves me, and I'm not going to let Mum spoil it all.'

Daphne would be having her baby in a month's time, early September, and was spending all her time at her mother-in-law's rather than at her own mother's. She had apparently had six children and saw Daphne as a strong healthy woman who did not need coddling apart from motherly support and advice. Daphne however was nursing herself ready for her event with her husband's mother waiting on her hand and foot, delighting in taking over.

Bob had got leave twice in all that time, and Daphne was all on tenterhooks that he might not get any more when the baby was born.

'He said he's trying to get compassionate leave,' she told Brenda in the quiet living room of their mother-in-law's home. Tears of apprehension glistened in her light blue eyes as she hugged her lump in both hands. 'Oh, I don't think I could go through with it if he can't get leave.'

Brenda bit back a chuckle. 'You can't push it back, Daph. It'll come when it's ready to, whether he's home or not.'

'I don't think I can cope.'

'You'll cope very well,' Brenda said, trying not to feel impatient.

'Who'll cope?' Mrs Hutton came bustling in with a few slender stems of pink Dr Van Fleet roses, rescued from the rambler over her garden trellis before they could get overblown from the heat of an August sun, and a small vase of water. Brenda turned to look at her.

'Daphne's worried about Bob not being home when the baby comes.'

Mrs Hutton placed the vase on the mantelshelf and popped in the blooms, rearranging them tastefully. 'I'll be looking after her for 'im.'

'Your mum will be with you as well,' Brenda pointed out. But Daphne gnawed at her lips, her fair brow creasing.

'It's our first baby. They ought ter let Bob 'ome ter be with me for a little while. Me mum says I'll cope. She had six with no bother and I know she'll be with me. But it ain't the same as me own husband being 'ome.'

Clucking with sympathy Mrs Hutton went to offer a little comfort to her favourite daughter-in-law.

Brenda turned to gaze through the window at the back garden. Sid Hutton was bent over his vegetable patch, forking up potatoes. She could see him framed between the criss-cross strips of gummed paper over the panes of glass that, with air raids seeming a thing of the past and with the full heat of summer's sun on them, had begun to lose their gum and curl up. If any more air raids did happen, how much glass they would stop from splintering, she wondered idly.

Mr and Mrs Hutton's house had suffered only superfluous damage: a few windowpanes cracked, a few tiles broken. They had been lucky. Mum and Dad were still having to live downstairs in their house; no one at the Town Hall showed any apparent interest in them.

There had been air attacks of course, around the country, but no real repeat of the Blitz. Hitler had too much else on his mind these days. His own cities were getting their turn now, from the British and the Americans. And the Ruhr especially, that important industrial area, had last month suffered its first daylight raid by the RAF. The German people were living in terror day and night. Brenda thought momentarily of the women and children, innocent as they themselves had been, then dismissed it – they were all the enemy, after all. But even so . . .

It was Hitler's fault, wasn't it? Him and his Nazis. Now he was being stymied by Russia, foiled by a winter his troops didn't understand but which Russian people did, and by their determination not to be overrun. And since last month, with the Eighth Army beating back Rommel's advance and holding the line at El Alamein, the war in North Africa seemed to be finally turning their way.

But even while they crowed, more stringent rationing was reminding everyone that war was tightening its grip, air raids or no air raids.

'It seems such a wicked shame having to deny Addie a little bit of chocolate,' Brenda had said to her mum after sweet rationing came into force. 'Poor kids, they don't understand things like rationing, do they? She looks so blessed bewildered, I just have to give her mine as well. Though God knows I can always do without sweets,' she'd added with a laugh.

But it was good to know how well the North African campaign was going, because Harry might be allowed home again. Feeble-hearted Daphne, sighing over her Bob possibly not being allowed compassionate leave! What of herself with Harry all those thousands of miles away? What if she fell ill, desperately ill, or his daughter did, would they send him home on leave from a battle zone? Not on your nelly. The fighting in North Africa might be turning round, but there was still the possibility of Harry being wounded, or . . .

Well, she wouldn't think about that. Maybe it would all be over out there soon and Harry would come home. Perhaps by the end of the year.

That thought reawakened the worry of how she was going to face him with her new business. What if he displayed disapproval, told her to sell up and be an ordinary housewife again, insisted that he should be the breadwinner for his family? As a warehouse assistant, going back to square one was the only route she could see for him. He'd be a fool to tell her to pack this business in, and surely he'd see that. Even he couldn't be that daft. But you never could tell. In her letter she had made a point of saying that she'd had so many clients that she had needed to find extra space and when the shop fell empty she had grabbed her chance. But that was no guarantee of his being pleased. He might see it as his authority being ousted in his absence.

Brenda had begged his mother not to say too much to him until the place proved itself and had kept her sweet by doing her and Daphne's hair free of charge and even Harry's sisters' hair when they came to black their noses. She prayed that they wouldn't write and tell him too much either, but then they and their brothers had never been that close and she doubted he had ever written to them or even to Bob.

With that thought Brenda settled down to making it a business to be proud of, if only to prove to her husband

313

that to let it go would be stupid. This was her place and no one was going to take it away from her.

Place was right though. Her place. It was what she'd ended up calling it after much careful thought. Brenda's Place. It sounded right for the area, better than some trite play on words. Locals seemed quite happy with its name, though within months customers started to come from slightly further afield than the surrounding turnings. Her reputation had begun to spread.

Now, she thought exultantly towards the end of summer, let Harry come home here turning his nose up. Though his homecoming seemed as far away as ever. For all that the widely admired Montgomery was finally beginning to gain mastery over Rommel, the North African campaign still looked a long drawn-out one. Brenda found herself not just praying for Harry to come through with no more than the now-healed wound he'd already had, but in a way looking forward with relish to winning the argument she was sure would occur when he found himself confronted with her achievement. She could hardly wait.

'Orright fer me ter go 'ome now, Miss Brenda?' She insisted on Joan calling her that rather than Mrs Hutton. Customers called her Brenda, because her married name rather detracted from the skills she displayed. But Joan being so young, it wasn't proper to address her employer by her Christian name.

Brenda glanced at the wall clock with pink cherubs around it, which had replaced the original plain second-hand one. Ten to six and well dark, it being October. They closed at five thirty, and with the blackout up, Joan had finished all the sweeping up of hair and cleaning of sinks and mirrors.

'Yes, of course.' After Joan had gone, she would make herself a cup of tea then go up to relieve Mrs Page who came to give eye to Addie. Such a luxury was affordable now, well worth the three and six a week she paid her.

She was just making her way to the back room when there came a tapping on the glass of the door.

Brenda tutted and glanced toward the drawn blackout blind on the door. Again came the tapping. Now she called out sharply, 'Sorry! We're closed!'

A familiar voice replied, muffled by the glass and blind. 'Brenda?'

Galvanised into action, her heart having begun to pound fit to bruise her ribs, Brenda practically aimed herself across the salon, though with a presence of mind born of habit she remembered to switch off the lights before unlocking the door with fumbling fingers and yanking it open.

In the perfect darkness she couldn't make out the figure at all but she knew too well who he was as with a gasp of joy she threw herself into his arms.

Chapter Twenty-three

The moment of joy lasted but seconds. Following on it came a mixture of sensations she couldn't define. And questions. Why had he turned up unannounced? What would he have done had she left? Would he have gone upstairs to her flat to find her? And what was she doing here in his arms, all her resolve gone to pot?

Coming to her senses, she moved back from him. His hold on her had not been strong and it wasn't hard to move away.

'I'm sorry, John, you'd best come in.' How could her invitation sound so formal?

She waited as he stepped inside what had once been his shop. That knowledge in itself added its odd sensation to those crowding her breast. Carefully she closed the door, locked it, and switching a light back on, just one this time, she turned to face him. Then as if formality had been but a weak dam through which joy now burst unable to be contained any longer, his name spilled from her lips. 'John – oh, John, darling!'

His arms were already opening out to her and again she let them close around her. No thought existed in her head but her happiness at seeing him, all the well-trained restraints she'd built up on his leaving falling like fence posts before an axe as she lifted her face to his to receive his kiss. That kiss contained almost twelve months of yearning, its hunger pressing down on her lips all but suffocating her.

She couldn't remember how they got to the kitchen. The small back room, now reflecting a woman's touch, gave far more space than when he'd used it. In place of the old wooden table and couple of rickety chairs was a folding table, two chairs with padded seats should any customer need to recover from the overheating effect of the electric perming machine, and a host of feminine touches: little ornaments, a vase of paper flowers, a pretty clock, a small mirror.

It was on to the chairs standing side by side that she and John sank. One arm still about her, he whispered, 'I've longed so often to see you again, my sweet, to be with you again.'

What could she say? 'I've longed to be with you too?'

That was true if she were honest with herself, but common sense was beginning slowly to return. That old relationship mustn't start up again, not after all those months of pulling herself together enough to put him firmly from her mind. Yet he had been there all the time in the hidden recesses of her brain. All she could do was stiffen her body a little – not too much to seem cold but enough to convey the message she must express. And beside that, a certain amount of anger against him was making itself felt.

'You never wrote,' she heard herself accusing him. 'I never really thought I'd ever see you again, John, when you didn't write.' Immediately she hated the frigid tone of those statements.

If he noticed he made no sign. 'I've thought of no one but you, my love,' he continued. 'No matter where I was, you were there in my mind. I wanted to write but I wasn't sure you'd want me to.'

'Where've you been all the time then?' she cut in, tension giving the question an edge.

Her chagrin had got through to him at last. His voice lost some of its entreaty and became formal, conversational.

'Atlantic run, mainly. Merchant vessels.' He might have been talking merely to a friend.

'How was it?' she asked. Safer to keep to friendly tones. Easier too.

'Scary,' he replied briefly. 'U-boats, you know.'

Yes, she knew; tons of shipping were still being sunk, lives lost, all to get food to the nation. She shivered. 'But you were all right?'

'I'm here.' There was a hint of humour there, his arm tightened fractionally across her shoulder. But rather than give in to his hold, Brenda felt her muscles immediately tighten again. He must have felt them too for though his arm remained around her, its grip relaxed a little.

'You've not been sunk.' It sounded so lame that she added, 'Thank God.'

'No.' There was a pause, then, 'Not yet.'

Her reaction was immediate. There came an image of him lying on a raft in the middle of a featureless ocean burnished by a merciless sun, his lips cracked, his cheeks bearded, his comrades dying around him, of him too, close to death. Following immediately came another image, a body floating face down in that same empty ocean, its only movement a swaying with each oily wave. 'Oh, John! Don't say that!' she cried out.

Seconds later she was in his arms, being kissed by him, her hands behind his head pulling his face even harder against hers.

'I'm asking if you'd wait for me, Brenda,' he said, and she felt her relief almost attack her in a wave of guilt for thinking bad things of such a good man as he.

'Would you?' he pressed. But surely he knew that was impossible.

Misery swept over her. 'I can't do that,' she answered.

'But you love me. I know you do.'

Her mind was in a turmoil. 'There's Harry . . .'

She let her voice trail off. Did she still love Harry? No question that she loved John Stebbings, but was it only lust, an immediate need? Was she in such need that she could do this with him moments after seeing him again? Even now her heart was leaping towards this man. In frustration and sorrow she found herself beginning gently to weep.

'John, I can't.'

But already she had fallen into his arms again, lying weakly against him while he crooned against her ear, 'Wait for me, my darling, that's all I ask. I have to go back this afternoon. I came here only to see how you were. I didn't know this would happen. Now it has and I know you love me, I can never put you out of my mind. I'm not all that religious but I just hope the Man in Charge will see both of us safely through this war, and when it's over, you can make up your mind whether you want me or Harry. I don't want you ever to let yourself be swayed by false loyalty to either of us. It has to be your decision, my darling. I can wait because I know you love me.'

He was putting her gently from him. 'I have to go.'

In panic she reached for him as he got to his feet. 'No, not yet, John!'

'I have to. I have to meet my ship at Southampton. There's a train. The moment I am back in England I'll come straight here to you, darling. Just wait for me. Will you do that, my sweetheart?'

Would she do that? With Harry thousands of miles away with no likelihood of coming home in the near future, there was little else she could do but wait. She took charge of her wits and stood up.

'I'll wait,' she heard herself promise.

He kissed her and she went with him to the door to have him kiss her yet again. 'Keep safe, my own precious sweetheart,' he whispered and there was a catch in his throat.

'You too keep safe,' she returned, and the same catch was in her own throat.

She made herself swallow back the tears as she watched him walk away without looking back, as though to see her there would have made him retrace his foot-steps. And that he could not do. He was caught up in this war as much as anyone now.

Huddled in winter coats, scarves drawn tight over their heads, collars up against a bitter February wind, Brenda

320

and Daphne were glad to board the bus home when it finally decided to turn up.

They were only able to go to the pictures of an evening; Brenda now needed to have her salon open on Saturday afternoons. The bus was cold as they found seats halfway down and flopped gratefully into them, the pair of them still practically punch-drunk from seeing *Gone With The Wind* for the third time.

Showing in London since 1942, more than a year later it was still going strong, as Brenda and Daphne themselves could attest.

They'd taken to going to the pictures together once a week since last autumn. Daphne had suggested it in October on seeing how pale and drawn Brenda was looking, taking it to be because of concern over Harry far away in the thick of the fighting, even though the North African campaign looked to have turned their way.

The opening of the battle of El Alamein under General Montgomery's command had been startlingly spectacular on all the cinema newsreels. The desert night was lit up by the bombardment of over a thousand Allied guns, a continuous flashing of gunfire revealing line upon line of steel-helmeted Eighth Army infantry with fixed bayonets amid rapidly moving heavy armour. Even in the cinema it blinded the audience, bringing gasps of awe and pride from them, including the Hutton sisters-in-law.

It got Brenda out of herself going regularly to the pictures with her. Daphne would leave her baby son with Mrs Hutton, who was more than willing to have him and had practically taken over the rearing of him. The pliable Daphne seemed quite content for it to be so.

She'd had her baby with not too much trouble, though all through her labour she had bemoaned Bob's inability to come and see her and his new little son, whom she immediately christened Robert after his daddy.

Bob had been given leave a few weeks after, so Daphne hadn't had much to moan about after all.

'Wasn't it lovely?' sighed Daphne in retrospective appreciation of *Gone With The Wind* as the nasal command of the clippie assaulted their ears with 'Fares please!'

'I could see it all over again,' Daphne said as she offered their money to an uninterested clippie with scraped back mousy hair. On extracting the appropriate colour tickets from a flat board holding a large selection of colours depending on length of journey, she punched a hole in each with a ping of the ticket machine strapped to her chest, handed them over and passed on down the bus, continuing to call, 'Fares please,' all without looking once at the two women.

Daphne sighed again as she passed Brenda hers. 'I just love Clark Gable. I can't take me eyes off 'im.'

'Too sure of 'imself for me,' observed Brenda, taking her ticket to fiddle with the corners the rest of the journey. 'I like Leslie Howard the best. He's so kind and gentle and he gets so done down by that Scarlett O'Hara.'

In reality Leslie Howard reminded her of John Stebbings except that Howard was fair-haired and blue-eyed where John's hair was brown and his eyes so dark that in their sockets they looked like velvet.

Where was he now? The thought prompted a small prick of hurt anger. Not a word had arrived from him since he left, last October. Four months and not one single letter. So much for those promises to write to her.

At first she had waited on the post day after day, but the days of waiting for a letter had grown into weeks, then months. She'd given him the benefit of the doubt realising that he wouldn't be able to contact her when probably he was at sea in the mid-Atlantic most of the time. As time went by she'd grown fearful for him, then angry again, for if anything had happened to him she'd have found out. Then it occurred to her that nobody knew of their relationship, so who would be able to tell her? Fear and foreboding had taken over again.

But as time went by, though he flitted into her mind from time to time, she was coming to terms with it, as she must, except for an inner pang that he'd have contacted her if he'd been able to. This thought became one from which she turned stoically, trying to convince herself that there was nothing she could do in such a case. But if something had happened, surely she would have heard, would have known.

By February all that was left in an effort to still that fear was this diminished residue of anger: at him – no different from other men after all; at herself – fool to have believed him; finally resignation – far easier to bear than any of the other emotions because it took nothing out of her. She had to get on with life. There were Harry's letters to occupy her, to be answered swiftly. Often she wrote without receiving one, desperate to cling to a love that was sure and the hope of it being rekindled when he came home for good.

Brenda turned her mind to this evening's exciting newsreel in order to stop herself thinking.

'Things looking good in Tunisia according to the news,' she said to Daphne, breaking into her sister-in-law's train of thought about *Gone With The Wind* and the suave and captivating Rhett Butler. 'Let's 'ope it's the end of the beginning, as Churchill said, though what that's supposed to mean, I'm not sure.'

'What?' Daphne came to herself with a start. 'Oh, yeah, let's 'ope so. Though it don't seem much like it at 'ome. Not when we've still got blinking air raids.' They were now being blighted by occasional daylight raids, some of them disastrous. 'That one last month with that bomb falling on that school in Catford. No barrage balloons up, no air raid warning, nothing. It's a disgrace. Thirty-eight of 'em killed, poor little mites, and God knows 'ow many injured, and them only between five and eight.'

She shivered visibly, particularly touched now that she had a child of her own. So did Brenda, her thoughts turning to four-year-old Addie who this time next year would be at school herself. She consequently felt the weight of those tiny deaths perhaps more than Daphne did with her baby only five months old and not really a person yet.

'I had a letter from Harry yesterday,' she said to rid herself of feelings of dread. She adopted a tone of peevishness. 'Written before Christmas. I don't know what they do with our letters. He don't get mine regularly either.'

'It's the war,' Daphne said simply, and losing interest left it at that. Putting her ticket into her handbag she began gazing attentively as best she could towards the opposite window beyond the cluster of bodies standing in the aisle as their bus with its miserable pinpoints of dim blue lighting began to near familiar home ground.

This had to be estimated more by instinct than sight, for outside the windows there was only complete and absolute darkness as though no world existed beyond them.

Something in the back of Brenda's mind still leapt with anticipation at the flap of the letter box followed by the postwoman's sharp rat-tat-tat in the mornings. It was usually a postwoman these days with so few men other than elderly ones around.

She would make her way casually to pick up the post, bills usually, in their once, sometimes twice-used envelopes, sometimes an air letter from Harry bearing the unfeeling inscription ON ACTIVE SERVICE. But casual though she tried to be about it, there was no ignoring those brief heart-thumping seconds of hope that one day there might, just might, be a word from John.

It was now July. It would soon be a year since the day he'd appeared at her shop door. She should by now have put him from her mind but it wasn't that easy with the memory of that evening still lingering. Life, other than the joy her salon gave her, had become empty and humdrum. Those weekly Saturday night jaunts to the pictures with Daphne had come to a full stop. Daphne's baby, Robert, now on hands and knees, got into everything so that Mrs Hutton was not quite as rosy about giving eye to him these days. As a result outings had become few and far between.

All there was to look forward to each week was going to see her parents, going to see her in-laws, perhaps popping in to Daphne now and again for a chat. More than often this would be interrupted by Daphne running after little Robert as though the least movement away from her side would be his last. And of course she had the pleasure of waiting on Harry's letters.

Harry hadn't come home as she'd hoped. Once the North Africa campaign had been won, he and his lot had got sent straight on into Sicily. The greatly acclaimed Desert Rats did not have any leave granted in reward for all they'd gone through.

By the sound of his letters Sicily appeared a walkover compared to North Africa, but it still kept him away from her and Addie.

'Like your daddy said,' Brenda would say to her. 'You won't know him by the time he does come home.'

She would show her the photos he sent, of him all sunburnt and smiling with eyes squinting against the fierce Mediterranean light, his wide-brimmed hat cocked, his knees bared in shorts as he posed alone or with mates against a dry backdrop of flat white houses or pale bleached rocks or in the shade of a gnarled olive tree. He sent home little local gifts for Addie: a tiny hand-woven doll or a pretty coloured raffia bag, and some locally made bits and pieces for herself: a leather handbag amateurishly stitched, a leather purse, a brooch.

She'd tell Addie, 'Daddy sent this,' and would point him out in the photos he sent. 'This one's Daddy. Say Daddy. This one here. Say Daddy, darling.'

Dutifully, Addie would repeat 'Daddy,' parrot-fashion, but Brenda could never be certain if the word held any meaning for her. It was sad. It was hateful. It was this blasted rotten war!

Retrieving the mail that had been shot through the shop door, which was easier for the postie than climbing the iron staircase, Brenda picked out in a rush of gladness the flimsy blue air letter of Harry's from among the business stuff. It was then that she glimpsed another envelope, her name and address handwritten on its usual washed-out wartime paper.

Harry's letter forgotten, Brenda stared at it, turning it in her hands in an effort to guess its contents. Her heart had begun beating against her ribs with sickening thuds. The postmark looked faint and smudged, impossible to tell where it had been posted.

Well, read it! Urged an angry voice in her head, yet it took her a while to acknowledge it, until with feverish fingers she finally had to force herself to tear open the flap.

There was a single sheet of cheap lined notepaper. Unfolding it, she began to read with growing disappointment and anger. It was from her sister, the handwriting frantic. Not even beginning with 'Dear Brenda' but merely 'Brenda', it launched straight into the plight in which Vera found herself.

I'm in a terrible mess. I've written to you because you're the only one I can turn to. I'm being slung out of the forces because I've got myself pregnant. It's not Hank's fault. We got carried away and we forgot to take the usuals. When nothing happened I supposed we started to get careless and then it did happen. I didn't tell anyone but now I'm four months and the MO had to examine me. She tore me off a right strip and wanted to know who the father was, but I've not said because I didn't want to get Hank into trouble.

I hoped we could be married. He'd get permission from his commanding officer and we could make the baby legitimate. But now he's been sent overseas and I don't know where he is. He said he'd write and I'm still waiting for a letter.

I'm in a terrible state and I'm at my wits' end. I'll have to come home but I can't face telling Mum. I don't know what she'll say and how she's going to take it. I don't know what to do. I'll be home in a few days and I wondered if I can come and live with you and if you could break the news to Mum.

I know I can't keep the baby. I mean how will Mum and Dad face their neighbours with me all out in front and everyone knowing I'm not married? They'll point the finger and say there goes another tart got herself up the spout with a GI.

It's not fair, Hank and me love each other and I know he's going to write once he is where he's being sent to. But I don't want Mum to have to bear the brunt of wagging tongues, so that's why I wondered if I could come and live at your place. At least till the baby's born. I suppose I should of sorted out some way to of got an abortion, but it's Hank's baby and I love him – I couldn't of done that to him.

We will get married, when the war's over, or when he comes back, but he could even be sent straight home to the States for all we know. I'm in such a mess. Please help me Brenda. Love, Vera.

And here she had been expecting it to be a letter from John as she opened it. Her heart wrenched by disappointment, Brenda had to steel herself to think about her sister. How could she not help her? Nor could she bring herself to condemn her, knowing how exquisite, and foolhardy, it was to love someone so much that thought of the possible consequence fled in the heat of a moment. Hadn't she imagined she would never be caught out, and had she not almost rued it? No one had a right to point a finger at Vera, for there but for the grace of God . . .

After her day's work, and with Addie abed, Brenda wrote to Vera that, yes, there was a bed for her here for as long as she wanted, and yes, she would break the news to Mum, and she wondered even as she promised all these things, why she took on such problems. She only hoped that had anything like that happened to her, there'd have been someone there for her.

'I don't want nothink ter do with 'er. She ain't no daughter of mine!'

This burst forth from Dad, smoking one cigarette after another, just as Brenda was doing at this very moment in an effort to relieve her tension.

'Dad, she is yer daughter,' she began, but her mother intervened.

'You come and tell us news like this, Bren, and yer don't expect us ter be upset? 'Ow could yer come tellin' us news like this?'

'Mum, it's not me what's having the baby!' Brenda shot at her.

It calmed her mother and she lowered her voice. 'No, of course not, Bren,' but immediately she went back to her strident tone. 'But 'ow could she go askin' yer ter do 'er dirty work for 'er. She goes and gets 'erself in a state like that and leaves it ter ovvers ter sort it out fer 'er. Ain't got the courage ter face us, that's what.'

'She knew yer'd go off half-cocked, like yer doing now,' said Brenda, growing angry herself.

'Can yer wonder at it?' cried her mother. 'Me wiv a daughter what's got 'erself pregnant and then expects everyone ter welcome 'er 'ome with open arms an' say, "There ducks, we ain't angry, just come in and we'll let all the neighbours know our business when you start paradin' around like 'alf the size of a barrel, you go a'ead and 'ave yer baby 'cos we don't mind." If she expects that, then she's gonna get the biggest shock in the world.'

'She won't be coming home here,' explained Brenda. 'I've promised to put her up at my place.'

'Then yer a bloody fool! Takin' on a fing like that, yer a bloody fool! But then you always was,' said her dad, stubbing out his cigarette and with tense fingers starting to roll another while Brenda herself extracted a tailor-made one from an already half-empty packet.

She didn't want to smoke any more. Her throat was dry from it, but it was the only thing she could think of to keep her from tears as he continued, 'And don't fink yer can blackmail us inter takin' 'er in because you can't cope, because I'm done wiv 'er,' and Mum looked sad but nodded.

Later, Dad having gone off to his allotment, it being Sunday, probably to nurse his chagrin, Brenda and her mum were able to talk a little more rationally.

'Vera's being a fool ter believe this Yank bloke is goin' ter keep in touch,' Mum said as they sat on at the table over an after-dinner cup of tea. 'Everyone knows they're the love 'em and leave 'em sort. I mean, what 'ave they got ter lose, them from another country thousands of miles away. They can go back there after the war and forget all about the kids they left be'ind.'

She fiddled with the tablecloth, rolling it continuously between her fingers and thumbs in a nervous motion. 'I know I sounded terrible, talking about Vera that way. I still love 'er. She's me daughter. But I can't 'ave 'er bringin' 'ome shame like that. Can yer just imagine it, 'er all out in front and the neighbours talking be'ind our backs. I couldn't look no one in the face, as much as she's me daughter. But I'm worried. What's she goin' ter do? 'Ow's she goin' ter cope on 'er own wiv no 'usband, the baby without no father? 'Ow will she live? She'll never be able ter hold 'er 'ead up.'

Brenda leaned forward and covered her mother's hands with one of her own, stopping their fiddling. 'Look, Mum, she's going to stay with me. I'll look after 'er. We ain't got that many neighbours to worry about, so she'll be all right. And once the baby comes, Vera can help me in the salon. I'll teach her. She always did want to be a hairdresser. So now'll be her chance.'

'It'll 'ave ter be adopted,' went on her mother as though she hadn't heard. 'She'll never find 'erself a bloke ter marry, 'er with a baby in tow.'

Chapter Twenty-four

There had been tears from Vera when she arrived looking peaky and downcast. There had been abject apologies for putting her sister to so much trouble. There had been profuse gratitude, and promises not to make too much of a nuisance of herself. There had been recriminations, not from Brenda but from her family, aunts talking aside or covertly seeking details if the family met, the uncles openly ignoring the business, cousins smirking. Brenda had kept very quiet about it to Harry's family and although they finally did find out, none of them actually referred to it.

She wrote to Harry about it, because after all, Vera was living in his flat. He wrote back saying that she couldn't go on staying there once he was home. Brenda did not reply to that, deeming it best to let sleeping dogs lie for the time being. Perhaps by the time he did come home for good, Vera would have sorted herself out.

Vera proved to be no trouble. She had heard from her Hank and was reassured of his continuing love. His letters came from Italy where he was fighting the Germans,

Italy having signed an armistice with the Allies early in September. Harry too was now in Italy so she and Vera had plenty to talk about. It was good having her here giving eye to Addie while Brenda worked; Mrs Page would no longer be needed, which helped save money.

But as time progressed Vera, waddling about the flat with increasing awkwardness, talked of being cooped up and trapped. She had grown enormous and wasn't carrying her baby easily, so Mum was more often there than not.

'I think you should go back to the doctor's to be checked out,' Brenda advised. 'You look far too big for just one baby to me.'

Vera had mentioned that at one time Hank had spoken of twins being prevalent in his family.

'What if you was carrying twins?'

Vera looked aghast. 'I can't be! You can't look after two of 'em!'

Some time ago Vera had become agitated at talk of her baby being adopted, saying it was his baby, she'd told him about it, he wanted to keep it and so did she. She'd refused to see that it was out of the question. But Brenda and Mum had sneaky feelings that for all his letters, when it came down to it he'd chicken out, go home to Illinois and peace of mind to settle down and marry some nice untarnished American girl from his home town.

In the end, taking pity on her, Brenda had been fool enough to remark that she might be able to take the baby on while Vera went looking for a job or helped out in the salon. She'd immediately regretted it as Vera took it as gospel. She settled back in relief, saying that the baby could always be passed off to any outside nosy parkers as one Brenda was fostering for someone, having a natural affection for children and a need for a bit more money. Brenda had been taken aback by her assumptions, but hadn't said much until by now it was too late. Maybe she could manage, she had speculated. But twins?

'If it turns out that way, I couldn't look after two, Vera.'

The result was wailing and weeping and flopping about the flat in lethargic misery. But Brenda was resolute. She couldn't take on two babies. Not in a million years. If it did turn out to be twins, then the solution must be the more painful one. Hank or no Hank, they would have to be adopted. Brenda steeled her heart to it as, still tearful and full of fear, Vera allowed herself to be carted off to the doctor who'd been keeping a check on her, making sure she was drawing her allowance of vitamins and doing all she'd been told to do. All this occurred without a bat of an eyelid at her unmarried state though Vera made a point of visiting him as little as possible, even missing appointments if she could.

But when at his expert probing twins were confirmed and Vera went ashen-faced, all Brenda's resolve melted. 'Let's see how it goes,' was all she could say on the way home, at the same time biting her tongue that she was in actual fact already committing herself with those five small words as her sister's face regained its natural colouring, her blue eyes glowing again.

Within an hour of getting home, Vera was writing of the good news to her Hank.

*

Just one more day to go to the birth. Mum was coming round early, despite the cold January morning, so as to stay with Addie should anything happen and Brenda be needed to go in the ambulance with Vera to the hospital.

'Yer usually late with yer first one,' she predicted. 'But just ter be on the safe side, I'd better stay on overnight. Yer dad'll be orright on 'is own.'

That morning before Mum got here, Brenda went down to open up. Young Joan, now nearly sixteen, had been promoted a while ago to washing hair, and under Brenda's tuition was proving herself skilled at cutting and setting so long as it wasn't complicated. There was now another young girl, Betty, to sweep up, clean sinks and make tea for any customer bringing a little from out of their own rations. Brenda had wisely avoided taking any appointments for perms or other jobs that might tax Joan's new skills until after Vera had given birth, though it meant losing money.

With Joan and the other girl still to arrive, Brenda was contemplating making herself a quick cup of tea when the post flopped through the letter box. Leaving the gas unlit beneath the kettle, her heart going pitter-patter, she hurried to the door with her usual hope that one day there'd be a letter from John among it, though she told herself it was Harry's letter she was really awaiting. That way it made her feel better.

There was no letter from Harry, but there was an envelope of decent quality paper addressed to her personally, typewritten and with the name Duncan, Simpson and Peaking, Solicitors, etched in faded wartime ink across the top.

Why should unfamiliar solicitors be writing to her? Quickly she ripped it open, thinking as she did so that she should have paused to find the paper knife so as to save the envelope for re-use. Slightly bemused, she opened the single sheet with its heading in the same faded ink and found herself being requested to attend these people's offices in Leytonstone where she would hear something to her advantage. The letter went on to explain that the writer was acting for the late John Edward Stebbings of a Leytonstone address which she recognised instantly as the house John owned. But it was the single word 'late' that leapt out at her, hitting her like a hefty punch between the eyes.

Hardly able to breathe, she sank down on one of the chairs facing the mirrors, her legs too weak to bear her weight. Her half-focused reflection gazed back, chalk-white.

The *late* John Stebbings . . . The implication was unbearable. There had to be a mistake.

She became aware of Vera calling out to her from the back kitchen. Vera must have come down the outside stairs to find her. The thought came of its own accord even as she fought to make sense of what she had read. It came to her also that the voice was raised in panic. 'Brenda! Oh, God, Brenda!'

For a moment she had the impression that the voice was her own, then, 'I think I've started! Bren, come quick!'

As if propelled, Brenda started up, ran for the kitchen. It was a pure reflex action almost as if to escape that which was going through her head.

336

She reached the kitchen, an automaton. 'What's the matter?'

But she already knew what was the matter seeing Vera double over, clutching her stomach with one hand and holding on to the table edge with the other, her face screwed in agony.

'You can't 'ave, not yet,' Brenda heard herself crying as she grabbed a chair and tried to push Vera down on to it. 'You get nagging pains first – for ages.'

'I 'ad them all day yesterday and on and off all through the night.'

'Why didn't you wake me? Why didn't you say?'

'I just thought I 'ad wind. We 'ad that tin of baked beans yesterday. I thought it was them.'

Brenda's mind was flying in several different directions at once. Get to the phone and call an ambulance. But what if Mum didn't get here, what would she do with Addie? There were clients coming through the door any moment now, she'd have to tell them to go home. Could Joan cope? What a way to run a business. And all the time at the back of her mind was the contents of that solicitor's letter, making her feel sick . . .

'Stay where you are,' she commanded as a fierce cry was ripped from Vera. 'Try to relax. You'll be orright. I'm going ter phone for an ambulance.' Addie would just have to be dragged out of bed and go with them.

The phone to her ear, Brenda felt faint, felt the floor wanted to come up and meet her, that it was wavering unsteadily under her feet, no longer solid. The words *the late John Edward Stebbings* were pounding in her brain. She mustn't give way – mustn't faint. A woman's voice smote her eardrum and the floor instantly steadied, stopped moving about.

'Can you send an ambulance to Brenda's Place,' she began, slowly and distinctly, again in charge of herself. 'It's the hairdresser's in Mile End Road. For Vera Wilson – booked in at the London Hospital – she's having her baby.' She began to say the road number, but the woman stopped her with a cheery, 'Yes, I know, I've had my hair done there before now. I'm—'

But Brenda had no care for small talk. 'Can you send an ambulance straight away? It's urgent,' she interrupted and the voice became efficient.

'It'll be with you within a short while. OK?'

Brenda sat in Mr Duncan's cramped little office above the premises of Lee Dairies in Leytonstone, the room made even more sombre by the scudding clouds and driving sleet outside.

She had travelled here by bus, fighting the elements with an umbrella that threatened to turn inside out, water splashing up into her shoes, her raincoat and handbag streaked with wet for all the brolly's protection.

Now, with it draining off into the trough of the hatstand on which her damp mac hung, she sat tense and dry-eyed. The dull empty pain inside her ironically proved an effective barrier to tears as she listened to Mr Duncan telling her that his late client, John Stebbings, had made a will on entering the Merchant Navy last year to the effect that should he be killed – Brenda felt herself cringe from the cold sound of that phrase – his entire estate was to go to Mrs Brenda Hutton, named as his sole beneficiary being that he had no living relative.

'So, Mrs Hutton,' beamed the man, having read it out, appearing not to notice the pale, stiff features facing him, 'as you see, there is no money involved, merely a few items of jewellery, not terribly valuable, and the house and its contents. At today's prices the house itself will realise, being wartime and with few people interested in house-buying, I should say around seven hundred pound or so. It is quite a large house, Victorian, but in quite good order and you might find an interested buyer with an eye to the future after the war. As for the furniture, I don't think it will fetch in any great sums. But if you wish to sell the house, I could act for you, of course.'

No, she did not wish to sell. What to do with it she had no idea, but she didn't wish to sell. And erase the last trace of him? No. All the while the solicitor was speaking the dull pain persisted, spreading through her body from some region around her heart; not a true pain, more a dark void, but as awful as any physical agony. How could she be sitting here discussing the disposal of the house which the man she had loved so much had left to her when her heart could only long to have him here again beside her?

Her brain seemed incapable of thought, or rather it blocked thought as though not to would have had her bursting into tears, and that she was not going to do in front of this man with his cold, efficient smile. No emotion, no sympathy. She was a mere friend; it was in his expression as he beamed coldly (how a smile could be a beam and yet remain cold was one of the mysteries of his profession, she supposed) that the deceased could as easily have left it to some charity as to this woman, whoever she was. Apparently the documents had made

339

no mention of any relationship she and John once had, and if this man suspected anything, he wasn't letting on.

There would be no one she could tell about the house and already it was beginning to weigh on her. She came away from the solicitor's office feeling as though she had taken sleeping pills and was walking in a dream, the pavement seeming to be made of rubber. And all the while her heart was crying inside her for the man she would never again set eyes on. He had died at sea, sunk with his ship. Vanished completely. All she had left of him were her memories, and a large empty house!

Six weeks now and still Brenda hadn't been able to bring herself to go and see the house in Leytonstone. What state must it be in with no one there to tend it? Nothing would induce her to go and find out. The mere thought made it feel as though she'd be violating the love they had known, making it mercenary. It could stay as it was. People had grown accustomed to properties lying empty, but did they know the owner had died? Would they wonder if she presented herself there, letting herself in with the key that the solicitor had handed over? She didn't want to have to explain herself to some inquisitive neighbour. But one day she would have to visit there.

Anyway, for the moment her time was taken up by Vera's babies. The birth had been hard and prolonged, being her first. It had been strange to see no man present when finally Brenda had been let into the ward to see her sister's white and drained face looking up at her. She had said that Vera's husband was away in Italy, fighting, and whether the nurses believed her or not she didn't care. Poor Vera's hollow eyes invoked Brenda's pity;

there was no husband and no man to comfort her and hold his children with pride.

'He won't desert me, will 'e?' Vera had moaned at one time. Brenda reassured her with, 'Of course he won't. He's stuck by you so far, 'asn't he?'

After a month, Brenda had begun to wonder what she'd let herself in for. The two boys took turns to cry and often cried together. They were utterly identical. Henry was named after his father in the hope that one day it would be changed to Hank, and the other one was called Samuel. Sam sounded very American, rather like Uncle Sam. Vera was insistent despite faces pulled by Brenda and Mum. With Vera not coping too well as yet, Brenda would regularly find herself at her wits' end.

Vera was constantly weepy, bucking up only when a letter from Hank arrived but in between full of doubt as to his loyalty. It took all Brenda's resources trying to convince her that he'd never let her down. 'Look what you read in his letters,' she reminded her sister, 'saying how proud he is and can't wait to see his sons.' But at times she could feel it all getting on top of her, never mind Vera. And she had a business to run.

The place was growing ever busier. Many women had become sufficiently inured to the war to give more time to themselves. Some, now long liberated from absent husbands, had started going out and about with like-minded friends and needed to look good. This went on despite heavy air raids having started up again since the last week of January after a virtual lull since the blitz at the beginning of the war.

The Little Blitz, as it was being called, was still going on as February came and went. The duration of the raids was not as long as in the earlier Blitz and they were more irregular. But they were far more intensive and concentrated with larger bombs and more aircraft – on one occasion nearly three hundred reported – so that just as many homes were being devastated and people killed as in any raid during that first blitz. They went for other cities and regions too, Hull, Bristol, South Wales, though once more London was taking the brunt of it.

Churchill was warning everyone that there could even be newer and more devastating forms of attack. He never said what, only that 'Britain can take it!' and that 'the hour of our greatest effort and action is approaching', and that the flashing eyes of their soldiers, sailors and airmen must be fixed on their front and the only homeward journey for all of them lay through the 'Arch of Victory'.

These remarks generated the certainty that the long-spoken-of Second Front would not be long in coming. Though exactly when, no one knew. Meantime they'd put up with continuing air raids and *take it* just as Churchill said. Taking it, the women continued to pop into Brenda's Place to have their hair done so as to look nice – almost as a sort of defiance of Hitler. Consequently Brenda had her hands kept full.

'Perhaps you'd help me,' she suggested to Vera in an effort to get her sister out of her doldrums. But understandably Vera wasn't too keen as yet to leave her four-week-old babies. She'd spend nearly all her time cuddling and crooning over them so long as they were good. When they weren't, their crying would send her into fits of sobbing and seeking help, saying that she couldn't cope with it all.

Mum was a tower of strength. Despite the air raids which so far this time had left her still only half-restored home unscathed, she'd toddle round each morning, fair weather or foul, to give eye to them. 'I've got nothink else much ter do,' she would say. 'Livin' downstairs like we do, the place don't take much lookin' after, an' yer Dad's at work. I can be of more 'elp 'ere.'

Addie of course was now at the local infants' school, lapping up being with other children, and was no trouble to anyone, though Brenda died small deaths whenever the warning went if Addie was there at school.

The babies were crying in the background and Vera held a hand to her forehead while Mum replaced soiled terry-towel nappies with fresh ones as Brenda stood opening a letter from Harry while she fought to ignore the chaos.

His letters came slightly more regularly these days. This one was dated the first of June, to her relief saying that he hadn't been so much in the fighting but repairing and driving supply trucks.

'I'm getting to be quite a skilled mechanic,' he wrote. 'Maybe after the war I'll make it me trade instead of going back to being a warehouseman.'

This letter, like his others, was full of accounts of the Italian people, and the landscape too, maybe to give clues as to where exactly he was. But it was already being reported in detail. Now the Allies were forging ahead, Italy having last year declared war on Germany for all the Italians had let themselves be disarmed by the Germans.

Harry's letters from Sicily had hardly mentioned the place apart from a few words on Mount Etna and that it was a dry sort of island. He'd only been there for just over a month with Sicily falling quickly to the Allies. But of Italy Harry waxed poetic, about how easy-going the people were, how friendly they were, how he'd recently been made welcome by a family not far from Rome now that the area had been taken from the Germans.

Their name's Alvaro. They're a really nice family. Very sociable. They keep wanting to feed me up. Said I'm too thin and they stuff me full of pasta and things. Funny stuff pasta. I ain't all that keen on it but you've got to be sort of sociable. I was given leave so I've been to see them quite a bit. Mr Alvaro looks quite elderly really. Face all lined and creased. But he can't be that old because he's got two smashing daughters about twenty-something. Probably the heat and dry weather what does it. His wife's short and plump and keeps reaching up and patting my face. The girls are called Maria and Luisa. She spelt that out for me so I know I got it right. They're both of them smashing-looking. I'm being treated like a prince . . .

Brenda ignored a small stab of jealousy the letter provoked, her laugh somewhat caustic as she thought, 'I bet you are – with two smashing daughters at yer beck and call,' and went to tell Vera, a little sharply, that changing nappies should really be her job, not Mum's, before going down to open up the salon.

For some reason as she put the letter aside, her times with John Stebbings flashed into her head carrying the usual twinge of sorrow. A vague thought came that if she could do what she had done, Harry could easily do the same with one of those daughters, but she quickly and angrily shrugged it away. If there was anything developing, Harry would be keeping it quiet, wouldn't he?

His next letter held no mention of them, nor did the one after. Brenda put it out of her mind as he wrote of the possibility of eventually being moved on further north with one after another Italian town being won from the Germans. Besides, there was much more to think about now. Exciting news for everyone, yet sobering lest it end up another Dunkirk. Though this time no one really thought so.

It was on everyone's lips – the invasion of Europe. D-Day. For the last fortnight every ear had been trained on Home Service news bulletins with maybe the only bit of light comedy allowed to intervene being *ITMA*. Never had so many newspapers been sold; every face was buried in one, in the street, in offices, in factories and shops during break times, in the home, as every foot of progress by the Allies got devoured.

Like following the football results, Brenda thought as she read as avidly as anyone, with a touch of guilt at her own flippancy, because men didn't die in football matches. Even so, people's hearts needed lifting; for all the good news that was coming out of Europe and the Far East too there was still much to be faced at home.

It was only three weeks ago that Brenda and Vera had thrown open the window to an unusual sound like that of an aeroplane in trouble and gazed up at the night sky. In Bow Road a murmur of wonder had risen as dozens of others stood also gazing upwards at what appeared to be an enemy bomber on fire. As the engine cut out and the plane fell out of the sky to crash not far away with a gigantic explosion that lit up the horizon, a cheer went up, forgetting those on whom the stricken plane must have landed. Minutes later another plane appeared with fire belching from its rear end, spluttering loudly before cutting out to topple earthward with another mighty explosion. This time the cheering from below was slightly laced with bewilderment. Even Brenda turned in wonderment to her sister.

'Fancy shooting 'em down as easy as that. Funny though, I didn't hear any gunfire, did you? There ain't been any sirens either.'

With a third plane, again with its rear end on fire and its engine growling like some badly maintained motorbike to splutter into silence with only the sigh of the air over the wings, and again followed by an explosion, this time nearer, there was no cheering.

Brenda's own words echoed what others must have been thinking as she again turned to Vera with a shudder. 'Something very odd's going on. I don't like it.' Nor did Vera, her eyes wide with the same nameless uncertainty.

They were to find out a few days later that what they'd witnessed was one of the 'new forms of attack' to which Churchill had referred. Three days later a general alert sounded across London and the Home Counties. It lasted all night, everyone flocking back into air raid shelters as an endless onslaught of what was now termed the V1 growled low overhead to fall randomly on running out of fuel. After that they came by day and night.

Pilotless planes or the flying bomb the Government called them. 'Buzz-bombs' and 'doodlebugs' they were dubbed by an irreverent public.

But for all the sneers the now familiar ragged and ominous growl sent chills up the spine as listeners waited, tense, ready to duck as soon as the engine failed. Bated breath would be expelled if it continued on its noisy path. If it didn't then all eyes would be trained on the direction it took, each trying to calculate where it would fall. With the tall plume of smoke rising from an explosion a short way off, the response was a sigh of relief that this time it wasn't here. It was when it cut out directly overhead that people threw themselves to the ground.

'It's like one of them plague things,' Vera said fearfully. 'Yer can't even see 'em when it's cloudy, but they're there, and one could drop on us any time and we wouldn't know it.'

Oh, we might, thought Brenda but best not to frighten Vera any further. Her fear was more for her little ones than herself.

Brenda, too, thought of her child. Now Addie was at school, she prayed that no buzz-bomb would ever fall on that building. At night she could protect her, or at least felt that if they went, they would go together, so that neither one would be left to mourn.

She had reinstalled beds down in the cellar, made it into a little home from home for her, Addie, Vera and the little twins. Being down there often brought back a poignant memory. Sometimes she would look up from her pillow as one doodlebug after another growled overhead, and half expect to see John Stebbings ducking his head under the lintel over the stairs, one slim arm hanging on to it for balance, to ask if she was OK.

The memory always brought a hollow ache to her heart, but only momentarily as yet another grating roar passing overhead forced her mind back to the present. A direct hit could devastate even a basement, taking its occupants with it. But it was when Addie was at school that she suffered most. What if one day . . . and Harry away fighting, having to be told? God, it was an awful thought! What awful times they lived in!

Those who could afford it had left London. Another official evacuation of children started and Brenda was of a mind to let Addie go. She herself couldn't with a business to run but she urged Vera to take the opportunity being offered to mothers and babies to go away, taking Addie with her. Mum urged her as well, but for all Vera's fears it was like trying to move a block of concrete and by the time she agreed, it all came to an end. After two months with literally hundreds of the blighters coming over, their numbers had dwindled to just an odd few. Hitler's secret weapon had been defeated by a great massing of ack-ack guns all along the south and east coasts. London had taken it yet again and had again triumphed. Brenda wrote to Harry of her relief and to say that so far they were all fine and safe.

The raids had left her feeling much stronger in mind. Prior to that she had never been able to bring herself to set foot in the basement for the memories it held for her. Maybe she had laid John's ghost to rest by using it again, at long last able to face life without him though she would never forget him or the feelings he had aroused in her. But now she felt she could deal with them enough to turn her mind to other things – like taking a look at the house in Leytonstone, perhaps?

Chapter Twenty-five

In his room at the top of the Alvaro house where he was still billeted – his job these days was to repair trucks and lorries – Harry read Brenda's latest letter that the attacks by doodlebugs were a lot less frequent than they had been.

She'd written several letters during the height of the attacks and he had feared for Addie. For Brenda too, of course. But she seemed to be doing pretty well, talking about her hairdressing business. She sounded quite independent these days, didn't need his help. Reading, Harry would feel a sharp, almost hostile prickle of inadequacy. If he was home he'd put a stop to all that fancy lark of hers. She was his wife with him the breadwinner. But he wasn't there to win the bread, and the feelings of hostility mounted.

She wrote about Vera and her twins, producing a sneer from him every time. Bloody fool taking things on like that, making a rod for her own back. Hadn't got the brains she was born with. Well, when he got back home, he'd put her right and Vera would get her marching orders.

He knew it was distance that was making him feel so hostile. With Brenda so far away, any differences that would have been patched up in minutes if he were at home could not be mended from here. He did love her. He did fear for her. He did long for her. But after all these years away, sometimes she seemed a stranger. Probably he was a stranger to her for all her loving words. At one time her letters had lost some of their affection and he'd been worried. But now she was again full of all the lovey-doveys under the sun, and ironically it was that which was causing him some guilt.

'He says Davy and Brian'll be all right,' said Brenda, reading part of Harry's letter out loud to her mum and dad, who had come round to Sunday tea.

Her dad had at last come round to his younger daughter's situation and after all her babies were his grandchildren.

'Orright?' he echoed sourly. 'Them in the thick of the invasion and 'e thinks they'll be all orright. Because 'e's got through OK, don't mean—'

'He didn't get through OK,' interrupted Annie, looking hastily at her older daughter. 'He got wounded in North Africa, remember?'

'A scratch.'

'It weren't a scratch,' exclaimed Brenda. Needled by his attitude, her carefully nurtured accents went instantly out of the window. 'It put 'im in hospital fer ages. I thought they'd of sent 'im 'ome, but all they did was patch 'im up an' send 'im back, but it weren't no blooming scratch!'

'All I'm tryin' ter say is my boys could get wounded too,' insisted David. 'So 'ow can 'e say they'll be orright?

Just 'cos our blokes is forging ahead like a bloody 'ouse on fire, don't mean none of 'em won't get theirs.'

'I don't want ter think of that, thank you!' cried Annie. 'P'raps it don't touch you like it do me, but yer could think of others' feelings, sayin' things like them gettin' wounded or . . .' She did not further that thought.

'And there's my Hank,' said Vera, 'out in Italy. Harry might be OK at the moment, out of the fighting, but Hank ain't.'

'We don't want ter 'ear nothink about your 'Ank,' her father cut in, banging his teacup down into its saucer. ''E ain't yer 'usband and the least said of 'im the better.'

It was mid-August, the idyll of these last two months gone as Harry said goodbye to the Alvaro family, and it felt like his heart was breaking.

He was being called back into the fighting. Churchill had been to Italy on a visit to Allied Headquarters and on a wave of elation, the British Army was surging northward. Florence was their objective, to sweep the Germans out of the country as soon as possible their goal. And now he was being ordered to leave this little paradise that he had mistakenly imagined he could inhabit forever.

Luisa, in tears, was being comforted by her mother's stout arms. The weeping girl stood far taller than her mother, and needed to bend to bury her head in the ample bosom.

'You will come back,' her mother was saying in Italian. Her words were translated by Maria, who spoke a little English, as did her sister, each often taking turns to explain what their parents said, though today it was beyond Luisa to do anything but cry.

Harry, having picked up a little of the language, lifted his shoulders despairingly in reply, and indeed felt genuine despair. In the weeks he'd been here, he and Luisa had grown close. Too close for someone who should have known he was only passing through. She was the sweetest, most gentle-natured, loving and most trusting girl he'd ever met, and he'd fallen in love with her. He had pushed away the guilt of knowing himself married. So many times he would think about it after they had made love, and it would tear at him knowing his infidelity would always have to be kept secret from Brenda.

It had come about almost without him realising it. He'd been attracted to Luisa from the start, both her and her sister. With their long, shiny, deep brown hair, their dark Italian eyes and the slim figure most young Italian girls seemed to possess, they had caught his eye, but it was Luisa to whom he had spoken the most, her command of English being more than Maria's. She had told him about her family, her father who was a shoe repairer. Living on the outskirts of Rome the war had more or less passed them by until, with Italy changing sides, the Allies had come swooping up from the south to fight Germans and shatter the tranquillity they had known.

Harry listened to it all and felt more sympathy for a girl caught up in war than he needed to, and he had loved the way she spoke. One evening when they were alone he'd kissed her, on impulse because her lips had been so close to his and so tempting. She hadn't drawn away and from then on it had been a matter of each wanting something more than just a kiss. Her parents, simple folk who did not see beyond their small world, smiled and nodded, happy to see their daughter courted by – and they had been very candid about it – such a handsome young soldier. Probably they, like him, thought it could go on forever. But the war still went on and he had to follow orders. The lovely days and nights together had come to an end too quickly.

He would see Luisa again; he could not bear thinking that this was final. He told her so. Her parents too, with gestures and Maria interpreting. He said with his eyes on the weeping Luisa, looking so frail in her grief, 'I mean ter come back, no matter what, and that's a promise.'

It must have sounded far more romantic in Maria's Italian version, for as Luisa lifted her face from her mother's bosom to gaze at him, her eyes glistened with hope through their tears so that he smiled tenderly at her, his whole heart revealed in that smile.

'This ain't really goodbye,' he told her, and in halting Italian, added, 'I love you, Luisa. When the war is over, I will return to you.'

In response she propelled herself away from her mother to throw herself into his arms, and he held her tight while her family looked on, Maria with envious eyes, the parents beaming approval. He had never told them he was married. Luisa didn't know either. Maybe that had been underhanded but as he felt at this moment he really meant what he'd said. After the war, if at all possible, he would come back. There was a lump in his throat and Brenda seemed to be fading to a vague shadow, hardly discernible.

Two hours later, having joined his unit being transported north to the fighting around Florence, normality had taken over again. He would never come back. It wasn't logical to think he would. Here was the real world. Brenda, waiting for him back home, was his real world. Two brief months of Luisa had been just dreaming. But into his heart came a strong conviction that back there he had already left something of himself with Luisa; that nine months from now there would be a little likeness of himself whimpering in the tender care of the Alvaro family, for Luisa, as the strong Catholic she was, had refused any unsanctioned protection.

Time and the speeding miles reawakened his common sense to override the pain of separation and told him as they drove northward that of course he would never go back, that it would be senseless to make enquiries and heap a load of trouble on himself. If Brenda ever found out . . .

With that thought, Brenda grew clear in his mind again. At this very moment waiting for him, keeping herself for him, how could he ever spring a thing like that on her? Best not to delve. Luisa with her loving family would be supported by them, surely. How many other young Italian girls were being left behind in this war to bear fatherless children? It wouldn't stigmatise her. She would confess her sins to her priest, do a small penance and receive forgiveness, or whatever, and everyone would surely understand and be ready to help. Not like people at home who'd point a finger to every erring girl as they went by.

With this convincing if misguided argument, Harry was able to comfort himself. But he would never forget her, and he knew he'd always be left wondering at times that somewhere . . .

Quickly, Harry shut down the thought and turned to the future as the convoy sped onwards.

The invasion of Europe had uncovered many of Hitler's secret weapon launchers, though not all, and the doodle-bug, if in sparser numbers, still drifted on through the summer. Most people, even Vera, had become inured to them, though they still killed.

Harry's mother was more incensed by them than alarmed, and would chide her husband at his concern for his family's safety. It served to irritate Brenda into defending the mild-mannered man when she went round there, especially when the chiding was directed at Daphne. Despite having turned into a capable mother to the two-year-old Robert, she was still unable to say boo to a goose where her mother-in-law was concerned and seemed quite willing to accept being walked all over by her.

'Why don't you stand up to her more?' challenged Brenda after the senior Mrs Hutton had practically ordered Daphne to stop moping over Bob. 'You let her boss you about like you was some kid instead of a mum.'

'She don't realise she's doing it,' was Daphne's excuse. 'Besides, I suppose I do mope after 'im. It's that I get so worried with 'im over there. I don't know 'ow you've stood it with Harry away all these years out there in Italy. Bob's only bin away three months.'

Bob had gone over in the first wave of troops. But so had Davy and Brian, her own brothers, and she, Vera, Mum and Dad were all worried for *their* well-being. Daphne's husband wasn't the only one, and Brenda could quite see how Mrs Hutton would be short with Daphne at times.

'We've all got someone over there,' she reminded her. 'There, or in Italy, or in the Far East. We just 'ave ter pray they keep safe.' At which Daphne had given her a look as if she'd cast a spell on all their safety.

Early in September there came something else to worry about as, without a doodlebug anywhere near, came a low but tremendous explosion, more like a terrific blast wave, that rattled the windows of Brenda's salon. Everyone, apart from the one with her hair securely strung up to the overhead perming machine, rushed with wet locks or hair partly in curlers or only partly cut to see what was going on. Seconds later, joined by scores of other spectators along Bow Road, they saw the cloud of smoke rising slowly over the rooftops to the south-west, low down and paled by distance.

'I reckon that's a factory gorn up somewhere,' came a speculation.

'Alan an' 'Amburies in Bethnal Green, d'yer fink?' Alan and Hanbury dealt in medical supplies. It had been hit during the last war.

'More like somewhere round the docks?'

'It looks a lot farver off than that.'

'I bet it's sabotage. I bet it's Fifth Columnists.'

'They don't blow fings up. They just spread rumours an' fings and take secrets back ter old Adolf!'

'Them's spies, not Fifth Columnists.'

'Well, I don't know, do I? But it was a blinking big explosion fer bein' all that far away, don't matter what yer say.'

It took all Brenda's efforts to persuade them back inside which they did in a trickle, returning to their chairs for her and young Joan to get on with them while they treated the woman trapped by her heated perming curlers to their opinions on the distant smoke they'd seen. The woman's face turned pale. 'I hope nuffink's 'appened to me 'ome.'

'No – more like a factory of some sort gorn up near the docks.'

'I did say it weren't the docks,' insisted the woman with only half her hair in curlers, the rest of which Brenda resumed putting in. 'The docks is sarf of 'ere. That was west,' she added assertively, wincing and drawing in a sharply overdone breath at a too-tight curler. Brenda hurriedly apologised.

'Well, I don't know.' There came an easy-going giggle. 'I can't tell west from east, norf from sarf. All I know, somefink's got blown up. Some sort of accident I expect.'

Later they were to learn the truth. Hitler's second secret weapon, the V2. Packed with high explosives, launched fifty miles into the stratosphere to travel faster than sound so that the first intimation of it would be the detonation which many were never to hear at all.

'I don't think these rockets worry me as much as them doodlebugs did,' announced Brenda to her mother when she arrived one morning while Brenda was eating her breakfast of jam on toast. 'Them doodlebugs put the fear of God up you when you heard them coming, but not knowing these are coming ain't half as . . .' Hardly had the words left her lips than an unexpected if distant explosion rocked the flat, making her jump nigh out of her skin, and some of the tea she was sipping spilled into the butter dish with its two-ounce ration for the week.

Mum, unruffled, stared down at the dish now awash with tea. 'I see – orright then – look what yer done ter yer bit of butter ration then,' was all she said.

There was nothing one could do about V2s. No warning came either by siren or sound. You just had to get on with life, like it or lump it. Brenda, having plucked up her courage for a completely different reason, finally visited the house in Leytonstone one Sunday morning, leaving Addie with Vera and her two little cousins whom she loved dearly.

It took a while to find the street, then the house. When she finally did, she could only stand looking at it for what seemed ages. Terraced, it had a bay window on the ground floor and one upstairs, and a wide door with a stained-glass panel set back in a porch. There were heavy net curtains at the windows which she hadn't expected to see in an empty house. There was no gate to the front garden; most iron gates had gone for the war effort long ago.

Each step required an effort of willpower as finally she made her way along the black-and-white tiled front garden path. The lawn beside it had long got out of hand, the seeded grass obscuring any plants there might have been but for a straggle of bush roses now inundated by suckers, while weeds grew high against the wooden boundary wall to the next door house.

Finding the key the solicitor had given her, she put it in the door and feeling like an interloper turned it, the door opening to her tentative push. She was met by the musty, closed-up smell of any place left vacant for any length of time. She stood uncertainly in the hallway, which looked far larger than she had imagined. At her feet lay a few bits of mail; no doubt they had not been picked up by the solicitor's people who dealt with such things.

Feeling it wasn't her place to inspect them, she stepped over them instead, making her way slowly, quietly, as though any heavier footfall might disturb someone, to the door of the front room. It stood slightly ajar giving her the impression that someone was indeed in the house. There was no one, though, all was still. Taking a deep breath she pushed the door further open.

The room was quite large, the ceiling high. But what struck home most was the sense that someone had only just left. The large three-piece suite in brown patterned moquette still showed indentations, almost as if John had only this minute got up from either a chair or the sofa. A shiver ran through her leaving in its wake an empty place in her breast. The brown and fawn curtains looked as if they had only a moment ago been pulled back. On a side table lay a cigarette box, a bulbous chrome table cigarette lighter, a book, a small lamp. The rug in front of the fire-place still bore imprints of shoes. There was a sideboard holding a couple of ornaments, some writing material, a small mound of letters and envelopes, and several books. Two bookshelves had several of their books leaning at an angle against others just as he'd left them, and Brenda had the sensation that at any minute he would enter the room or get up from an armchair to put them straight.

It was eerie. Everything remained as he had left it the day he'd gone off into the Merchant Navy. The house still bore the traces of him, yet all was silent now and untouched. Taking it all in triggered a most strange sensation deep inside her, knowing that the last person to see it had been him, as though his ghostly hand was reaching out to her, to touch her, to join her to him in this place. She almost fled. But taking deep breaths she managed to control her wildly vivid imagination. Others *had* been in here, hired by the solicitors to keep an eye on the place. It was just a house. Yet in all this silence she almost thought she could hear John breathing.

Battling to regain a sense of normality, Brenda turned to other thoughts. What was she going to do with the place? She could never live here, not with the shadow of him drifting from room to room. Maybe she should try to sell it. But that was hardly to be contemplated, for the very reason she had told herself earlier. His memory would be desecrated if what had once been his home passed to someone else. Yet it couldn't stay empty forever. To allow it to fall into decay would be an even worse violation. It would still have to be maintained. For what? To stand here as a monument? He would be appalled. He'd given it to her – it must be used. Perhaps if she let it? But that would mean people trooping through it, filling it with their noise, altering things. Only she was permitted to do that. Maybe she could bring herself to come here periodically to clean and dust without needing to move any of the things from the places where he had left them.

Still undecided, Brenda let herself out, at the open door taking a final look behind her. It was a lovely house, large and roomy, one which she in her poky flat had always dreamed of owning. All around were trees and front gardens with flowers growing, and not far off open spaces, Epping Forest, Wanstead Flats, open country to take Addie to. It could be made so beautiful. But not yet.

Shutting her mind to it, Brenda locked the door, dropped the key into the depths of her handbag and without looking back, walked down the garden path, turning left towards Leytonstone Station.

Chapter Twenty-six

She hadn't gone near the place since that one time. In the months that followed, Brenda found herself confronting a constant dilemma. Having told no one, not even Mum or Vera, about the house – and if Mum had harboured any suspicion of her affair with John Stebbings, that suspicion must have died a long time ago – she could hardly start blurting it all out now. But how did one explain away a house?

Around Christmas she hit on how she might get away with it. Brenda's Place was doing marvellously well these days and she had accrued a nice little bank balance, to the envy of her mother-in-law who saw her becoming ever more independent of Harry. No one of course knew how much money she had made, some assuming it was quite a fortune. She dressed well, ate well all of which blared comparative affluence. She wasn't in reality as well off as she looked. Overheads took their share of income, and profits were still only modest. The business kept growing, but there were her two assistants to pay, and Vera, now that she had consented to teach her sister the trade. But in time she could let it be known that she had decided to buy a house while prices were at rock bottom. After the war, she'd explain, prices will rocket.

She would wait until after Christmas before telling everyone what she had purportedly done. It would arch a few eyebrows in the Hutton camp, but she was sure her own people would be overjoyed to see her reap the reward of all her hard work over the years. Yes, it was an excellent idea.

Christmas passed in its usual defiant wartime manner, provisions hoarded for half the year going towards making the Christmas pudding and a Christmas cake of sorts with carrot, apple, prunes and dried dates making up for a wartime scarcity of currants, sultanas and raisins. Eggs preserved in something called water-glass did their job, sugar hoarded spoonful by spoonful over the last seven or eight months got brought out with margarine being pooled by the whole family to go into the communal Christmas luxury. All this and the cook's own skill went to do a fine job.

Brenda, spending Christmas Day this year with her own family, had still not been able to broach this apparent business of house-buying. She hated to lie. Even with her own people it wasn't easy. They'd be astonished at her apparent wealth and success after starting out to earn just a bit of pin money. Not green-eyed or begrudging but certainly surprised. The begrudging bit she'd leave to her in-laws, or at least her mother-in-law, who would see Brenda as doing too well with her son not there – maybe much too well and how did she come by it all, and so on? She wasn't looking forward at all to Boxing Day with her in-laws while this secret lay inside her.

She needn't have worried. The talk was mostly of the way the war was going – the situation had become worrying after everyone had earlier been so optimistic. After all that forging ahead, with German troops on the run and even the first German town taken, the enemy had suddenly turned, and in three days had advanced forty-five miles towards Antwerp.

'I only 'ope it ain't goin' ter turn inter anuvver Dunkirk,' observed Mr Hutton, echoing what a lot of people were thinking.

'Not after all that's been done, it can't,' said Brenda. From the dinner table where she sat eating cold meat and bubble and squeak made from potatoes and sprouts left over from yesterday, she gazed towards the fire, wishing Mr Hutton would put some more coal on it against the draught seeping into the room from the coldest Christmas weather they'd had for fifty years, so it was being said.

'How much longer is this rotten war going on for? Sometimes I feel like my Harry's never going ter come home.' The British had sorted out Italy and were now in Greece. So was Harry.

'They should of sent 'im 'ome before now. 'E's done 'is bit,' said his father at which Daphne pulled a face and reminded him that his younger son was also in the thick of it.

'I get so frightened worrying fer Bob, if 'e should get killed fighting.'

'Oh, Daphne,' chided Brenda. 'You mustn't think that way. You've got to say to yerself, "He's going ter come home all right."'

Daphne turned moist eyes towards her and cuddled little Robert, who sat on her lap eating from her plate, a little closer to her. 'I can't 'elp meself lying awake at nights wonderin' if this poor little mite'll end up with no dad.'

'Daphne . . .' Brenda began, but Mrs Hutton intervened.

'I read they still ain't found Glenn Miller yet.'

She got up hurriedly to go over to her old mother who was hugging the fire to give her a bit more of the cold chicken with some pickle.

'Went down over the Channel goin' ter play to them in France. They still ain't found 'im or any wreckage of the plane. I used ter like 'is music.'

'I expect it'll still be played,' said Brenda, her mind temporarily taken off Daphne and the war, though still wondering how she was ever going to tell anyone about that house.

Around the middle of January she finally plucked up enough courage to embark on her tale of buying it. She would tell her own family tonight and tomorrow, Sunday, tell her in-laws when she went round there for dinner. Going over in her mind what she would say as she combed out the now-fashionable loose shoulder-length hair of a client, she was surprised to see a frantic Mrs Hutton come into the salon.

After a few visits following its opening when she'd come more to black her nose than anything, she hardly set foot here now. Whether out of resentment, misguided disapproval or just because nowadays she cut it herself, Brenda had no idea, but she preferred to think the latter.

Mrs Hutton almost ran to her, taking her by the arm and pulling her aside. 'Bren!' Her voice was a low, harsh whisper. 'Yer've got ter come 'ome with me, now. We've 'ad some bad news.'

Brenda felt her blood run cold. Harry! Already there was a whirling inside her head. Please God, no!

'Daphne's in a terrible state.' Her mother-in-law went on without taking a breath. 'We've tried to calm 'er down, but she don't 'ear us. P'raps you can make 'er 'ear you. Yer've got ter come. Now. It's Bob.'

The whirling sensation had grown worse, the relief every bit as bad as shock and foreboding had been. So was the guilt that she should dare feel relieved at someone else's bad news. Her heart went out to Daphne.

She gathered her wits. It wasn't easy to leave the salon on a busy Saturday afternoon. 'You go on back, Mum. I just need to finish off here, and then I'll follow.' But the demanding drag on her arm increased.

'Now, Bren! Daphne's in hysterics. We can't do nothink with 'er.'

Poor thing. To lose a husband at this time of the war. It had been bad with the Allies being pushed back like that, but the Battle of the Bulge was over, the enemy broken, the Allies rushing ahead once more. It had even so left something like eighty thousand Allied casualties – a terrible price to pay. And Bob was one of them. Brenda felt her heart grow heavy with sadness and sudden grief, knowing that it could have easily been for Harry.

'Vera, keep an eye on everything,' she ordered. 'And Joan, you carry on – I don't think there's anything you and Vera can't handle at the moment.'

Thankfully she'd done the two perms this morning. At this time in the afternoon only a couple of sets and three trims remained to be done before closing. She could rely on Joan, and Vera was coming along very well. Mum was upstairs looking after the babies and Vera had already collected Addie from a friend's flat. She thought of telling Mum what had happened, but there was no time. She'd tell her later.

Changing into heavy shoes, donning her coat, woolly gloves and thick scarf, Brenda hurried off after her mother-in-law through the snowy streets.

'When did you hear?' she queried as they went.

'Half-hour ago,' explained Mrs Hutton, gazing ahead. 'We was told they'll be sending 'im 'ome to a military 'ospital after a while. We don't know when or where that'll be yet. Daphne's beside 'erself . . .'

Brenda pulled up sharply, her raised voice dulled by the snow-laden air. 'Hospital! Mum, you made me believe he'd been killed.'

Mrs Hutton also stopped, turned and looked at Brenda. 'I never said. I said . . .' Confused for once, she fumbled for words. 'I don't know what I said. It's because Daphne's in such a state over it. The telegram said 'e's bin wounded, lorst a leg and they're goin' ter 'ave ter send 'im 'ome.'

Brenda was angry now. 'You dragged me away from me work, just over *that*?'

Mrs Hutton too had grown angry. 'What d'ye mean, *just* over that? He's lorst a leg! 'Ow can yer be so unfeelin'? If it was your 'usband . . .'

She stopped abruptly remembering that Harry too had been wounded in North Africa, but recovered herself. Though still angry, she went on, ''E didn't lose a leg. He weren't crippled. Daphne's got an invalid on 'er 'ands now, an' a toddler ter look after, an' she ain't strong.'

She was strong. Just didn't want to be. But Brenda held her tongue. Here, with the snow falling and the cold biting into their bones, wasn't the time to have a row. 'Well,' she said, 'Maybe I can 'elp to calm 'er down.'

She told her mum and dad about the house that night, after passing on the news about Harry's brother. They were sorry about Bob but were genuinely pleased over the house, and, as she had expected, surprised.

'I didn't think yer 'ad that much savin's, gel,' said her father. 'Good luck to yer, all the same. Yer must of saved bloody 'ard for it. Harry'll be pleased when 'e comes 'ome, an' proud of yer. Or 'e ought ter be.'

There followed a bombardment of questions about what it was like, how had she found it, why hadn't she told them all earlier, and when could they all go and see it.

Lying in her teeth to her own parents was an unpleasant business. More than once during the evening she was on the verge of confessing the true story behind the house. The only thing that stopped her was the volume of information she would have had to provide, all the time aware that she'd be disclosing what they'd see as an unsavoury affair. She wasn't going to subject them or herself to that.

'Once I get it straight,' she promised, 'we'll go and see it together,' and managed – with a lot of hard thinking and excuses that she wanted to get it looking nice – to parry a natural eagerness to 'just go an' 'ave a look from the outside'.

'P'raps in a few weeks' time,' she finally conceded, hoping that this interval might dull their curiosity if she did not refer to it any more than she need to. But she could see it cropping up time after time until she did let them view it.

The experience with her own people was a sobering lesson and it was ages before she could bring herself round to telling her in-laws.

The day Daphne had been told about Bob had certainly not been the right time with the girl going off into fresh hysterics the minute Brenda walked into the house, immediately looking to her for comfort.

'Yer the only one I can see what might 'elp 'er,' Mrs Hutton had told Brenda on that particular occasion with no grudge in her voice. 'She won't listen to me. She might of listened to my Sid, but 'e ain't 'ome from work till seven and I didn't want ter get a doctor, payin' 'im fer just an hysterical attack. That's why I came ter get you. You both get on so well tergether, you might be able ter 'andle 'er better than me.'

Brenda had asked Mrs Hutton to make a cup of tea with lots of sugar in it. The one already beside Daphne lay untouched and cold, but she would make sure of the girl drinking a fresh one. Once she was alone with her, Brenda had held her sister-in-law to her, then eased her away while keeping a tight hold on her arms, and looked into her face.

'Now listen,' she'd commanded. 'Listen to me, Daphne. Getting into a state ain't goin' ter do no one any good. You've got little Robert to look after. Bob won't thank you fer givin' way like this. And he's goin' ter be all right.'

'But 'ow will he ever get work, 'im crippled?' sobbed Daphne.

'Of course he'll get work. It'll be a while, but this ain't the First World War when they left men on the scrapheap to manage best they could. These are modern times. They do miracles and they'll fit 'im up with a new leg, and knowing Bob he'll be as right as rain. Him and Harry are a pair alike. Harry wouldn't let anything put 'im down. Neither will Bob. Just trust him.'

It had sounded so trite, so easy to say; how would she have behaved had it been Harry? But it seemed to work. Slowly Daphne had calmed. Her body ceased its jerking to the spasmodic sobs. Revived by the hot cup of sweet tea which this time Brenda insisted she drank all up, she was even able to smile, at last beginning to see a tiny light at the end of her dark tunnel, a light conjured up for her by her friend and sister-in-law.

It was the beginning of March, when with luck everyone would be more preoccupied with going to visit Bob some way off in the hospital than with anything she might have to say, before Brenda was able to find the right time to tell them her trumped-up story of house-buying. By that time she had practically come to believe her own story, so well-rehearsed was it.

Even so, she wondered why she had picked today of all days – Irene Hutton's birthday. Mrs Hutton had invited her to tea, and Brenda found she'd also asked her immediate family: Iris and Enid, her daughters, and Daphne. Each had their man away in the forces, so Mr Hutton looked utterly isolated.

With everyone there, Brenda was nearly tempted to shelve her long-held news until yet another time, when it felt right. But when would there be a right time? Then again, today might be that right time with so much going on. Enid and Iris were nattering away to each other and regaling their mother with their own family news;

Mrs Hutton had her hands full cutting sandwiches and cake into tiny morsels for her own mother who, as always, had taken her dentures out to eat. 'Can't chew wiv a mouth full o' china shiftin' about in me poor ole north an' south!' she always maintained.

Perhaps all the distractions were a godsend in a way. What she had to say might be submerged by it all and it wouldn't be a lie to say later that she'd told them and they'd probably been too busy to take a lot of notice. And the jolt would have gone out of it.

Taking in a deep breath, Brenda chose the noisiest part of the birthday tea. 'I thought I ought ter tell you – I bought a house. It's all gone through at last and I thought now's the time ter let you know.'

If she'd hoped for a few casual nods with the conversation picking up where it had left off, it wasn't to be. Dead silence fell, followed, just as she'd feared, by a rash of raised eyebrows from around the table and about as many responses:

'Yer what?'

'Bought an 'ouse?'

'Well I never did!'

'Yer mean, yer *bought* an 'ouse?'

To which she could only nod in agreement.

It was Mr Hutton who came out with the longest string of words, his sense of isolation amid all these women cured instantly, his masculinity coming to the fore.

'What'yer mean, Bren, yer bought an 'ouse? What for? Yer got a nice flat, ain' yer – right over yer work?' They had begun to accept that she did work. 'Why d'yer wanna uproot yerself now for? You ought ter 'ave waited till yer 'usband got 'ome. The war'll be over soon – I'd of waited till then an' let 'im do it. Not you. Anyway, how'd yer manage ter find that much dosh ter buy an 'ouse wiv?' It was a demanding question yet delivered not too unkindly.

'Must of set yer back a pretty penny, gel,' he continued, not waiting for a reply. 'Bet yer've left yerself wiv nuffink. Yer should of bin careful, y'know, doin' a silly thing like that. Should of told us before you went and did it. Yer could be lettin' yerself in fer a lot of trouble. Us sort of people don't go buyin' 'ouses. Fer us sort of people it's always best ter pay rent. Yer don't get no comeback that way. Out of our league, *buyin'* an 'ouse.'

'I've been saving for ages for it!' The lie as well as indignation at being questioned and advised made Brenda's reply more terse than it might have been. Mrs Hutton's eyebrows shot up even higher, her tone hardened by shock.

'Probably at the expense of more important things, I suppose.'

'No.' Brenda's back was up, even though she tried to control it. She'd expected this sort of reaction, had steeled herself for it, but it still rankled. 'No one's gone short over it. Addie's well clothed, she's well fed, and she has everything any other child could 'ave with a war on.'

Addie, of course, was her first line of defence, knowing she'd be the main target. 'And I've made sure there's still enough in the bank for when Harry comes home.'

'Must of bin coining it,' observed Mrs Hutton as if such coining had been kept from them like some wicked secret.

'No. Just been careful,' replied Brenda. 'Not throwing it around.'

Mrs Hutton had always been first to believe that was exactly what she'd done in the past. Even if it was an unfair thought, she couldn't help thinking it.

'My Bob's got nothink ter come 'ome to,' mumbled Daphne despondently, while Enid and Iris, who had kept very quiet, suddenly looked towards their offspring sitting at the little table with two-and-a-half-year-old Robert, busily stuffing himself.

Mr Hutton leaned forward, protective and kindly. 'Yer ought to 'ave waited fer 'Arry, Bren. He'd know more about 'ouse-buying an' all the pitfalls than you would. I just 'ope for your sake, and 'is, you ain't done nuffink silly. Buying 'ouses ain't a job for a woman. Yer should of arst me. I might of bin able ter put yer right. What's it like, this 'ouse?'

Brenda bit back irritation at being given to understand that women's brains were pea-sized, that she could not be expected to move without a man to advise her. She'd been a businesswoman these past two years and had made a decent fist of it. Harry, a warehouseman prior to the war, lived in a rented flat. What more could he tell her than she already knew? Neither had his parents ever owned their own home. And here was his father offering to advise her on house-buying, well intentioned or not.

It was in the midst of this last thought that she remembered with a rush of humility that she too knew nothing of buying houses. The house, and the salon too, had been bequeathed to her. She'd not had any hand in it, so how could she crow, sitting here believing her own lies?

With that reminder to herself she forced a tolerant smile at her father-in-law.

'It's Victorian,' she told him.

'Ah,' drawled her inquisitor as though that said she'd definitely gone and bought a pig in a poke. He shook his head slowly. 'Yer should of got expert advice on its condition, gel. If it was structurally sound and fings.'

Brenda forced another smile, this time not quite so tolerant. 'I did. It's in tip-top condition and I've bought it with all the furniture and everything in it – lock stock and barrel. The asking price was low fer all that, and I believe that when the war ends, the price of houses will start ter soar. So I've done the right thing, buying at the right time.'

That put paid to his advice. She saw him nod, stumped, if not fully convinced. She also caught a glimpse of his wife's expression. She looked piqued that her son's wife should consider herself above the need to consult a man. And not only that, but going behind Harry's back, said her look.

Well, we'll face what Harry has to say about it when he comes home, thought Brenda, and turned to reprimand Addie who had started quarrelling indignantly with one of her cousins, who had apparently grabbed the piece of cake she'd had her eye on.

Chapter Twenty-seven

Everywhere people were already preparing to get back to normal after five and a half years of war.

Blackout regulations had been relaxed for a couple of months now to what was known as dim-out; some shops and places of entertainment were even displaying subduedly lit signs, and on buses and trains passengers were able to see to read again at night. Doodlebugs and rockets – the last at the end of March scoring a direct hit on Hughes Mansions in Bethnal Green and ironically taking a hundred and thirty-four lives just as the war was about to end – were largely being consigned to memory, only their devastating results remaining to sober any over-joyous mind.

Where children had played freely on bomb sites low wooden hoardings were going up. Elsewhere clusters of bungalow-like prefabricated homes were being put together for the bombed out. Those who moved into these prefabs, as they were called, had already been creating little gardens around them with flower beds and an ornamental tree or two as though seeing them as permanent.

Around the middle of April Brenda's parents had a pleasant surprise – council men arriving to 'do up' their upstairs. It was simpler to repair such partially damaged places first. They yanked off burnt door frames and replaced them with new wood, also putting in windows, renewing charred floorboards, refitting ceilings, scraping and repainting walls. If that faint smell of burnt wood did still linger, the Wilsons once again had the use of their upstairs rooms. They celebrated it by hanging new curtains and buying bedroom furniture and by going up and down the newly painted stairs several more times than ever need be in a day. Dad even attempted to carry Mum up them, though four years had made him just that little less agile than before.

All that remained was to await the capitulation of the enemy. To most it seemed a long wait; as the saying went, the last mile home is always the longest. Hitler remained determined to have his defeat go right up to the wire. Even the war against Japan was proving protracted, yet another determined foe refusing to realise that its days were numbered. In the meantime fine men were still dying.

Brenda prayed long and agonisingly for Harry's safety, all the while half-tortured, especially at night with her brain freed from daily concerns, by how easily something might happen to him practically on the last day of hostilities. In the last war men had fallen moments before the Armistice had been signed. Why not Harry? It seemed to her that she and her family and his family, even Bob in a way, had got off too scotfree these five and a half years for their luck to go on.

She prayed for her brothers too. Let them all come home safe, dear God! And especially my Harry.

Willing him safe home, it was easy to forget that when he finally did return, she was going to have to face him with all she had achieved in his absence: the salon, the house, the money she had saved. His letters hardly mentioned any of these things and she too, feeling it best not to raise too much dust, wrote little about her success. But once Harry was home . . .

Well, she'd face that when it came. Meanwhile, she prayed.

Much of the good news coming out of Germany had been marred by the shock of the good President Roosevelt's death, and now the newsreels in all the cinemas were inflicting with awful and startling clarity upon totally unsuspecting audiences the atrocities of Nazi concentration camps like Belsen and Buchenwald, showing stunned Allied soldiers entering them.

Sprung on them as they sat contentedly in a picture palace watching the Pathé Gazette News, Brenda and Daphne sat with their decent senses numbed by what they were seeing. Sickened and stupefied by how humans, even Nazis, could do such things to others, a profound silence descended over the entire audience, broken only by quiet spasmodic weeping. People felt too shocked to utter even gasps of horror. It was as though they too stood there in the camp alongside the liberators as bodies, skin-covered bones, were lifted, light as feathers, to be dropped in mass graves, limp body atop limp body that seemed to move in death as each

377

settled – an abomination to English eyes regardless of all they themselves had gone through – despite the care given to those dead forms. And all the while the still-living shuffled without aim, with vacant stares, eyes unnaturally large and sunk deep into sockets, teeth grinning without mirth from shrunken lips and abnormally enlarged by skeletal cheeks, limbs so stick-like they seemed incapable of supporting each wasted frame.

Those who had come to see a lively Hollywood song and dance film rose silently as the newsreel faded, and to the last person filed from the cinema. Brenda and Daphne went along with them, their interest in the rest of the programme lost. Certainly the happy musical which they'd paid to see would now have seemed utterly inappropriate.

All the way home no word passed between them as automatically they produced their bus fare while people around them, who hadn't been in the cinema, babbled away.

Only once did Daphne say anything. 'We did right ter fight that kind of tyranny,' she muttered before falling silent again.

Brenda opened Harry's letter. 'Hope to be on my way home any day now,' it said.

Clutching the letter to her bosom, she burst into tears. Her prayers had all been answered. Italy, Greece, no longer had need of occupying forces. Mussolini had been shot dead, then strung up by his own people. Berlin lay crushed between the British and Americans in the west and the Russians in the east, Hitler and his mistress, Eva Braun, had reportedly committed suicide in a Berlin bunker. The war was virtually over, all bar the shouting.

Mum had heard from Brian yesterday saying much the same thing as Harry – he hoped to be home very soon. He was looking forward to seeing the girl he'd been corresponding with since one of his leaves from way back. She lived in the very next street and he intended asking her to marry him. Mum had known nothing about this.

Davy's letter had a bit more to say. He was writing to a girl he'd met near Paris, hoped that once home he could send for her. They were very much in love, he said, and he too had plans of marrying.

'Ooh,' said Mum. 'I don't think I fancy some gel what's foreign fer me daughter-in-law. Wouldn't know what ter say to 'er. What if she don't speak no English – 'ow am I goin' ter cope with 'er? I've got ter tell 'im I don't like it. Not when there's such a lot of nice English gels around. Fancy, all these years and 'im never so much as lookin' at a bloomin' gel. Now 'e wants ter marry a foreign one. No, I don't like that at all.'

It was May. The eighth of May, a Tuesday. The war was over: officially.

For days everyone had been expecting it. When it came, excitement had already preceded the official announcement, and the whole of Britain joined in one huge celebration. Victory in Europe, VE Day, got going strongly with bunting and flags hung out of every window, coloured fairy lights draped around front doors, tables and chairs dragged out of homes to line the centre of every side street in readiness for a children's party.

Mums in aprons were spreading tablecloths and sheets end to end, laying out vast varieties of cups, glasses and plates ready to take the mountain of sandwiches and jellies and trifles whose ingredients they'd managed to hoard for this very day.

With the official announcement given over loud-speakers at three o'clock the cheer shook the whole of London, people leaping fully clothed into the fountains of Trafalgar Square. Whitehall and the Mall became a mass of cavorting humanity, people with arms linked. Girls in bright dresses wearing servicemen's caps, embraced by every contingent of British and American forces, waved little flags while people singing at the top of their voices belted out British favourites. A massive conga snaked around Queen Victoria's statue. At the Palace a solid crowd singing 'Land of Hope and Glory' yelled for the King and Queen.

In the warm May air, every town and village saw children of all ages stuffing themselves to bursting point at the party tables beneath red, white and blue bunting and flags last used for King George VI's coronation. By evening pianos had been dragged out; adults now took over from the children, and the night sky grew lurid with countless bonfires and was split by exploding fireworks – as if the people hadn't had enough of fire and explosion. This however was different.

Across the length and breadth of Britain there was hardly a square inch of any town that didn't have dancing and not a mile separating any habitation where singing could not be heard. The relief that the war was over and done with and that the Allies were the victors resounded from every corner of the nation. Brenda and Vera, having rushed round to their parents with their children in tow, were just one small item in that grand jollification.

By evening Dad had drunk too much and was cuddling Mum while she tried her damnedest to extricate herself. 'Not in front of everyone, yer silly old sod!'

Hardly anyone heard her and if they did, they took no notice as squibs and bangers were set off to make people jump and in passing remember the louder explosions that had once made them more than jump.

In the midst of it, Brian came home, sunburnt and jolly. Having been kissed and cuddled by the family under a hurriedly fashioned banner made from an old bedsheet that read WELCOME HOME BRIAN – they'd had a telegram that morning to say he'd been sent home on leave – he went straight round to the other turning to bring back his fiancee, for whom he'd promised to buy an engagement ring as soon as he could afford one.

'Can't afford a bloomin' thing on my pay,' he told them as Cecilia, more often known as Cis and sometimes Ceil, was introduced.

'But we'll make up fer it when I'm demobbed and get meself a decent job, won't we, Ceil?' he added while Ceil, a slightly built blonde of eighteen with upswept hairstyle, gazed at him in dewy-eyed adoration.

'I like that gel,' Mum said much later, gazing into the street bonfire that was finally being allowed to die down. Neighbours were tiring and beginning to drift off. It had been an exciting day. Tomorrow would see the anticlimax of knowing they were no longer at war; it created a sort of vacuum they were going to have to get used to.

That night, Brenda and Vera with their children slept together in Brian's old bedroom. He had gone off to stay at the home of his fiancee's parents at their invitation, sleeping on their couch. He maybe had ideas of getting a little more cosy with Ceil when all was still.

'Been a good day,' murmured Brenda, her eyelids beginning to close. She received a sleepy grunt.

'Nice, Brian coming 'ome out of the blue like that,' she went on.

'Sooner it'd bin Hank,' came a mumbled response. 'Wish 'e was 'ere. I ain't 'eard from 'im fer ages. I reckon 'e must of got fed up with me.'

'You'll hear from 'im soon,' Brenda encouraged, but there was no reply. Whether Vera had already drifted off or couldn't bring herself to express her doubts about ever hearing from him again, Brenda felt it best not to push things. It was true, he'd not written for over a month.

Two weeks later, Brenda had Vera bounding into the salon like a gazelle, almost knocking the magazine out of the hands of a customer sitting awaiting her turn.

Totally out of breath, not all from hurrying down the iron stairs, her face was lit with happiness as she waved a telegram in her sister's face.

'Brenda! It's from Hank. He's got leave from France and he's coming 'ere. Look, see what it says.'

Not pausing for Brenda to finish trimming her customer's hair, Vera began reading loud enough for the whole salon to hear:

'"Got seven days leave STOP be there tomorrow STOP you get dolled up STOP I'll bring the ring STOP"' She thrust the telegram at Brenda to read for herself. Vera's voice continued in the same breath. 'Bren, Hank wants me ter marry 'im!'

Brenda lowered her comb and scissors to take the telegram being pushed at her. 'It don't exactly say to marry you, Vera.'

'Of course it does!' came the hot retort. 'What else would 'e bring a ring for? He can't go inter detail in a telegram, can he? It costs.'

'What about Mum?' asked Brenda, her customer forgotten. 'What's she going to say?'

'It ain't up ter Mum,' blurted Vera.

The neglected customer, rather than feeling ignored, was grinning with pleasure. 'That's right, dear, it's your life.'

'Exactly,' Vera told her. 'Mine and Hank's. I'm so 'appy, Bren – don't put the mockers on it. I've gotta lot ter sort out. He'll be 'ere termorrer.'

'You best go and explain to Mum,' advised Brenda. She was pleased for Vera, but at the same time wary. It had come about all too suddenly. Was Vera really thinking straight? Did she know what she could be letting herself in for? Marrying – if that's what he was asking – someone from across the other side of the Atlantic who no doubt had no intention of settling down in England? Hers could be a different life, maybe one she wasn't prepared for.

But Vera was already off, leaving Brenda to return to her still-grinning customer.

'It don't 'alf sound romantic,' said the middle-aged customer, who settled back into her chair, adding, 'Good luck to 'er, eh?' ready to enjoy a nice long discussion on love and romance while the remainder of her coarse, greying hair was being trimmed.

*

Hank was of middle height and rather thickset, but his face with its straight nose, square jaw and bright blue eyes was exactly as Vera had described, remarkably handsome beneath a regulation bristle of sandy hair. His surname was Cameron and for that at least, Annie Wilson was relieved. It could easily have been something quite unpronounceable. He'd told Vera his stock was Scottish, though a good three generations back.

He stood now, filling her doorway, slightly braced against Vera's ecstatic onrush into his arms, her heart on her sleeve. Dropping his pack to catch her, he was looking over her shoulder in silent appeal at her parents standing in the passage to receive him.

'I'm sorry to have bust in on yah like this.'

Annie, having recovered from her initial awkwardness, saw in the smile a self-conscious young man who had probably never been out of his own state of Illinois before joining up, and immediately warmed to him.

The day before, confronted by an excited Vera, she had said, 'We ain't never even met 'im, and now 'e's comin' 'ere askin' yer to marry 'im. Where yer goin' ter live? I know what's goin' ter 'appen – he's goin' ter take yer back to America wiv 'im and we'll never see yer again. No, Vera, yer've got ter look at this one sensibly. An' then yer must tell 'im yer can't leave yer family.'

Now, although at first sight she found herself warming to a likeable young man, she could see the pitfalls and the heartaches that could lie ahead – for Vera and for her, those two little boys she'd never see again. Tears crushed her heart even as she stepped back for Hank Cameron to come in, having to force her husband aside to allow entry.

He'd said nothing but she knew he was feeling exactly as she did. He would have his say later, when he and this Hank were in serious discussion together out of the hearing of women. He might not even tell her what was said, but she would know.

Whatever was said and whether it was objected to or not, who could prevent a woman with two little children doing what she wanted? It was up to Vera, who would have to bear the brunt of her own decision. Having made her bed she'd have to lie in it whether she liked it or not. It was out of her parents' hands. But it didn't stop the tears filling Annie's breast yet still managing to leave this vacuum stemming from a premature, already aching, sense of loss.

It took three days for all the paperwork to come through. By then Hank's leave was half over.

'I always 'oped yer'd 'ave a white weddin',' whispered her mother as, in a pink plaid skirt and jacket on which Vera had squandered most of her clothing coupons and some of Mum's, she went to meet Hank at the register office, followed by the family, none of whom appeared to feel in a celebrating mood. Mum stayed well back, holding one of the twin boys. Brenda held the other, Adele at her side.

Vera looked radiant, he too looked fetching in his sleek American uniform and his American corporal's stripes; the pair brought oohs and aahs from onlookers while a bunch of his buddies who'd come over with him on leave formed a guard of honour for the wedded couple. The ring he had bought in France was a splendid one, the thick heavy gold set with diamonds which Vera proudly showed off to family and friends. That was as far as her joy went with just two nights together in a hotel comprising their honeymoon. Hank had to go back to his unit in France, crooning tenderly, 'I dunno when I'll see yah again, Vera, but come hell and high water I'm gonna make damned sure it's soon,' lovingly calling her Mrs Cameron which made her cry even more.

With Vera drooping on his arm he said his farewells to her parents and thanked them for their hospitality. 'It's been a real pleasure knowin' yah, Mr and Mrs Wilson, and I'm lookin' forward to meetin' yah again.'

But he didn't meet them again. Letters passing between him and Vera written at least twice weekly numbered just six before he was sent home to the USA.

He wrote from the ship: 'Soon as I get back home, I'll start to get things moving.' His home was Springfield, Illinois. 'I'll get you over here the first chance. My people can't wait to meet you. They must be sick at hearing me talk about you, but they're looking forward to seeing their grandsons. I'm real proud of you, darling, for producing our two sons, and I miss them already.'

Their honeymoon days had been largely spent at her parents' so that he could see as much of his two boys as possible. Hurried arrangements had been made that Mum would have them there rather than at Brenda's, so that she could make the most of their presence. At the back of her mind lurked the knowledge that Vera would one day take them far away, and then when would she ever see them again?

'There'll be a lot of paperwork to go through,' Hank wrote, 'before you and the boys can be brought to the States. There'll be a lot of forms for you to fill. And you'll need a passport and to get yourself inoculated against smallpox. Then before we know it, we'll be together again. I can't wait for it. I love you so very much, darling and I can't wait to have you here.'

Vera read it all out to Brenda through a welter of tears. 'I'm looking forward so much to going over there. He says he misses me. Well, I miss 'im. I really do. Trouble is, it's goin' ter be a terrible wrench leaving all of you. But I do miss 'im and I want ter be with 'im. It's only natural ain't it?'

'Well, you won't have too long to wait,' said Brenda, sad that she was soon to lose her sister to those thousands of miles, but wondering more as to when on earth she would get to see Harry again.

Chapter Twenty-eight

There was to be a celebration party.

Harry's homecoming more or less coinciding with Bob's discharge from hospital at last, their mother had organised a do. It would be on Saturday the twenty-fifth of August. Bob was due home on Tuesday and Harry had said to expect him on Thursday.

'So a party on Saturday'll be perfect,' she told her husband. 'That'll give yer time ter scout round for enough beer and stuff fer all the family an' friends an' neighbours. Me an' Daphne an' Brenda, we'll do the food in. And yer'll 'ave ter make a Welcome Home sign ter go over the front door and get them fairy lights up over the windows and 'ang up that buntin' again what we 'ad fer VE Day.'

'It don't seem to occur to 'er Bob mightn't fancy a big party,' Daphne said to Brenda. 'It's taken all this time ter get used ter walking on that new leg of 'is without coming out of 'ospital to a bloomin' big party.'

Most of his time there had been fraught with despair as he tried to regain a sense of the man he'd once been.

Daphne chivvied him on, helping him combat his flagging spirits. She had grown surprisingly strong and resolute. No longer the wilting lily Brenda had first known, she hardly seemed the same girl.

'It took something like that to get her moving,' Brenda told Mum in awe when she popped round to see her two days before Bob was due to come home. 'What a difference to what she used ter be, too scared to say boo to a goose. I tell you it's certainly put Bob's mum in her place. Funny how people can be such bullies until the worm starts ter turn. Daphne just runs rings round her now.'

'And 'bout time too,' said Mum, getting up to feed the meter with yet another shilling as the gas jet under the kettle for a cup of tea began to die. 'I seem ter do nothink but put money in that blessed thing – I'm sure they've cut down the power rather than put up the cost. Yer wouldn't think the war was over, all this rationing still on an' Attlee tellin' us we've all got ter tighten our belts. Fine prime minister 'e's turned out ter be. Should of 'ad Churchill back – 'e'd of got things right like 'e did in the war. Shame, votin' 'im out like that, after all 'e done. Gas don't seem ter last no time these days.'

'I expect Vera being here don't help.' Vera had stayed on at Mum's after her marriage, Mum needing to see all she could of her two grandsons before they were whisked away forever. And besides, Brenda didn't want the flat cluttered by mothers and children when Harry came home. It had all worked out quite well really.

'Daphne being like that makes me feel I'm the one being told what to do,' Brenda went on. 'I'd give anything ter say to Mrs Hutton that me and Harry don't want no big do. Trouble is she got carried away organising that street party on VJ Day. Made up for not getting a look in on VE Day, I suppose. So now she wants to 'ave another go, doing a party for her sons. I mean Harry's not even out of uniform yet. All they've done is send him back home. Could be December before he's demobbed.'

The day following Bob's homecoming, he and Daphne were installed in their own house. Daphne told his mother she would manage him well enough on her own without need of help in a manner that must have sounded very pointed. On that same day Harry got off the bus in Mile End Road.

His telegram had considerably heartened Brenda, feeling they were all sharing a small conspiracy against his mother. All those words must have cost him a packet: HOME TOMORROW NOT THURSDAY — DAY TOGETHER BEFORE MUM GETS LOOK IN — CAN'T WAIT TO SEE YOU.

The telegram just about gave her time to alert her customers that she'd be closing that day. None of them raised any objection seeing it was only a Tuesday and not as important as a weekend appointment might have been.

CAN'T WAIT TO SEE YOU. The words had sent a thrill through her where earlier she'd been having collywobbles wondering what they would find to say to each other, whether each would find the other so changed that they would feel awkward. Now, her heart bubbling with eagerness as she waited for that first glimpse of him getting off the bus, she stood at the window where she had been half the morning while Addie played on her own. Finally she saw him step off the rear platform of the No. 25, very agile for someone toting full kit.

She stood just a second longer to see him swing the heavy kitbag over his shoulder as he strode across the road in the brilliant late August sunshine, sidestepping first a chugging motor car then a cyclist. Then gathering her wits, Brenda swept a startled Addie up from where she'd been playing with a home-made stuffed toy dog. 'Daddy's home! Oh Addie, yer daddy's home!'

Giving her no time to protest, Brenda was through the kitchen and out on the iron landing as he came in by the side gate. Seeing her there, he yelled in alarm that she could trip trying to rush down with Addie in her arms, and dropped the kitbag to bound up the stairs two at a time and embrace her.

Laughing and crying both at the same time with Addie now loudly protesting at this unaccustomed rough treatment, Brenda felt her breath hugged out of her as she returned Harry's embrace with her one free arm. 'Oh, darling! Thank you, God, thank you . . .' was all she could say as Harry twisted her round and round in his joy at being reunited with her.

How beautiful it was. Adele had been put to bed, no one else was in the flat but herself and Harry. It was as though they were enjoying a honeymoon all over again.

'I wish yer didn't have to go back after the party,' she whispered as they lay side by side, fulfilled. 'Why can't you be demobbed straight away? There ain't any reason now not to be, surely.'

She felt his arm, still lying beneath her neck, tighten comfortingly. 'I'm only in Essex. I might even get a sleeping-out pass – just like I was an ordinary civvy. It won't be long, Bren, before I'm out altergevver.' And with that he leaned over her and gave her another lingering kiss.

'Goodnight,' he murmured. 'It's good ter be 'ome.' He turned over, wearied by lovemaking, and went to sleep.

Brenda had expected to lie awake for ages thinking of today's excitement, of how to approach the matter of her work, but remembered nothing.

'I'm so fed up of waiting,' Vera told Brenda in December, at the same time eyeing Harry, home on yet another weekend sleeping-out pass, and soon to be demobbed.

They had gone round to Brenda's mother for a couple of hours this Sunday before he was due to return. Stationed in Essex, he was home every weekend now and Brenda supposed that her sister felt it keenly with her American husband so far away after only a few days of wedded bliss and no sign as yet of her going over to the USA to be united with him.

'People are so rotten,' Vera complained. 'I'm fed up of people saying the same thing. "Ain't 'e sent for yer yet?"' In an effort to mimic them she put on a high smirking tone, then let her voice drop in bitterness. 'They make it sound as if he's deliberately forgotten me. I'm sick of it! And don't you look at me like that, Mum, as if you believe it too.'

This was spat out in response to her mother's glance of sympathy.

Brenda always felt so guilty when she and Harry came round, but she needed to come. She in her turn had got fed up with his mother always demanding he pay her a visit every single weekend he was home.

'It's not as if yer going ter be sent off somewhere these days,' Brenda would complain. 'I need you as much as she does.'

She stopped short of adding anything about having more right or even as much right. Mrs Hutton was his mother after all. But she was his wife. Yet going round to see her own parents had become every bit as much of a trial with Vera there, always going on about her own absent husband and looking at Harry as though it were his fault.

Sometimes she too wished that Vera would hear from the American authorities. It wasn't Vera's fault. She'd have been much more patient if it were not for other people's comments, probably innocently voiced, though she never saw it that way.

'He writes to me every week regular,' she proclaimed. 'But it don't make no difference to some people, everyone's too ready ter be convinced I'm making it up about 'is letters. I can show yer 'em if yer don't believe me.'

'I do believe you,' said Brenda at this attitude of defiance, while Harry nodded affirmation of his belief in them too, coupled with sympathetic looks because of her frustration. The war should have taught everyone how it was to wait for some word, some hope that never seemed to arrive.

'Jus' be patient, Ver,' he advised kindly, 'It'll all come round in time.'

Everything comes round in time, thought Brenda, wondering if he would be as understanding about her

393

business as he was with Vera's ever-present and exasperating fretting. She just prayed he would be, though sometimes she was far from sure about it.

So far he hadn't said too much about it because by the time he arrived home on Friday night the salon was closed anyway so he saw very little of it or any interruption it might cause in his life. Saturdays she was able to leave in the capable hands of Joan, now almost a fully fledged hairstylist and very adult for her seventeen years; those clients wanting perms, which Joan wasn't yet able to handle, had been persuaded to have them done during the week so as to settle down and look more natural by the weekend. So it only needed her to pop down for a moment or two on a Saturday to see all was well. It always was. Joan now had an assistant of her own, the girl who'd once done all the clearing up promoted to washing hair, taking out rollers and combing out, with another young girl to do the menial tasks of sweeping and cleaning of sinks and making tea.

There was so far no need for Harry to get on his high horse about being neglected or even be aware how much work running a hairdresser's entailed. Time enough for that when he returned to civvy street.

Brenda put all those morbid thoughts behind her on the day Harry was demobbed, two weeks before Christmas. She was only too overjoyed to have him home permanently, to know they could at last pick up the threads of their life together. That was all she needed at this moment. Problems could come later and be ironed out as and when they arose. After all that's what real marriages were about, wasn't it?

There was another party, this one blended in with a Christmas do and again held at his mother's house, this time with her own people coming. Vera came too, still waiting to hear from the American authorities and threatening to put a damper on the spirits of everyone she spoke to.

'I don't think I'm ever goin' ter 'ear,' she complained to the hostess, a glass of sherry rapidly warming up in her rigid grasp. 'I feel a real outcast, the lowest of the low in their eyes. But I am 'is wife, and them two, poor little sods . . .' she eyed her sons being played with by Addie and Harry's sister's children. 'They're 'is kids too. I don't think the American officials even care 'ow he feels. He's always writing saying 'ow much 'e misses 'em.'

'I know what it's like to miss someone,' agreed Mrs Hutton. 'I missed me two sons fer years. And now I miss me muvver, fer all she was 'ard work in the end.'

The senior Mrs Hutton, having passed away in early August, had been given a quiet funeral, which rather got lost in the throes of the homecoming party given for her two sons.

'She'd got very frail, yer know. By the end I 'ad ter do everythink for her. But fer all that, I miss 'er. She was me muvver. But I'm glad she saw the end of the war out. That must of bin a comfort to 'er, knowing we was all safe again. Though I don't think she knew much about that. She'd just lie there, yer know, not knowing nothink much. I 'ad ter feed 'er an' wash 'er an' do everythink for 'er and I don't think she knew a thing of what was goin' on. Took up all me time, it did. Should of bin in 'orspital, but most of them seemed ter be taken up by wounded soldiers. But I do miss 'er.'

But Vera, still clutching her sherry as though clinging to some lifeline and with her own thunder stolen for the time being, focused more on when, if ever, she'd hear that she would finally be allowed to sail off to America to be reunited with her husband.

The second welcome-home-cum-Christmas-party had been good but Brenda had been glad to get back to her own home and have Harry to herself again. All day he had been hugged and kissed. She'd hardly looked up once without seeing someone commandeering him. Out on the perimeter of all this enthusiasm, she'd not really had a look-in the whole day.

Not that she wished to be the centre of attraction. She quite accepted that she wasn't. But she did wish just to have a moment on her own with him now and then. At times it even seemed he too was ignoring her as he accepted the whisky and beer thrust on him until he was visibly swaying on his feet.

'Harry, come and talk to me. Leave the others, love, and sit down beside me just for a little while.'

'I can't b'rude t'em,' he slurred happily. 'I's me fam'ly. C'm on, Bren, c'm on, get up 'n 'av 'a dance wi' me.'

She did, having to hold him upright, but there was little pleasure in it at two in the morning.

Everyone started nodding off; some of the men were getting the playing cards out. Harry, revived with a cup of strong Camp coffee after chucking up his Christmas dinner and tea along with the beer, could now at least stand. Brenda finally managed to haul him off through the streets, but he kept upright only by holding on to her, a sleepy, whimpering Addie clinging on her free hand. Thank God it wasn't too far to home.

She thought of Daphne. She too had looked as if she hadn't been enjoying it. Sitting beside Bob all night, she'd held his hand; his face looked bleak and he said little. A blanket tucked round his legs hid the false one which he preferred not to try walking on in front of everyone and which she had told Brenda still hurt him terribly when he did try. 'He says it rubs the stump ever so tender even through the bandages,' she'd whispered, while he had sat looking as if he'd rather be anywhere than there.

'D'yer 'ave to be down there messin' about all blinkin' hours? Look at what time yer've come up. And me waiting fer supper.'

With an effort Brenda refrained from snapping back at him that it wouldn't have hurt *him* to rustle something up. He spoke as though it were a game she was playing, a silly pastime to be sneered at, but retaliation would only start up yet another argument. One a few days ago had narrowly missed causing a virtual breakdown to their marriage, so angered had she been as he told her to give up this bloody soppy business idea or else! But it was hard to keep quiet.

It was only mid-January and here he was already complaining of her absence when he was around. He wandered aimlessly about the place and grew irascible at Addie getting under his feet when she came home from school, for all he adored her.

The place was beginning to prove too small for all three of them. Many times she thought of the large house in Leytonstone, still lying empty and which so far she'd managed to sidestep. Harry too never referred to it though he knew of its existence. Still believing she'd bought it cheap, his only mention of it had been to mutter that it must be some tumbledown old ruin on which she'd thrown away good money and that he for one had no intention of going to look at it. So far it had been easier not to start another quarrel by suggesting he did. And just as well, for she could never have lived there, with the memory and feel of John Stebbings all around her. It had in fact become a thorn in her side. Meantime, here in this cramped place, all three were under each other's feet, since Harry had no job at present.

'*Business!* Anyone'd think we'd fall apart wivvart you doing yer *business!* It ain't even a proper job. Not that I'd allow yer goin' out working, respectable 'ousewife like you.'

'Allow?' she burst out, her temper now matching his. 'What d'you mean, *allow?* Times have changed, Harry. While you was away I had to fend for meself and Addie. All the women had to. And we're not prepared to go back to being the nice little housewives we were just because you men 'ave come 'ome. We've proved our worth, proved we can work as well as any of you.'

'Yeah,' he sneered, a little taken aback by her show of force. 'But you weren't away fightin'. That's men's work.'

'Women was in the forces too, y'know,' she reminded him. 'And they ain't going ter stand being expected to go back into the kitchen, expected ter knuckle down under a man's thumb any more.'

He was wilting, blustering. 'I still say you're playin' at business. What's a woman know about business?'

'I know enough to bring in good money.'

She wanted to have done with this argument. She was tired after a full day's work perming two lots of hair while Joan got on with the trims and sets. She began laying the table. But he wasn't done.

'And what's there ter show fer all this money yer bringin' in? Not enough on the table ter feed a flea.'

'That's because of rationing, not money,' she replied wearily.

Rationing, rather than easing with the end of the war, had grown even more austere with resultant mounting unrest against the government that had seen them through it all. There *was* a world food shortage. Some in Europe were said to be living on scraps, the German people were starving. Here rationing had mercifully prevented all that, but it was hard trying to make reduced rations go round. That had nothing to do with money, and she was getting sick of his carping.

'You've no right to talk like that,' she went on, needing to have the last say in the matter. 'Especially as what I do brings in enough for us to sometimes come by a little extra under the counter.'

Lots of people dealt in the black market, though she preferred to call it 'under the counter', but they had to have money to do it. So what right did he have to sneer?

He too was beginning to tire of the argument, and besides, Addie was looking from one to the other, her little face filled with concern.

All he could say as Brenda put his tea on the table, was, 'I suppose yer think *you're* running the family now.

It's like I said, I begin ter wonder why I ever come 'ome.'

Weary of it all, Brenda didn't answer though quietly under her breath she said, 'Sometimes I wish you hadn't.' But to say such a thing aloud would have been like saying she wished he'd been killed. In truth at this moment she almost found herself wishing that at least he'd found himself a bit of foreign stuff, perhaps in Sicily or Italy, and stayed there!

Without warning the face of John Stebbings came to hover, bringing such longing and regret that she had to keep her face averted from Harry in case he thought the sudden welling of tears stemmed from what he'd said. He was the last one she felt like crying over at the moment, filled with anger at him as she was. She felt an unbearable need for the one who'd been taken.

If only she hadn't turned John away that day, he might be alive now. How would her life have panned out had she taken up his offer, broken up her marriage and stayed with him? Feeling as she did at this particular moment, she wouldn't have been the least put out how Harry took it. But that was all hindsight and it was no good crying over spilled milk.

Yet it was more than mere spilled milk – it was how different her life could have been. She had chosen Harry. That didn't mean he could come home playing the lord and master he'd seen himself as before the war. The war had changed all that sort of thing and she refused to return to it, even if this marriage threatened to break up as a result. Better that than be bullied into the way it used to be. But it wouldn't come to that, or so she prayed.

Though the tears refused to be controlled, Brenda called out to Adele who had gone to play in her bedroom away from the arguing. Hardly waiting for her to reply she went off to fetch her.

By the time she returned to sit her daughter up to the table, her tears had dried, and she had put the memory of John Stebbings firmly out of reach as far as it could safely be put for the time being.

Chapter Twenty-nine

'That's it!' Harry threw himself down in one of the armchairs, his face dark as a thunder cloud. 'Got me washin' bloody floors and cleanin' urinals. They said they wanted a mechanic. They didn't say they wanted a blinkin' lavatory cleaner. Said I'd 'ave ter work up ter bein' a mechanic. Like I was a bleedin' kid out of school instead of someone what fought for 'is country when sods like that stayed sittin' all cushy at 'ome. I told 'em ter stuff their bloody job!'

'Oh, Harry.' Brenda laid his plate of lamb stew steaming on the table. 'That's the third one you've walked out on in a month.'

'So bloody what! I ain't bein' treated like some snotty-nosed kid.'

'No, of course not. They've got no right to treat yer like that.'

Of course she supported him in this, but thoughts were in her mind which she was loath to voice, for the month hadn't gone smoothly. When she had finally persuaded Harry to go and find something, anything, her suggestion that he try this resettlement training lark had met with a storm of rage. He insisted he was already a skilled mechanic and didn't need no fucking retraining.

He'd never sworn this bad before going off into the army. Now every sentence was punctuated with one oath or another, some really vile. She too had become angry and told him not to use his foul-mouthed army language in front of the child and to go and clean his mouth out before he said any more. It would work for perhaps a day or two before he was off again.

'See what you've done?' she railed at him last week as she caught Addie telling a doll that she was an 'orrible little sod! 'I won't have you effing and blinding all over the place, Harry. And especially when she's around. You ain't in the army now.'

But it wasn't even that which bothered her. It was how she was going to gentle him towards this idea she had, an idea that kept raising its head but to which she knew even before saying anything he would never agree. He'd see it as her putting him down – as if he no longer had control of his family. The truth to her mind was that he didn't and he knew he didn't and it irked him.

She would never ever be able to bring herself to live in the house in Leytonstone, much less ask him to. It should have been tempting to have space in which to breathe, instead of this cramped flat in a largely bombed-out East End. Many times she'd wondered if she could bear that sweet ghost that would always lurk there, each time knowing she could never do so – such bitterness, so much self-recrimination lay in that direction. And now to fly in the face of Harry's self-esteem; was she sticking her neck out too far?

Yet she couldn't turn away from this idea in her head. If she were to sell the house, though it would tear her apart to do so, the money could go towards getting Harry a small garage of his own. The price of houses was rising fast with a housing shortage now the war was over. People were crying out for somewhere to live. She would get a good price. And with a business of his own maybe Harry would let her get on with hers. With both of them bringing in money they could buy a nice house without him feeling patronised.

It all sounded so easy. The problem would be getting him to agree to her suggestion without feeling himself in her debt. His pride and his self-respect, the things she had always loved about him, could present an insurmountable barrier. It was natural for him as the man to want to be the one to make decisions, but the war had changed a lot of things. Women left on their own had learned to become more independent, but already she was hearing about how it had started breaking up marriages. Did she want that for her and Harry? But it wouldn't come to that, not with her marriage, and it was worth a try.

'That place in Leytonstone,' she began one evening with Harry home after a miserable day in the garage he was working at and Addie tucked up in bed. 'I was wondering, what if we was to put it on the market, I reckon it'd sell with no bother at all. With this housing shortage, it'd get snapped up. We'd get good money for it.'

She kept her eyes on the sock she was darning, one of Harry's demob socks that was already going threadbare. 'With what we make on that you could find premises somewhere and start up a repair garage, your own business.'

For a moment his silence sounded as though he were in agreement. Then, 'With what *you* make, not we. It's your 'ouse not mine, and I'm not 'avin' you provide *me* wiv a business – bloody patronisin' me.'

She let her darning fall into her lap. 'Don't say it like that, Harry. I'm trying ter help, trying ter do what's best for all of us.'

'I'll save up me own money, thank you.'

'What on?' she couldn't help snapping. She felt angry at having her offer thrown back in her face.

'On what I earn.'

'And how long is that going to take, on *what you earn*?' She couldn't help the sarcasm. He was being so silly.

'Let me worry about that,' he answered tersely. 'I don't want your money. I can get it together meself.'

'When?'

'When I'm ready.'

'That'll be never,' she shot at him. 'Meantime there's a bloody good house in a decent-class neighbourhood sitting doin' nothink.' She couldn't help swearing, she had become so angry with him and his foolish pride. 'On top of it I'm paying good money in rates that we could well do with here.'

'Oh yeah, *you're* payin' good money – not me, not us, you. Always you!' He'd jumped up out of his chair and reached for the packet of cigarettes on the mantel-piece. Now he was furiously searching for a box of matches. 'Well, I'm the breadwinner 'ere, not you. And the sooner you give that bloody so-called business of yours up and learn to be my wife proper while I go out and keep us, the bloody better.'

'And throw away all we 'ave?' She too was on her feet. 'No, Harry, I'm not going to give up my hairdressing just to succour your conscience.'

'Oh, *succour,*' he burst out, viciously throwing the cigarette packet down on the floor. 'Don't we use bleedin' posh words these days. *Succour*! What's that mean when it's about then? Gone all bleedin' 'igh an' mighty, ain't we, since we run our own so-called business. Well, get this inter yer 'ead, Brenda, I ain't 'avin' nothink ter do wiv your *business* or that bloody 'ouse of yours. Yer can do what yer like wiv it, I don't want none of it – you boastin' to everyone in years ter come that you 'ad ter keep me, I couldn't look after me own family. Yer was soddin' mad ter buy it in the first place. And now yer fink yer goin' ter keep me? No one keeps me! Least of all you, me own wife. I'd rather not be married than be dictated to by you.'

'Right!' Brenda's heart was thumping savagely in her fury. 'If that's what you want we can start gettin' divorced immediately. I managed without you all them years you was away. I can do it again. I ain't strapped for cash, if you are, and I don't want to live on what you earn when there's money to keep us in comfort. You're the silliest sod I've ever come across, Harry, and you never used ter be. I 'oped we'd be able to pull together, but if you want to end it, that's orright with me!'

Flinging herself from the room, she went to bed in a welter of fury and some regret at how it had all erupted. Raging inside it took ages for sleep to come. Harry hadn't come to bed and when she woke next morning he had already gone to work although it was too early to leave. No doubt he was walking the streets.

The settee showed signs of having been slept on and as Brenda tidied it she went over and over their argument the night before. Surely he hadn't meant what he'd said about ending their marriage? But if it came to it, she could go it alone. Trouble was, she didn't want to.

On the last Saturday of April, Brian took Ceil out and bought her a modest little engagement ring from a little backstreet jeweller. On their way to tell their happy news to their parents, they popped in to show Brenda the loop of three chip diamonds.

'What d'yer think of it?' asked Brian as she congratulated them both and forced a smile of appreciation, remembering how happy she and Harry had been when he had slipped his own modest little ring on her finger.

She and Harry had been somewhat distant towards each other since that row they'd had in March. He'd come home giving no apology for going off without saying cheerio to her or sleeping on the sofa all night. It was as though it hadn't happened except for this relative silence between them. Although he was now looking for a better job, not that he'd found anything to suit him so far, Brenda felt that rather than to win her approval it was to show that her income should always take second place to his.

'You are glad fer us, ain't you, Bren?' queried Brian, noticing her glum face so that she had to force herself to perk up and smile at them.

'Of course I am. I'm thrilled for you both. And I know you'll have a really happy life together.'

'I wonder,' she thought after they'd gone. Maybe they would; starting their new life together with the war a thing of the past, there would be no thought of him being torn from her. The war was to blame for so many broken marriages. A man expected to come home and pick up the reins, not realising that for four or more years his wife had been coping alone and now resented being relegated to the background once more. After looking forward with eagerness and hope to his return she would often see her illusions of joy totally shattered.

'We ain't 'avin' no engagement party,' Ceil told both parents on displaying the three tiny diamonds on which Brian had blown most of his demob money. 'We can't really afford it now.' But she said it cheerfully.

'Our first concern,' he agreed, 'is ter save as much as we can fer the wedding we're planning fer this time next year, and of course finding somewhere ter live.'

Both parents looked doubtful. People were snapping up the tiniest couple of rooms; with so many homes destroyed and thousands coming out of the forces to get married and settled down, demand far exceeded supply. Living accommodation was almost impossible to come by, though if you had money you were all right, but mostly that was beyond ordinary youngsters.

But Brian was confident. 'We'll get somethink by next year,' he said, gazing fondly at Ceil. 'But we can't go wastin' money on parties.'

'No, we can't, love,' she agreed, returning his gaze that said she was sure he'd find them the most beautiful love nest there ever was.

'Anyway, I don't want all that palaver of sendin' out invitations ter people what only want a free booze-up,' he announced.

'I ain't sorry,' Mum said to Brenda. 'Having ter get all that bloomin' food tergether with rations gettin' worse instead of better. An ounce down on this, an ounce down on that. Worse'n in the war. If that's what come of us winnin' it, I'd 'ate ter think what it would of bin like if we'd lorst it. Next year we'll 'ave a really good wedding ter make up fer it. By that time things'll all be off ration, we 'ope. Besides, I ain't ready ter start keepin' up with people like your Harry's mum. From what I can see of it, it's all show with 'er. Not one but two welcome 'ome parties! Blimey, it was enough fer me with my two boys, without trying ter keep up with the likes of 'er an' do another one.'

Brenda was inclined to agree. Mrs Hutton couldn't help the way she was, but she was inclined to grab the lion's share of attention all the time and was still doing it even now.

Harry had taken to going round to see her in between looking for his perfect mechanic's job. She was still interfering, offering bags of sympathy for his dull existence after his exciting army life. He'd come home saying, 'Mum says she'd look after Addie if we want ter go out tergether,' or, 'Mum thinks yer go on at me too much fer not getting a better job and that somethink'll come along eventually,' and again, 'She says I've only been 'ome a couple of months and ter give it time and not get so impatient.'

Brenda seethed in silence. To ask where he thought the money would come from for them to go out when he'd never agree to her forking out for it would only add grist to the grindstone of this teetering marriage. To say they hadn't any real money worries would be like saying she could afford to keep them and put his back up anew. Again and again arose the dilemma of how to approach the subject of selling the place in Leytonstone so as to put the money into a business of his own.

Coming up to April and still Vera waited. 'December they told us it was all OK,' she fretted. 'But we're still 'ere.'

In December an act had been passed by Congress allowing admission into the United States of alien spouses. 'What an 'orrible word,' she'd burst out on first hearing of it. 'I'm not an alien. I'm English!'

At the time it had been a step in the right direction, but the months had passed and no more appeared to have happened. 'A lot of the wives 'ave bin 'olding marches and 'anding in petitions to the American Embassy,' Vera told everyone. 'Somethink's got ter 'appen soon.'

Her mother nodded, pressed her lips together and kept her own counsel. But Brenda could read her mind.

'I don't want her to go,' she saw in her eyes. 'I don't want to lose her, but I'm going to. I'll never see her again, never see the grandchildren again.'

If it were the last thing she did it would be to send her and Dad over there for a visit to Vera and her husband and the two boys.

Again came thoughts of the house in Leytonstone and silently she blessed John Stebbings. If Harry refused to recognise it as their salvation, she would do what she liked with it – sell it and put the money into the bank to accrue interest. John would never know what good he'd wrought, when some of it paid for Mum and Dad to visit the United States.

It would make a hole in the funds but that was what the money was for: to help her family as John had meant to help her. And then, who knew, maybe after a while Harry would get used to it being there and agree to get his own garage. At the moment though she was heartily sick of this stupid attitude of his. A change of heart would come sooner or later, she vowed, but if it didn't, what of their marriage? She preferred not to think of that just now, but one thing she did know. Either way she wasn't prepared to knuckle down under Harry's rules. After all these years on her own she'd become her own woman and come what may there was no going back to the old ways now. But again she preferred not to think about it, and would concentrate on her mother.

It must feel to her that everyone was leaving her. The war had wrenched her sons from her; though they had come home she must now suffer this other wrench, in fact more than one with Vera sailing to the other side of the world and Davy hardly setting foot in the house before he was off to the home of his French girlfriend, Monique, at St Maur near Paris. No doubt when they married, as he was sure they would, they would settle down there. He was even talking about adopting the Catholic faith, which, to his mum, was like throwing his upbringing in her face. Next year Brian was getting married except he'd only be round the corner, which was not quite so bad; he planned to live with his future in-laws until they found a place of their own, if and when.

It had become accepted, this living with families. Thousands found themselves without a home of their own, after coming out of the forces. And they needed somewhere to live, what with all those wartime marriages. Couples kept their noses to the ground like deerhounds and would pester the milkman, the coalman, the postman, even the rent collector who might know of a couple of rooms going before they got snapped up. Meantime people stayed stuck with parents and in-laws, getting under each other's feet; quarrels broke out, marriages broke up, normal marital pursuits became a furtive business with so many ears to hear the squeak of bedsprings, the unguarded sigh, the smallest cry of joy.

Brenda felt so sorry for those starting out married life in someone else's home and she cringed in guilt knowing she had a house standing empty. But that house was her means of keeping the job she loved doing. She was prepared to sell it to help out others, yes, but not to give it away, and ruin hopes of her own for the future. She didn't think she was being selfish. At least she hoped she wasn't.

'The place ain't 'alf goin' ter feel empty without them all,' Mum lamented briefly, but squared her shoulders, ready to face it. 'As all mums 'ave ter at some time or other, I s'pose. Though yer dad says it'll be nice to 'ave the place all to ourselves. An' I suppose he's right so I mustn't really grumble an' upset 'im.'

Her stoic remark wrung Brenda's heart. But mainly it irked – Mum was knuckling down in the old way of women subservient to their menfolk. She was blowed if she was going to be subservient to hers after all she'd achieved.

*

'I feel so guilty and rotten,' Vera had said, 'leaving Mum like I'm goin' to.' But that second Monday in April, all guilt seemed to leave her as she rushed over to Brenda who was working rapidly on an elderly woman's hair before snatching a moment to go up to her flat to enjoy a quick cuppa and a Spam sandwich for lunch. Adele was at school and Harry was out, having found temporary building work. It was not his cup of tea, still hankering as he was to be a car mechanic, but it paid more.

Vera was out of breath from running as she burst into the salon. 'Oh, Bren, I've 'eard at last. It come this morning. I 'ad ter rush round as quick as I could ter let yer know because I could be goin' at any moment. Mum's in a right stew. It could even be termorrer, I really don't know.' Vera's face began to pucker as Brenda stared at her, the comb she was using poised above her client's head.

'Quick as that? Oh, Vera, they couldn't do that to you – or to Mum.'

'It's what they've said. I've bin told ter be in a state of ready – that's 'ow they've put it – ter leave within twenty-four hours.'

'Twenty-four . . .' Brenda broke off in shock while her elderly client, sensing some drama, clicked her tongue in sympathy despite being unaware of what it was about.

'They say it's the present shortage of shipping and they can't estimate an approximate date any of us'll be able ter sail. We come under the United States Transporting Office what used ter move men to the war, and they're using the same ships ter move us off to America. Bren, it's come so sudden.'

Brenda breathed in a sigh of relief. Vera was exaggerating again. It could be weeks yet. She bet Vera had already frightened the living daylights out of Mum too with her tendency to panic over the smallest of things.

'It might not be all that sudden,' she soothed. 'They mean you to be ready to *leave* in twenty-four hours, Vera. They don't mean it will be twenty-four hours from this very minute. It could still take ages.'

Vera's face grew even more distressed at the statement. 'It's so unfair! They've bin keeping us apart all these months, and they still want ter keep us apart. I don't think they really want their men ter marry English girls. They look down on us. I'll never get ter see Hank at this rate.'

Vera could be so exasperating, one minute panicking that she might have to leave her home and beloved family at a moment's notice, then on being reassured that it might not be that quick, turning things completely round to complain of delays. What did she want?

'Vera, I've got customers to see to. I'll see you at the weekend, love. Then we can talk more about it.'

'I might not be 'ere by the weekend,' Vera said, despondently and not a little ominously. But Brenda wasn't to be cajoled into spending more time and sympathy on her.

'If you want to go up and make yerself a cup of tea,' she suggested, but Vera shook her head.

'I want ter get back ter see if Mum's orright. I left 'er in tears – or nearly in tears.'

Brenda didn't doubt it and decided to tell Harry she would pop round there this evening to see if there was anything she could do. Lately she and Harry were on better talking terms; the matter of selling the house had been shelved with all this business of Vera leaving to go half across the world, although he was still carping about this 'bloody hairdressing lark' as he called it. He might even consent to come along with her.

'I ain't 'alf goin' ter miss them little ones,' said Mum, her eyes on the robust little boys, blissfully ignorant of their imminent new life in another country, playing happily on the floor. Vera was out shopping, getting things together for her journey, though it seemed the USA would be providing an awful lot of it.

Two years old now, Vera's boys, Sam and Henry, had become Mum's whole life. She spent time with them constantly, urging Vera to go out with friends to the pictures while she gave eye to them. It was as though she was drinking them in, the last sip of precious water to sustain her in her barren world when they finally departed for a new land, a new life with different grandparents fondly gazing at them. She would become consigned to the mists of the past, would become just a name written on a letter: Nanny Wilson.

Watching her gaze at them, Brenda was conscious of just the tiniest stab of uninvited jealousy. Mum used to give Addie all her attention in that way but with Vera's twin boys in her home now it was practically as though they'd taken Addie's place in her heart. But naturally they would and should – all three of them were her grandchildren but after the other two had gone, only the one would be left and her attention would return to Addie.

With that in mind, such puny envy dissipated; such sadness for her mother took its place that it was hard to stop her eyes from filling with tears. She too would miss Vera dreadfully, and the children, so how much worse must it be for Mum? But she was taking it so stoically, the only sign of her breaking heart the words, 'I ain't 'alf goin' ter miss them little ones.'

It was the first of May and Vera was in a flap. Tomorrow evening she and her children would be on board ship. She should have been relieved that the wait was over, that soon she'd be with her husband, the children with their father, but all she could do was weep, throwing her arms about her mother's neck with each fresh burst of tears with Mum patting her gently on the back to console her. Mum's own eyes remained fixed upon some distant point, arid with grief, while Dad looked on uselessly.

It had turned into such a terrible rush, with Vera torn between excitement and sorrow, anticipation and apprehension, having signed all the forms and read the booklet sent to those leaving for America, *A Bride's Guide to the USA,* from cover to cover and got together all on the list of things to take with her. She wore the outfit Henry (the name his family knew him by, Hank having been for the benefit of his pals in the forces) had sent her in a parcel. She'd bought wine-coloured shoes with matching hat and handbag to go with the grey suit, and looked very smart.

'It's like I'm in America already. I look just like Betty Grable does,' she enthused and failed to notice the bleak look these words brought to her mother's face.

416

Henry's parcel had also contained outfits for the boys that made both toddlers look American the moment she put them on Henry and Sam: long trousers, chunky sweaters, tiny baseball caps.

'As if they're already livin' there,' said Mum, and Brenda, waiting with her and Dad to leave for Waterloo Station where Vera would board a train for Southampton, heard the lonely bitterness in her voice. She wondered if Vera had. But Vera was too taken up with the hastiness of the moment.

It was a painful train journey to Waterloo. The station was crowded; a lot of uniforms could be seen still despite the war having been over a whole year. But they were drab British uniforms, British men still waiting to be demobbed. The GIs had all gone back home. Now Vera was following them, bound for the unknown.

In the while it took for the train to leave, Vera leaned from the carriage-door window, having dropped it down as far as it would go, for a last conversation with her family. Among all those saying their farewells, nostrils filled with the warm odour of engine oil and of acrid smoke, ears deafened by the echoing noise of a busy main station, the rattle of mail trucks, the shouting of porters, the whistle of release steam, thunderous puffing of trains leaving and the shriek of others arriving, they had to practically shout to be heard.

Talk was stilted. 'You take care now, won't yer?'

Dad had gone inside with her to hoist her suitcase up on to the mesh luggage rack. He now stood ineffectually on the platform, gazing up at the daughter he would never see again. How would he ever afford for himself and Mum to go all the way to America?

Vera nodded, eyes glistening with tears. 'I will, Dad.' The words had become choked in her throat. 'You take care too.'

'I 'ope the sandwiches are orright. I 'ope they're enough.'

Mum had lovingly cut them that morning, opening a precious tin of ham kept back from Christmas. Not the great doorsteps she usually made, but cut thin, each sandwich of ham and cucumber sliced into four dainty triangles reflecting all her love for the daughter who within minutes would be leaving her forever.

'There's plenty there, Mum. I'll look forward to 'avin' 'em.'

Her voice, harshly Cockney, would eventually soften with the adoption of an American accent. If they saw her again in some future year they'd hardly know her. Again Brenda made her silent vow that if it was in her power to send them over there, they'd get to know her again. But was it wise? Any visit would always be a short affair. They'd suffer this pain of parting all over again.

Sending them, she wouldn't be able to afford to go herself, and she wouldn't go without Harry and Adele. She would never see her sister again. It was all she could do not to turn away and hide her tears. She needed to feast her eyes on her sister to the very last moment, consign that face, that way of talking, that way of standing, to memory, even though the reality would change, unseen other than in photos sent back, and the voice would maybe one day be heard only in a long-distance, distorted phone call.

'There's a bit of cake in there as well. A bit of me own cake.'

This brought a fresh glistening of tears. Cake made by her mother's own hands – the last thing she had that had been made by Mum. The look on her face said that she didn't want to eat it but to keep it until it grew hard and crumbled away.

'I 'ope there's enough there fer you and the babies.'

They weren't babies any longer, but in her eyes they were and always would be.

'There's plenty, Mum. Thank you, Mum.'

The whistle was blowing, the guard waving his flag. Doors slammed. People sat back in their seats. Last-second travellers sprinted for the train before it could begin moving, yanked open doors and reached out to slam them shut behind themselves. Scores of women, alone, leaving for the same destination, leaned down to kiss loved ones and wave a last goodbye.

Vera leaned down too, kissed her parents, grabbed Brenda's hand and pulled her close for a cuddle. 'Thanks fer everythink you've done in the past, Bren,' she whispered. 'I'm gonna miss you.'

Breaking away she picked Sam and Henry up and held them to the open window for each to be kissed by everyone in turn, a hasty business, an all too brief touch of lips on the cool, silky, baby skin.

The train was beginning to move, steam erupting from it, the funnel letting loose explosive puffs of dark smoke, the whistle valve giving out a high-pitched, ear-splitting shriek. Carriages shuddered, their passengers jerked forward then back.

Vera held her two boys in one arm against the door support, then held up her free arm to wave.

'Bye . . . Take care . . . 'bye . . . love you . . . love you, Mum, Dad, Bren . . . 'Bye, Mum. Mum, look at me, please . . . turn round and look at me . . .'

But Mum had turned away, merely raising a hand, her back view the last Vera saw of her as the Southampton train bore her and her children off.

Brenda and her father stood until the last carriage disappeared from sight. Brenda came to herself and hurried ahead of her dad to put an arm round Mum's thickened waist as they walked from Waterloo Station. Neither of them said anything. There were no words to be said.

Chapter Thirty

Vera was gone. Davy was gone, living with his fiancee's people in St Maur. She didn't miss Davy so much; he had been away so long in the forces that childhood closeness had melted away long ago.

But she missed her sister dreadfully, missed the times she'd loaded her problems on to Vera: Harry's refusal to take her hairdressing business seriously, sneering at it though apparently willing for her to pay the bills he couldn't; his refusal to have anything to do with the house everyone believed she'd bought herself; the rows and arguments they'd had over it and her own refusal to bow to his dictates – all of which Vera used to listen to with little noises of sympathy that, while offering no solution, made her feel she at least had a listening ear. Now there was no one to talk to about it. She couldn't burden Mum with it. Mum was of the old-fashioned type of woman and would judge her unfair to a husband who had fought for his country and now by rights should resume his life as head of his family.

With no one to consult or take her side, Brenda could only ponder on how to raise the question of the house yet again without causing a ruckus. For a while it seemed better to keep her mouth shut. But somehow one summer evening it just sprang up out of a perfectly ordinary conversation while they were having a bedtime cuppa.

It was a perfect evening, the sky still faintly tinged by afterglow. Addie lay asleep, and a shared moment or two of talk would hopefully lead to one of their frequent bouts of snuggling close in their own bed and making love. But her mind seldom strayed far from the thing that forever bugged her.

Harry had in fact been talking about property, about how 'them with money' seemed to reap yet more. 'Buyin' old places an' doing 'em up inter flats, makin' a bomb lettin' 'em out ter people what'll pay anyfink fer a roof over their 'eads.'

'You know, love,' she said casually, 'we're wasting an awful lot of money we could be living on, still paying rates on that place of ours in Leytonstone. Why don't *we* let it out then, like other people are doin', and get something back from it? It's standing there all empty and—'

'Your place, not ours,' he cut in, his tone grown suddenly harsh. She shouldn't have felt surprise. Reference to the house always provoked this reaction. But she did.

Trying to ignore it, she continued in an unruffled tone, 'Think about it, Harry, we could get a decent income if we let it out. I don't know why we never thought of it before. We could live quite well on it if you don't want us to sell it outright.'

'That's *yours*,' he growled in reply. 'What *you* bought.' It wasn't said generously, more an accusation, and now she couldn't help but rise to the bait.

'Why d'you keep sayin' it's mine? I bought it because it was cheap at the time, thinkin' it'd stand us in good stead when you came out of the forces.' She hurriedly closed her ears to her own lie and ploughed on. 'We're married, Harry. What's yours is mine and what's mine is yours. I saw it as somethink for us to fall back on if we ever hit hard times.'

'And wivvout consultin' me. Goin' be'ind me back.'

'How could I consult you when you was miles away?'

'Fortunate, weren't it, me bein' miles away? Didn't 'ave me ter tell yer not ter be such a bloody fool.'

'How could I of been such a bloody fool when what I bought fer next to nothing is worth lots more now?'

She was near to believing her own lies. 'Enough ter keep us in comfort the rest of our lives if we sold it, an' if we didn't, rentin' it out. You can be such a bloody fool when you want ter be, just because *you* want to hold the reins. You'd cut off yer own bloody nose fer that, wouldn't yer? Yer can't stand the thought of me bringin' in money. Grow up, Harry. Things ain't like they was before the war. This is today, and women work!'

Furious with him, she was aware of the deterioration in her speech. Of late she had let it go, having on one occasion come upstairs from her salon and listened to him mimic the nice accent she used to her customers. 'All bloody la-di-da, nowadays, ain't we?' he'd said, his unkind and unexpected sneer stunning her rigid.

'Yer can keep what bleedin' money you make on that 'ouse yerself,' he was saying, slamming down his nightcap

423

cup of cocoa and leaping up to stride across the room to turn off the wireless that was broadcasting a late evening drama. 'It ain't nuffink ter do wiv me.'

'Course it's somethink to do with you,' she blazed, she too putting her cup down on the floor to stand up and face him. 'We could be doin' bloody well on what that'd fetch. You'd 'ave a garage of yer own and I'd 'ave me 'airdressin'. But no, you want—'

'Oh, that's what's in yer mind?' he shot back at her. 'I ain't bright enough ter get a job of me own. I ain't that good a mechanic ter be taken seriously and need you ter set me up on *your* money an' make me look a right chump in front of everyone. Let everyone see I can't stand on me own two feet wivvout your 'elp. Poor old 'Arry can't do nuffink wivvout 'is wife to 'elp 'im get a job. Well, no fuckin' thanks! Yer can stick yer bloody money and yer bloody 'elp an' yer bloody business – stick it all up yer arse fer all I care.'

How could he swear at her like that when she wanted only to help him? At this very moment she felt she could go for him with both fists or better still, aim her cocoa cup at him. But what good would that do?

'And sod you too!' she yelled back. 'I'm stuck with a silly bugger what don't see somethink good when it stares 'im in the face.'

'What stares me in the face is that yer can do wivvout me,' he bawled, shoving past her and almost knocking her over. 'Well, maybe we can sort that one out too. I'm orf ter bed!'

'Thank you for all your faith in me!' she yelled after him.

In the silence he'd left in his wake she sank back down in her chair in a welter of misery and confusion as to how all this had started. But didn't it always start up out of nothing? Why couldn't he accept what she had to give? Why hate her having a business, her possession of that house? She'd thought only of him when she'd bought . . . She pulled herself up. God, she really was believing her own lies. Were he to know how she had really come by that house it would certainly finish this marriage.

Another day, another argument, Harry standing morose, staring out at the warm June sunshine of this Friday evening as she came upstairs after closing the salon a little late.

The shop had been so busy, women wanting their hair done in time for their first proper summer break in seven years, a weekend or a week at the seaside with the whole family. Some had probably tried it last year to find most once out-of-bounds beaches still cluttered with rusting barbed wire and reinforced cement blockhouses, even though a portion of wire was pulled back to allow them to paddle in the sea. Cleared at last, Londoners could enjoy their first real taste of the seaside since 1939. Especially the kids, the little ones, who would be experiencing their first-ever visit. Perhaps after the summer rush was over and the salon became less busy she and Harry could take Addie.

After working flat out, Brenda was worn out, looking only to get their tea and settle down on the sofa. But as she came into the room Harry spoke without turning round, his tone almost a snarl.

''Bout bloody time too.'

'Yes, I'm so sorry,' she agreed. 'It has absolutely been hectic all day.'

She was stopped by his cynical laugh. As he turned she saw his lips drawn down in sarcasm at her salon talk.

'H-oh, h-as it, now? H-as it been h-absolutely h-ectic, h'all day, then? H-ain't you the busy one!'

A small spurt of anger touched her. He was harking after yet another row, as ever jealous of her skill, her success in the job she loved, where he had still not settled down.

Sometimes she wondered if he wasn't deliberately trying not to, spiting her, jealous that rather than being the little wife who relied on him alone, she might very well be capable of doing without him altogether.

Maybe that was being unfair to him, but that was how she felt. And so did a lot of other wives towards their husbands judging by what she gleaned as she did her clients' hair.

'Stupid old fool!' one had muttered after recounting some incident with a husband. 'Cock of the North now he's 'ome, but 'e can't even mend a fuse wivvout cryin' out ter me ter run around gettin' this an' gettin' that for 'im. When I fink 'ow many times I've 'ad ter mend fuses, and build shelves, and keep the kids in order, doin' two or three fings at once, and all on me own too, I could swipe 'im one.'

And another: 'I ain't gonna doff me cap to 'im every time 'e snaps 'is fingers. We're rowing like blazes all day, then 'e thinks he's entitled to a bit of the other the moment we get to bed. Well, no thank you! He can get

426

'is oats somewhere's else! Me, I've got out of the 'abit. Once in a while, yeah, but not every blessed night.'

It was like this with most of them so why should she be any different, having Harry run rings round her with his moans and his jealousies?

'Don't start, Harry,' she begged wearily.

All she wanted was a sit-down and a few minutes of normal chat before getting tea. It would have been nice if he'd started cutting the bread or peeling the potatoes, but that wasn't a man's job! The least he could have done was butter a bit of bread for Addie, who, having heard her voice, came running into the room from her bedroom where she'd been playing to fling herself at her. 'Mummy! I'm hungry. I wanna drink of orange juice.'

Brenda sighed, and picking her up gave her a kiss on the cheek. 'Yes, I know, love. I'm getting something right now.'

She was blowed if she would drop her genteel talk for Harry. At this moment she couldn't care less if he did take the rise out of her. To think she'd been saving her dreams of blissful married life all this time – for this? She should have gone off with John . . .

'She ain't the only one what's 'ungry,' Harry butted into her thoughts. 'I bin waitin' 'arf-hour fer you ter come up ter make a bloody cuppa tea. S'pose you 'ad yours downstairs.'

Brenda sucked in a fierce breath, then let it out in a torrent of sarcasm. 'You know where the kettle is – you know where the tap is – and the gas stove. You fill the kettle from the tap, put it on the stove, light a match and turn on the blooming knob!' Her voice rose on those

427

words. 'After that it does itself. At least we'd of 'ad the kettle boilin' fer the tea. Can't you even do a simple thing like that?'

'I've bin workin' all bleedin' day.'

'Hod-carrying on a building site, making a blessed point of not findin' a proper job just so you can 'ave a dig at me working.' In her annoyance all the nice talk went out of the window. 'Sometimes I wonder if you ain't come 'ome not quite right in the 'ead, you've come 'ome so bloody unreasonable.'

'Don't yer swear at me,' he bellowed. 'I'm bleedin' worn out.'

'So am I,' she shot back at him.

'Then give up that bloody job you keep callin' a business.' His words became a taunt. ''Ow would we exist if you wasn't bringin' in the dosh? My, it's more'n I can ever make 'cos mine's only a bloody pittance, an' we can't live on that, can we?'

'If you was ter . . .'

No, she wouldn't make an issue of the opportunity staring him in the face, his own business. It would only provoke a worse row, with him again insisting that he wasn't going to be patronised by her and her money. Addie was looking from one to the other, her little face tense, her little mouth gaping, her blue eyes wide. No, not in front of Addie, that same old damned argument.

'I'll get tea,' she said wearily and hurried out to put the kettle on and start on the meal.

'Listen, your place is ter look after me,' he was shouting, 'Not ter muck about down there.'

July was as busy as June had been. Harry had got a job in a garage at last, which he appeared to be sticking to this time though still not earning what she was bringing in. And that was the crux of it.

Brenda sighed and went to get tea. It was hard not to retaliate. It upset Addie. She would tackle him later, keeping her voice down with Addie safely in bed. Maybe she would tackle him on the house too. Her first idea of renting it out seemed not so good now. A weekly income was of no use; she earned enough. What was needed was a lump sum to buy that garage.

The house continued to sit all empty and forlorn; were local people wondering about its untreated paintwork, its yellowing curtains, its overgrown garden, maybe even annoyed knowing that so many were looking for homes? John Stebbings' ghost must be lonely indeed, and fancifully she often imagined it wandering through the empty rooms looking for her.

In between working, taking Addie to school and looking after Harry, where was the time to do it up? Anyway it needed a man to sort it all out and Harry wasn't going to do it, that was for sure.

Harry had followed her into the kitchen. 'Did you 'ear what I said? You an' this 'airdressin' lark. I've bin 'ome fer months now, and I'm telling yer it's time for yer to give up working now I've got a decent job.'

Her patience snapping, she turned to him. 'You could have an even better job if you set up on your own.'

'Oh yeah,' he sneered. 'You'll buy me my own garage and set me up. Well I ain't having no wife of mine *setting me up!* D'yer hear? As fer that blasted job of yours, I ain't askin' yer, I'm telling yer – yer can give that all up too. In me own 'ome I say 'oo works and 'oo don't!'

Brenda's blood seethed through her like soup in a hot cauldron. 'You what?' Her eyes blazed at him. 'You'd sooner cut off your nose to spite your own face just so you can feel satisfied, you an' yer bloody pride!'

'I don't want ter 'ear any more about it,' he warned, but nothing was going to stop her now.

In anger she threw down the tea towel with which she'd been about to get his tea out of the oven. 'Well, you're going to, Harry, whether you like it or not. I've just about 'ad it up to here with all of this. You and your stupid bloody pride, you don't want ter look beyond your stupid nose, that's your trouble. With the money from that place you could be laughing. Your own car repair shop, your own car, all of us livin' in luxury. But no, you want it your way, but I tell you what I think. You ain't got the gumption to start out on yer own. Well, I have.'

She didn't give him a chance to butt in as her tirade stormed on. 'All the time you was away I looked after myself and because I made a success of it and didn't write to you crying that I couldn't exist without your 'elp, it got up your nose. You're bloomin' jealous that I've got on and you haven't – or don't want to more like!'

As she ceased, breathless from yelling, he faced her, leaning forward, fists clenched as though to launch himself into a physical fight.

'Right, if you think yer can get on wivvout me, you can go on an' do just that. I don't want no more of takin' second place in this marriage. We're finished. We can sort out the details, and when that's done I'll pick up me old life an' go back ter bloody Italy where I was 'appy wiv that—'

Shocked by the path this argument had taken, Brenda felt more shock as he broke off sharply. He was blinking as though he'd nearly come out with something he hadn't intended to.

Something inside her was asking just what had he been up to out there in Italy that she didn't know about, suddenly aware of that part of his life which had lain hidden from her just as hers had been from him. A woman? No, not Harry. But why not? He'd never imagine her going with another man; she would never have imagined it of herself. But she had. Why not him then, out there in that warm and romantic Mediterranean climate?

For a moment jealousy consumed her before reason returned with the realisation of how close they were to ruining this marriage. What would she do if their marriage broke up? For all their arguments it was the last thing she wanted. If it were to, what of her business? She'd done all this for him. What would be the point of going on if he threw it all in her face?

She could only stand there gaping as he turned on his heel, saying, 'Bugger it, and bugger you!' Bluster perhaps to cover his tracks after what he'd threatened, maybe frightening himself.

Wild thoughts began racing through her head. What if he really meant what he'd said? Even if he hadn't it was the thin end of the wedge and with both of them pulling in opposite directions it could only grow worse.

She couldn't see this marriage lasting now. What would she do if it did fail?

As though someone else was inside her head, rationality started to take over. The first thing would be to sell the house. There'd be more than enough there to keep her and Addie. Having managed alone these five years it was possible to do so again. She pushed away the thought that she didn't want to manage alone any more and kept her mind trained on rational things. With someone in charge of the salon for a while she could go and see Vera. She so needed Vera at this moment, someone to talk to, who might understand.

Vera's first letter had arrived earlier in the month and hadn't been as happy as all that. She and her husband were having to live in his parents' home on the edge of Springfield, the house, according to her letter, built only of wood.

The place feels flimsy, not like our brick, she wrote. The main room is huge, not like our cosy back room and front room and kitchen, it's all in one with no doors. Stairs go up from the main room too. But the bedrooms are really titchy. There's a veranda we sit out in. They call it a porch. Everyone can see you there. No one minds though. People are nice. His mother goes out in her dressing gown to take the mail from the box by the road. It's ever so odd. We wouldn't dream of going out in the street in our night clothes.

She had said that Henry and his father worked in a factory making steel cylinders 'and things'; that his mother didn't work, enjoying helping her with the boys, and that Henry had a younger sister and brother living there and his dad's mother and father.

When we're all round the meal table it's a real big crowd. I like them all, but I'd rather we had a place of our own. I miss our house, and London. It was so cosy. I always thought it was cramped but I can't get used to all this space. The streets are so wide and the houses so spaced out. The country is so flat, I feel that if I went too far from town I'd fall over the edge. The sky seems to go on forever. It makes everything look real small, sort of unnatural. A real uncomfortable feeling though the sunsets are beautiful. Henry says I'll get used to it in time. He couldn't get used to our funny little squiggly roads and odd little hills. I am trying though, and we are happy. It's just that I wish we had our own place so as we could be on our own.

Maybe she could help set them up in their own home, send some money from selling the house. Maybe she'd sell her business and go over there, set up there in hair-dressing – get a work permit or whatever. But that would mean leaving the familiar comfort of Mum and Dad and the rest of her family, and uprooting Addie. All she wanted deep down was to have her marriage intact. Yet still not at any price. She needed to talk to someone about it. Vera, now her mind had begun to sort itself out, was out of the question. But Mum was still handy.

The next day, when Harry had again gone to work without so much as a goodbye, neither of them speaking,

Brenda left the salon in the hands of the others for the morning and went to see Mum.

Sitting over a cup of tea in the kitchen, she told her all about it, the rows and Harry's threats, with Mum listening attentively to every word.

'So the upshot of it is,' she finished, 'if I refuse to give in to 'im our marriage is on the rocks and I don't want that to 'appen – for Addie's sake. It'd be 'orrible for 'er, but I can't just stand by while Harry tells me what I can and can't do, just so he can feel the 'ead of the 'ouse. Expecting me to give up a business I've worked so damned 'ard for, just because it all makes 'im feel inadequate. It's just not fair after all I achieved.'

Her mother's reply was disappointing. 'I can't see what else yer can do,' she said slowly, raising anger in Brenda.

It was all she needed, Mum taking sides with Harry. This wasn't what she'd come here for, to be told her role as a wife. She'd had enough of that from him. The trouble was, Mum belonged to the old school; she still believed a wife should play second fiddle to her husband, be subservient to the breadwinner, the master of the house. But she controlled her annoyance with her mother. 'And there's that place I bought in Leytonstone while he was away. He says he won't touch one penny of it if I did put it on the market – says it's nothing to do with 'im and he ain't 'aving people think I'm keeping 'im. It's the nasty way he says it.'

'Yes, now that is silly.'

Brenda looked at her with renewed hope. 'I really thought he'd be pleased with a little nest egg for 'im ter come back to. But he ain't. He says he'd rather us part company than 'im touch a penny of it. I really don't understand his thinking when he could have a nice little business of his own out of it all.'

For a moment or two her mother ruminated on this fact, saying at last and very slowly, 'I s'pose yer can see it from 'is point of view in a way. It could look to 'im as if he'll be living on your money an' no man likes the thought of that.'

'It's *our* money, Mum,' Brenda persisted. 'And it's that what he won't see. I don't know why he won't.'

'Men can be funny about that sort of thing, Bren. They ain't like us. Their pride is everythink to 'em.'

'Even ter wantin' ter break up a marriage? No, Mum, if it's just 'is pride what's at stake, he's just goin' to 'ave to learn to swallow it, because I ain't changing for 'im. I've worked 'ard for what we 'ave and I ain't ready ter let it all go just because he says so. What about my pride?'

Again her mother pondered at length, but Brenda's patience was wearing thin.

'I kept our family 'ome together all through the Blitz, livin' down in a basement, almost bombed out, puttin' up with rationin' an' doin' without,' she went on. 'But that don't seem to count for much. He sees it as a piece of cake after what he says he went through in North Africa an' Sicily an' Italy.'

'It couldn't've bin an 'appy time fer 'im neither.'

Brenda's eyes narrowed over the cup she still held, the tea now grown cold. 'Sometimes I wonder. He once told me that a lot of 'is mates 'ad a good time with Italian girls. I wonder if he didn't have a good time as

435

well. I asked him once and the way he got all shirty in an odd sort of way made me think for a while.'

Mum found her voice. 'I don't wonder, a man bein' asked a question like that. Yer probably put 'is back up.'

They were getting away from things. 'It don't alter the fact that he expects me to give everything up an' go back to bein' the little wife again. Well, I can't and I won't. Things have changed, Mum, from what they was before the war.'

'Yes, I s'pose they 'ave,' sighed her mother, then she perked up. 'But don't be silly and let it break up yer marriage. There's more'n one way ter skin a cat, Bren. I've learned that in my marriage ter yer dad. 'Ow do yer think I've kept it workin'? Yer do it bit by bit, nibbling a bit orf here, a bit orf there, until yer've whittled 'em down ter your way of thinkin'. It's no good blusterin' an' arguin'. You 'ave ter learn just 'ow ter get round 'em. Let Harry see 'imself as the man of the 'ouse, keep yer temper an' do it crafty like. Yer've got heaps of time. You ain't in no mad rush, are yer? Yer've all the time in the world. Yer don't 'ave ter go in like a bull in a Chinese shop.'

Brenda found herself smiling at the malapropism. It was perhaps the first time she'd smiled in ages. But Mum wasn't finished yet.

'Harry'll never know you've got the upper 'and of 'im. But you'll 'ave ter put up for a while with 'is nastiness and 'is sneerin'. In time he'll come round so long as you don't push things in 'is face. One day you'll find '*im* suggestin' sellin' the 'ouse. And you tell 'im what a lovely idea and how clever he is and make sure to let 'im deal with all the negotiations fer sellin' it. You see, yer'll end up the winner and 'e won't ever know. Ain't no good gettin' the upper 'and if all yer goin' ter do is ter cut it orf at the wrist in the end, is it?'

She was right of course, but it went against the grain somewhat. Were Mum's old-fashioned methods best? She didn't truly want them to be, but if it was worth a try – if she could stomach it? Mulling it all over but determined she wouldn't be the loser in all this, Brenda left her mother's house in a thoughtful if uneasy frame of mind.

Chapter Thirty-one

It was no good. All through summer she had tried to keep up this role of the easy-going wife as Mum had advised, but it was driving her round the bend, the way Harry was behaving, seeing himself as lord of the manor. The more he flung his weight around, or so it seemed to her, the angrier she grew and the more determined that this wasn't going to last much longer, even if it did mean the end of their marriage.

Maybe Mum, brought up in a different era, had taken a back seat, but this was today's world; and maybe peace had reigned throughout the summer but she was the one who was suffering, and she couldn't see herself going on forever saying yes to everything Harry said.

It was a Friday evening in September when the crunch came. Addie, who had been at a little friend's flat after school for an hour or so, was due to be picked up and brought home around seven. Harry had come home from work ready for his tea.

These days Brenda made sure to be upstairs in time for him so that he had nothing to reproach her for. Even

438

so, he still uttered the occasional snide remark about her working for all her efforts to be more obliging.

This evening Harry had come home thoroughly disgruntled. 'Had a bloody run in with the boss,' he explained, tucking into the fried fish and chips she always brought in on Fridays. 'I ain't 'avin 'im tellin' me to stop workin' on this car and do that car, then moanin' 'cos the first one ain't done in time. He should get anuvver bloke to 'elp out if there's too much work. I'm sick of bein' bossed around. I've a good mind ter chuck it in.'

Brenda paused over her own meal and said sharply, 'No, Harry, don't, that'd be silly,' while managing to refrain from reminding him that he had no need to work for others. 'It's not that bad a job and the pay's good.'

Now he looked up. 'What d'you know about it? You don't 'ave ter work there. I'm sick of bein' treated like I was a bloody skivvy instead of a skilled man. All right fer you ter say don't chuck it in. What if I told you ter chuck your work in?'

She couldn't help it. 'You do, Harry. Every blessed day.'

'An' I'll go on sayin' it! I can't 'old up me 'ead at the garage wiv everyone knowing me wife works.'

'Don't you tell them she doesn't just work – it's her own business?'

Inadvertently she'd brought her salon accent upstairs with her and now he looked across the table at her, his lips thinning in resentment.

'Hoh-hah-h-ere we go again, puttin' on the fancy talk.' The smirk faded. 'Listen, Bren, I've bin a patient man since I came out of the army, but I've 'ad it up to 'ere wiv *your* work, *your* earnings, *your* business.'

Here we go again indeed, came the resigned thought. He could never leave it alone, could he? But he was in full flow, continuing to rail and taunt, saying how small she made him feel, deliberately he sometimes suspected, while he had to work for some ungrateful boss who didn't appreciate him.

'Then do something about it!' she railed back, all her good intentions suddenly snapping. 'You could work for yourself just as I do if you wasn't so high and mighty about it. But if you think I'm going to give up a perfectly good business just to make you feel better, you must be out of your mind.'

How many times had they had this very same old argument, getting nowhere?

'Yer don't need ter work,' he was yelling at her, his nice supper forgotten, ruined. 'I bring in good money now, overtime, bonuses. We don't need you workin' too, an' I don't need ter 'ave it pushed in me face every time I come 'ome. I tell you this fer nuffink, much more of it an' I'll go down there an' burn the 'ole bloody place down. Then yer'll 'ave nuffink ter brag about, making it look like yer can do wivvout me.'

I *could* do without you, don't worry about that, she wanted to shout back at him across the table. Instead she said as calmly as she could, 'The salon's insured, so what good would burning it down do?' But she couldn't resist adding, 'You stupid idiot,' she was that angry with him.

His response should have been expected. 'Idiot, am I?' he bawled, leaping up. 'I'll show yer 'oo's an idiot. I ain't bein' insulted by me own wife. I'm gettin' out, right now. An' I ain't comin' back, not 'till you come to yer senses and get rid of that 'airdressing lark yer fancy yerself so clever at. I bring in the money round 'ere, not you. And until you get that into yer 'ead, I'm staying elsewhere.'

He bolted from the room. She heard him storm through the kitchen and out through the door, heard his boots rattling on the iron stairs, then silence.

For a while she sat on at the table, surveying her half-eaten meal and the one Harry had left. The house was unnervingly quiet. Where would he stay? At his mother's no doubt, telling her his tale of woe, how his wife thought herself above him. Brenda almost smiled at the thought, but seconds later her mouth took a downward slant as sudden tears welled and her heart seemed to lurch. It was the first time that Harry had ever walked out on her with such force, such purpose. She felt strangely shaken by it.

Slowly she got up from the table. She had to collect Addie from her friend's flat. On the way home she would warn her that Daddy wouldn't be home tonight, answer the child's questions as best and brightly as she could.

Perhaps he was bluffing, as he had those other times he'd hurtled off to work, his threats to leave proving empty when in the evening he returned. Would he return after a while, having calmed down? Something told her that this time he wouldn't.

Walking Addie home, she came to a decision. If he did come back he would not find her here waiting for him. Not this time.

'We're going on a little trip,' she told her daughter as they reached home. 'I'm going to pack a suitcase for me and you and tomorrow morning we'll go and see Nanny and Granddad Wilson.'

'Is Daddy coming?'

'No – he has to go away for the weekend.'

Would it be just the weekend or forever? Hard to face, that last possibility. Unbelievable that a situation like this had arisen from just a few unguarded words. She was in shock of course, dry-eyed from it, dead inside, feeling nothing as she carefully put essential things for her and Addie into the case.

Mum too was shocked as she listened to the story.

'I tried to do what you said,' Brenda told her. 'But I couldn't keep it up. I tried, but I couldn't.'

'I thought it was all working out,' said her mum, while her father looked on in silence. 'I really did.'

'Well, it wasn't,' Brenda said tersely, abruptly putting an end to her mother's questions. Her mother sighed, giving in.

'Well, yer'd best stay 'ere and we'll just 'ave ter see what envelops,' she said, this time without Brenda mentally smiling at the misuse of words. 'Yer old room's got a bed in it. The room ain't bin used since it was repaired by them council men after it was burnt out. It might still smell a bit even after all this time, but yer dad did decorate it, so's it ain't too bad.'

'It'll do fine,' Brenda said, grateful for her ready help.

'You an' Addie'll 'ave ter share it.'

'Fine,' Brenda said again. To have the warmth of Addie sleeping with her would be a crumb of comfort at least.

'Right then,' said Mum, getting up from where she'd sat to listen to her daughter's tale. 'Dad, you play wiv Addie while me and Bren make us all some cocoa and a couple of Spam sandwiches. You 'ave brought yer ration books, I 'ope, Bren. I don't want ter be stingy, but . . . you know.'

'Of course,' Brenda said. The war might have been long finished, but with rationing as tight as ever, old habits persisted. No one visited for any length of time without automatically packing those essential items. Indeed, putting them in her handbag had brought home the fact of her leaving even more vividly. There was no word from Harry. Whether he'd thought better of it and gone back home, Brenda had no idea. If he had, he wouldn't find her there. Maybe he was wondering where she'd gone. Would he notice some of her and Addie's things missing and realise what had happened? Would he come searching for her – at her parents' home first, the most likely place?

But as the weekend passed and he failed to appear her determination grew. She wouldn't go back to him and there was an end to it. He'd pushed her too far this time. She'd done her best but it hadn't been enough. The marriage was finished. On Monday she would start divorce proceedings. She was well rid of him, she told herself time and time again, she could look forward to her freedom. So why did she feel so low, so lost?

Her first intended port of call on Monday after taking Addie to school was a solicitor's office. Instead she found herself in an estate agent's, trying not to acknowledge her move as an excuse to delay embarking on her first intentions.

The man sitting across the desk to her beamed. She could practically see him mentally rubbing his hands together.

'So you want to put this house of yours on the market,' he repeated unnecessarily after she had already said so. 'And you want to know how much it will bring. Well, let's see.'

She waited as he thumbed through a sheaf of papers, finally looking up with a wide grin meant to imbue her with joy. 'I reckon we could command a very good asking price for a property like this, Mrs Hutton.'

Brenda nodded without smiling. 'I'll be selling it vacant possession. It's in very good condition.'

'Oh, I don't doubt it from what you say,' he went on breezily.

'It's probably a bit old-fashioned,' she continued. 'It's fully furnished. The furniture goes with the property but that too is rather out of date. Still, whoever you get to buy it can do what they like with it.'

'Indeed,' he smiled agreeably, but Brenda rattled on in a welter of nerves.

'I haven't been there for a long time so the curtains might look very dingy from the outside. You will impress that on any likely buyer?'

He pursed his lips. 'I can't see that being a problem, but I will impress it on viewers.'

'And inside must be very dusty. But it's only dust. There's no rubbish or anything lying around. It's in very good order, just as I got it from . . .' She paused, her mind conjuring up John's face, wearing such a gentle, dark-eyed look of love that her throat constricted suddenly. Swallowing hard, she forced herself to go on. 'From the previous owner. He was very fastidious.'

'I don't doubt that for a moment from what you say,' agreed the agent hastily, suspecting nothing.

Brenda took a deep breath to dispel the bleakness that had lodged itself inside her. It did little to help but she kept her back straight and businesslike.

'The outside appearance might turn people away.'

'Not at all. The market is very buoyant at the moment, housing being in great demand. I expect it might even be bought up for flats – since the war many people are jumping on the bandwagon so to speak. From my knowledge of property in that area, it would convert to two very spacious flats, three at a pinch. That sort of property has very adequate attic space that could make a third, smaller, flat. I wonder you hadn't thought of this yourself.'

She had, many times, but to have let it out as flats would only have aggravated the rows between her and Harry. Now it was hers to do as she pleased with.

'I'd rather get rid of it,' she said firmly. 'So what asking price are we looking at?'

John had once mentioned that he had bought the place for seven hundred and fifty pounds. A bit extravagant, he had said with a laugh, that low wonderful laugh of his, but it had been close enough to London and in a good area so that he had thought it worth the money. She had never been able to bring herself to have it revalued after he'd left it to her – it would have dishonoured his death – and she still had no idea what it would fetch. She tried not to think about it, but common sense told her that getting rid of it was what she had to do to give her daughter a good life if she was to grow up without her father, and help others of her family. If Harry could be so small-minded as to throw her offer of help in her face, then others would benefit.

The man had leaned forward to deliver his good news. 'I reckon we could ask two thousand. Perhaps more, say two thousand two hundred.'

Brenda heard herself gasp. What she couldn't do with two thousand quid! Help Vera, Brian, Mum. Davy was all right, now living well in France.

She could give Brian enough for a mortgage, Mum would be able to decorate her home, for she had expressed a firm wish to stay in the neighbourhood she was familiar with: 'Bomb sites or no bomb sites all round us, it's me 'ome and I've got me old neighbours. I couldn't ever move, not unless they tore down the 'ole street an' invicted us all ter somewheres else.' And Vera, she could go over to America, have a nice time with her sister and at the end of it, make sure Vera had a home of her own that she could do up and feel proud of. Perhaps she could even settle there herself, though she doubted that would happen. She couldn't leave Mum and Dad. But she could send them there for a visit as well. After all, she could live quite well on what came from her hairdressing. She might give up Brenda's Place and get another place away from Harry, never need to see him again. Thoughts stopped suddenly there. She did want to see him again. She had to turn away from the man opposite her as her eyes misted over. How had all this come about?

'Right, we'll put it on the market straight away, Mrs Hutton. I have no doubts that it'll be snapped up the moment it goes on. Give us a week or two to finalise things. Meantime, have you a property in mind you want to buy? We can—'

'No.' Brenda stood up sharply. 'I'm well settled at the moment, thank you.'

The man looked just a little disappointed but produced his bright smile as he too stood up to shake hands with her. 'Leave it with us, then,' he said as he showed her to the door.

She'd done it, at long last. There could be no changing her mind, taking it off the market again – no going back now.

'I'm sorry, John,' came the words in her heart. 'I had to.'

Was he smiling at her? A thought crossed her mind. Had his gift of the house been given out of love or had it been more a curse, paying her out for turning him down as she had after all they'd been to each other. Perhaps he had foreseen that it would bring conflict between her and his rival. But John had never been like that. He'd been gentle, generous, kind. It was her own lies that had cursed this place. That was over now. There'd be no need to lie ever again.

Once the money was gone, she would rest easy, and hopefully so would John Stebbings' ghost.

Now she must look to the future. Harry was gone too. She would never go back to him to have him throw everything in her face for the rest of her life.

With Mum getting Addie from school, Brenda made her way to her salon. She didn't relish going there, fearing to bump into Harry, though he'd no doubt be at work. For a moment she wondered how he was feeling, then swept it from her mind. Perhaps when the money came through, she'd close the salon and find another further away. Would he leave the flat, no doubt go to stay with his parents where he could cry on his mother's bosom and tell her how cruelly his wife had treated him? A sardonic smile touched Brenda's lips. That would give his mother pleasure. It would go round the family like wildfire; his sisters would relish tearing her to pieces. Would Daphne be sympathetic? They had become good friends, but now she didn't really care. That part of her life was over. All she wanted to do now was look ahead. Yet the thought of Harry belonging to the past and not the future induced a heavy sensation in her heart, a feeling she brushed angrily aside as she reached the salon.

The place was already busy. The staff had a key and all of them knew what to do. Instead of going in immediately, Brenda turned into the backyard and went up the iron staircase. She needed to get a few more things and the best time to do it was while Harry wasn't there. She would only take necessities, Addie's toys, and a few more of her belongings. He was welcome to whatever else she left behind, she didn't want any of it.

Letting herself in by the kitchen door, she was relieved that the place was quiet. There was a letter on the mat just inside the door. Picking it up she saw it was addressed to her. It bore a United States stamp. She'd read it back at Mum's.

Pocketing it, Brenda made for the bedroom, pulled down a somewhat battered suitcase and began packing it with what was left of Addie's clothes, a few favourite toys going into carrier bags from the kitchen. She could buy Addie all the toys she wanted from now on. The next thing would be to find a place to live, a nice place, something she could be proud of, call her own. But without Harry . . .?

To combat a second wave of depression, Brenda sat on the double bed they used to share and opened Vera's letter, imagining the joy on Vera's face when she turned up in the not-too-distant future with the means for Vera and Hank to acquire a house of their own.

The letter, as always, was filled with what she and her husband were doing: news of his job, bits about his family, how hot and overpowering the weather had been this summer. Her scrawl was hard to decipher. Then came a passage that caught Brenda's eye, making her read it twice over.

I'm having another baby, Bren, and Henry had a promotion a month or two back so we've been able to save well and we've gotten a place of our own, not too far away from his people, so we'll see quite a bit of them. We're painting and decorating at the moment and there's lots of room for the larger family. Oh, Bren, I'm so happy.

There was not much else in the letter. Brenda folded it slowly. So her scheme of getting Vera her own home would not be needed. Still, she could go over and see her, perhaps at Christmas. She could take Mum and Dad with her. She could afford to live the high life well enough. Why was it that the prospect stirred her not at all?

Brenda put the letter in her pocket, stood up and looked round the room. She could see nothing she wanted as a keepsake, or could she? She reached out for a small ornament Harry had bought her at Hampstead Heath. It had been at Whitsun 1938 – another world, yet at this moment, holding the cheap little trinket, so near. No, she wouldn't take it. Better to cut and run.

She was putting it back on the windowsill when she heard the door to the kitchen open. Maybe one of the staff had seen her come up and needed advice or help.

'Who's there?'

The voice that answered her was masculine, alarmed. 'Who's that?'

For a moment Brenda hesitated. But she would have to emerge from the bedroom at some time. Gathering her dignity together, she walked out to the kitchen where Harry was standing stock-still.

Seeing her his first words hit her like a bullet. 'What're you doin' 'ere?'

Brenda felt her lips thin. 'I have every right to be here. It is still my home.'

She expected the retort, 'Not for much longer.' Instead, he looked at her for a moment longer then without speaking brushed past her, going into the living room.

Brenda followed at a pace to find him sitting on the sofa and gazing down at the carpet. Out of the blue she experienced the faintest touch of sympathy, already expecting to hear him plead with her to come back.

'I've lost me bleedin' job,' he said instead.

Sympathy turned to irritation. How dare he act as though they hadn't split up at all? She said nothing. If he had cared to glance up he'd have seen the cold look of indifference creep over her face, but he merely continued talking as if to the carpet.

'Had a run in with me guv'nor again. Told 'im ter stick his bloody job up 'is arse, and when he said right-o, he would, I picked up me tools and walked out. So now I'm out of work.'

Brenda found her voice, startled by how icy it sounded, especially as there had been none of the usual belligerence in his tone. 'What do you expect me to do about it?'

'Nuffink,' he replied, almost meekly. 'Ain't your worry no more. Just thought I'd tell yer, that's all. I expect I'll find somethink.'

She couldn't help herself. 'And make another doormat of yourself for some other jumped-up employer? With your own business you'd never have to kowtow to anyone ever again.'

To her surprise he did not leap down her throat but merely shrugged, encouraging a feeling of power inside her.

'I've put the house on the market, you know,' she informed him in a tone that brooked no argument. 'The estate agent says it could definitely be snapped up inside a week of the board going up. I'm putting the money in the bank. If you and me do part company, then I'll vacate the salon and set up somewhere else away from here, buy a place for me and Addie, and what's left can be put away for a rainy day.'

Still he remained silent, merely sitting staring again at the carpet. It was strange having the upper hand for once, not meeting opposition to every one of her suggestions.

Gaining strength with every word was a wonderful feeling. She was calling the tune. There came a strong sense of independence, dominance even. It surprised her. She'd always argued, protested fiercely, but this felt different. She could go it alone if necessary, could do without him. She didn't need him.

Yet in the midst of these thoughts came sudden doubt. Did she really want to spend her life coming home to an empty house, bringing up Addie alone? She might remarry. But better the devil you know . . . came a voice.

'Or you could . . .' Brenda hesitated, swallowed hard. One final attempt. If he didn't respond to this, she was finished with him. Even as the words formed themselves she knew she was burning her bridges.

'Or you could put it into that garage business you've always wanted and be your own boss. It's your choice, Harry. It's not my money, it's ours, so don't throw it back in my face ever again!'

Her own strength continued to amaze her. 'That money we could both use, and if you want to make use of it then take charge of it neither of us will mention where it came from ever again, right? Otherwise I'm leaving – no arguments, I'll just leave.'

She was speaking as though they had already agreed to get together again, but nothing had been said. She stopped short.

'That's if we're going to stay married,' she began hurriedly. She was surprised to see a half-nod from him, but managed to hold herself together despite sudden elation and relief. She still couldn't be sure if that had been a sign of agreement or not. She needed to keep talking to allay the threat of caving in to some kind of compromise. She needed to win this one or else go her own way. Whatever way it went, she mustn't be the one to break down. After all, this was all his fault – him and his silly pride!

'It's something to start off with,' she hurried on, giving him no chance to have his say, if in fact he had been about to. 'You're a good motor mechanic, Harry, and it'll be your skill and your business sense that'll make it grow. You could go a long way. We could go a long way. But it's up to you. If you'd sooner we part company, then . . .' She broke off, unable to explore that possibility. All she could do was to repeat, 'It's up to you – your decision.'

She waited, her heart pounding in her throat. Laying herself wide open with her ultimatum, that was what she was doing. No going back now.

He looked up. 'And what about this 'airdressin' lark of yours?'

Couldn't she have bet her last penny he'd ask that? She stood her ground. If this was to be the deciding factor, that she give up her hairdressing, bow to his dictates, she would walk out right now and never come back.

'I'll go on with it,' she said firmly. 'It's something I love. Maybe one day I'll get fed up with it. Or maybe you'll earn so much money I'd feel it's not worth me worrying about. Or maybe I'll have another baby to keep Addie company, and all my time'll be taken up with that.'

Where had that notion come from? She almost startled herself. She saw his eyes light up at the mention of enlarging their family, and realised suddenly that she would like that too. Even so, she had to be firm.

'It's up to you, Harry. There'll be no humble pie to be eaten by either of us. Not ever. Your choice.'

Harry got up and moved to the window to stand staring out.

Brenda waited, already preparing herself to gather up what she had come to collect and go.

'I could take on a decent bloke to 'elp,' he said from out of the blue. 'If I did expand – did get bigger – I'd need ter employ someone.'

It took a moment or two for her to absorb what he had said. With those few words he'd spoken volumes: of their marriage continuing, of his acceptance of her offer, of his capitulation to her terms regarding her own business. So much.

She didn't rush into his arms as he turned round to face her. She merely stood there looking at him, relief and tenderness showing on her face. The time for embraces would come later, as would the baby they would produce.

This was what she had wanted – not to triumph over him but to share a simple, uncomplicated married life with him, the two of them pulling together rather than against each other all the time. It had taken all this while since his demob from the forces to get it correct. Maybe there had been faults on both sides, she wasn't sure. But the knowledge that she had won brought no sense of triumph. Yes, she had won, but he must never be allowed to realise that. Not ever.

'Yes, you could,' she agreed simply to his suggestion. Any more than that would have spoilt the moment.

Can't get enough of Maggie Ford?

Read on for a sneak
peek of her
brilliant WW1 saga

A GIRL IN
WARTIME

Available from Ebury Press

EBURY
PRESS

Chapter One

June 1914

Louise Lovell glanced over her sixteen-year-old daughter's shoulder as she passed the kitchen table; in her hands were several large spuds which she would peel and cut into chips to go with the cold roast lamb left over from Sunday.

About to tell her that she'd have to clear the table ready for that evening's dinner, she paused, gazing fondly at what the girl was doing. She was wasted working in a factory making cardboard boxes.

'Wish I'd been given your gift, love,' she remarked. 'That's really lovely.'

Connie looked up from the pencil drawing she was doing. 'You think so, Mum? Thanks.'

'Ran in me family, drawing, y'know, but passed me by, didn't it?'

'Maybe it's in you too, Mum, somewhere,' Connie said absently, returning her attention to the country scene she was copying from a black-and-white picture she'd found in an old newspaper.

Later she'd colour it in, using her own imagination for the hues from the cheap box of watercolour paints she'd got for her twelfth birthday four years ago. The little pallets of bright colours were hollowed from much use. Soon they would be all gone but when she'd be able to afford a new box was anyone's guess. Dad said she was too old for such soppy childish things.

'Time you got out of them kids' toys,' he'd said. 'You're sixteen now, and in work. It's about time you started acting your age.'

Dad didn't – or wouldn't – understand how essential they were to her. Drawing and painting were her life. She had a gift, as Mum said. Even at twelve she'd been able to look at a person's face and draw it well enough for people to instantly recognise the owner. Under her bed in the back bedroom she'd once shared with her sisters, both now married and moved away, were pencil portraits of the current silent screen stars, men who'd made her heart go pit-a-pat: Maurice Costello, Charles Ray, James O'Neill, each a perfectly recognisable likeness.

Alone, she'd dream of one day meeting one of them, becoming his adored lover, showered with gifts, envied and rich, though chance would be a fine thing. It was only a fantasy. In the real world she worked in a factory, standing at the assembly line for hours on end turning the cardboard edges of boxes into place and dabbing them with sticky paste as they passed, and it looked as if she'd be staying there doing it until, like her sisters, she got married and became a housewife.

'Come on, love, best clear away,' her mum said. 'Your dad'll be home soon, and you know he likes to sit straight down to his meal.'

Obediently, if reluctantly, Connie got up from her chair and began carefully to collect all her bits and pieces, the two pencils, the India rubber, the nearly completed drawing on its sheet of off-white paper she'd smuggled out with a thin stack of similar sheets from her workplace – for how could she afford proper parchment on factory wages?

Carefully she rolled up the landscape drawing so that it wouldn't crease, and, with her arms full, went out of the kitchen and up the dark, windowless stairs of her terraced home in Cardinal Row, Bethnal Green, to stash all her stuff away under her bed.

Soon she would be vacating this room, with its cheerful sunshine coming in first thing in the mornings, for the back room downstairs. It wasn't a prospect she looked forward to. She had no option but to comply with the wants of her family.

This house being two-up-two-down like all those around here, she and her two sisters, Elsie and Lillian, had shared this room for as long as Connie could remember; the other bedroom was occupied by her parents. But since her sisters had left to get married, Elsie the year before last and Lillian just a few weeks ago, she'd had the room all to herself. And lovely it had been too, but not for much longer.

Her brothers, George, Albert and Ronald, had slept in one bed in the downstairs back room since they were kids, two at the head and one at the foot. But now they were grown men: George twenty-one, Albert – Bertie – nineteen and Ronnie seventeen. So, as from next week, they'd have her room and she'd have the downstairs back room. No more privacy, just the curtain around the bed behind which she'd retire after everyone had gone up to their rooms around ten o'clock.

Of course, if they were home late they'd go straight upstairs, so there was no fear of her being bothered. But there'd be no more lingering at a window to gaze down into the neighbouring backyards, or the pleasure of having the early morning sun pour through the window on to her face.

Her mother's voice calling up the stairs interrupted her thoughts.

'Hurry up back down here, love, I need you to lay the table while I dish up your dad and brothers' dinners. It's getting late and they'll be home any minute now, hungry as blessed hunters.'

Connie couldn't see why they'd be hungry as hunters, except Dad, who was a coalman delivering heavy sacks of coal to households by the hundred and needed lots of sustenance. The boys had far less energetic jobs as far as she could see.

Ronnie was a packer in a sweet factory while Bertie was a milkman, which meant admittedly he was up early, but it was not exactly hard work. As for George, he was a law unto himself, doing casual work on and off but he was more than decently involved in his Free Church pursuits, which were held in a small hall half a mile away. Its pastor was his mentor, and he hoped to be one himself one day.

He was always going on about it to his family and how enlightened a person would become if they joined.

Not that there was anything wrong in that, except that it got a bit tiresome sometimes, none of the others being all that religious. It was more that he wasn't in proper work as often as a young man should be. How he'd ever be able to save up to get married, much less support a family, was beyond her.

'Connie, love, the time's getting on.'

'Coming, Mum,' she called back. Dismissing her meandering thoughts she hurried downstairs.

Arthur Lovell opened his paper, and being a bit politically minded more than usual these days, made a point of scanning the headlines before turning to the sports pages to see if there was anything on his local football team, Tottenham Hotspur, not that there'd be all that much, it being Monday.

This evening, though, it was the headlines that caught his attention, making him pause in shovelling his dinner into his mouth. Letting the still full fork fall back into the bowl, he let out a deep, irascible growl as he squinted against the June evening sunlight that slanted through the kitchen window directly on to his newspaper.

'Gawd – I dunno what's wrong with this bloody world! What with that bloody Ireland making trouble and them perishin' suffragettes causing even more bother! I don't know what they expect to gain. What do women know about politics, I ask you?' He eyed his family but they knew better than to respond.

His bushy eyebrows met in indignation, his large moustache bristling.

'Now it says 'ere someone's gone and shot some archduke in the Balkans. That's going to cause trouble,

462

you mark my words. Always trouble somewhere on the continent, countries squabbling among themselves. Thank Gawd we live in England.'

Peering closely at the smaller print while Connie and her mother paused to gaze at him, though his sons continued eating their dinner, he went on, 'Some damned upstart or other wanting to prove a point, I suppose.'

Dad loved shouting politics each time he opened his paper. Having now got this bit off his chest, he turned abruptly to the sport pages, the newspaper rustling noisily. His wife gazed at him for a moment or two, the bread knife paused in the act of slicing bread.

'Never mind, love,' she said quietly, not all that interested, before resuming slicing the loaf. 'Finish your dinner, there's a dear, before it gets all cold and horrible.'

Chapter Two

July 1914

'Wouldn't be a bit surprised if this don't develop into a perishing full-scale war,' muttered Arthur Lovell, glancing up from his paper. 'So long as it don't involve us.'

Connie glanced at her father from where she was sitting at the kitchen table, covertly sketching his likeness on a bit of paper, one hand shielding it in case he noticed what she was doing and made some mocking remark.

He wouldn't get that annoyed but she would feel an idiot as he tossed his head and tutted – that to her was as good as ridicule. Mum, on the other hand, would smile and nod, might even voice her pride, which would make him shake his head even more and ask lightly whether she hadn't got better things to do, again inadvertently making her feel a fool.

'Goin' out tonight, love?' Mum asked her now, though it was obvious, Connie having already changed into nicer clothes than those she wore for work.

She was meeting a couple of friends, Cissie and Doris, and the three of them were going Up West to gaze in all the big London shop windows for an hour or two and dream about wearing the lovely expensive garments they saw displayed there that they could never afford. It was a pastime of which all three never tired.

Later they'd come home to hang around for a while by the shrimps and winkles stall outside the Salmon and Ball pub under the railway arches to laugh and chat and maybe flirt a bit. Connie was tall for her age and boys often made a beeline for her, even though her friends were just as pretty.

She brought her mind back to her mother. 'Meeting Doris and Cissie at half past,' she replied.

'Then you'd best be off, love, or they'll be wondering where you are.'

Connie got up from the table, folding the paper with her drawing and tucking it into the pocket of her hobble skirt, already thinking of the evening ahead: the bus they'd catch, boarding it as ladylike as possible with her tight hem hampering her ankles. If any man watching dared smirk, she'd be ready to glare at him as haughtily as she could until he finally pulled a straight face again.

There were several more bits of blank paper in her Dorothy bag along with a couple of pencil stubs, for, if she got the time, she intended to quickly sketch one or two of the garments that most caught her eye. Later she'd have a go at running up something similar on Mum's sewing machine, the material bought locally and far cheaper. This was how she kept up with the fashion, to the envy of friends and workmates. To her mind the talent for dressmaking was another art, going hand in hand with that of drawing.

Giving Mum a quick kiss on the cheek and her dad a peck on the top of his slightly balding head – to which he growled, 'Get orf!' – she was away to enjoy her evening of window shopping.

'Let's just hope our government keeps its own nose clean and stays out of it – all this squabbling between Germany and Russia and now France. Ain't none of our business, and besides, this country can't afford to dabble in other people's wars.' Connie heard her father growl contemptuously from behind his *Daily Mail*.

Tension was beginning to mount daily, the newspaper full of this growing unease in Europe. Connie could see it in her own parents' faces as foreign governments began glaring at each other across borders.

These last few days there had been reports of Austria breaking off diplomatic ties with Serbia; Serbia mobilising its army; the Tsar warning Germany that he couldn't remain indifferent if Austria invaded Serbia.

Recent news had been of Austria declaring war on Serbia and of Russia ordering the mobilisation of a million troops, then, as July turned into August, came reports of the Kaiser warning that if they didn't cease within the next twenty-four hours, Germany too would mobilise. That deadline ignored, Germany had declared war on Russia.

Connie could see the concern on Mum's face, but all her father said was: 'Bloody storm in a teacup!' as he turned to his beloved sports pages.

But Dad's words, meant to reassure himself as well as those around him that in no way would Britain let herself be dragged into conflict, held a note of anxiety and for once Mum didn't lightly change the subject by asking if he wanted the window opened wider on this hot evening or did he fancy another cup of tea. She merely stood looking at him, her round face blank, her mouth slack, her plump shoulders slumped, the tablecloth she was still holding, limp and only half folded.

Connie, in the process of getting ready to pop over to Cissie's house, felt the tension her father's comments had brought to them all: Bertie on the point of going outside to light a cigarette, Mum not minding pipe tobacco but hating cigarette smoke; Ronald, his younger brother, about to follow him out, their older brother George doing nothing as usual. Having finished their tea of ox tongue sandwiches, her three brothers had their minds more on going out to find girls, or whatever young men did when well away from the house of an evening.

Bertie was already courting: a pretty, fair-haired, easy-natured girl, Edith Kemp, or as he called her, Edie. He'd brought her home to meet them all earlier this year and it was recognised that come next Christmas the two of them would get engaged, both sets of parents happy for that to happen.

Young Ronnie said he'd be seeing a few mates this evening but beyond that gave no more away. George was off out to yet another of his odd chapel meetings, saying he was taking part in helping organise a fete for August. To Connie it seemed he hardly ever went anywhere else but there. In a way it touched her as being just a bit unhealthy but she said nothing and carried on getting ready to go off to Cissie's house. Their friend Doris would be over too and they'd probably play gramophone records and giggle over one thing and another.

'Well,' Connie heard her dad burst out. 'Didn't think we'd be foolish enough to end up being dragged into this war too.'

No one responded to the irascible remark as they all crowded around the morning paper which was spread out on the parlour table, its headline staring up at them: *Britain Declares War with Germany*.

Yet as they read, Connie felt she detected more a sense of euphoria than dismay among her brothers at least, a feeling of pride more than fear. Germany would quail before the might of the British bulldog and, before it knew it, they would soon have Germany on the run, tail between its legs. The Government was already saying it would be over by Christmas, although Lord Kitchener was declaring vehemently that the Government was wrong, that this could prove to be a far more drawn out process than they imagined – or at least were trying to convince the country.

It was hard to credit how swiftly everything had moved on in a matter of days. Three days ago Germany had asked France, Russia's ally, to remain neutral, but France had declared that impossible, leaving Germany to demand the right to send troops through neutral Belgium so as to invade France. Yesterday Belgium had refused, while Britain warned Germany that if it did march on to Belgium soil, she would have no choice but to stand by an old treaty with Belgium and declare war on the invader. In the small hours of this morning Germany had ignored the threat and now every newspaper carried the headline in huge letters that Britain was at war.

Beyond the front-room window, even in this small side street, Connie could already see a more than usual amount of people passing, mostly men, each with a set look of fierce determination, or so it seemed. Her first instinct had been to find paper and a pencil to sketch that look she saw. But there were other things to think about. As they had finished breakfast, both her sisters had come knocking frantically on the front door in a panic. Now they sat around the table, straight-backed with fear.

'I've had a busting row with Harry,' Elsie was saying, her face taut as she sipped agitatedly at the cup of tea Mum had handed to her. 'As soon as we read the paper he started going on about how it was his duty to sign up as soon as he could. I ask you, where are his brains? We've got a little'un now. He can't go and leave us. What if he got killed, and me left on me own with just me and a little kiddie?'

She'd had the baby just before Christmas. They'd named him Henry after his father, for all he'd always been called Harry.

'I told him, point blank,' she went on, her voice rising, 'if he went out that door and signed up, he'd never see me again. I'd leave him. I would.'

Her words made Connie shudder involuntarily. If her brother-in-law did join up, how easily those words could prove true.

'My Jim's saying the same,' Lillian put in. 'And me having just discovered we're going to have a little'un of our own. How would *I* cope if he got killed?'

'It won't come to that, love,' Mum said, sipping her own tea as if her life depended on it. 'We've got our regular troops and the Government is already saying it'll all be over by Christmas.'

'That Lord Kitchener don't think so,' Elsie put in harshly, 'says it could go on for years. He's already talking of calling for ordinary men to volunteer. Harry says they're already opening up recruiting offices all over the place and expect thousands to enlist. But I don't want my Harry to be one of them.'

'If I was younger, I'd be there, up front like a bloody shot,' their father said, his voice grating with harsh determination. Now that the inevitable had happened, her father had been the first to change his tune about the war.

'Then bloody good job you aint!' her mother burst out, sharp for once, even to the extent of uttering a swear word, which she rarely did. Dad shut up and she turned to Connie's sisters.

'You two had any breakfast? I could make some. The baby'll be fine in his pram. You can take him in the other room when he wants feeding – give you some privacy. Though your dad'll be off to work as soon as he's finished his breakfast. The boys aren't home. Bert's already off finishing his milk round, and Ron has to be in work by seven thirty. Neither of them has seen the paper yet. George was here but as soon as he read the news he was off to have a chat with that minister of his, so he said. So I don't know when he'll be coming home.'

Connie wasn't interested in her eldest brother's pursuits but her sisters' words had set her thoughts working, and deeply concerned thoughts they were. Ron

470

and Bert would have seen the newspaper placards on the way to work or heard the news from their colleagues. Had either of them already gone to see if they could enlist? Mum had said the country already had professional soldiers: the British Expeditionary Force – the BEF – proper soldiers who'd soon have Germany on the run, and the war would indeed be over by Christmas, if not sooner. And Lillian and Elsie's husbands and the boys, all full of impetuous eagerness with no idea of what fighting could entail and what could happen to them, wouldn't be wanted. At least that's what she hoped.

She shuddered, imagining her brothers and brothers-in-law fighting in a foreign land, maybe killed. Mum and Dad – their sons gone . . . Hastily she turned her thoughts back to the present.

'I'd better be off to work too,' she said. 'They'll be wondering where I am, and be upset with me if I'm late.'

She made to leap up from the table but her mother countered, 'I don't expect many people will get to work on time on a morning like this, love. It ain't exactly a normal day, is it? Same with your dad, I think.'

Glancing up from the newspaper he was still reading, he looked as if struck by lightning. 'Good Gawd, I forgot all about work!'

He glanced at the ornate mantel clock over the fireplace as though it might bite him. 'Look at the bloody time! I should've been on my rounds an hour ago. War or no war, housewives expect their coal to be delivered.'

'I don't suppose anyone'll be fretting over late coal deliveries on a day like today,' his wife said, murmuring somewhat absently, turning her attention to her eldest girl. 'Look, love, I'm sure if you go home and have a

471

quiet talk to your Harry, without getting all riled up and
starting another row, I'm sure he'll see sense and not go
galloping off like a wild bull.' She looked at Lillian.
'You too, love. Go off and have a proper talk with your
Jim. At the moment everyone's running about like head-
less chickens, doing things they might regret. If we give
ourselves time to calm down, we'll all be better off.'

Anxious about what her employers would say to her for
being late, Connie rushed out of the house even before
her sisters left.

From the short street where she lived, she turned on
to Bethnal Green Road only to find herself caught up in
a hurrying mass of people, most of them heading in one
direction – westward. Some were on foot, others on
bicycles – loads of bicycles – the buses that passed her
crammed full. They usually were, but today everyone
looked obviously bent on joining those already gathered
in front of Buckingham Palace or Downing Street. There
they would be cheering themselves hoarse, she imagined.

Resisting the urge to join them, she crossed the road
as best she could towards Dover Street, where her firm
was situated. Inside she was met by almost complete
silence, hardly a soul to be seen except the foreman she
saw striding towards her – a heavy-set, stern but fair
man in his forties. One hand was raised as if waving
her away.

'I'm so sorry I'm late,' Connie began automatically,
half expecting to be handed her cards.

'You're not late. You're one of the few who's bothered
to come in and you probably won't be working at all
today. Everyone's too riled up. Bet they're all cheering

like mad up the West End, I shouldn't wonder. You might as well go back home or go and join them. Tomorrow it will all calm down and when you come in, see that you're on time. The company can't put up with any more of this.'

His tone had sounded agitated, but she guessed it was more from a sense of excitement that had caught the whole country, it seemed. Sighing, thanking the war itself for giving her a day off, even if it would be unpaid, Connie turned and left, remembering to say a polite thank you as she went.

What to do now? Back in Bethnal Green Road, she decided at first to resist following the crowds, but moments later found herself joining them. In her jacket pocket were some scraps of blank paper and the stub of pencil she always kept handy, together with a piece of India rubber. She would spend time drawing the expressions on people's faces, maybe a crowd scene, maybe Buckingham Palace itself. And if Their Majesties came out on the balcony to show themselves to the cheering crowds, she would sketch them too, as best she could from where she guessed she would end up, standing at the back of the vast throng.

Excitement at the prospect caught at her. Those drawings would be something to add to her scrapbook. As she walked with the crowd she silently thanked her school teacher who'd taken her under her wing when she'd been twelve, recognising her talents, and had given her art lessons when she should have been outside at playtimes and lunchtimes.

'You've a rare gift,' Miss Eaves had said. 'When you leave school you must protect that talent, nurture it, practise it at every moment you can spare. Then one day you will become a good artist and even make money from it. And please, don't let it drop once you leave school, thinking it all a waste of time. Make quite sure to do as I say, won't you, my dear?'

Overawed by such dedication and earnestness, she had nodded and, to this day, that tutor's words still rang in her head. But how did a factory girl like her go about becoming a real artist? She didn't know. Yet she was sure that one day it would come about. Until then all she needed was faith and dedication. Dad and her family – except Mum, of course, who showed such pride in her – could say what they liked, make fun of her if they wanted. At this moment her heart was filled to the brim with determination.